Cursed King

Ringdweller Series Book 2

Brady Hunsaker

Lightfire Publishing

Published by Lightfire Publishing LLC

Cover art illustration by Miblart

Contents

Dedication   VI

BW map   VII

Fullpage Image   VIII

Fullpage Image   IX

1. Chapter 1   1

2. Chapter 2   7

3. Chapter 3   14

4. Chapter 4   18

5. Chapter 5   25

6. Chapter 6   31

7. Chapter 7   36

8. Chapter 8   42

9. Chapter 9   52

10. Chapter 10   62

11. Chapter 11   69

12. Chapter 12   80

13. Chapter 13   87

14.	Chapter 14	95
15.	Chapter 15	104
16.	Chapter 16	107
17.	Chapter 17	115
18.	Chapter 18	120
19.	Chapter 19	130
20.	Chapter 20	133
21.	Chapter 21	148
22.	Chapter 22	166
23.	Chapter 23	170
24.	Chapter 24	181
25.	Chapter 25	185
26.	Chapter 26	199
27.	Chapter 27	212
28.	Chapter 28	223
29.	Chapter 29	231
30.	Chapter 30	241
31.	Chapter 31	245
32.	Chapter 32	248
33.	Chapter 33	250
34.	Chapter 34	254
35.	Chapter 35	259
36.	Chapter 36	263
37.	Chapter 37	274

38. Chapter 38 — 279

39. Chapter 39 — 289

40. Chapter 40 — 293

41. Chapter 41 — 306

42. Chapter 42 — 311

Afterword — 318

Pronunciation Guide — 319

About the Author — 322

Wow, massive shoutout to the absolutely amazing beta team for helping me finalize some things in this book—Penny, Chelsea, Hannah, Alyssa, Pallavi, Rebecca, Celine, and Melody—you're all absolutely awesome.

Also to my wife for being so accommodating for all my crazy tangential blurting, clearly indicating that my brain spends so much time on Mala-hem. My wife has done so much to teach me about love, working together through struggle, overcoming pain, finding hope, forgiveness, and change.

Malahem
FROZEN WASTE
SCORCHED WASTE
MAZANIS
IAZEEM
HABKAMAL
JEHRIBAL
PAL-IRAD LAKE
SANADIL-ATAR
CATABAN
MALORIA
ASMALAM
WANAY
WANAY LAKE
SHIBAN

Mal
MAZANIB
HABKAMAL
SCORCHED WASTE
MALORIA
WANAY
WANAY LAKE
SHIB

ahem
FROZEN WASTE
LAZEEM
JEHUBAL
DELIRAD LAKE
BANADIL ATAR
CATABAN
ASMALAM

Chapter 1

Migo Rikaydian hadn't been allowed inside this room. That was before he had his mother assassinated. Now, he was soon to be the king. The moment he entered, bitter coldness dropped over his body like a bucket of water. He stepped lightly, though musty air kicked up from his boots, filling his lungs with each breath. The sound of the creaking door closing behind him was all but lost amid the boom of crackling thunder. A magical storm raged outside. Sand and ice pattered loudly against many small, thick windows lining the far wall.

A near constant stream of lightning provided enough stroboscopic light for Migo to see. The room was equally orderly and messy as he remembered from years before. He paused, allowing the dust to settle before closing his eyes and taking a deep breath, savoring the familiar smell of polished wood and new paper. The scent had changed. The paper was aged, and the polish was stale. Nobody had entered the room in ten years.

Or so he thought.

He opened his eyes and looked across the floor. It was subtle, but the dust *had* been disturbed. He stooped low to inspect. The footsteps were small, as if made by tiptoes. Whoever it was, they'd moved slowly, or perhaps he was only imagining things. The steps were difficult to trace in the ever-changing light, but he followed them to his father's desk. There, the evidence was more apparent. Half a handprint had smeared the dust across the smooth wood.

It was recent. Very recent.

Migo growled as he scanned the surface of the desk. A candle, a knife, an old logbook, a bottle of varnish, a bottle of ink, a pen, and a half-finished carving. All untouched. An ache grew in his gut.

He opened the single drawer on the desk. Just as he'd feared. A rectangular space was completely clear of dust. His father's journal had been taken. He slammed the drawer shut.

Who else even knew about it? Why would they have taken it? They'd gone straight for it, of all things. And they must have done so immediately after the queen's death. He pounded a fist into the ironwood desk with a dull thud. Instead of answers, he only had more questions.

The implications were jarring. Agents of the queen still lurked in the palace. She would haunt him even in death. He'd never be free of her scorn. He clenched his fists, determined to root out all of her agents and destroy them.

The worst part about it was that he didn't know what they were hiding from him. What could be in his father's journal that they didn't want him to read?

Migo sighed and looked around the room, heart warming at the sight of his father's wooden battle stave. They had often sparred together. Above the stave was a plaque that read "The greatest battle is not in the field of war against your enemies, but in your mind against yourself. Once fear, or anger, or shame, or malice becomes your driving force, you have merely subjected yourself to instinct as the animals. Temperance and wisdom are the necessary elements of true humanity."

No wonder his mother had outlawed entry to this room. Such a statement decried all that she'd enforced ever since his father's death. Anger and malice were all Migo had known from her. Rage flared in his chest.

Temperance. He resisted scoffing, not daring to sully the memory of his father.

He continued perusing the room. It was difficult not to clean things off, but he wanted to be sure that nothing else had been disturbed or removed. His father's ring, complete with the rangola insignia of the Rikaydian family, lay on the floor by the desk. He picked that up and immediately placed it on, though it only fit over his smallest finger. It was strange to think that he was perhaps bigger than his father had been. He always remembered him as a giant of a man.

He could find no other sign of activity, but there was a document on the floor beside the chair. The parchment was half covered by a detailed map of the area around Delirad Lake. He pulled it out from underneath and found it unopened, sealed by unmarked, yellow wax. The document bore no marking either.

Migo let out a slow breath and glanced about the room before popping the seal open and holding the letter up to the flashing light from the windows. It was addressed to his father.

Lord Kidem Rikaydian,

I hope that you are still well when this letter arrives. I have been pursuing your assignment with all earnestness. Any trace has been difficult to find. One of my men has gotten lost in the canyon, but in greater urgency, I have been able to confirm some of your suspicions. There is indeed a fabrication, and the origins are as you'd feared.

I worry that I will be discovered and this information can be traced back to you. If so, all is vain and I have failed. Your public efforts have been recognized without sympathy. I do not question your activities, but only worry about the attention it draws.

Steer clear of the Maedari.

~ R

Migo stroked the back of his neck in thought. "Sleet, what was my father doing?" he muttered to himself. The last line also seemed like some sort of premonition. Whoever this person was, had they anticipated the assassination attempt against his father?

He'd never discovered who was responsible for the murder. With his mother out of the way, no longer forcing him into some blind rage, he could finally focus on the matter at hand. Who really killed his father?

A deeper question occurred to him. He rushed out of his father's office and hurried down a flight of stairs to the throne room.

Hatan stood in the room with a couple soldiers, including Captain Falshon. "I've placed a soldier at each of the balconies on the second floor as requested," Falshon said. "There were no signs that those doors had been opened."

"That's all the entrances then," Hatan said. "So there's no evidence of any door being opened except for the one through which the assassin fled."

"That is the case, sir," Falshon replied. "Nobody has been in or out since the storm started except for her."

"Hatan," Migo said. "A word."

Hatan bowed his head. "Certainly, lord." He nodded dismissal to the soldiers.

Migo strode into a side room and sat down in the cushioned chair. He sank into its softness, closing his eyes for too short of a time before Hatan entered and closed the door behind him.

"How can I help you, lord?" Hatan said.

Migo rubbed his temple. "I don't think I can get used to that. Please just call me Migo."

Hatan smiled. "I've been waiting to call you that for a long time. I have to indulge myself."

"Indulge yourself some other time, cousin. Somebody broke into my father's office and stole his journal."

"His journal?" Hatan said, features hardening.

"Yes. I feel like it had to have been during or after the assassination. If our lockdown was successful, then the culprit should still be within the building."

Hatan nodded. "I'll make a point to search for it. That's a peculiar thing to steal, and very specific."

"Did my father have many friends or enemies? How many people would have known about his journal?"

"I'm sure several people knew about it, Migo. He sometimes kept it with him to jot notes. He had more enemies than friends. His opinions were not extremely popular."

Migo nodded. "He was not a supporter of the shamanfolk extermination. Wasn't he often looking for peaceful resolutions with the local tribes?"

Hatan nodded.

"Then why would a shaman be the one to assassinate him? Could somebody have hired someone to look like a shaman?"

"Possible," Hatan said, "but they were stormwading. It would be a rare thing indeed for a ringdweller to stormwade."

"Perhaps not. All you need is their equipment. And somebody could still hire a shaman. Sands, Hatan, I practically hired a shaman to kill my own mother. I want to know who killed him. I need to find out."

Hatan's eyes softened as he stepped closer. "Migo. I don't know who killed your father. The options are endless. It would be almost impossible to figure it out now, but I will help you in any way I can."

Migo held out the letter to Hatan. "I found this. It was unopened."

Hatan took the letter and scanned it.

"Any idea who 'R' might be?" Migo asked.

Hatan groaned. "I was not part of your father's covert team. He wanted me in charge of the army. I was aware that he was running some secret operations and who some key figures were, but not any other details. I think he structured it that way on purpose. I used part of that network and a few loyal soldiers to establish my own group when your mother took over. All of those who were part of his secret operations vanished, however."

"Of course," Migo said, grinding his teeth.

Hatan tilted his head. "With one exception." He held up the letter. "R?"

Hatan smirked. "Yes. He's no longer in Jehubal, but as long as he's not dead, I know where to find him."

Chapter 2

It burned as Katsi's feet pounded against the hot, desert sand, leaving a trail of dust behind her. She used her magic, creating a cloud of sand that blotted out the sun. This offered only meager protection from the pervasive heat that dubbed this place the Scorched Waste.

A dull pain lingered in her chest, right over her heart. The image of sliding her blade across the queen's throat wouldn't go away. She'd become the assassin. The murderer. The very thing she'd loathed for years. All her troubles had started with an assassination when King Rikaydian was murdered years ago and the queen swore her revenge against shamanfolk. Would another assassination really end the troubles?

Even Damani had rejected her. After all she'd gone through to save him. It was for him that she killed the queen. She instantly doubted herself. When she was faced with the choice of fleeing or fighting the queen... she hadn't thought of Damani even once. She'd thought of Migo. She'd thought of the pointless war and the countless lives that would be lost as long as the queen maintained her rampage. But not of Damani. Perhaps she didn't love him as much as she thought. Perhaps it was only the idea of being loved and cared about that drew her to him.

She clenched her fists and ran harder, shaking her head to clear the thoughts. Scales had followed her all the way to the edge of the Ring, gliding in the wind that she'd created. He stayed behind when she crossed into the

Scorched Waste, chasing after insects. She worried about leaving him like that, but she had a feeling he'd always be around.

The stone outcropping indicating the Bayvana Tribe's hideout was only a few steps away. No fear of attack entered her thoughts at all. The tribe wouldn't dare turn against her now. They knew she was a stormcaller. Aside from the elders, there was no official rank among shamanfolk, but shamans, those who possessed magical abilities, were always honored. And stormcallers were the most revered, along with the seers.

She slowed and jumped down into a crevice between the rocks. It widened and sloped down into the ground.

A young shamanfolk woman emerged from the darkness ahead, pulling down her black veil to reveal her face.

"Katsi," Shinaseh said with a wide smile. She approached with outstretched arms.

Katsi was so taken back that she stood frozen as Shinaseh clapped her on the shoulders.

"I can't believe you did it."

The cheeriness was unfamiliar. Nobody from the tribe had *ever* greeted her like that. She could only nod. Any affirmative response felt like a betrayal to the memory of her pacifist parents.

"Everyone's been waiting for you," Shinaseh said, ushering Katsi into the coolness of the enchanted cave. The temperature changed instantly as Katsi passed through a wall of magical energy that kept out the blazing heat.

"Word travels quickly," Katsi said.

"Oh, scouts came sprinting as soon as word got out. We were preparing for an attack at the end of that Maedari, but they called it off. It's a shame you didn't get the prince too."

"I wasn't planning on killing the prince. He's supposed to become king and call off the war."

"Oh. And were there other people helping you? We thought you were solo."

Katsi cocked her head. "What other people?"

Shinaseh brushed a couple braids of black hair out of her face and smiled at Katsi. "The word is that some other Ringdwellers tried to take out the prince, but he killed them all."

"I see. No, I acted alone," Katsi said. Shinaseh was probably referring to Migo killing Captain Tarahan and the other men. She wondered how Migo was going to get away with killing his own soldiers.

They entered the large chamber. Cheers and applause echoed off the stone walls as soon as people caught sight of Katsi. She smiled despite noticing that their numbers were painfully slimmer than the last time she'd entered the chamber. How many had died? It only solidified her resolve that the queen's death was necessary. She'd saved lives.

Despite their recent devastation, the tribe was happy. Shinaseh ushered her on as everyone continued cheering, clapping her on the shoulders as she walked by. She couldn't decide if she should smile or cry. She couldn't remember the last time anybody from the tribe had been happy to see her. Emotion gripped her chest, and she had to take deep breaths to keep the tears from forming. This was what she'd wanted for years. Peace. Happiness.

They made it to the back of the large chamber and proceeded down a narrow path that eventually opened into a tall, long room with several enchanted holes at the top where natural light bled through. Three statues carved from the stone lined either side. Despite preservation enchantments, bits of the statues had worn away, and one statue in particular was completely decapitated, something that likely didn't happen by accident. The icon of distortion and death.

All the shamans were gathered in the room. Katsi counted 17 of them. So few. Shinaseh patted Katsi's shoulders once more before retreating the way she'd come, leaving her with the other shamans.

A brief round of applause passed among them before the five elders stepped forward. Mashe stood foremost among them, her brown skin darkened and wrinkled. She was old, but strong and steady. As much an able warrior as any of the youth. Manahae stood beside her, shaking his head with a smile. He must have officially been inducted as one of the elders.

"You surprised us, Katsi Danan," Mashe said, clasping her hands in front of her. "We've long sought the death of Queen Rikaydian, but I never thought it would be you who'd make it happen."

Katsi shrugged. "Me neither, but it's better that one person should die if it means saving many others. Especially if those other lives are innocent." Her chest burned as the words left her lips. The statement sealed her abandonment of her parents' beliefs. She still thought peaceful resolutions were the higher, preferable sort, but no longer believed it was the *only* way.

Mashe blinked at her. "This is true. You said you would bring peace. Who's to say that the young prince won't be as cruel as his mother."

"He wants peace. He cares for his people. I trust he will do better," Katsi said.

"Trust." Mashe looked over her shoulder at the other elders. "Trust is too strong a word for a man who would rule over lands that were forcibly taken from us."

Katsi clenched her fists. "That was many generations ago. Everyone in that city was born well after those sins were committed. We had a semblance of peace before the king was killed."

"I know this, Danan," Mashe said. "I only make a point. They will not have our trust, but we can respect a new ruler while yet untested. This is the problem with their monarchies and empires. Too much power with one person means each ruler can bring a new age of policy. As an elder council, we have discussed the matter before you arrived. The tribe will hold its peace unless the new ruler proves himself a tyrant."

Katsi nodded and bit her lip.

Mashe's features softened. "Peace is what your family wanted. We too desire it, Danan." She looked around the room at the statues. "Have you been in this chamber before?"

Katsi glanced around at the six icons again and shook her head.

"There are six orders of shaman magic," Mashe continued. "Brewers, like your father, who helped bring growth, and life, and healing. Earth-melders like Manahae, who move the stone and shape our homes. Enchanters like myself who use the industrious magic to create shields against the heat, bewitching our armor and clothes. Seers who are granted wisdom and glimpses of what could be. Stormcallers, like you, who may shape the weather itself. Shamans are not limited to using one form of magic, but typically display greater strength in one order or another. In fact, many potions are often imbued with enchantments during the brewing process. You have displayed an aptitude in stormcalling, but we must offer caution."

"Stand beside me," Mashe said. Katsi hesitantly approached. Mashe turned to look at the sixth icon, the one missing its head. "Do you know much of the magic of distortion and death?"

Katsi had heard plenty of stories about it, but never directly from the elders. She shook her head. "Not really."

Mashe closed her eyes. "The members of their order were called bleeders. The use of its magic requires the blood of animals or humans. Our ancestors, the Shavarani Tribe, used this magic to do terrible things, often sacrificing other humans. Eventually, the elders became aware of the horrors they committed, and they ordered a stop to such magic, but most of the bleeders persisted. The bleeders were thrown out, all record of how to use the dark magic was destroyed, and the tribe was renamed the Bayvana Tribe."

Mashe opened her eyes and snatched Katsi's arm just below her shoulder muscle, the exact location she wore the armlet she'd stolen out of Nedro Wajek's manor. The armlet that bore a symbol of the Shavarani Tribe. It was as if Mashe knew where it was despite it being hidden beneath Katsi's robe. "Do not. Touch. The magic of distortion and death, Danan. No good can come of it. If you ever meet a bleeder, never give them your blood. They will try to bargain for it. I give you this warning because you are powerful, but you are also rebellious. You do not stand unified with our tribe. You will always be running off on your own, but do not forget my warning."

Mashe's gaze was so sharp and intense that it bored through Katsi's skull. Katsi gave a quick nod, and Mashe released her grip.

"But aren't the swords you made—the seculas—aren't they made with bleeder magic?"

"Sands, no," Manahae said, his deep voice growling. "True seculas killed any whose skin the blade pierced. We placed no such curse on our weapons."

Mashe patted Manahae's arm. "Will you stay here to receive any training, Danan? Our shamans are willing to teach you what we know despite your independence."

Katsi bowed her head. "I am grateful for the offer, elder, but I will go to the shaman woman from Banadil-Atar in the canyon, the one you call the spirit. She has offered me direction on how to learn more about stormcalling specifically."

"I see," Mashe said. "Then we wish you well. Be wary of the spirit. A seer's work is never certain."

"Okay," Katsi said. She looked around the room again. At the statues. At the shamans. She'd half expected them to make her stay, but instead, they sent her off. They had never spoken to her in such a way. Perhaps now they saw her as an adult. Whatever the case, she nodded to them and turned to leave.

Shinaseh was just outside the entrance, folding her arms as she leaned against the wall. "No more war then?"

"If we're lucky," Katsi said.

"Shame," Shinaseh said. "I was just getting good with this." She patted her secula then laughed when she saw Katsi's expression darken. "I'm only joking. I hope we see peace for a long time. But in case we don't." She pulled another curved sword out from beneath her robe. "Take this." She held it out to Katsi.

"No," Katsi said, prepared to push it away, but Shinaseh insisted.

"You might need it. Wherever you're going. We have... a few extra ones now, anyway."

Katsi sighed. This was what she'd become, despite all her efforts to prevent it. She was a warrior. She took the sword. Her training with weapons and fighting was minimal, but not entirely foreign. She'd trained with them two full years before leaving to live at her parent's old hideout.

"Don't look so grateful," Shinaseh teased.

Katsi rolled her eyes.

"How'd you do it anyway?" Shinaseh said. "With the queen, you know."

"I just got lucky," Katsi said. Her fingers were wrapped where the throwing disc had sliced through skin. She felt lucky they were all still attached.

"Stay lucky."

"I'll try," Katsi said, tucking the sword into her belt as she moved to leave. If she mastered stormcalling, maybe she'd never need to use the weapon.

Chapter 3

Nagesh kept his arms to his side and regarded his new client from behind the enchanted veil that covered his face. He was prepared to escape if the man was planning anything, but this was a location of Nagesh's own choosing, near to the gravesite the client wanted him to inspect.

The client was a man in his mid-forties. He only wanted to go by the name Bodhi, but Nagesh knew that was a cover. His clients typically used aliases. For good reason. Ringdwellers hiring shamans for their magic was not something very popular. Nagesh didn't care who they were. As long as they paid.

"We have access to the bodies for about half a mark," Bodhi said, his voice rushed. "Will that be enough time?"

"Plenty," Nagesh said. "You know the rate?"

"I prepared accordingly," Bodhi said, voice hardening as he pulled his robe tighter against his body. It was a cheap robe. Part of the disguise. But the well-manicured hands and the scented beard oil were definite give-aways. Bodhi was some kind of merchant or lord. Probably the latter. From what Nagesh already knew about the bodies, this was likely something political.

Nagesh smiled behind his veil. The ringdwellers always got tight when he mentioned money. "Very well. Show me the bodies."

Bodhi turned without a word and strode towards the sun. They were already relatively close to the Scorched Waste at the edge of the jungle north of Jehubal. Most of the dead from Jehubal were taken out here to be burned, unless they died on the south side where it was too far to move them.

But not the queen. Nagesh took a warm breath. Her body wouldn't be here. There'd be a place in the palace where they'd burn her more discreetly. Now that was some blood worth its weight in silver.

When they reached the burn site, nobody guarded the bodies. Bodhi must have bribed them off. "There are seven of them. Killed in battle."

"Who were they?" Nagesh asked, testing the man's response.

"I was hoping you might tell me," Bodhi said with a level stare.

Nagash's smile was hidden behind his veil as he withdrew a knife, approached the bodies, and bent over them. "There are only six bodies," Nagesh said, counting them twice. This job just got more interesting. He looked up at Bodhi, but the trained politician squinted down at them as though counting them for the first time himself.

"I must have been mistaken," Bodhi said.

"We'll find out soon enough," Nagesh said. All six bodies were men, and they wore only pants. They certainly looked like they'd been through a terrible fight, but they were still fresh enough to draw blood without too much trouble. "You may not want to watch this part," Nagesh warned just before sliding his knife across the back of the first body's neck. Blood came in a slow trickle. He pulled out a vial and collected some. He'd mix it with the blood of the others. This would strengthen the bond and help show what connected them all together.

After collecting a couple drops, he ran his finger across the incision and brought his hand to his face, rolling the blood across his skin. He pulled his veil down and spoke a word. "Duga." Images and feelings entered his brain, though they were fuzzy. Through the blood, he could access the memories of the deceased, though they were weak. It worked better when the blood was fresh. Nobody realized how powerful blood was. Nobody but bleeder shamans. Blood connected with everything. With it, Nagesh could know many things—what the subject had eaten for the last few years, their age, who they'd kissed, or even on a deeper level, what made them angry, or the last few things they'd seen. Heightened emotions at certain events in their lives also strengthened the vision.

"Who killed them?" Bodhi asked.

"There was a fight," Nagesh said. "Inside the palace." He moved to the next body now, repeating the same action with all six, collecting a few drops and rubbing some into his hand. The image and memories became more vivid. He closed his eyes, clearing the picture and spoke aloud to relate it to Bodhi.

"There was a duel with the prince. He won. Everyone here was killed by him. His scent is riddled in their blood. A woman was there. Young. A prisoner. She watched. Another soldier had also been there, but his body is not here."

"A duel?" Bodhi said, impatience on his breath.

Nagesh leaned over, rubbing the blood deeper into his hands. "The prince had been a prisoner. They thought of him as a traitor. He taunted the captain until he accepted the duel and let him out of the cage."

"A traitor? Why?"

The visions were fuzzy. Pinning down motivations was always difficult. "It has something to do with the girl." She was a shaman. Nagesh snapped his eyes open and stood. "That's all I have for now. I need to run a test on this blood. It will allow me to connect better with some of the other elements of their memories."

Bodhi's face had turned slightly red. "This better not be some scam."

"Don't worry," Nagesh said, tucking the vial away. "My price doesn't change. I just need to run the test. It might take a couple marks. I'll deliver the final results for you when it's ready. Pay me half now, half after I deliver the results."

Bodhi muttered a curse and slapped a small bag of coins over to Nagesh. "Two marks then. I want to know what connection the prince has with the girl."

"You will have it." Nagesh pulled the veil back over his face, ignoring the drying blood on his hands. He turned and disappeared into the warm jungle. He already knew the answer, but whoever this Bodhi was, maybe he didn't need to know that Migo Rikaydian had been the one to release a shaman assassin inside the palace.

Chapter 4

"Cataban?" Migo asked. He had yet to replace his glaive, so he instead gripped the pommel of Hatan's knife. "Do you know where specifically I would find him in Cataban?"

"Yes," Hatan said, leaning against one of the throne room serving tables. "Judging from the letter, I'd say he might know more than I even suspected. I would have gone to find him myself, but I wanted to remain with you. When you left to train on shaman hunting, I was too focused on developing a network in your absence that I'd forgotten all about your father's other connections."

"I want to go to him," Migo said. "Immediately. I want to see if he knows anything about my father's killers. With such a specific warning, he had to know something."

"I agree, but I think it should wait until after your coronation. It wouldn't be good to leave the city in disarray."

Migo closed his eyes and let out a long breath. "When will that be?"

"Tomorrow at the earliest. We'll want to announce it and give time for the local nobility to prepare."

"And for the coronation itself," Migo said, "I want to do it in the palace courtyard."

"Typically that is done here, in the throne room."

"No, this room isn't large enough. I want any citizen to attend. They'll need to hear what I have to say."

Hatan smiled and patted Migo on the shoulder. "Very well, my king. And I'll make sure there are enough pastries for everyone."

Migo shook his head. "Of course you will."

Migo struggled to remain still as two attendants helped don his attire, which included an intricate silver and steel plate over his right shoulder. A rich maroon cape was clasped over his left shoulder. It bore his family insignia, the feline shape of a rangola, sewn in black. Golden lace trimmed the edges.

An army of seamsters had worked all cycle to create Migo's outfit, much to his dismay. He'd had to stand there for hours while they measured and remeasured, excluding him from much of the other preparations.

Hatan insisted it was necessary. The lords and ladies would expect a certain level of professionalism and decorum.

Migo rehearsed a speech in his head. He had enough enemies to go around. The queen had made sure of that. At least Tarahan was dead, but Migo had been so disconnected from politics that he was not at all prepared to deal with court. All he'd done for the last several years was focus on destroying shamanfolk to please his mother.

Until Katsi.

His whole way of thinking was shattered.

Maybe he wasn't much of a politician, but he could still use his strengths to his advantage.

Hatan entered the dressing room wearing his finest uniform. Accompanying him were two soldiers from Migo's old division. The queen's guard had been disbanded after her death. After this cycle, they would be restructured into a palace guard.

"It's almost the sixth mark," Hatan said. "The moon is nearing its peak. The palace courtyard is full and the street outside is packed. It seems the whole city has come to see the coronation of Jehubal's savior."

"Please don't call me that. There were many I didn't save."

"Don't let the death of some diminish the gratitude of those you *did* save." Hatan smiled. "And until your coronation, I can call you whatever I want, cousin."

The dressers backed away, having completed their job. Migo dismissed them from the room and regarded himself in the mirror. He'd seen kings and queens before, and he absolutely fit the bill. Jehubal was a wealthy nation, rich from its sale of produce, pastries, and fabrics made of soft plant fibers. He hadn't dressed as royalty since his father's death. The cycle after his father died, his mother burned all he possessed and sent him to live with the soldiers. He didn't get his own room until after he'd returned from training as a shaman hunter.

But now, dressed in an intricate outfit, with such comfortable clothing, he had to admit that he looked good. The pain of guilt that struck him, however, was staggering. He was the reason both his parents were dead.

No.

He had to remind himself of what Katsi told him. It was not his fault his father died. He, like any good father, was trying to save his son.

Hatan must have seen a shift in Migo's expression. He stepped in front of Migo, blocking his view from the mirror. He gripped Migo's shoulder and lowered his voice. "You deserve this, Migo Rikaydian. You are the rightful king of Jehubal. Your people need you."

"I have made so many mistakes."

"Haven't we all? Such is life. Be your best man now, for this is the cycle you will be reborn."

Migo nodded, feeling the truth ring. "You're right. I will need your help."

"And you have it," Hatan said, looking deep into Migo's eyes.

Migo took a deep breath, warmth filling his chest. He nodded. "Let's put a crown on my head."

Hatan laughed. "That's the spirit."

They left the room together and navigated through the palace halls until they emerged out onto the courtyard. The whole space was packed, though with enough room to allow people to move around. True to his word, Hatan had some servants walking among the crowd with trays of pastries.

Soldiers held a cleared path all the way to the stairs of the palace walls. Some onlookers cheered Migo's name while others glared at him. His only weapon was Hatan's knife, hidden beneath his cape. Today he was not coming before the people as a soldier, but as their king.

The voices on the other side of the wall grew like a coming rainstorm, getting louder with each step that drew him closer. When he reached the top of the steps, the cheering crescendoed. People stretched down the whole street. Many of them climbed up on the roofs of nearby buildings. He may not have been able to prove himself to his mother, but at least the people had begun to believe in him. He forced a swallow past the lump in his throat.

The ceremony itself was not grandiose. Migo was the undisputed heir to the throne. Hatan was the only other living relative Migo had. "Try not to be too poetic," Migo warned him before Hatan raised his hands, and the crowd grew silent.

Hatan spent a couple minutes reading aloud a script about loyalty and honor before tucking the sheet away and smiling at Migo. "I present to you Prince Migo Rikaydian, heir to the throne of Jehubal."

Migo raised a hand to the crowd on both sides of the wall and took three steps toward Hatan. He clasped both hands in front of him and remained silent.

A servant opened an intricate chest and held it out to Hatan. Hatan reached in and withdrew a crown. It was a simple thing, crafted before the age of Jehubal's wealth. It was built of brass with three yellow-brown gems at the peak of three prongs. The etching of a single rangola graced the front.

"I always knew this day would come," Hatan said, lifting the crown up. Many people started to clap and cheer. A small scuffle broke out inside the courtyard, but it stopped just as quickly.

As soon as Hatan touched the crown down on Migo's head, the applause grew so loud it vibrated in Migo's body. His skin warmed, and his face flushed.

Hatan immediately offered a deep bow before adding his own applause.

Migo faced one side of the crowd, then the other, basking in the moment of jubilation. He waited a couple minutes before raising his hands to silence them. A deep breath filled his lungs. Though he'd rehearsed his speech a dozen times, words fled from his mind. He'd have to make it up as he went.

"Our city has been bashed by storms for generations," Migo shouted. "We've not only built strong walls to weather these storms, but we've built strong people." He waited as a round of cheering erupted. "We have been wading a storm for many years now. I promise to bring us peace. The war with the shamans is over. They will not attack us, and we will not attack them. My mother let rage blind her into disregarding the needs of our people in order to enact some form of revenge. We must discard this notion. The deaths resulting from this war have been needless. No evidence has indicated the Bayvana Tribe as responsible for the murder of my father ten years ago. My mother led no investigation to uncover the true suspect. I will do my best to discover the real murderer. This will take me away from the city for some time, but Captain Hatan Padarro will govern in my absence. We will continue to weather the storms, and become stronger by doing so."

The crowd's reaction was mixed. The group gathered inside the courtyard, comprising mostly of the upper class, was more subdued. A few of them cheered, but most remained silent. The general public however went wild, as if it was the greatest thing they'd ever heard.

Hatan gave Migo a narrow-eyed expression that said he would have wanted to talk about this first.

Migo just hoped most people were scared of war enough to look past the hatred the queen had rooted in them. They'd lost almost half their army in the last battle. How many families were now missing sons or father?

The crowd started dispersing after his short speech. The next full mark passed slowly as various lords and ladies climbed the wall to publicly bow to Migo. He scarcely knew any of them, with the exception of Nedro Wajek, a merchant lord with an infamous history of murdering and robbing any shamanfolk his caravans ever came across.

"I know I have a history of fighting shamans, Majesty," Nedro said. "But no war means safer roads. Safer roads means more travel and greater prosperity. They'll see your wisdom even if they don't agree now. This is why I always came to you instead of the queen." It was comforting to know that at least one person had confidence in their new 17-year-old king.

Once the ceremony was complete, Migo caught Hatan alone on their way to a meal they were hosting for the local nobility. "I want to find R immediately, Hatan. With my father's journal missing, perhaps somebody else would go after him. I don't want to risk losing the one chance I have at finding answers."

Hatan nodded. "I understand fully." Then he laughed. "I just wish I didn't have to run the city in your absence. Both of us are merely warriors."

"The way I see it, leaders are leaders, Hatan. Besides, you've already been running your own secret intelligence network. I'm sure that's all the experience you need. But just as you have agents, I'm sure there are enemies with agents of their own. Somebody close enough to know about my father's journal. Find them. And if anyone speaks out against me, just let me know when I get back and I can quietly take them out myself."

Hatan's lips curled slightly in amusement. "I'm sure that last bit was your morbid attempt at humor."

"Possibly," Migo said, turning down the hall to hide his smirk.

Chapter 5

A light breeze blew blazing hot wind through the air of the Scorched Waste. It whistled through the canyon with a deep hum. Katsi stood at the edge of the cliff, looking down into its rocky depths. The sun burned at her even through her enchanted armor.

She glanced up. The moon, Aivar, was already at its peak. She needed to get to the bottom. Anybody who fell would most certainly die. They'd have to be crazy to jump on purpose. Maybe she *was* crazy. She checked all her pouches and pockets. Everything was secure. Another glance down almost convinced her not to try, but she summoned her magic. Sand filled the air.

"You're not about to jump, are you?" A voice called from behind her.

Katsi screamed and nearly fell off the cliff. She dropped and grabbed at the rocks as one foot slipped off the edge. Her fingers easily caught the rough sandstone. With a heave of her magic at her back, she pulled herself to her feet and faced the ancient woman.

"I thought I had to meet you in the canyon," Katsi said, trying to play off the fact that she almost died.

"You're welcome to jump off the cliff to get down, though I recommend other methods that are more intelligent."

Katsi bit back a snide remark. "You don't think I could use my magic to make it down?"

"I'm sure you could, you just wouldn't be alive after your body hits the bottom."

Katsi remembered soaring over the rooftops of Jehubal in great leaps and bounds. Surely her magic could carry her down safely.

The old woman smiled at her. "There's an easier way to use your magic. Come." She walked to the edge of the cliff. Without pause, she stepped off the edge and dropped until her body was horizontal, then proceeded to walk down the side of the cliff.

Katsi ran to the edge and dropped to a knee. The woman stopped a few steps down then turned, looking up at Katsi as if lying on the air. "How? I've never seen magic used like this," Katsi said.

"There is much you don't know. The Bayvana Tribe's knowledge has been withering for generations. I was surprised you were born to them. Your father had great strength as a shaman, but didn't know how to channel it. Instead, he only focused on making simple potions. You, on the other hand, will do much greater things."

"Show me," Katsi said. She was done with all the words.

"I'm using a combination of earthmelding, enchanting, and stormcalling," the woman said. "I am not strong in any of those elements, but I am proficient enough. You only know stormcalling and some mixing enchantments. Your stormcalling is strong enough that you might use it alone. The alterations I'm using are too delicate. With stormcalling you will need to rely on strength to create a force strong enough to push your body up enough to reduce the fall. More experienced stormcallers would be able to connect with the air itself, but that's too advanced for now. Connecting with the stone will be much easier."

Katsi did so. She touched the rock with her bare hands.

"Breathe it in. Taste it with your senses."

Katsi took a deep breath. She could smell the rock. It was similar to the smell of sand, but not so dusty. She could sense its gritty texture against her tongue, and it tasted slightly of metal.

"Now grab it."

Instinctively, Katsi knew what that meant. She gripped the rock, not with her hands, but with her mind. Her hands as well as her knee and feet locked onto the surface.

"Loosen your grip."

Like a muscle, she relaxed her mental grip on the rock and was able to move her hand across the surface, relocking when she paused. "Amazing," she muttered. She never knew she could be so connected with an object. She could hardly wait to apply the same concept to air or sand.

"It's simple and doesn't require much strength. You can do the same thing with the air, but it often requires more motion to create a stronger force, so create wind as a counterbalance to your horizontal body as you go down the side of the cliff." The woman proceeded to walk down the cliff. "It's too hot up here. I'll see you at the bottom." Her voice echoed off the canyon walls.

"I suppose this is one way to make learning exciting," Katsi muttered to herself. What she was really uncomfortable with was trying both magics at once. She tested calling the wind while taking steps to see if the connection remained. It worked.

A wave of fear clenched at her insides as she leaned over the edge, using the air to keep her steady. She used too much force at first and had to ease off to let her body drop to a horizontal angle. Her breathing came in rapid bursts. She struggled to move her feet, shuffling them at first. Slowly, she descended, dodging around parts of the cliff that jutted out or sank in. She gained more confidence as she kept at it and gradually increased her pace.

The old woman reached the bottom and folded her arms as she watched Katsi.

As soon as Katsi was close enough, she released her bond with the cliff and jumped, using the air to turn and land softly on the sandy ground. The shamanic artifact wrapped around her upper arm tingled. She smiled triumphantly.

The woman grunted. "Find me any shaman in the Bayvana Tribe who knows how to scale a cliff with magic. You could use that same earthmelding technique to climb the cliff using both hands and feet. You wouldn't even need to use stormcalling." She shuffled through the canyon, sticking to the side where shade prevented the sun from melting them.

Katsi followed silently as they entered a small cave where the temperature cooled as soon as she passed the magical threshold.

The old woman sat at a chair carved from the stone, and Katsi sat on one opposite her.

"There is much left for you to learn," the woman said. "If you'd been raised properly, much of using magic would already seem natural to you. Your impulsiveness actually proves beneficial there, and you have great power."

Katsi scowled. "My parents died when I was young, so there's not much they could have taught me."

"I mean no insult to your parents, stormcaller. They taught you what they could, but your tribe has been stifling shamanic learning for years. Less use of magic reduces potency. This is why there are fewer shamans among them than in previous years when a majority of our people could use magic." She leaned back into her seat and closed her eyes.

That answered a question Katsi didn't know she had regarding dwindling shaman numbers. Katsi leaned forward. "Why do you care? Why bother showing me anything?"

The woman opened her eyes and squinted at Katsi. "Stormcallers are rare. Especially ones with as much strength as you. You've also shown some proficiency in the other classes. You can't tell now, but you possess greater power than you realize. I am a seer, and I've seen many possibilities, but the fate of our people rests with stormcallers. Your very choices might save or destroy us."

Katsi felt a weight descend on her shoulders, so she rose to her feet as if to push it off. "I want to save us. I've seen enough people die on both sides."

"This is bigger than Jehubal and the Bayvana Tribe. The entire Ring is balancing on the edge. I cannot teach you enough about stormcalling to maintain our precarious balance. That must be taught by a proficient stormcaller."

"You want to send me to somebody else?"

"Yes. You need to learn how to use your powers." She leaned forward, placing her elbows on her knees. "There is another, more immediate quest at hand, however. Jehubal is in danger. There is an organization seeking to destroy the peace that you have fought to create. By now you understand that some violence is necessary for maintaining a collective peace."

Katsi's heart filled with dread. She'd essentially stated the same thing earlier while speaking with the shaman council. "Yes," she said, her voice a whisper.

"Then you must do one more thing." The woman's face darkened. "There's a man in Cataban who needs to be killed. I can share with you a vision of the place you need to go and what the man looks like. You would need to leave immediately to make it in time." She rose to her feet and held out a hand.

Katsi rubbed at her forehead before dropping her hands to her side in fists. "Fine. Show me." She placed a hand on top of the woman's, and her sight went blurry for a while. When it cleared, she saw a domed building with two distinctive pillars to either side of the main door. Next, she saw a man with dark skin, long black hair, and a thick beard. The vision disappeared.

"You saw him?" the old woman asked.

"Yes," Katsi gasped.

"Then go. Do not hesitate to kill him. If he utters even a single word, it could threaten more than the kingdom of Jehubal. Two warnings: pay no mind to the birds, and if you see King Rikaydian, flee from him. He will bring nothing but discord to you."

Katsi cocked her head at that. What threat was Migo?

The woman shooed Katsi away, so she turned and ran, feeling the urgency. She fought back the agony coursing through her veins. Had she somehow become an assassin? Who was she even fighting for at this point? She'd changed, and something told her it wasn't for the better.

Chapter 6

Migo stood in the now empty courtyard. The crowd had been ushered off. Those who remained were running about their business. A group of over forty mercenaries had been herded together. None of them were native to Jehubal.

"Have they been interrogated?" Migo said.

"They have," Captain Falshon said in his gruff voice. "I interrogated them myself. They've all said the same story—they did nothing but exterior wall patrols."

"Get them out of our barracks and off the payroll. They can find work somewhere else."

"Will do, Your Majesty," Falshon said.

"One more thing," Migo said in a low voice, grabbing Falshon's shoulder before he left. "Watch after Hatan while I'm gone. He needs all the allies he can get."

Falshon's eyes darkened with understanding, and he gave Migo a nod, then rushed over to herd the mercenaries off the palace grounds.

Migo shifted his weight from one foot to the other, trying not to watch as two servants prepared Genda, his rangola, for his trip. The massive, scaled feline let off a rumbling purr as one servant distracted it by scratching under its chin so two other servants could lay the saddle across its scaled back. He wanted nothing more than to be on the road. Every second he wasted was another opportunity for his enemies to locate R first.

A small group approached from the other side of the courtyard including Hatan, Engineer Cosova Dia, and Lord Obet Ilanitan—the commerce director. Migo's family never had a good relationship with the Ilanitans. He suspected his mother kept him in his position merely to keep an eye on him.

Migo glared at Hatan. His cousin knew he didn't want to talk to the commerce director. He'd been avoiding the man since the coronation.

"Your Majesty," Obet said before anybody else could speak. Obet was a plain man in his early fifties, not built like a warrior, though he had no need for such a thing when his profession involved sitting in a chair. He bowed his head.

"You speak out of turn, Lord Ilanitan," Hatan said. "You are supposed to wait for the king to address you before speaking."

"My apologies," Obet said, bowing deeper.

Migo sighed and glanced at his rangola which still wasn't ready. "Speak. We may as well address whatever it is you want."

Obet raised his eyes, brushing a thick braid of brown hair over his shoulder. "Your Majesty, I understand you are leaving soon, but we've had an issue that I wanted to bring to your attention before you left."

Migo nodded for him to continue.

Obet straightened and squared his shoulders. "There's a secondary street off the main road in the city that is in need of repair. It has several local artisans and trades on it, but they have not been able to benefit from the through traffic. I tried discussing this with the late queen, but she was... not enthusiastic."

Migo frowned and folded his arms. "Did she provide a reason?"

Obet shook his head. "No, your majesty. She dismissed me without listening to the proposition."

Migo often checked the streets adjacent to the main road, and he could immediately picture which street Obet was referring to. He'd often thought of the disrepair of the road as having some correlation with decrepit tenants, but perhaps he'd been misguided.

"Hatan," Migo said, "reallocate resources to the repair of this street immediately."

"As you wish," Hatan said, inclining his head in a short bow.

Cosova stammered as she spoke, "If I might speak, Your Majesty."

Migo nodded to her.

"Our teams are currently constructing a new watchtower by the Frozen Waste."

"Pull them off that project," Migo said. "Maintaining the livelihood of our people is more important than having soldiers stare at ice. Funding for such projects becomes easier when the needs of our people are met." Hatan turned his face away, but Migo glimpsed his smile. "Coordinate with Director Ilanitan to see what resources are necessary, then run it by Regent Padarro for approvals."

"Yes, your majesty," Cosova said, bowing her head.

Obet smiled. "Thank you, your majesty." The two of them departed, leaving Migo with Hatan.

"I don't think I'll get accustomed to anybody calling me Regent Padarro," Hatan said.

Migo grunted. "You will. You've been leading for as long as I've been alive, Hatan. Everybody in this kingdom respects you. Even your enemies."

"You seem to be managing the role well so far. You handled that scenario better than I could have. I wish I could go with you."

"We all have our part to play," Migo said. His rangola was about ready. "I should only be gone a few cycles. Keep things afloat until I return." The servants brought Genda over, her thick paws pattering against the stone.

"Watch your back, Hatan." Genda lowered herself, purring deeply as Migo scratched behind her ear.

"I'd say the same to you, but I know you always are."

Migo threw his hood over his head, then leapt onto Genda's saddle.

Hatan and every other soldier in the courtyard saluted as Migo steered his way out the gate. He kept his veil down so the people could see him. A warm breeze blew from the Scorched Waste, leaving the air dry. Migo nodded or waved to those who greeted him in the streets, but he weaved his way through as quickly as possible. Most people were afraid to be anywhere close to a rangola, so they naturally hurried out of his way.

Migo let out a sigh of relief when he got out of the city. Traffic south of Jehubal had somewhat resumed as people returned to their farms, but it was still lighter than before the battle. Genda growled. She liked to run, so Migo sped up to a trot. He had one last stop before heading straight to Cataban.

They passed through a strip of jungle before reaching the farmlands where marshy soil stretched from one side of the Ring to the other. Migo steered to a single farmhouse where the door hung open. He dismounted. "Stay," he said. Genda sat on her haunches to wait.

Migo approached the door cautiously. He could hear movement from inside. "Damani," he called, stopping in front of the door.

Silence.

It took a few seconds, but Damani emerged, a woven basket held under one arm. His expression was somber. "Yes, Your Majesty," he said in monotone.

"Did she come to see you?" Migo asked.

Damani sighed. "She did."

"And what did you say to her?"

Damani looked at the ground, shoulders sagging. "I told her that I couldn't be with her. She took off after that. I doubt I'll see her again."

Migo let out a breath and unclenched his fists. He took a step closer. "Did you tell her about your betrayal?"

Damani gave Migo a hard glare, eyes hardening. "No. You forced me to betray her. I had to tell you the truth about her or you'd kill me. What was I supposed to do?"

Migo sneered. "You did the right thing by proving loyal to the kingdom, but you still betrayed her. That is all." He'd wasted enough time. A pain pulled at his stomach, urging him back to his objective. As a loyal subject, Damani had truly done the right thing for his country, but he'd been unfaithful to Katsi in the process. The morality of the decision clashed with Migo's own reasoning. All he knew was that if Damani truly loved her, he would not have betrayed her. That was enough.

Migo clicked at Genda, and she lowered for him. He mounted in a quick motion and put Genda into running speed. For all he knew, R was long gone, but he sensed the man was still there, waiting. He just couldn't shake the feeling of dread that clawed at him. Something was wrong, and he couldn't go fast enough.

Chapter 7

Loud footsteps echoed on the stone floor of the hallway. Hatan sat at a desk in the clerk's office, a smaller office adjacent to the throne room. The door to the office was left open, and light spilled into the room from a large storm window up above. The light reflected off two mirrors to either side of the room, providing plenty of illumination as Hatan scrutinized the ledger. His worry grew with each line he read.

The footsteps halted outside the open door, and Hatan looked up from the ledger, folding his arms. "Hello, Penym."

"Regent Padarro," Penym said, hands on hips. She wore an elegant, dark blue dress with golden trim, shoulders peeking out from slits in the long sleeves revealing her smooth, light brown skin. "What a pleasant surprise." White teeth flashed behind plump lips. She was pretty. Too pretty to be single in her thirties, especially when working in the palace. It made Hatan suspicious. But who was he to question such things when he had his own difficulties?

"The shoes are new?" Hatan asked, glancing at her high heels before standing.

"No detail escapes you, regent."

"You may as well address me as Hatan. We'll be working together a lot over the next few cycles, I'm sure."

Her smile widened. "Very well, Hatan. But no, they aren't new. I've had them for years, I simply couldn't wear them here in the palace. Queen Rikaydian wasn't too fond of it." She bent down and removed the shoes. "I can't say I like to wear them though. I feel like people can hear me coming from halfway across the palace."

"You're right. I certainly could." Hatan chuckled and stepped aside as Penym entered the room, placing her shoes on the floor beside the desk.

"So, what can I help you with, Hatan," she said, taking every opportunity to say his name.

Hatan resisted the urge to shake his head. "King Rikaydian wanted me to focus on regaining financial stability, so I came to review expenditures." He looked back down at the ledger. "It would appear we are in debt."

"Very much so," Penym said, opening a drawer.

"We need to remove quite a few people from staff."

Penym withdrew another notebook. "Which we can do. I've already identified some positions we can remove, primarily service staff. Some of them could be reallocated to profitable positions, like the Rikaydian orchards or ice harvesting, but there are also skilled craftsmen who we can't necessarily relocate."

Hatan nodded. "Very good. I'm glad you've already thought of this. What if we employed the craftsmen and sold their services?"

Penym tapped the desk in thought. "Like running a business?"

"Exactly. Especially if peace with the Bayvana Tribe brings an economic boost. There's a street we're cleaning up off the main road with a couple empty buildings. We could even set up a shop there."

Penym set down the notebook, dabbed a pen in ink, and highlighted a few jobs listed on the sheet, including dressers, seamstresses, inkmakers, and hydrators. "This will help some."

"What else do you recommend?"

"Perhaps not ordering mass quantities of pastries to feed to the whole city."

Hatan grunted a laugh. "It's not every day we coronate a new king."

Penym smirked up at him. "Most of the throne's income is from taxes—merchant tax, business tax, and land tax. Land taxes have always been the same, but we can expect merchant and business tax income to increase as more merchants are willing to visit from the south. Potential visitors have been stopping in Cataban, then turning back south rather than proceeding to Jehubal. Many of our local merchants would transport goods to Cataban and establish shops there to sell their goods. If we can do that locally, it will shift the revenue to us instead of Cataban."

"Right," Hatan said, despite most of the information going over his head. He wasn't sure what any of the taxes meant.

"But it will take some time for that to trickle back to the throne's coffers. Several cycles at least. Some of those debts could very well take years to pay off."

Hatan looked back at the ledger. Much of the debt was owed to local nobility and merchants, Nedro Wajek included. Mercenaries were not cheap. How had the queen become so frivolous? Then again, he had to remember she wasn't a very stable person. "Now we just need to convince everyone we're doing well."

"Not we, regent. That's your job." Penym laughed. "I'll handle the finances, you handle the relations."

"Regent," a voice said from the doorway.

Penym yelped at the sudden sound, and Hatan's hand settled over the pommel of a new dagger tucked visibly through his belt.

"Sands, Emil," Hatan said, addressing the soldier who now stood in the doorway. "Did you walk on the air? Don't you normally report to Captain Falshon?" He cast a sideways glance at Penym. She seemed harmless enough, but there was still an unidentified traitor in their midst. Or at least someone that was intent on keeping information from the current ruling body.

"Yes, regent," Emil said, dipping his head. "Captain Falshon is on an escort to the south gate, but I have some interesting news to report."

"Very well, I'll walk with you," Hatan said, then turned to Penym. "Thank you for your work here. I'm glad we have a plan in place. Let's meet with the head of staff at seventh mark to review those rearrangement options."

She flashed him another smile. "I'll look forward to it."

Sands.

Hatan followed Emil into the hallway. The soldier was in his young twenties and stood even taller than Migo. He was built like a mountain, but his voice was soft, and his steps were light. Instead of a glaive, he was equipped with a poleaxe and a short sword. The black hair on one side of his head was trimmed nearly to the skin, while the rest of his hair curled down to his chin.

"What news do you have?" Hatan asked.

Emil looked down both sides of the hall. The only other person was a palace guard hanging outside the throne room.

Hatan needed to do something about that. The palace certainly didn't need a whole army guarding the palace. Dismissing all the mercenaries was a good start. Now he needed to redistribute. Technically, they were no longer at war, which meant the vast majority of soldiers could easily be dismissed and they could simply run a trained militia. Yet another item to discuss with Penym...

Emil's voice was but a whisper when he spoke. "There were only six bodies at the burning earlier. The king killed seven people in the throne room."

"That's... odd," Hatan said. He indeed remembered seven bodies. He'd counted them himself immediately after the deed had been done. It was

Migo's way of defying the queen and releasing Katsi without any witnesses. He killed everyone who'd witnessed his betrayal. Everyone but Hatan and Katsi. "And you were involved in moving the bodies?"

"I was, sir. I volunteered to help. I loaded seven bodies. Unloaded six." Emil bent his head down. "There were only four of us involved in transporting the bodies. My brother and I walked out in front, and two others sat at the front of the cart."

"Could one have fallen out?"

Emil shook his head. "Not likely."

Hatan's thoughts whirled. "Certainly you're not suggesting that one of them survived?"

"Wild as it seems, regent, that's exactly what I'm suggesting."

Hatan had seen people survive terrible wounds before, so it was certainly possible. He reviewed the gruesome scene in his mind, but couldn't remember a person that seemed like they should be alive. But he hadn't checked the bodies. Nobody had. They just assumed everyone was dead.

"Do you know which person it was?" Hatan ventured.

"I do," Emil said, eyes hardening. "It was one of Tarahan's men. He had a stab wound in the face, so there was blood all down his front. Easy for us to mistake him as dead. I suspect he blacked out and maybe woke up in the back of the cart. Either that, or he was extremely good at pretending to be dead."

Hatan's heartbeat pounded in his ears. The truth of Migo's betrayal would spread. They had to find him. "Please report this to Captain Falshon. We need eyes on the street. A wound like that would be easy to spot, but he'll most definitely be hiding behind a veil."

"Will do. Anything else you need, regent?"

"No, thank you, Emil."

Emil nodded and hurried off, footsteps somehow making almost no sound.

Hatan sighed. Was there a way to get ahead of the enemy? Maybe people would buy the truth as a valid argument for Migo's actions. Migo released an innocent person, who then promptly killed the queen, but this saved the city from getting annihilated by war. But Migo's actions were still illegal. If the truth got out, Migo would be detained, deposed, and executed.

And that, of course, was not an option Hatan would allow.

Chapter 8

A deep sigh seeped out between Katsi's lips as she regarded Scales in her hands. She had to use both hands now to hold him. "You may have heard the rumors by now. I should have told you sooner," Katsi said, trying not to look too deeply into his large, trusting eyes, "but it was me. I... I killed the queen."

Scales closed his left eye as he rubbed that side of his face against her thumb.

"This is a big confession here, Scales," Katsi said.

Scales sat on his rump and looked up at her unblinkingly.

"Thank you," Katsi said. She leaned back against the wall of the Scorched Waste, hiding in the shadow it cast. The stones were hot against her back, but she felt like she needed to get this off her chest. "The tribe was really happy to see me. I've never had such a warm welcome from them, and it felt so nice to be accepted. Now I'm being sent out for another assassination, supposedly to save Jehubal again, just so I can learn how to use my powers better. This is the opposite of what I wanted to do, Scales. I feel selfish for focusing so much on becoming more powerful, especially if it means doing something very questionable."

Scales slid his tongue over an eye very slowly before nipping at Katsi's palm.

"Killing bugs to stay alive is not the same. It would be like you killing other scailas or... whatever you are." She eyed the spikes folded against his back. "But I'm basically an assassin now. And I'm not even getting paid!" She hadn't even thought about that part. How much money was a life worth? What would it be like to actually have money instead of scrounging around for food? How many cycles had she gone to sleep hungry because she couldn't find food or Damani didn't give her a handout?

She shook her head. Certainly working as an assassin for hire was not her destiny. The entire train of thought gave her a shiver, despite the hot air shimmering around her.

She sighed. "I'm not doing the wrong thing though, am I?"

Scales tilted his head and let out a small croak.

Katsi nodded. "You're right. I'm not doing this for myself. I'm doing it to save others. The seer said there was much more at stake than just Jehubal. I need to hone my skills for the sake of Malahem. Who knows, maybe Migo's right, and I can control a lot more than I think. What if I could stop a Maedari?"

Scales hummed and stretched the spikes on his back as he observed a black beetle buzz by.

Katsi rolled her eyes. "Go for it." She gave Scales a short toss upward, and he glided after the beetle, chasing it under a withering rockberry bush. "I'll be back in a few marks." She rolled her shoulders and took off at a run, wind at her back as she descended the sandy bank of Delirad Lake.

Talking with Scales had become a lifeline of sorts. Sure, she might be a little crazy, and Scales didn't actually talk back to her, but even though he didn't understand the words she said, she wanted to believe he could *feel* them.

The water beneath her frothed as Katsi flew across it. A spray of vapor left a misty cloud in her wake. She squealed, chest bursting with excitement. She'd decided to use the connection method the spirit had shown her with both the air and the water, and now she was running across the surface of Delirad Lake, her steps carrying her further and faster than she'd ever moved before.

She hoped ringdwellers waited on the other side, watching her coming. Not so that they'd fear her, but so they could see how amazing shamanic power could be. At the same time, the attention wouldn't do her any good. She stayed near the Scorched Waste in the shade of the massive dam that kept the water from spilling out into the canyon.

Ambient heat and sticky humidity permeated the air. Several shelled creatures, startled by her passing, shuffled off the rocky dam and into the water. As she neared the far shore, she could faintly see a few people at the edge of the water, further from the Scorched Waste. If they tried spotting her, they probably would, but hiding in the shadow of the dam would at least make it hard to pick her out.

She quickened her pace, strengthening the force of the wind that helped carry her. Her feet barely grazed the water's surface. When she reached land, she dropped to her knees on the hardened sand. She dropped her head, exhausted, not only from running, but from using her magic. Her armlet glowed warm against her skin.

After relaxing her muscles, she took a deep breath. Bright energy blossomed in her chest. Her fingers and toes tingled. She'd never been on this side of the lake before. She wanted it to feel magical or unique, but it was much the same as the other side. Vegetation was scarce this close to the Scorched Waste, but a few gulbas melon vines sprawled intermittently across the sand and dirt. They were all empty of fruit, however.

She was slightly annoyed at her constant assessment of what food she might be able to scavenge, even though she'd just eaten quite well with the tribe before visiting the canyon. She rose back to her feet. The sooner she was done with this task, the better.

The people further up the beach noticed her then. One pointed in her direction, and their voices echoed toward her.

She ran ahead. Thick jungle wasn't far away, but this was unfamiliar territory. On her side of the lake, she knew all the nooks and crannies to hide in, but she'd have no advantage here. The land sloped up. From what she'd heard, Cataban was on the side of a mountain, so it received a lot of sunlight even on the far end of the city.

She kept glancing back at the group of people by the shore, but none of them pursued her. Instead, they all picked up and started moving further upshore. Maybe people in Cataban felt differently about shamanfolk than the people of Jehubal.

Once she came to the jungle, she slowed down. Thick leaves provided a canopy cover, but the air was warmer and even thicker with humidity than it was on the lake. Her sweat turned sticky as she dodged around the large tree trunks. She pulled out her canteen and took a few deep swigs. The jungle here was thicker than she was used to. Rockberry bushes grew in large patches and were woven through with vines, often creating impassable walls, so the going was slow until she found a narrow animal trail.

She must have wound through the jungle for a full mark before emerging on the other side. The ground was covered in rocks, but she scrambled over them and climbed a large boulder to get a better view. She sucked in a deep breath as she reached the top and caught sight of Cataban. The entire city sloped up the mountain that peaked somewhere in the Frozen Waste. The city's border ended halfway up the mountain. None of the buildings were very tall, save for a single tower near the Frozen Waste.

From what her parents had told her, the city had originally been built by some of her ancestors. There was a labyrinth cave network built into those mountains, and a complex water filtering system running down from the mountain that provided more than enough water for the citizens. Cataban quarries had supplied the stone for most of the walls around the Ring in this part of Malahem.

Katsi's world had felt so small until now. She shook her head at the realization and jumped down from the boulder. Caution warned her not to get too close until she was able to observe the people. Were the walls guarded? Would they stop and question her? Did they dress or act differently? She'd seen plenty of Catabani people visit Jehubal and they'd seemed the same as anyone else, but she wouldn't dismiss these questions too lightly.

She headed to the road that came up from the docks. As with Jehubal, Cataban had only one entrance open to the public. There were smaller gates, but these were exclusively for local tradesmen.

Traffic was light, but Katsi was more worried about one of the people from the beach reporting that they'd seen somebody running across the water. From the few people she saw, none of them wore veils over their faces, so she pulled hers down around her neck and dropped her hood. She waited behind a few rocks until the road was clear before taking a deep breath and emerging.

The sounds of city life echoed down like the dull hum of a distant storm. A light breeze was constant, but instead of blowing toward or away from the sun, it flowed up from behind her. The humidity she felt in the jungle quickly disappeared as she gained some elevation.

Ahead of her, the gates were open. Two soldiers stood to either side of the opening and two more stood atop the wall. She wasn't worried they'd harm her. She was confident enough in her powers now that she felt like she could take on the world, but she didn't want to complicate the mission any further. Her heart still pounded as the soldiers looked at her for the first time. She averted her gaze. She'd never feel comfortable with a soldier looking at her.

Except for one of them. She bit her cheek as soon as the thought came to her. The memory of Migo's kiss and his big arms wrapped around her still burned hot in her mind.

The spirit's warning was clear. She needed to avoid him. Whatever crazy ideas she had about him needed to be discarded. He was scarred and traumatized by his own horrible life, and she'd shown some semblance of caring. Those were the only reasons he'd expressed any interest in her.

No matter what she told herself, her cheeks still burned.

Katsi was cautious until a group of three people walking ahead of her went through the gates without a second glance from the guards. She avoided looking at the soldiers as she got closer and was almost through the gate.

"Wait," said one of the guards as he stepped up to her. "I don't think I've seen you before. You're new?"

Wow. These guards actually recognized people coming through. Katsi gulped hard. "Yes." Best to keep her answers simple. She had to force back the elaborate story that came to mind.

"You came through Jehubal?"

"Yes. I didn't want to stay there. My father died in the—" she turned her head away and sucked in her lower lip, feigning emotion. Word of the devastating battle had no doubt reached them. She had a whole fake backstory prepared if they asked more.

"I see." The two soldiers shared a look. "Well, you're not the first one to come here. You might try visiting Terivahn in the lower district. It's a sleephouse where some Jehubalins are being looked after."

That was all the permission she needed. "Thank you. What's the lower district?" Katsi said, taking a few steps forward.

"To your right," he said, pointing. "The city is split in two. To the left is the upper district."

Katsi gave him a small smile and entered the city.

The main road was different than what she expected. Stone walls rose to either side, but temporary shops were set up against them. Several intersecting streets led up to the left or down to the right. She continued down the road for a while, hoping to blend in with the crowds before trying to find the right building. Something about the angle of the vision the spirit had shown her gave her the impression that it was in the upper district.

She was about to ask about it when something caught her attention. It was a cage of metal wires, and flitting about inside of it were small animals with wings that fluttered rapidly as they darted from one side of the cage to the other. They occasionally stopped, two taloned feet grasping at twigs that had been placed through the cage, little heads twitching from side to side as they looked around. They were bright colors of red, blue, and yellow.

"Ah, first time seeing one of these, eh?"

Katsi jumped at the voice, placing a hand over her chest. Her arms tingled with magic. The shop owner, a middle-aged woman, had come and stood by her side.

"Um, y-yes," Katsi responded.

The woman smiled kindly. "We brought these ones all the way from Brejael, halfway around the Ring. They say Malahem used to have millions of them, all different kinds, all different sizes, but these ones persisted because of their beaks."

"Beaks?" Katsi asked. She wanted to back away. She had a mission to do, but the woman grabbed the hem of Katsi's cloak, not aggressively, but it made Katsi nervous.

"Yes, their mouths. They have very hard beaks that can act like hammers to reach grubs inside of the tough trees. And the birds are covered in feathers instead of scales, so they can fly quite well."

"The what?"

"Birds. They're called birds."

Katsi jerked her arm free and hurried down the road, away from the birds. The spirit had warned her about those. What was threatening about them? They were small enough to fit in her hand. It must have been the shopkeeper. She looked over her shoulder, but the shopkeeper was gone.

"Sleet," Katsi muttered to herself. She stopped the nearest person, an older man with very dark skin. "Hey, do you know where I can find a domed building with two pillars on either side of the entrance?"

He eyed her up and down. "Ah, I've seen a couple like that in the upper district. You'll want to head up that next street and go a few blocks."

"Thank you." Katsi all but ran as she turned the corner, hoping to place some distance between herself and the birds.

She had to fight to resist the urge of pulling her hood and veil on. She felt too exposed, like everybody was watching her. The low stone buildings passed in a blur until she stopped after ascending a few blocks. Her breath came heavy as she looked around, but none of the buildings fit the vision. She wanted to keep looking and find it on her own, but she knew that could take too long. Still, she wandered aimlessly for two more blocks before pausing to ask someone. After providing details about the diamond shapes etched into the pillars, the person gave Katsi specific directions.

It was three blocks away.

She hurried off at first, but her pace slowed. Anticipation clawed at her. She checked her belt and pockets. Everything was in order. She'd purchased another paralytic potion before leaving the tribe. It was the same way she killed Queen Rikaydian, but she wasn't sure if she needed it this time.

Her fingers trembled. She shook out her hands, then clenched her fists. The building came into sight. It took up a fourth of the block. The street wasn't busy, but every person that passed made her more nervous. She yearned for the cover of a storm. No hiding this time. It wasn't too late to turn back. Nobody was forcing her to be an assassin. She was making this choice herself.

And for what? The spirit mentioned that this man risked the destruction of cities. She'd be working to save them.

Katsi blinked away tears.

She wasn't here to save anyone.

Her true purpose in coming to kill someone was so that she could learn more about her power. She loved the freedom it gave her. The strength to make things different on her own accord. The acceptance and warmth she'd received from the tribe. Where was Scales when she needed him?

She released a shuddering breath and strode across the street to the building, forcing her thoughts aside. Enough second guessing. She'd already made up her mind.

Katsi passed the two pillars and approached the door. Sand scraped beneath her boots on the unkempt path. The door was unlocked, so she shoved it open, its hinges creaking. She stepped inside, realizing how unprofessional she was being. Normally she would have checked the whole perimeter from the outside, looking for other openings for means of escape. She would observe for a while to see who came and went. She would have memorized any patterns and planned her approach at the perfect timing.

She'd done none of that. *Magic is making me reckless.* She stepped further into the dusty corridor. The building looked abandoned. Debris was shoved up to one side of the hall's wall, but a clear path led straight ahead to a large, open room. Light filtered in from grimy storm reinforced windows in the domed ceiling.

Air whistled through the corridor as Katsi walked ahead, ignoring the smaller, empty rooms to either side. The domed room beckoned her. She pulled out her knife and held her breath, stepping lightly across the floor.

There was a figure at the center of the room, stooped over a crumbled, stone table, back turned to her. He was alone. She stopped at the end of the hall, watching him.

"You've finally come for me," the man said in a deep, quiet voice. "I wondered how long it would take."

Katsi was frozen in place. She wasn't supposed to let the man speak. His words would bring destruction. She forced herself out of the stiffness and continued to approach him.

He held his hands to the side and turned around slowly. When their eyes met, he tilted his head, eyes squinting in confusion. "You're not who I expected." A ragged sigh escaped his lips. "You must be the one who killed the queen. I should have known I'd be next, but I stayed. I hoped the king would find me."

Questions popped into her head. She needed to kill him. Kill him and be over with it. "Do you mean Migo?" she asked. She wanted to clamp a hand over her mouth.

"Few call him Migo." His eyes narrowed. "You know him."

"What do you have to do with Migo?"

"I served his father, the late king." He reached into his cloak and Katsi summoned her magic, stones and sand lifted into the air. The floor of the building trembled. Without skipping a beat, he withdrew a parchment. "Please, if you see him. You must give him this."

This conversation wasn't supposed to be happening. "But I'm here to kill you. Your words are dangerous." She summoned a strong wind that blew across the man, whipping the parchment from his hand.

"I understand," he said, dropping his head.

Footsteps echoed from outside. He had help coming. She shouldn't have spoken with him. Her stomach lurched. It was a trap.

Chapter 9

Dread coursed through Migo's body as Genda thundered up the street. He pulled her to a stop just outside the domed building. He couldn't shake the feeling he was too late.

"Stay," he said, giving Genda a hand signal as he swung off her back.

Migo charged through the open door. An unnatural wind blew through the hall. He held Hatan's knife in one hand as he pumped his arms in a full sprint. He reached a large room in the ruined building just as the assassin withdrew a knife from R's chest and stood up.

"No!" Migo shouted. He hurled his knife at the assassin, but it clattered away, knocked aside by a rock. When she turned to look at him, he froze. The wind stopped. Rocks and sand hung suspended in the air.

Her eyes widened, mouth open.

"Katsi," he whispered, shaking his head slowly. "No." His hands balled into fists. "Why?"

"He was dangerous—"

"He was going to help me find out who murdered my father," he snarled. He stomped over to her and grabbed her by the cloak. She made no move to flee. The sand and rocks dropped from the air. "Don't you understand? If I can find out who actually killed my father, I could seek justice. We could turn Jehubal's anger away from the Bayvana Tribe. This would have bought us the long lasting peace we've been looking for."

Katsi's hazel eyes widened even more as she looked up into his. "I'm sorry, Migo. I didn't know."

His face grew hot with rage. "How did you know about him? Did you steal the journal?"

"I don't know what journal you're talking about. A seer told me to come here. Seers can see things—whatever information he had—it was dangerous. She was trying to protect us."

He shook his head. "Sleet, Katsi. After ten years, I was finally going to know the truth."

"Maybe the truth would destroy you," she said softly, eyes glinting.

"Is that a joke? You killed the queen, the one responsible for murdering your parents. Don't you sleep better knowing that justice has been dealt? All I want is the same relief."

"You're afraid."

"No, I'm angry," he said, voice rasping. "Have you ever been angry enough at someone," he lifted a trembling hand, stroking her neck with his finger, "that you wanted to rip their head off their shoulders?"

"Yes," she whispered, eyes glistening with tears. "And yet you're still alive."

He dropped his hand. The softness of her flesh burned him. He felt the urge to peel his own skin off just to shed the anxious pain that coursed through his veins. He couldn't be mad at her. She was hurting. Something wasn't right.

She placed a hand on his chest. A chill rippled across his body. "You're in so much pain, Migo. I hoped you were getting better." She blinked and a tear escaped down her cheek. The sight of that single drop of water completely disarmed him. When was the last time anybody shed a tear for him? "I didn't kill the queen for revenge. I killed her because I wanted to save you."

Migo closed his eyes and let out a long breath. Katsi's hand soothed the burning in his heart, melting his rage. "It's not all about revenge." He opened his eyes and looked down at her, wishing he could take away the tears that glimmered on her cheeks. "I need to know who killed my father. Who ruined my life. Who turned my mother into a monster. I need to know why."

"Will it heal you to know?"

"I'm not sure anything can heal me. I'm still me, after all, but at least I could maybe move on."

She stepped away from him, hand dropping off his chest. "I should go," she said, but made no move to leave. She stared down at the bloody knife in her hand.

Migo knelt beside R. His eyes stared lifelessly, so Migo closed his eyelids. Blood pooled on the stone floor around him. "Did he say anything before you killed him?"

Katsi took another step away. Her breathing was staggered. "No... I...." Her skin had paled.

"Katsi." Migo rose to his feet. "What's wrong?" He'd seen this look before in soldiers after battle.

"I don't want to be an assassin, Migo."

"I doubt anybody aspires to the role," he said, stepping closer. "Let me clean that off for you." He took the knife from her hand, then turned to wipe it off on R's cloak. "Did he say anything to you?"

"He-he mentioned you. Almost as if he knew you were coming."

Odd. Migo coming to find R was known only to Hatan. "Did he say anything else?"

Katsi let out a shuddering breath. "No. Nothing else."

He squinted at her. His training as an inquisitor urged him to dig deeper, but it didn't feel right to press her. The timing was off. He kept her knife in hand and proceeded to check through R's pockets. He found a few coins, some sort of balm, a glass lens, worn, blank paper, charcoal, leather cords, and an ornate silver dagger. It seemed he hadn't tried to defend himself. If he was a spy, he would have had combat training. Migo tucked the silver dagger into his own belt.

The tips of the fingers on his right hand were smudged black. Charcoal. He'd written something recently. "Was he alone?"

"Yes," Katsi said.

"Did you check the other rooms?"

"No."

He rose back to his feet and regarded her. She'd backed away a few more steps, but her breathing had steadied. Her hands were clasped together.

"Katsi, you're not doing a good job at masking your emotions."

She glanced away, pursing her lips. "I don't know what you're talking about. I'd like my knife back."

Migo walked to her, placing the handle of the knife in her hand. "I was trained as an inquisitor. You're conflicted. You're afraid of me. Why?"

Katsi rolled her eyes. "The seer said I needed to avoid you."

Migo smiled. "Of course she did. She's right to be cautious. I'm the king of Jehubal now, Katsi. The shamans don't trust me. I'll work to fix that. But you know better than that." He stepped closer. Close enough to feel the heat of her breath on his neck as she looked up at him. She cared about him. Maybe not in the same way she'd cared for Damani, but it was genuine. She cared about him even when he'd been her enemy. "I would never hurt you. I'm the last person you need to fear."

Katsi bit her lip before smirking. "How far you've fallen, princeling."

If only she knew. "The correct term is 'Your Majesty.' I'm a king, thanks to you."

"That's the second time I've saved your life."

"Third, truly. You also saved me from myself." He placed a hand on her elbow. "You once told me about defining myself on my own terms. If you don't want to be an assassin, that's up to you. Maybe you're a hero instead."

"Sleet and sand, Migo." She shoved at him with a laugh, but he didn't budge. "I certainly don't feel like a hero."

"But you were my hero when I needed you. And I didn't feel worthy to live. Things change."

"That's too optimistic and profound to be coming from your mouth."

"It proves my point even more." He gave her a smug smile. It was amazing to him how quickly his anger had dissipated, replaced by determination. "Now help me search the building. It's likely that R recently wrote a note or letter, but he didn't have it on his person."

Katsi sighed. "Yes, he... he held it out to me. Asked me to give it to you, but it got blown away when I used my magic. It's probably here in the room somewhere."

Migo nodded without pointing out that she'd lied to him. Best to keep her on good terms. He started looking around the perimeter of the room. He knew she'd been hiding something. Somewhere along the way, he'd lost her trust. Asking her to kill his mother had been asking a lot. Perhaps too much, but it had bought his freedom, and hers. No more hiding.

Finding the letter wouldn't be too difficult. The round room had no nooks or crannies for things to get lost, but there was significant dust and rubble. It could have gotten buried. He kicked rocks aside and found a piece of parchment, bending down to pick it up without telling Katsi. She shuffled slowly on the opposite side of the room, still looking.

Migo unfolded the parchment, expecting to find a letter, but instead it was a map with scattered phrases and paragraphs. It was a section of the Ring north of Jehubal. Several landmarks were noted.

One paragraph at the bottom was scribbled out in hasty handwriting. It read, "Lord Migo Rikaydian, by now you know of the agents embedded at

Jehubal. We found what they were looking for. All attempts at entry failed. Silver and magic are the keys."

That was all it said. Did this mean his father's murderer was at Jehubal? And what were the agents looking for? He scanned the map, looking for any other distinct markings.

Katsi started coming from across the room.

He spotted a single mark along the Frozen Waste, a circle drawn in charcoal around a distinctive mark in the wall.

"What is it?" Katsi asked, pausing as she reached Migo and looking over his shoulder.

"Just a map."

"I thought you said he would tell you who killed your father."

"He probably would have, but he's dead." Migo looked at her pointedly, trying not to sound as annoyed as he still felt. "I assume he would have elaborated on this map further, but it looks like this is all I get."

Katsi didn't meet his eyes, but focused instead on the map. "Silver and magic are the keys. What does that mean?"

Migo sighed. "It means I can't get in there alone." He rose to his feet, folding the map back up.

"Oh, no."

"I need your help, Katsi."

"Come on, Migo." She shook her head.

"I know this seer told you to stay away from me, but I'm no danger to you." As their eyes met, his heart pounded, his ears and cheeks warmed. There may as well have been static crackling between them. It was just one cycle ago that Migo thought he'd never see her again, yet here they were, brought together again in a different city, against all odds. "I've had plenty of opportunities to hurt you, but I never have, and I never will. I've risked myself for you. Has anybody else ever done that?"

"You're trying to manipulate me."

Migo shrugged. "If telling the truth is manipulative, then yes, I'm guilty."

She folded her arms and narrowed her eyes at him. She chewed her lip in thought. He almost had her. If magic was necessary for unlocking whatever R had found, then Katsi was his only chance at getting in. "I swear I won't ask you to kill anyone."

"I didn't kill your mother because you asked me to. It was my own choice."

"Okay, I get it." Migo held up his hands. "You always make your own decisions. I'm saying I won't force you into anything."

She raised an eyebrow at him. "You couldn't force me if you wanted to anyway."

"Fair enough. So will you help me?"

Katsi ran a hand through her hair, then flicked it over her shoulder. "We don't know what it is yet, so I'm not making any promises, but I'll go with you to check it out. Deal?"

"I accept."

"You're unhealthy for me, you know that?"

"I don't see how I have a negative effect on your health. It's not like I poison your food. That doesn't make any sense."

She slapped her forehead. "No, I don't mean physically. I forgot you still don't quite know what a joke is. You know what? Nevermind. If I have to explain it, I've already lost the kicker." She started bouncing off to the exit.

"Wait," Migo said, pushing his confusion aside. "We should take care of his body."

"You're right." Her face dropped with a twitch of pain as she regarded the body. She walked towards R and paused a couple steps away. She knelt on the ground, placing her palms against the stone. Dust vibrated on the floor. She dragged her hands across the floor and R's body sank into the stone as though the stone had liquified. Katsi stopped a couple seconds after his body disappeared.

She stood with a gasp.

Migo tapped the stone where R's body had been; it was solid. He forgot how to breathe as he looked at her. "Have you always been able to do that?"

Katsi shook her head. "No, I-I made it up. I just learned shaping a few marks ago. I can connect with the stone. I was trying to open it like a door, instead it... did that."

Possibilities whirred. She could sink soldiers in battle. She could sink *him* right now. The image of his father's blood spattering across the stone flashed through his mind. *Such power shouldn't exist.* He'd heard that phrase every day while training as a shaman hunter.

"Migo, you've got that look in your eyes," Katsi said, patting his arm. "I'm not a monster, remember?"

He blinked at her touch. "I know you're not a monster. I've never seen anything like that before, and I... had some training trigger when you did something that ordinary people shouldn't be able to do."

"That's because I'm nothing less than extraordinary," she said. She started walking to the exit again. He followed as she spoke over her shoulder. "I have to stop a couple places before going on your little quest."

"You need to report back to the seer? I'm not familiar with shamanfolk politics, but I'd like to know more. Does she hold a position of authority?"

Katsi sighed. "Not necessarily. She's not even technically part of my tribe, but a seer isn't a position or rank, it has more to do with the type of magic she possesses. At the same time, seers are regarded with a higher level of respect than other types of shamans, especially because of how rare they are. The Bayvana Tribe has no seers."

"So there are different types of magic, and no formal type of political structure?"

"Yes, different types of magic, but the governing structure is not what you're used to." Katsi paused at the door as she saw Genda laying on the ground just outside.

"She's tame," Migo said, quickly stepping out in front of Katsi.

Genda lifted her head to regard them and unfolded her paws.

Migo hummed at Genda and scratched under her neck. She thunked her massive head against his chest. He laughed at the sour expression on Katsi's face. "Not all of nature hates ringdwelllers."

"Right. How fast can you reach Jehubal while riding a rangola?"

"I'll need to cross the lake by ferry, so a little over one cycle."

"Okay, that should be enough time for me."

"Katsi, Jehubal is three cycles walking distance from here."

Katsi smiled and lowered her voice. "Who needs to walk when you can fly?"

"You're joking, right? You can't actually fly."

"Well, maybe not flying, but I did run across the lake to get here."

Migo raised an eyebrow at her. He tried to picture her running on the water. It was wild, but she just made a man sink into the stone. He could believe just about anything at this point. "Incredible."

"So let's meet up in two cycles. I need to sleep and collect a few things if we're going near the Frozen Waste. Is my home still being watched?"

"No."

"Will people in the city be looking for me?"

"No, not actively," Migo said, running a hand through his hair. "Even though I've put an end to the war with the shamans, you may be recognized. Many people saw your face when the queen had you imprisoned. You have been identified as the queen's murderer."

Katsi's face went blank, and she looked off to the side.

"Not ideal, I know. As long as you have your veil on, you should be fine."

"I'm accustomed to hiding, Migo," she said flatly.

He conceded with a nod. "Northeast gate on the fourth mark in two cycles then?"

"See you then." She dashed off down the street.

Migo watched her until she was out of sight. He never thought he'd be relying on her again. He hoped for her sake that he wasn't putting her in danger.

Chapter 10

Katsi's stomach twisted as she bounded through the air. The rush of wind roared by her ears, her loose robe whipping and flapping behind her. Instead of crossing the lake, she jumped the wall into the Scorched Waste, deciding to risk the heat rather than people seeing her. She couldn't shake the feeling that she was being manipulated. If not by Migo, then by the spirit.

She barely knew the spirit. She didn't even know the woman's name, and yet she'd run off and assassinated somebody for her. The spirit told her to avoid Migo—the only person who'd ever stuck himself out for her. It was everything she'd feared. Migo forgave her too easily, and the guilt gnawed at her. She had to believe there was still hope to find whatever he was looking for.

Sand swirled about her as she came to a stop at the edge of the canyon, looking down into the depths. The yawning chasm stretched for miles into the Scorched Waste. The desert was endless. Nobody knew why the whole planet stopped rotating. She wondered how many more people must have lived on Malahem before that happened.

I'm stalling. She smiled to herself. Best not to think about it. She took a deep breath and jumped, grasping at the air with her magic. She still fell too fast, then tried to connect with the stone wall of the cliffs, panic gripping her chest. Nothing happened for a moment until a fountain of stone erupted out of the cliffside and crashed into her legs, her body smashing down onto the abnormal protrusion.

Katsi burst into anxious laughter. She was laying on a horizontally suspended pillar of stone, held there mainly by her own magic. She'd only fallen a few feet from the ledge. The air managed to slow her, but not enough. She summoned it again, this time using a strong, upward push, then leapt off the pillar. The stone crumbled once her connection ceased, and she fell through the air once more, though much slower this time. The powerful, upward draft roared through the canyon, throwing sand into the air, but it slowed her descent enough to bring her all the way to the bottom of the canyon with a stumbled landing.

"That looked fun." The aged voice echoed off the canyon walls.

Katsi looked around until she spotted the spirit, walking toward her from deeper in the Scorched Waste.

"Try melding with the wall next time and keep a hand connected. It's much more controlled."

Katsi stood upright, watching the spirit carefully as she approached. Perhaps Migo was right. Maybe she'd been too quick to trust the spirit. Even Mashe had warned Katsi about seers and their visions. If anyone had turned Katsi into an assassin, it was her.

"It is done, then? You killed him?" the woman asked. She stuck to the shadows.

"Yes."

"And the birds, did you see them?" Dust kicked up as the woman walked.

"Yes, I ran as soon as I saw them," she lied.

The woman paused at arms length from Katsi. "Good, good. And he wasn't able to speak? Relay to me what happened."

Katsi took the opportunity to drink from her canteen, giving her time to think. She had no idea how much a seer could see. "I felt a sense of urgency, so I ran straight to the building. When I went inside, he was just standing there in the middle of the room. I didn't want to approach him, so I used a new idea. I basically turned the floor into liquid. He sank right into the ground and it returned to stone when I released my connection."

The wrinkles around the spirit's eyes grew deeper as she pursed her lips and squinted at Katsi. "That is a complex use of earthmelding. I'm not sure even any of the earthmelders among the Bayvana Tribe have had that level of intuition with their own proficiency." She continued scrutinizing Katsi long enough to make her uncomfortable.

"Alright, so what now?" Katsi said. "Just tell me where to go and who can teach me. I'm not your assassin."

"Of course," the spirit said, stepping further back into the shadows. "I am simply impressed by your skill in a class of magic that isn't your primary proficiency. I can only fathom what you might be able to do with stormcalling once you are taught properly."

Katsi shrugged. "I'm here to learn."

"What do you know of seership?"

"Practically nothing. The tribe hasn't had one for a long time."

"Probably for the best. It can sometimes cloud one's judgment between truth and possibility. Earthmelding and stormcalling are quite similar. They are very physical and instinctive, which can make them easier to learn. Enchanting and mixing require study and practice. Seer magic is not so straightforward. It takes self-awareness, sensitivity, and mental training. Without training, it can be difficult to discern between visions and your own ideas. I say all this because you have great strength. You may have the capacity to effectively utilize all classes."

All of them. Katsi tried to ignore the tight feeling that gripped her chest. She still just needed to grasp how to use stormcalling. "Even bleeding?"

The seer's face didn't change. "Yes. Using any of them without proper training comes with risks as you thoughtfully demonstrated by jumping off a cliff. Your instincts are sharp but wild."

"Then where do I go?" Katsi asked with a shrug, her voice a little snappy. "How do I learn? Who can teach me?"

The wrinkles around the woman's mouth deepened as she smiled at Katsi. It was the first smile she'd ever seen the woman make. "You must go to Mazanib."

Mazanib. She was sure she should know the name. She'd heard it before. "Mazanib. Of course," she said, tone laced with sarcasm. She at least knew it was a place. "Where is that?"

"It's the capitol. On the north of the Ring."

Katsi shook her head. "Impossible."

The woman's expression didn't change, and she said nothing.

"That's a death sentence. Why would I go there?"

"Because if you want to master stormcalling, that's where you must go."

"I don't believe you."

"With power like yours, Katsi, you could change the world. The only one who can help you achieve that is in Mazanib."

Katsi folded her arms. Her ears burned, a combination of the heat and her frustration. "I find it hard to believe that there are many shamans that close to the emperor."

"I understand your hesitation, but there are in fact shamans there. Not many, but they are close to the emperor." A smirk lifted her lips. "Very close."

Of course they were. A shiver went down her spine despite the heat. Perhaps they were assassins too. Biding their time. Maybe that's what the seer really wanted from her. Maybe it was less about training and more about another assassination. "What's your name?" Katsi asked. She needed more from this woman. A name was a start.

"I have had many names over the years," she said, her voice suddenly weary.

"I don't care about your titles," Katsi said with more flare than she'd intended. "What's your true name? I deserve to know at least that much."

"Very well," the seer said, picking a long, black hair off her robe. "My name is Alishara."

"Alright then, Alishara," Katsi said with a nod. "How am I supposed to get in there and not die?"

"Simple. You need to memorize some names. Can you do that? Don't want to strain your brain too much."

Katsi rolled her eyes. "Sands, just give me the instructions."

"There's a sleephouse called Elen-Fidtan. When you arrive there, you must ask one of the cooks for Venach. Venach will ask you for the name of a root. You will tell him Shavarani and show him your armlet. Got it?"

"Yes. That's it?"

"That's it. Don't repeat this information to anyone. Don't write it down."

"Do I look like I own paper?" Katsi raised her arms. She did actually own some paper. She had half a sheet back at her parents' old hideout. One of the perks of her occasional robberies.

Alishara didn't respond, but she inhaled deeply and lifted her chin, looking down her nose at Katsi through lidded eyes. "Do not linger in Jehubal. You've done all you can here for now."

"Excellent advice," Katsi said, looking up at the canyon walls. "Anything else I should know before I go get myself killed?"

Alishara clicked her tongue. "You've got enough experience hiding and sneaking. I'm sure you'll get where you need to." She cast her head to the side as if hearing something in the distance, then regarded Katsi again. "Is there anything else you need to tell me about your visit to Cataban?"

Katsi shook her head and shrugged. "No. I did the job and came back."

"You didn't see King Rikaydian?"

She knew. Somehow she knew. "No," Katsi lied. "What would he even be doing in Cataban?" She fought back the intrusive thoughts. There was no way she could have known about her interaction with Migo. Seer magic didn't work like that, right? She understood too little. The pressure to know everything was suddenly mounting on her. Change the world? She was too young, too inexperienced, too weak.

But I can change all that, she reminded herself, taking a deep breath and staring back in the old woman's brown eyes, noticing for the first time that they were flecked with blue.

"Don't mind that," Alishara said. "As long as you avoid the king, we'll all be safer."

"Right," Katsi said, walking to the cliff wall and placing her hand against its rough, sandy surface. The stone molded around her hand as she became a part of it—or did it become a part of her? She couldn't tell the difference. "Anything else?"

Alishara shrugged and turned away. "I suppose not. Try not to be as snappy with the shamans in Mazanib."

"No promises," Katsi said, then started scaling the wall, stifling her smirk until she was out of sight. Climbing by connecting with the stone was like second nature already. Her very skin tingled with excitement as realization settled in. She was one of the most powerful shamans in years, not only in stormcalling, but in other classes as well. She had a feeling she'd only scratched the surface of what her magic could do.

When she reached the top of the cliff, she burned with energy as the hot sun licked the sweat from her flesh, leaving her salty and dry. She *wanted* to meet with Migo again. She *wanted* to see what he needed her magic for. Not just to repay him for killing his informant, but because she wanted to test her own limits.

There was one place left to stop. If they were going anywhere near the Frozen Waste, she needed to bring some additional supplies.

Home.

She summoned the air and sand at her back and burst ahead with a massive leap.

Chapter 11

Migo stood on the roof of Rikaydian Palace. It was the tallest point in the city. The view was spectacular, and yet he hardly ever came. He felt surprisingly emotional as he watched Agwe, the head servant, spreading Tilayna Rikaydian's ashes into the wind. A dark emptiness squirmed its way up his stomach, and the lump in his throat pained him. Their land was free of an oppressive tyrant, but that woman had still, at some point, been his mother. Tears threatened to well in his eyes as he pitied her existence, so harrowed up by grief and anger that she'd lost all pleasure in life.

Katsi hadn't killed his mother. His mother had died years ago.

But Migo had never had the opportunity to mourn her. And now that sense of loss mounted. The loneliness he'd felt for years hung on his back like a wet coat. As the last of her ashes disappeared into the distance, he felt no anger towards her. No resentment. No shame.

Perhaps that's what mourning felt like.

He wanted to say something. To express somehow what he was feeling, or even whisper a goodbye, but the words caught in his throat, and all he could do was stare.

A strong hand gripped Migo on the shoulder. Migo turned to look at Hatan, surprised to see tears on his cousin's cheeks.

Only the three of them stood on the rooftop. Perhaps they were the only people left who remembered the old Tilayna. The one who'd loved her family and her people more than revenge.

He looked out towards the Frozen Waste. She was the one who finally took him to the Frozen Waste just so he could see the stars. He'd begged his father for cycles, and then she suddenly surprised him while an astronomer was visiting. They bundled up in the warmest clothes and hiked up a rise right behind the wall by the Frozen Waste. A few stars would barely be visible on the horizon, but the astronomer knew them all, and Migo absorbed everything his little mind could.

Agwe turned and gave a solemn nod to them before retreating down the stairs.

Migo cleared his throat and turned to Hatan. "Anything interesting happen while I was gone?"

Hatan wiped his face and sniffed. "It's a whole kingdom, your majesty. Of course there were interesting occurrences."

"Do you need me to kill anybody?"

Hatan burst with laughter. It instantly warmed Migo's broken heart, and he joined in. Perhaps they were both hysterical.

"You let me worry about it," Hatan said after regaining control. "But you are the one I'm hoping has news." He clapped Migo's shoulder. "And I made something for you while you slept. It's in the kitchen still."

"I thought they stopped letting you in there," Migo said.

Hatan barked a laugh. "That's before I was regent, my dear king. Now they can't say no." Hatan led the way down the stairs, and Migo was only too eager to follow. Not for whatever food his cousin had planned, but just to get off that roof.

"I have other news, Hatan," Migo said darkly as he closed the stormlock behind them.

"I'm sure you do," Hatan said. "Tell me it's good news."

"R is dead." And Katsi was the one who killed him, but he didn't share that detail. Why was he defending her? What was he even protecting her from?

Hatan was silent for several steps before he responded. "I'm sorry. How did you find out?"

"I found his body. He had a silver dagger and a map." Migo withdrew the dagger. It was a hand-and-a-half in length, certainly a step up from Hatan's knife.

"I suppose that means I get my knife back, then," Hatan said. He glanced back at Migo, searching. "Anything good on the map?"

"Possibly. There is a location marked. I'm determined to find out what it is. I'm assuming they couldn't access it before because there's a note stating magic is required."

Hatan gave Migo a knowing look and a small nod. "I see." They turned a corner and entered the kitchen where a coal-burning stove was still warm. A stone plate of rounded, baked goods cooled on the work table.

Migo rolled his eyes. "Cookies, Hatan? You know I don't like sweets."

"Ah, but these aren't just any sweets, Migo." Hatan's eyes lit up, and he bounced across the room to scoop up a cookie. "These are Padarro Pastries. I made them myself—just for you. I packed them with a balance of disgusting, nutritious ingredients that you like as well as sugar, salt, and everything nice that the rest of normal society enjoys. I even experimented with adding a couple selaha eggs to the mix."

"Selaha eggs?" Migo raised an eyebrow. Hatan responded with an excited nod. Selahas were aquatic reptiles that lived in large numbers in the waters northeast of Jehubal. People had only started farming their eggs in the last few years. Migo had hesitantly tasted one a few months ago only to find that it was... remarkably delicious. And Hatan clearly hadn't forgotten.

Hatan handed the cookie over, beaming as Migo rose it to his mouth and took a bite. It practically melted in his mouth with a creamy, grainy texture. The sweetness was mild, balanced well with a hint of nut and salt. He swallowed and was tempted to take another bite, but Hatan was perspiring with anticipation.

"Sleet and sand, Hatan," Migo said with a chuckle. "I've never seen you more animated about anything in my whole life."

"What do you think?" Hatan said, his muscles straining as he gripped the table.

Migo shook his head. It almost pained him to admit it. "It's delicious, Hatan."

Hatan roared as if he were charging into battle. He pumped his fists and clapped Migo on the shoulder so hard he almost dropped the cookie.

All Migo could do was laugh.

"All things are possible, your majesty," Hatan shouted. "If I can make something that King Rikaydian finds delicious, no obstacle is too great."

Agwe peeked through the door, along with an armed guard, but they quickly scuttled away when Migo looked over at them. "Alright, you made your point, cousin," he said, still chuckling.

"This is a proud day for me," Hatan said. He whipped a cloth out from under the table and immediately started wrapping all the cookies into it. "I'll pack them up for you. But go ahead and close the door. Tell me more about this... finding of yours."

Migo popped the rest of the cookie in his mouth and closed the door before pulling the map out from a pocket of his shirt coat. He unfolded it and placed it on the table in front of Hatan.

Hatan's demeanor changed as he squared his shoulders, face growing serious as he scrutinized the document. "I feel like I should know more about this." His frown deepened.

"Well, I intend to get some answers. My father was looking for something, and somebody was trying to stop him."

Hatan shrugged. "Perhaps it was the other way around."

"I'll find out soon enough."

Hatan handed Migo the wrapped up cookies. "I have something else for you before you go."

"Oh, better than some treats I regrettably like?"

Hatan smirked. "Much better." He led Migo outside the kitchen and down through the throne room to the office he'd taken up. The room smelled of oiled metal and polished wood. When they got inside, Hatan stepped to the side of the room and gestured to the desk.

There, resting atop the desk was a new poleaxe. "For me?" Migo asked.

Hatan nodded.

Migo looked up and down the length of it. Poleaxes were versatile weapons. The tip was a sharpened spear, with a curved ax on one side and a hammerhead on the other. He picked it up, testing the weight, running his hands along the polished wood.

"I know it's shorter than your glaive, but I figured this would be more appropriate for travel. Carrying a massive pole around isn't always convenient. Oh, and there are a few silver studs intermingled in the steel which should help create a bit of magical resistance, should that need arise."

"No, this should be perfect, Hatan. Thank you." Migo squeezed the handle. It wasn't the same as his glaive, but still, holding a heavier, thicker weapon brought with it a measure of comfort. "Any idea how to carry it?"

"Ah, yes," Hatan said. He pulled a leather strap and a wrap from under the desk. The wrap went over the ax portion of the weapon, and then the strap looped around the shaft. "Then you just sling it over one shoulder or the other."

"Thanks again," Migo said, swinging it over his shoulder. "I should be off. I'm supposed to be meeting with Katsi soon."

Hatan nodded and then opened the door to the office.

A spear tip slipped through the gap in the door as soon as it was open, poking right into the side of Hatan's chest. He gripped the end of the spear as he stumbled away.

Migo bellowed and charged out, shoving the shaft of the spear into the door, snapping the weapon in half. A different spear jabbed at his head. There were two of them. He ducked. It came again, right for his gut. He shifted to the side, hurling the broken spear at the attacker, then charged in. The other would-be assassin swung his broken spear at Migo like a cudgel. Migo raised his arm, taking it in full force, then kicked the man square in the stomach, sending him back.

The second attacker dropped his spear and withdrew a shortsword. This gave Migo enough time to swing the poleaxe back off his shoulder.

The man's eyes widened.

They knew who he was, right? They knew what Migo was capable of. And they'd hurt Hatan. Perhaps that first spear had been meant for him. They'd wish it had found its mark.

Migo didn't wait. He stepped in, swinging lightly before the first attacker could get back to his feet, batting the man's knee with the hammer end of the poleaxe. Then he thrust the spear point into the man's chest.

The other attacker rushed in, jabbing his sword. Migo barely parried in time, then barreled down on the man, swinging the poleaxe over and over. The man's shortsword wasn't able to deflect the attacks. He actually gave up, throwing the weapon at Migo. It glanced across Migo's hip.

"Migo," Hatan's voice called from behind. Hatan peeked out from the office room, hand clutched over his chest. "Keep one alive."

Migo growled and sprinted after the remaining attacker who was already running away at full speed. "Assassin!" he bellowed, hoping others in the palace would hear.

The door opened just before the assassin reached it, and a soldier came inside.

"Assassin!" Migo repeated.

The attacker slipped as he tried to turn, and the soldier hacked across at him with his longsword, scoring a gash across the man's back.

When Migo arrived, the assassin sprang up, stabbing a knife at Migo's chest. Migo swung, bashing the arm down, smacking the ax side of his weapon into the man's throat. The leather sheath was still on, but the assassin collapsed on his back.

"Who sent you?" Migo demanded.

The assassin only wheezed. A pool of blood spread out beneath him.

Migo kicked the knife away for good measure then glanced up at the soldier. "Find something to bind his wounds. Quick."

The soldier nodded and sprinted off.

Hatan walked across the room, still holding a hand to the side of his chest. "This one looks familiar," Hatan said, looking down at the wheezing man. "He's suffocating. Won't be able to talk."

"Your wound?" Migo said.

"I'll live."

"What about the other one?" Migo pointed to the other assassin who lay on the other side of the throne.

"Dying."

They walked back to the first assassin together. The one who'd stabbed Hatan. He looked to be in shock, face twisted as he panted, blood seeping out between his fingers as he pressed them against his stomach.

Migo kneeled down beside him. "Who sent you?"

The assassin made no response.

Migo placed the hammer of his poleaxe down against the man's hands, right over the wound, and pressed. The man screamed. "Who sent you? Give me a name and I'll end it."

"L-L-L," he struggled to pronounce the first letter until his face suddenly went still. He blinked up at the ceiling, took two slow breaths, then stopped moving.

Migo groaned and got back to his feet. "We got one letter. Not sure that'll help. It could be lord or lady for all we know."

Hatan prodded at his wound. The bleeding appeared to have slowed down. "I just want to know how they got in here."

"Likewise. You said one looked familiar?"

"Yes. I've seen him around the palace. I think he was one of the mercenaries we'd dismissed after the queen's death."

"That didn't take long for them to get in somebody else's pocket."

A gasp echoed through the room as Agwe entered, a hand over her mouth. "But I just finished cleaning all the other blood off the floors a few marks ago." She glanced up at Migo. "Your Majesty."

"Yes, Your Majesty," Hatan said, "you should really try to keep all your killing limited to the exterior of the palace."

Migo blinked back at him then spoke as flatly as possible. "I'll try my best to carry them out next time before I stab them."

"That's the spirit," Hatan said, patting Migo's shoulder.

The soldier burst back into the room with some cloth in hand then looked down disappointedly at the dead assassin.

"It's alright, Rivar," Hatan said, taking the cloth and stuffing it under his own shirt. "You'll come with me and His Majesty to the courtyard."

Migo glared down at the two dead assassins one last time before leaving the room. If he had to guess, they somehow knew about the passageways in the palace. The ones only his family were supposed to know about. How such information had leaked, he could never figure out. They'd have to seal most doors off in order to secure the palace better, but Hatan knew this. He probably already started.

Migo returned the poleaxe to his shoulder.

"Sir, what about the bodies?" Rivar asked.

"Somebody else will take care of them," Hatan said. "Right now we need to get King Rikaydian safely off on his mission. Ensure there's safe passage out to the courtyard."

"Yes, sir." Rivar trotted ahead with his weapon drawn, slowly edging around the intersections until he confirmed both sides were safe.

Migo kept a hand over the silver dagger. As a mostly silver alloy, the weapon would really only be much help for fighting against shaman magic. In most other cases, silver was too soft a metal to really deflect a blow should a fight come to that. But still, as long as it could stab and slice, he'd be fine.

"Are you taking Genda?" Hatan asked.

"No. She doesn't like the cold." Anticipation started tingling across Migo's skin as he wondered what would happen if he found what his father had been after. What would he do if he identified his father's true killer? He'd want justice, certainly, but what would justice require?

And he was still unsure about Katsi. He liked to think that he was good at determining whether someone was lying or telling the truth. He'd scored considerably well at it back in training, which is why he'd undeniably been appointed the official inquisitor upon returning to Jehubal. But he wasn't flawless. And Katsi had told him herself that as a shaman hiding among Ringdwellers, she often had to fabricate elaborate lies.

Why would this seer have wanted Katsi to kill R? What did they have to gain by burying the truth? He suspected there was more that Katsi wasn't telling him, but he would get the truth. One way or another.

When they emerged into the courtyard, they were greeted by Captain Falshon and about a dozen other soldiers.

"Lord King," Falshon said, bowing his head. "Regent Padarro."

"Has everything been properly adjusted, captain?" Hatan said.

"Yes, regent."

"What adjustment?" Migo asked.

"We've downsized and restructured our military personnel," Hatan said. "We've got four groups whose responsibility is primarily policing. One group watching the north, one in the south, and in the city, and one for special assignments and investigation."

Migo grunted. He was right. Hatan was already working on getting things straightened out. "The palace needs a thorough sweep," he said to Falshon. "Two assassins somehow made it into the throne room. They managed to stab Regent Padarro with a spear."

"A spear," Falshon asked, mouth agape, then added, "my lord?"

"Yes," Hatan said. "Likely taken from off the wall of the throne room. There are three or four of them stashed in there."

"I'll see that a sweep is done immediately," Falshon said.

"One more thing," Hatan said, turning to Migo. "You are heading somewhere that is potentially extremely dangerous. I'd like you to consider having some soldiers accompany you."

Migo immediately started shaking his head, but Hatan jumped in again.

"Lord, please. Even one or two soldiers could make a significant difference, and you know it."

Migo sighed and put a hard look between Falshon and Hatan. "Who would you suggest?"

"The twins," Hatan said without hesitation. "Emil and Rivar. They are both excellent warriors who've served loyally under Captain Falshon since they were your age."

Migo knew both of them. He'd been their captain for almost a year while Falshon was lieutenant.

Rivar still stood beside them as they spoke... but where was Emil?

"I would be honored to serve," Emil said from directly behind Migo.

Migo nearly stabbed down at him before realizing who it was. Emil knelt on one knee, head bowed, hands clasped in front of him.

Migo held back a growl. He hadn't agreed to this yet.

"Would that be agreeable, Your Majesty?" Hatan asked.

A deep breath filled Migo's lungs. He knew the two men would be loyal. They were even among the group of soldiers he'd saved during the battle against the Bayvana Tribe when the Maedari arrived. He regrettably agreed with Hatan that additional soldiers would have its advantage. "Very well," he rumbled. "As long as they don't grovel." And as long as they didn't mind traveling with a shaman...

Rivar clapped his brother on the shoulder and urged him to stand back up. "We'll serve you with our lives," Rivar said.

Their lives were the last things Migo wanted. Hopefully it wouldn't come to that. Hopefully this would be safer than here at the palace where assassins from other lords were hunting for his throat.

"Let's be off, then," Migo said. Looking up at the sky, he was surprised to see something like a scaila gliding high over the city. Odd. They usually didn't do that unless they were traveling in large groups. No matter. It was almost time to meet back up with Katsi.

Chapter 12

K atsi held her hand out as the breeze whispered across her skin. It gave her a strange sensation every once in a while, as though she might be able to grab the wind itself and hold on.

She kept a careful eye on those coming and going from the city. Jehubal's northeast gate was much more active than the single south gate. She hadn't been up here very often, but the effects of the war on the local populace were undeniable. She wondered if commerce would pick up more in the south now that she and Migo had brought peace.

Scales flitted around somewhere overhead, chasing insects. He seemed excited to be exploring somewhere new. He'd followed her across the city, gliding much higher than she thought he could. He had an excellent sense of direction. No matter where she went, he always seemed to know where to find her. It offered her some small comfort to know that she wasn't ever alone as long as Scales was around.

Katsi yawned and leaned against the wall to the gate. So far, nobody gave her any trouble, and hardly anyone even looked in her direction. She'd seen other groups meeting up and departing from here, so it seemed like a common enough event that it didn't catch anyone's attention. In fact, there were only two guards manning the gate. She couldn't see the moon from her vantage, but it had to be well into the fourth mark by now. She'd fully expected Migo to be a punctual person.

Her thoughts must have summoned him. At that moment, he emerged from the gate, but the going was slow. Almost every person stopped to greet him. Instead of shirking it off like she expected him to, Migo responded to everyone, talking, shaking hands, nodding. And they loved him for it. What a difference. How many people had even seen the late Queen Rikaydian? But he wasn't alone. Two soldiers accompanied him, similar enough in appearance they may as well have been twins.

Migo alighted his gaze on her, brown eyes sparkling.

She pushed off from the wall and folded her arms as he approached. Scales flitted down from above, landing on the gravel in front of her. A guttural sound escaped his throat as he looked at Migo then back at Katsi.

"All is well, Scales. They might be coming with us."

He retracted the spikes on this back, then croaked and sprinted off into the nearby shrubs.

Katsi checked her veil for the hundredth time as Migo got closer. Yes, it was still securely covering her face. Only her eyes peeked out from the slit. Apparently that was all Migo needed to see to recognize her. He stopped a few steps away. She reflexively looked over her shoulder. Nobody was coming behind her. It wasn't some trap. Either way, she was prepared to flee. All she'd have to do was touch the stone wall, zip up its surface, then with a gust of air she'd be deep in the jungle.

"Let's be off, then," Migo said.

"What's with those two?" she asked, pointing at the other soldiers with her eyes.

"I decided it would be best to have additional support in case we need it," Migo explained. "Many people have died in pursuit of whatever this is we're after, and we have no idea how dangerous it will be."

"I'm Emil," said the taller of the two. He was even taller than Migo. He stepped forward and extended a hand.

Katsi ignored the hand and thought she heard a rustling in the bushes to her right. She imagined Scales preparing to jump out and bite Emil's fingers. It was more than slightly irritating that Migo had brought others along without informing her first.

When she didn't shake his hand, he shrugged and stepped back. "Not a people person. That's alright."

"I like her," said the other one in a gruff voice. "I'm his brother, Rivar." He stayed behind with his hands on his waist, flashing a crooked grin as if to woo her. He was shorter than his brother, with a thicker build and a scar that split one of his black eyebrows in two.

"Well, make yourselves useful then," Katsi said. She picked up a rolled blanket by her feet and tossed it over to Rivar, then handed another one to Emil. "You can carry these. Shall we go?"

"Yes," Migo said. "I'll lead the way." He turned down the trail.

So that was it? She was just some other minion now? She half felt like disappearing and heading north, abandoning Migo's quest altogether. What had he done to deserve any loyalty from her?

Well... he did save my life. She also felt the crushing guilt of killing his only contact. Two lives. She'd taken two lives now, and the second one was somebody she didn't even know. Would the weight of their blood ever leave her mind? She could only imagine how Migo felt, and he'd done things much, much worse.

The brothers followed after Migo, so Katsi shouldered her bag with a sigh and jogged up to him. She caught up and struggled to keep pace with his long-legged stride. "How much do they know?" she said, keeping her tone quiet enough that the brothers wouldn't hear.

"Enough," he said without looking over at her.

She waited, expecting him to say more. He didn't. "Wow, you're quite the conversationalist. Why so sour?"

"I'm not sour."

"And sensitive."

Now he looked at her. A blank stare. The muscle of his jaw twitched.

"Don't worry, your secret is safe with me." She gave him a fake slug on his arm.

"That's not it," he said, half looking over his shoulder.

"Ah, yes. Embarrassment," Katsi said. "The true culprit. Can't be seen talking casually with the girl that killed your mother."

His eyes widened, and he glanced over his shoulder again. "Sands, Katsi."

"What about the mission itself? Do they know what they're getting into? Do they know I'm a shaman?"

"I didn't share those details," Migo growled. "They know that they need to keep us alive."

"What did you tell them about me, then?"

"I said there was a woman who'd accompany us that has specialized experience. They understand this is a covert operation, and they haven't asked me any other questions. It's what they've been trained to do."

"Not asking questions? That's a miserable existence."

"And your many questions make it a miserable existence as well."

"Hm." Katsi backed away. Migo was different. She realized she'd hardly interacted with him around other people. She'd have to see if she could sneak an opportunity to talk to him one-on-one and see what was going on. She could have sworn even a couple cycles ago that Migo still had some interest in her. After all, he had kissed her once upon a time, and had practically sworn to defy the empire to keep her safe if needed.

"Emil, Rivar," Katsi said, slowing down enough to walk beside them. "I wonder, has Mr. Scowlface been short with you as well?"

"Who?" Rivar asked.

"His Majesty?" Emil said, eyes wide. "He may speak with us how he pleases."

"But to answer your question, yes," Rivar said. "I'm not sure he's particularly keen to work these kinds of missions with a team. In combat, I've never seen a better teammate and comrade, but when he was captain, he used to swap places with Lieutenant Falshon and run his own little scouting missions."

"You are loyal to him, then?" Katsi asked.

"We've sworn to obey," Emil said. "I'd lay down my life if needed."

"Were you also loyal to the queen?" Katsi added. She was prodding them. Weighing how much they could be trusted. But she had to remember, even Migo had once been loyal to the queen.

"Absolutely," Emil said, hugging the rolled blanket against his chest. It looked small in his hands.

"It's different with His Majesty, though," Rivar added. "You seem to not know much about Rikaydian soldiers, but when we join the force, we're sworn to serve the throne. Rarely, however, do we ever take direct orders from the king or queen. This is a rare exception. We typically serve under a lieutenant, who serves under a captain. We served under His Majesty when he was a captain for less than a year. You'll find no group of soldiers more devoted to him than those who worked under Lieutenant Falshon."

"We're only soldiers," Emil said, "but he cared for us, he fought for us, and nearly died for us. I'd say we aren't just loyal, we're devoted."

Rivar shrugged and offered another smirk. "Devotion was something the late queen had never earned, no disrespect. So don't you worry about us, lady. We're all on the same side here."

"What about you?" Emil said with narrowed eyes. "What is your loyalty to the king?"

"I guess you could say his *lordship*," Katsi's mouth shivered at the word, "has a knack for saving lives." Even though she saved his life first, but she kept that bit to herself, though part of her yearned to tell somebody besides Scales.

"You never told us your name," Rivar said.

"It's Katsi. Katsi Danan."

"Danan?" Emil asked, looking to the sky in thought. "This reminds me of something." He dug into a pocket of the coat he wore over his leather armor and pulled out a tiny booklet.

"Cloud and storm," Rivar grumbled.

Emil turned a few pages. "Aha." He quoted from the pages.

Though mists fog the eyes

And clouds cover the skies

Though the stone and sleet

Thrash a terrible beat

Though there be flashes and thunder

And the ground tear asunder

Know this, know the canon

Fear the wrath of the Danan

The final word sent a shiver down Katsi's spine. "Nonsense," she said. "Did you just make that up?" She snatched the book from his hand and read the same poem word for word.

Emil and Rivar shared a look as Katsi slapped the book into Emil's chest.

"Rubbish," she muttered. Why would her family name be mentioned in some random book?

"Normally I find all that poetry of yours dull, Emil," Rivar said, "but that one sounds a bit eerie."

"Where is that book from?" Katsi asked.

"It's *Malivari's Compilation 11*," Emil said, his voice taking a higher pitch. "Each compilation highlights different thematic elements and includes her own work as well as the work of other poets that fit the theme. I've read—"

"Alright, Emil," Rivar interrupted. "We get it. You read lots of poetry."

Emil frowned and tucked the book back into his pocket. "We're all allowed our interests," he mumbled.

"Who wrote that poem?" Katsi asked.

"I would love to answer your question. If I have permission." Emil raised an eyebrow at Rivar.

Rivar simply rolled his eyes.

Katsi was ready to shove both of them. "Just tell me."

"It's marked as written by an unknown author," Emil said. "It's not one of Malivari's own."

Probably because it was written by a shamanfolk. Danan was a shamanfolk family name after all, not that they knew that. It was well known among shaman tribes that the Lahanawe Archivists did a thorough job at plagiarizing all shamanfolk documents and purging their names from complete record. She'd never personally felt wrathful, but she wanted to believe that it had even been one of her own ancestors who'd written it.

"Thank you for sharing," Katsi said.

Emil jabbed an elbow at Rivar. "Ha, she appreciates poetry."

Katsi preferred not to respond. She'd certainly heard better poetry before. The twins seemed normal enough, but all that could still change once they learned she was a shaman. If magic was truly needed to unlock whatever Migo was after, there wouldn't be much hiding it.

As they reached the jungles, Katsi split off. She preferred to have her distance. She felt Migo could be trusted, but not the brothers. Scales appeared from above and landed on her shoulder. "Hey, Scales. I'm not sure about this. Maybe you can keep an eye on things for me. I have a bad feeling about this mission."

Chapter 13

Migo tried his best to ignore whatever Katsi was doing. He wasn't handling this right, and he knew it. He was doing something wrong. The soldiers were bound to find out more about her eventually, and she was a questionable ally to say the least, but he would defend her if needed. No matter how nonsensical it seemed. Despite the fact that she'd murdered R simply because an old shaman woman asked her to.

He still needed to ask her about that, but not with Emil and Rivar so close. In fact, shortly after Katsi disappeared into the jungle without a word, the two brothers caught up with him.

"Lord King," Rivar said in a sharp whisper as he hurried up beside him. "Lord King."

"Yes, Rivar," Migo said.

Rivar eyed the jungle cautiously before continuing. "I'm concerned that the woman accompanying us may very well be the shaman that killed the late queen."

Sleet. That didn't take long. "Can you be certain?" Migo asked, his voice deeper than he'd intended.

"Completely," Rivar said. "I saw her when she was brought in. I'd recognize those penetrating eyes of hers anywhere."

"This was part of the plan, wasn't it, your majesty?" Emil said. "You wanted us to help detain her."

Migo stopped in his tracks and turned to face them, hand resting over the pommel of his silver dagger. "About that." He didn't have it in him to lie. He'd tell them everything, and if they didn't accept it, he'd do what he needed to do. "She did kill the queen. But I have no intention of arresting her."

Emil's face paled.

"Lord?" Rivar said.

"If she didn't kill the queen, then the Bayvana Tribe would have overwhelmed the city. They were planning a slaughter during the Maedari. We would have been unable to stop them. Thousands would have died on both sides. The queen knew this and refused to call off the war. The only option was to take her out and install me as the king." He looked at them both in turn. "I asked Katsi to kill her. This was the price of our peace."

"Understood, sir," Emil said, the color returning to his face.

"I've been honest with you. If you're questioning my decision, I'd prefer to know." Migo's eyes settled on Rivar.

"Not at all, Lord," Rivar said. "I think you made the right choice. I simply wouldn't dare soil the queen's memory by saying anything further."

"I understand, Rivar," Migo said, "but the queen was a tyrant. She put hatred above the needs of her people, and I have no intention of making that same mistake. My hunt for my father's assassin is for justice, not for revenge."

Emil nodded to his brother. "I can see the reason for your decision, lord."

Rivar cleared his throat. "So that whole bit about Captain Tarahan's coup..."

"Fabricated. Much of the nobility would turn against me if they knew the truth, and I needed to quickly become king in order to establish peace."

"Will this not be a sign of weakness, lord?" Rivar pushed.

"That's certainly possible, but it was all over a war that was unjustified to begin with."

"But the shamans are still to blame for the Maedaris, are they not?" Rivar asked.

Migo shrugged. "Some shamans, possibly. But not any of those in the Bayvana Tribe. None of them have the capacity to summon storms like that. Katsi is the only stormcaller among them, and she has no knowledge of the origin of the Maedari."

"You told them?" Katsi said, emerging from the jungle, veil pulled down off her face.

"They already figured out who you were on their own. They have a right to know," Migo said. "I won't lie to them."

"I trust your judgment, lord," Emil said.

"Good, because Katsi here saved my life twice," Migo said.

Rivar nodded slowly. "She's the reason you survived after the battle, isn't she? When you went missing for a few cycles."

"She is," Migo said. They were certainly sharp.

Katsi folded her arms and watched them closely.

"I'm with you, lord," Rivar said. "You have my word."

"Swear it," Katsi said, stepping up to Rivar. "Swear your loyalty to Migo or return to Jehubal."

Migo couldn't help but burn at the passion Katsi displayed.

Rivar smirked. "Not a difficult decision." he bowed his head to Migo. "Lord King, I swear myself to you. Till the day you or I die, I'm your man."

"Emil?" Katsi said.

Emil bowed even deeper. "I swear I'm your man, King Rikaydian. It is my honor to serve you."

"Satisfied?" Migo asked Katsi.

She shrugged. "That'll do."

Migo shook the brothers' hands in turn. "I accept your allegiance. You are the first soldiers to swear to me directly. Know that I regard you not as servants, but as brothers. We have fought and bled together on the same battlefields. That brotherhood runs deeper than any oath."

"Here, here," they said in unison, chuckling afterwards. Migo patted them both on the shoulders. He had to admit, a weight shifted off his back. Keeping the truth from everyone was taking its toll, but sharing it with at least these two made that burden lighter.

"I suppose I should share a bit more about where we're headed," Migo said. "We have to head straight east to the Frozen Waste. We'll need to cross between the two lakes on either side and then head north along the Ring's wall until I can identify some landmarks. My father was looking for something out here. Something that got him killed. We're hoping to discover what that is.

"And according to some information I collected, it requires a bit of magic. This is why Katsi is here. She has graciously agreed to aid me in figuring this part out. We're unsure of the dangers that may be presented there, which is why Regent Padarro recommended the two of you accompany me as well."

"Not to mention the assassins trying to kill you, My Lord," Emil added.

Katsi raised an eyebrow at him.

Migo couldn't help but smile. "The life of a king," he said. "To the end, then?"

"To the end," the brothers said.

"Take the lead," Migo said. "I need to discuss something else with Katsi." The brothers nodded and walked out in front as they turned towards the east. A cool wind whipped through his hair, a gentle reminder of the freezing pain that awaited them.

A lizard glided down from the trees, landed on Katsi's shoulder, and stared directly at Migo, its half-lidded eyes almost glaring. Migo looked between the two of them. "You have a pet lizard?"

"I bet you didn't know scailas could be trained."

Migo frowned. "That's definitely not a scaila," he said, observing the webbed spikes protruding from its shoulder. "Scailas only have webbing between their legs. That thing has... almost wings."

"Since when were you an expert on animals?" Katsi asked, slowly walking up the trail. The lizard kept its unblinking eyes on Migo.

"I'm not. I've... seen scailas. I think I know the difference. That lizard isn't one of them." The lizard croaked and pumped up on its front legs. He'd never seen such behavior from lizards before.

"Well, maybe he's not a scaila," Katsi said. "But his name's Scales."

"That's creative. Did you name him yourself?"

"I did, actually," Katsi said, her voice animated. "And you like that name, don't you, Scales?" Scales scuttled around her shoulder so his face was next to hers as she rubbed under his chin. He croaked in pleasure, eyes closed.

Migo couldn't help but smile. "How long have you had him?"

"I rescued him during that Maedari when I broke into Wajek Manor. A rock had crushed his back legs. He actually just looked like a really small scaila back then."

"How have I not seen him before?"

"Why such an interest?" Katsi curled her lips in a smile, white teeth flashing. And her eyes, light with amusement, sent tendrils tingling across his chest.

Sands. He averted his eyes to the lizard. He'd felt it again. There was wonder in those eyes. A deepness more immense than all the stars in the sky. But the thing about stars was that they were too far to ever reach. He couldn't get lost in impossibilities.

"I've never seen it before," Migo said finally. "No harm in curiosity."

For the most part, the lizard's scales were dark green and brown, but red diamond shapes grew brighter along Scales' side, as if looking at them somehow made them more vibrant, and hues of blue shimmered along his belly, with shades of yellow interspersed. Under the scrutiny, Scales looked directly back into Migo's eyes, hinting at an intelligence uncommon among most creatures.

"I still get the feeling it has less to do with curiosity and more with assessing a potential threat," Katsi said. "Don't worry, Scales only eats bugs, fruits, and sleeping nobility."

"Funny," Migo said.

"But I know Scales isn't what you wanted to talk about. What's on your mind?"

"I'm concerned about that shaman you mentioned. The seer who asked you to kill R." Migo forcibly unclenched his fists. "I still don't understand why she wanted him dead. What would she have to gain from that?"

"I... I don't know," Katsi said. "I just assumed she wanted peace. That's why she told me to do it."

"Yes, but it was all very ambiguous. And she's not part of your tribe?"

"She's not."

"Do you know her well?"

The frown on Katsi's face deepened. "Hardly at all." She wiped her hands on her cloak. "I only just learned that her name is Alishara."

Silence stretched for a moment as Migo thought. Dust kicked up beneath their feet. "Has it ever occurred to you that Alishara might be the one who asked another shaman to murder my father? Maybe she's just protecting herself or whoever she works for."

"I." Katsi paused and let out a breath. "I believe that's possible. She's all alone in the canyon though. I don't know who she could possibly be collaborating with or what ulterior motive she could have."

"I don't like it, Katsi," Migo said. "The more you talk about her, the more it worries me. What does some solitary woman care about the fates of Jehubal, Cataban, and the Bayvana Tribe? It's suspicious. And you're sure she's alone? I don't know much about the canyon, but I know it has elaborate cave networks. Does your tribe use those? Is it possible there are others present?"

Katsi groaned. "I don't know, Migo. I know it's possible. I've been an idiot. Is that what you want me to say?"

"No," Migo said. "Not at all." He grabbed her elbow, and Scales looked like he was about to pounce off her shoulders and bite Migo's nose. "I just want to know what we're up against. Somebody is playing with our lives! I don't want to see you become a pawn, and I don't want any more people to die."

Katsi was silent, but her frown disappeared. Fire ignited in her eyes. "She's also the first one who asked me to kill your mother."

"Ah." Migo nodded. "That's why you did it then?"

"No, at least, not entirely."

"What aren't you telling me? What's your motivation, Katsi? What did she promise you?" He realized his grip had tightened, so he let go of her arm and took a step away.

"She promised to provide me a way to learn my powers."

Power. That was it. For an orphan girl where everything had been taken from her, of course she'd want the power to control her own destiny.

"I see," Migo said. "Of course, now you can see that they've turned your own desires against you. Did you get it, then? The control you wanted over your powers?"

Katsi looked away, her steps growing heavy. "In a way. I'm learning quickly, but not everything."

Migo remembered well the trick she did by absorbing R's body directly into the rock. Quickly was an understatement. "Alright then. Last question: did she ask you to kill again?"

Katsi shook her head. "No. I have no need to report back to her about anything. I didn't tell her that I saw you either. She believes my assassination went perfectly, and that R didn't share any information, though I'm not sure how seer magic works. I'm hoping she believes me."

"You don't know how seer magic works?"

"She's the only one I've ever met, and I've only heard stories about seers."

Migo ran a hand through his hair. "Let's hope she didn't catch your deception, then. For all we know, there could be a group of assassins waiting for us when we get there."

Katsi bit her lip then said, "Let's hope it's not as large a scheme as you suspect. And just in case it is, maybe your two lackeys will come in handy."

For all their sakes, he hoped he was wrong.

Chapter 14

Katsi emerged from the forest empty-handed. This far east, the jungles faded away into a strange mix of ancient, massive trees that only had a few leaves at the very top of their tall trunks, and some short shrubs and grasses. She didn't know of any fruits that grew in the colder climate, but there was the occasional nut or root. She came across none of them. Or perhaps she wasn't experienced enough to know what to look for. She'd brought some food with her, but had been hoping to scavenge some more. It reminded her why she didn't like the Frozen Waste.

Scales had stopped gliding around marks ago. Instead, he would glide ahead and cling to a tree until they caught up. His scales had shifted to a greyer shade. It was clear he didn't like the colder air.

"Let's settle down here for a rest," Migo announced, stopping at the base of a small rise.

They'd just walked past the edge of the two lakes to either side and finally arrived at a storm shelter. These were built to provide refuge for those who needed to travel. They'd probably been walking for almost a full cycle. The moon was nowhere in sight.

The temperature was surprisingly not as bad as Katsi expected. Though well accustomed to the heat, her clothes, stormwading armor, and cloak provided plenty of warmth. She also knew it would get much, much colder.

"We've been lucky so far," Migo grumbled as Katsi got closer. "We've had the wind at our backs this whole time. As soon as it shifts, we'll have freezing air coming at us from the Frozen Waste."

That explained it. Katsi felt out of her element this far from the Scorched Waste.

Emil and Rivar headed into the storm shelter to start setting up.

"Ever stayed in one of these?" Migo asked.

"Never," Katsi responded. She'd avoided them like a disease. "Merchants frequently use them. I probably would have been accused, captured, and killed."

Migo only grunted, his brow creasing. "Well, there should be room for all of us. Including your lizard."

"Scales."

"Yes, Scales. They're made to fit twenty."

"I'm not sure I want to sleep in there." She hadn't slept in the same room as anybody else since leaving the tribe. And she still didn't trust the twins enough to dare fall asleep by them.

"It will be safe from the wind and also the storms in case a Maedari comes along." He looked off to the side as he spoke to her, as if he was avoiding looking her in the eyes. She noticed him doing this when speaking to her, especially the closer they got in proximity.

"I don't think I'm ever in danger from the storms anymore. I'll find my own place to sleep, but I do need one of my blankets." She strode toward the storm shelter just as a chillier wind picked up from the east. As Migo had predicted. She poked her head through the open door. It was already significantly cooler. Inside was a large, open room with no windows. Several stone pillars supported the rounded roof made of reinforced brasswood.

The twins had settled on one side of the room, unpacking their bags.

"I need one of my blankets," Katsi said.

Emil quickly tossed one over to her.

Migo entered the building from behind her.

"These are enchanted blankets," Katsi explained. "*Inita*," she said, activating the enchantment, then threw it back.

Emil didn't catch it. Instead, it flopped on the floor beside him.

Katsi sighed. "It's heated. There's nothing to fear. Feel it."

Migo chuckled. "Their educational background is similar to my own. They'll have been taught that magic corrupts." He went and picked it up himself then nodded to Katsi. "It does feel quite warm. It's incredible." He handed it to Rivar, then tossed Katsi her other one, which she activated as well.

Rivar and Emil both felt at it, jaws slowly lowering in awe.

Katsi smiled. She couldn't wait until they saw her use her magic. "The three of you can cuddle up and share that one. I'll be staying out here somewhere."

"Thank you, Katsi," Emil said as Katsi left the building.

Scales was there clinging to the wall's exterior, basking in the fraction of sunlight that lighted upon it.

"Come on, Scales," Katsi said, throwing the warm blanket around her shoulders. "Let's find somewhere to sleep. I'm exhausted." Scales flitted over to her shoulder and hummed in satisfaction, flattening himself against the blanket. She skirted around a particularly large tree. Even if ten people held hands, they probably couldn't stand around its trunk.

She found herself wishing she'd traveled more. Here she was, several miles from her home, and it felt like foreign territory. If only she'd discovered her powers sooner, she could have easily gone around the whole planet or something. However, she wasn't so sure about Mazanib. The very idea of going there filled her with dread. Right under the emperor's nose? A shiver trembled up her neck. She wasn't so sure it was caused by the cool wind blowing at her ankles.

Leaving her home. Leaving southern Jehubal. She was out of her element. But maybe she wouldn't have to be gone for long. She could follow Alishara's instructions and find the shamans in Mazanib. She'd learn to use her power. As a fully capable stormcaller, who knew what she'd be able to do? Would she be able to stop a Maedari altogether? Protect a whole city? What would such an act teach people about shamans?

She found a good spot to lie down. Right at the base of two trees, a bristlebush covering one side. The ground was a mixture of sand and dirt. She moved a few rocks aside, tossing them over to the base of the bush to possibly block off more of the wind, but the ground there was already a little higher. Her stormwading armor had been enchanted with decent resistance to both the heat and cold, but that didn't cover her extremities, and the chill wind from the Frozen Waste was getting stronger.

She set the blanket down and took off her bag, pulling out a small bit of sun-dried meat. She bit off a chunk and threw the rest to Scales. He chomped away excitedly, the scales on his neck changing to a deeper shade of blue. She laid flat on her back and pulled her blanket over. Most of the wind was blocked off and she felt quite warm. Scales settled down by her feet, and her thoughts slowly drifted.

***

Something sharp pinched Katsi's chin. She jolted up, reaching for her knife. Scales launched off her chest, flipped, and glided back to her feet. He bit at her blanket and tugged.

"What is it?" Katsi hissed, getting to her feet, shivering in the cold wind. She rubbed the grogginess from her eyes. She must not have been sleeping very long.

But then she heard it. Boots crunching lightly on gravel. Slow steps. And there was another sound, like a distant, hollow thud. She couldn't pinpoint its location. She prepared her magic, reaching out, connecting with the stone, the sand, the air. Everything was ready to move at her command.

Scales leapt onto one of the trees, climbing higher as he went around it. Katsi followed on the ground. The footsteps were just on the other side of the tree. Her knife was somewhere on the ground, but she wouldn't need it. Whoever was sneaking up on her would face the full force of her power.

When she came around the other side of the trunk she saw none other than Migo, a finger over his lips, his strange ax held in the other hand. Katsi looked around. What was Migo onto that she was missing?

That deep sound still lingered in the air. Was it the wind? She tried to listen closely, but it was Migo who looked up first. High, all the way up the massive trunk, something gave a loud, guttural cough. It fell from the great height, spreading out as if broken into pieces.

Katsi took a few hasty steps away and ducked behind another tree.

Migo stood his ground and swung at the scattered mass that fell around him. Scales dived down after it as pieces broke apart.

"Sleet," Katsi said, taking a closer look at it. "It's a fruit." Scales ate voraciously.

"It just exploded up there," Migo said, slowly looking back up. "I never would have thought there'd be exploding fruit."

"A first for everything, I suppose," Katsi said. Far away, she could hear another one doing the same thing.

"Odd. We didn't hear any of this when we were first approaching."

"Maybe it's triggered by the cold air," Katsi said, then smiled widely. "Thanks for killing that piece. I don't know what would have happened to us if you hadn't been so quick on the swing."

"Funny," Migo said flatly, but she could tell he was holding back a smile. "What kind of fruit explodes?" He crouched down and looked more closely. "I've never seen this in the market."

"Me neither, but Scales sure seems to like it." Scales was practically drowning himself on the insides of the fruit. She didn't know he could even eat so much. She almost missed the tiny little lizard she found in the storm that could fit in the palm of her hand. She picked up a piece of the fruit. It had a leathery skin with reddish-orange insides. Seeds the size of her fingernails had scattered all over.

Against her better judgment, she took a small bite. Her parents had taught her never to try any mysterious plants in the wild, as some things could be poisonous, but Scales' enthusiasm bypassed her senses. The texture was smooth, and the taste was almost oily. She didn't risk trying any more.

"Is this what you came out here for?" Katsi asked. "To protect me from exploding fruit?"

Migo sighed and placed the butt of his weapon against the ground. "I suppose. I couldn't sleep, and I worried—" he paused and glanced at her. "I was concerned that you might be in danger." He rubbed his hand across his arm as if to warm it up.

"Cold?" Katsi asked.

"The wind gets through the bricks. I had the brothers share the magic blanket. They passed out rather quickly. Rivar snores."

"You should have taken the blanket."

"I have my own."

"Nothing beats a shamanfolk's enchanted blanket. I originally brought one for me and one for you. I didn't know you'd be bringing anybody else. I figured we'd wrap up in them once we reached the Frozen Waste as well."

"Ah. Wise." He picked up his weapon. "Well, I'll see you when we wake."

"We could share," Katsi blurted. She didn't want Migo to get poor sleep. He was likely the most capable fighter among them. It wouldn't do any good to have him exhausted in case they needed it. "If you grab your blanket and bring it here. We could lay on yours and put mine over top. They were made to accommodate two people that way."

A wordless sound escaped Migo's open mouth as he regarded her from beneath his deep brows, wavy black hair whipping in the wind.

"Just don't be weird about it. We'll lie back-to-back," she said.

"But what if there's a storm?"

"Migo, that's the last thing you should be worried about if you're right next to me."

He stood there frozen, as if he couldn't decide.

"It's cold, and I'm tired. Please hurry."

His expression darkened, and he turned away, tromping back to the storm shelter.

She didn't know why he was being awkward about it. They'd already spent a few cycles together in a small cave, and he'd been wearing a lot less clothing then. Albeit, that *was* against his will. She shrugged and squatted next to Scales. She'd never seen him so excited to eat before.

Migo reemerged from the storm shelter, blanket carefully folded, scowl fully settled into his features.

"There's that scowl I know so well," Katsi said, more than a little irritated at his response to her generosity. What was the big deal anyway? She almost wanted to tell him to go back inside and forget it.

He didn't respond, but he spread his blanket out on the ground, oddly particular about how neatly it settled. "I'll face outward."

"Great," Katsi said, tossing up a hand. Despite the cold, heat rose in her cheeks. Energy boiled in her stomach as she felt increasingly frustrated. She grabbed her blanket and settled down beside him, facing the bristlebush between the two trunks so that they were back-to-back. Katsi tossed the heated blanket around them, resting her head on her bag. Migo's body was stiff.

"The blanket is pleasantly warm, isn't it?" Katsi prodded.

Migo grunted.

Katsi resisted the urge to jab him with her elbow. "I thought you were over all your distaste. I didn't think lying next to me would be so painful for you."

Migo's body tensed even more. "I don't have any distaste towards you, Katsi."

"Then what's your problem?"

"My problem is that you stabbed me and then told me to..." He released a long sigh.

Katsi's heart thundered in her chest and her fingertips tingled. What was going on with her? "I told you to what?" she whispered.

"Forget it," Migo said, his voice a deep rumble.

She clenched her fists, definitely ready to jab him with her elbows now.

"You told me to forget it," he said.

"Oh," Katsi said, realization dawning on her. The kiss. Of course. He didn't want to develop feelings for her. She folded her arms. Her heart still thundered away. The blanket was more than warm, it was hot, but she didn't move. "Right." She swallowed. Why did it feel like there was a hole in her chest? "You can still be nice."

Migo shifted. His first time since laying down. Even through her robe and armor, she swore she could feel every bit of him. Every muscle of his back that pressed against her. He seemed even warmer than the blanket. "I hope you sleep well," he said softly.

"That wasn't too hard," she said, trying to lighten the mood, even though she herself felt as impassive as ever. She closed her eyes and added, "You too."

Scales croaked as he crawled over her feet and settled down between their legs, wheezing stuffed little lizard snores as he almost instantly fell asleep.

Even Migo slipped off into sleep, his breathing steady.

But the feeling of some kind of hole in her chest didn't go away. It writhed. It ebbed and flowed. Migo hadn't denied that lying next to her was painful. Maybe this was what he felt. She squeezed her eyes tight and took deep breaths until eventually sleep delivered her.

Chapter 15

Hatan unlocked a door at the back of Rikaydian Palace. There were several mechanisms to remove, including a crossbeam, two deadbolts, and a heavy chain link at the top. He peeked through the reinforced window that provided vision into the walled-off garden beyond. Once he was sure it was safe, he opened the door and stepped outside.

This was not the most secure location of the palace, which was the reason for all the extra locks. The garden formed a small rectangle with four walls, vines growing over the surface of each of them. The scent of flowers and sweet fruits sizzled in the air, mingling in a way that, on any other cycle, might have eased Hatan's worries. This was not one of those cycles.

On the other side of the north wall was an unfrequented street, which created a good opportunity for unwanted visitors to scale the wall. Or, in Hatan's case, for him to smuggle in conversations with his network. A secret door had been carved into the wall to allow access to and from the street. Hatan unlocked this door with a brass key and coughed loudly enough that somebody on the other side would have been able to hear.

The stone door swung open, and a shrouded figure rushed inside, closing the door behind him with a grating thud. The figure shirked off the hood and pulled down his veil, revealing an angular, brown-skinned face and short black hair. "Sir," he said in a hushed tone, dipping his head at Hatan.

"Kyel," Hatan said. He rubbed a hand across the stubble growing on his chin. "We need eyes. I need you to run an investigation on any house that maintains its own military presence here within the city."

Kyel nodded. He was accustomed now to receiving succinct orders. He'd been little more than a thief a few years ago, before Hatan caught him. He stole food for him and his sister who lived alone together in an abandoned home. Instead of arresting him, Hatan paid for the food and offered Kyel and his sister a job. A little bit of mercy could go a long way when extended to the right person. And Kyel was certainly the right person. "It will be done," Kyel said. "There may be anywhere from ten to fifteen of them though. It'll spread us thin."

"You'll have to weed some out. Focus on the ones with the largest forces. They shouldn't have reason to keep too many people on staff. It's also likely that any hired arms will simply be on-call. If we have mercenaries hanging around sleephouses without a clear reason to stay, they're probably in somebody's purse already. I trust your judgment from there."

Kyel nodded. He was a sharp lad, and Hatan didn't doubt that he picked up on all the implications this mission entailed. "You suspect a coalition against the young king."

"More than a suspicion."

"Understood. We'll find who it is."

"I know you will. I'll want a report next cycle, ten marks from now. Stay safe."

Kyel dipped his head again before disappearing through the door.

Hatan locked the door then returned to the palace, putting all the other locks in place. If someone was trying to assassinate him and Migo, that meant they were hoping to seize the throne for themselves. Migo was the only Rikaydian who remained, and Hatan, as the queen's nephew, was the next in line. The rest of their relatives had all died. After them, the throne would be up for grabs to whoever gained enough power or influence.

He only made it halfway to his office when footsteps came pounding down the hall. One of the few remaining guards came to a halt before him.

"Regent," the man huffed with a bow.

"Speak on."

"A woman ran here to report. Fire. In the city."

"Sleet," Hatan muttered, clenching his fists. He had a feeling this was only the beginning.

Chapter 16

Migo awoke as Katsi shifted, tugging the heated blanket off his feet. He had no idea how long he'd managed to sleep, but he stealthily extracted himself from the blankets. Scales blinked a lazy eye at him as he stood. The lizard looked a lot bigger than he remembered, but that was maybe due to its bulging stomach.

A few clouds had rolled in overhead, but the wind had weakened. He yawned and stretched his arms and back before scooping his poleaxe off the ground. He snuck back into the storm shelter and dug through his pack until he found the wrapping of cookies Hatan had given him. Emil and Rivar were still sound asleep. Migo might not have slept long enough, but there was no going back now.

He could scarcely believe what he'd done. Sharing a blanket with Katsi? It was wild enough that Katsi suggested it. He'd been insane to accept. He could have easily said no and avoided the whole thing. Was he really so disarmed by her that he abandoned all logic? Maybe she was just trying to put him back in his place, or maybe it had been a joke that he wasn't supposed to take seriously.

He went outside and sat down against the wall to eat some of the cookies.

She truly seemed to have forgotten about their kiss. He envied her. He could hardly think straight as the memory of it replayed in his mind. It had been the briefest of moments, but he still remembered it with vivid detail, from the sunbathed scent of her skin to the softness of her hair brushing the back of his hand. And laying beside her? Yes, it had been agony. Not because he hated her. Quite the contrary.

Sands.

Forcing himself to think of something else, he pulled the map out and unfolded it, double checking the notes and landmarks. His prediction was that they were perhaps one more cycle away from the location marked. He accepted the possibility that whatever he was looking for was gone. Perhaps the others, whoever they were, had already found it. But he wouldn't give up either way.

The moon was rising.

As if on cue, Rivar and Emil stirred from inside, chattering about how incredible the blanket was. Migo had to agree with them. He wasn't sure how magical enchanting worked, but there was no denying that shamans could make incredibly useful things. He could only imagine how much more productive their society might have been all these years if not for the war.

"I'll fetch Katsi," he said to them before heading back over to her nook.

Scales was awake, watching Migo from his perch on the trunk of the tree. He croaked loudly as Migo got closer, but Katsi was sound asleep. She lay flat on her back in the middle of his blanket. He was about to wake her, but the tranquility on her face gave him pause. It struck him how young they both still were. Seventeen years old. A king and a shaman with rare abilities.

"You know, if Scales' warning wasn't loud enough to wake me up, you're breathing sure is," Katsi said, opening her eyes only after she finished speaking.

Migo breathed a laugh. "My breathing wasn't making any noise, but good joke. Aren't you the one who said something about being nice?" He held out his hand to help her stand. She took it, but there was no humor in her eyes. He helped her pack up before they all met by the storm shelter and started heading northeast.

The wall of the Ring was built in a line where, generally, life stopped growing. This also mostly coincided with where the last rays of sunlight reached. It was far from a straight line, but varied quite a bit based on elevation or anything that blocked the sunlight, like a bulky tree or boulder. Even in this close to the Frozen Waste, there were still several plants growing, especially some bushes with dark green leaves and vibrant, red berries. The ground was covered mostly in rocks and sand. Further to the east, beyond the wall, there was a light fog, suggesting rain or snow, much to Migo's dismay. He was hoping that they'd have clear enough skies that he'd be able to sneak a peek at the stars.

Katsi was wrapped in her blanket, with the hood up, and her veil on.

"Katsi, are you well?" Migo asked. "I thought you practically lived outside."

She glared at him from the side. "The Scorched Waste is a lot different than over here, clearly." She pulled one of her hands out. "And my hands feel all dry."

"Ah," Emil said, turning around and pulling a small metal tin from his bag. "Try some of this. It's buttered garaso oil. Rub it on your knuckles. It will keep them moisturized."

Katsi took some out and applied it without hesitation. "Thank you. I didn't know Ringdwellers used garaso oil too. Shamanfolk use it for some of our potions. Who knew it was so practical."

"I thought everyone was a Ringdweller. Shamans included," Rivar said.

"That's news to me," Katsi replied.

"He's right, but most people share your confusion," Migo added. "You may not have been aware of the distinction because you and your tribe have been living in the Scorched Waste most of the time. People who live in the wastes are called outlanders. From what I know, most, if not all, outlanders are shamanfolk, but not all shamanfolk are outlanders."

"So then what do I call people who aren't shamanfolk?" Katsi asked.

"Probably just people," Rivar said with a laugh.

"Marems," Migo said. "We're called Marems. It's an old term. But I agree with Rivar. We're all people. Someday, hopefully, we can live without discrimination of heritage. This was one of the things my father was hoping to accomplish. I believe it's part of why he was assassinated. That's why I want to figure out who killed him and what he was trying to find out here. I would guess that somebody wants this war to go on. They want us to be filled with hatred. I only wonder what that person is trying to cover up."

Katsi's eyes lingered on Migo for a moment before she nodded and looked away, tucking her hands back under the blanket.

"Rivar, Emil," Migo said. "Have either of you two been this way before?"

"No, sir," Rivar said. "We've always been with Captain Falshon in the southern fields."

"And before that, lord," Emil added, "we lived northwest of the palace before getting sent to the Rhian Academy in Lazeem for training."

"Rhian?" Migo said. "That's where the queen sent me off to. You are trained as shaman hunters, then."

"Yes, sir," Rivar said.

"Good to know I'm in such excellent company," Katsi said.

"We know the academy taught all kinds of indoctrination," Emil said. "We could see through that much. You're safe with us. As long as you don't turn against the king here."

"Why did your parents send you to the academy?" Migo pressed.

"Bah," Rivar said. "Well, lord, we're the youngest sons of the second wife to an old man—his first wife died. It was practically our oldest brother who sent us off, hoping we'd come back and lead caravans through the south, all the way to Wanay or Maloria."

"Wouldn't that kind of trip take a couple years?" Katsi asked.

"With a decent team of varman oxen, you could get there and back in three and a half, maybe four years," Rivar said. "It's a long time, but if it's a skilled trading team with good starting supplies, you'd return and never have to work another day in your life."

"Then why are you here, defending me instead of a caravan?" Migo asked.

Emil and Rivar shared a look.

"I wish there was a more chivalrous answer, lord," Rivar said, "but we simply have no loyalty to our brother or father. Neither of them are particularly honorable men. Of the wealth that we'd amass by leading such a trade mission, most of it would end up in our brother's coffers. We knew Captain Falshon as a good man and opted to join his team almost just to spite our family."

Emil held up a hand and inserted his own comments. "That being said, lord, we have seen much higher purpose since you returned. Your dedication to peace and stability is honorable indeed. And after you saved our lives, you have done more to earn my respect than anyone."

Migo shrugged. No special thanks seemed necessary. "It is my duty to protect Jehubal and its people." He didn't fail to notice that they were likely the sons of a local lord, and a man they deemed dishonorable. "Who is your father?"

"Vitori Kesten, lord," Rivar said. "You would know him as a merchant lord, no doubt."

Migo scratched his chin. "I can't say I know him at all," he said. He couldn't recall having much interaction with the Kesten family, though it was likely that Vitori or their brother had attended several gatherings at the palace. They were no doubt the kind that turned up their nose at Migo and avoided contact with him.

"Be grateful for that, your majesty," Emil said.

They walked on for another couple marks, steering ever closer to the wall. Warmer wind continued to blow by and cold, light rain drizzled down. Getting wet was the last thing they wanted, especially if they were going to be passing into the Frozen Waste.

A rock formation was barely visible through the fog on the other side of the wall. It had two distinctive, rounded shapes, one on top of the other. Migo double checked the map for reference. He could have sworn that it was one of the landmarks. "Does that look right?" he asked Katsi, pointing at the drawing on the map.

Katsi scrunched her eyebrows in thought. "I can't tell." Then she summoned her magic, blowing a force of wind across the formation. The fog swirled in defense, but slowly retreated, revealing the shape more clearly.

"Definitely looks right to me," Migo said.

Katsi dropped the magic. "At least we're heading the right direction."

"That was incredible," Rivar said. "I've never seen anyone use magic before."

Katsi smiled. "That was nothing. Wait until you see me run across water."

"Impossible," Emil said.

"I wouldn't doubt it," Migo said. He was positive this was only the beginning. Katsi was inexperienced and untrained. Part of her motivation for the assassinations was so that she could receive better training. He wouldn't be surprised if Katsi would eventually be able to summon her own Maedari, despite her protestations to the contrary.

Some rocks clattered in the distance.

Migo held up his hand, unslinging his poleaxe with the other, eyes on their surroundings. Emil and Rivar caught the sign and pulled out their weapons as well.

"What is it?" Katsi hissed.

"I heard something," Migo whispered back. The three soldiers automatically formed a triangle with Katsi at their backs. Migo removed the leather sheath from the ax and tucked it into his tunic.

"Where?" Katsi whispered again.

Migo held a finger to his lips. They weren't alone. He whistled and pointed to a small rise to their northwest. Best to have the higher ground, and if they were further sunward, they were less likely to have sunlight in their eyes if it came down to any kind of battle. The team slowly made their way over, all eyes on the horizon, scanning for signs of movement.

They made it to the top just as Migo heard another clattering of stones.

"There," Emil whispered, pointing to a gravelly pile of stones that were right up against a damaged portion of the wall.

Migo nodded and signaled the two brothers to move in on the south side while he would maneuver in around the west.

They moved in, boots grating on the stones. It was not an easy place to walk stealthily. Katsi followed behind Migo, as he suspected she would. He had to admit that if something attacked them, Katsi's magic was likely their most formidable weapon.

As they got closer, the stones shuffled again, this time with the distinct sound of something scraping against the rocks. Whoever it was, they knew Migo's crew was approaching.

A deep growl emanated from behind the stone. It was deep. Guttural. Almost... monstrous. Migo's first thought was that it might be a wild rangola, but as the creature emerged and charged at him, nasty face curled into a snarl, he couldn't have been more wrong.

It was a blur of dark gray as its massive, taloned stride ripped through the gravel. Its body was mostly covered in short gray hair, but spines ran down its back. It was about the size of a rangola but stood more upright, its front legs looking more like long arms.

Migo stood his ground but had a feeling no level of intimidation would work against this monstrosity. Instinct alone kept him alive as the beast launched itself at him, massive talons slashing at him like blades. He dove to the side but still felt a sudden pain on his lower leg. He rolled back to his feet, preparing to hack down at it, but it charged on, straight towards Katsi.

But Katsi stood there, paralyzed, knife held loosely in one hand. She would die. It would tear her apart, and there was nothing he could do about it. He'd never experienced more fear or more rage in his life. "Katsi!" He bellowed her name, racing to reach her, but knowing he was too late.

Chapter 17

Hatan's body glistened with sweat as he threw bucket after bucket of water and sand on the blazing inferno. Other townsfolk worked alongside him for a full mark to help bring the fire under control and keep it from spreading to the other buildings that practically shared walls with it.

He didn't dare think of the implications. That would come, he knew it, but he needed to quell his emotions. Instead, he focused on the repeated motions. Grab the bucket from his right, throw the contents in the correct trajectory, place the bucket down on his left.

By the end of a full mark, they managed to keep the fire from spreading, but the Rikaydian warehouse had become a charred, blackened skeleton. Its contents, a full stock of grain and harvesting equipment, had been reduced to ashes.

Hatan coughed and wiped the sweat from his brow. His light brown skin had been blackened with soot. He removed his shirt and used it to wipe his face as he went and stood inside the smoldering ruin.

The warehouse manager, Telsala, stood in the middle of the room, staring blankly at the rows of rubbled urns that once filled half the space inside. Her clothes were slightly burned, her brown hair singed at the ends. She'd fought fiercely to bring down the blaze. This was her job, her livelihood, that had burned away.

"Anything salvageable," Hatan said, voice dry and raspy.

"A few urns are unbroken," she said. Her tone was lifeless. She crunched over the ruined urns and grabbed a whole one at the back, tilting it to the side as she looked inside. "Most of it is spoiled. If we sold the rest, it would have a burnt, smoky taste to it."

"That's not too bad. Some people like that flavor," Hatan said, still attempting some semblance of optimism even though it was all he could do to restrain the anger that wanted to boil up.

"I'll recover what I can, sir," she said, then blinked over at him, eyes glistening with unshed tears. "I'm sorry this happened. I don't understand how fire got in here. We didn't use torches or anything."

Hatan shook his head. "It's alright. I know this wasn't your fault. I'm quite certain this was intentional. Somebody is targeting me and His Majesty."

Her eyes widened. "Who would dare?"

"I'm still working on suspects, but was the building locked? Who had access? Anybody new on staff?"

Telsala pulled out a key from within her burnt tunic. "No, nobody new. There are only three keys. I have one, another is kept at the palace, and the third is held by the assistant manager, Lesandri."

"Where's Lesandri?"

She blinked at the ground. "I haven't seen her for a few marks."

Hatan clenched his jaws. "Where does she live?"

"I—I can take you."

She shuffled towards the door, her tired footsteps leaving traces in the blackened soot.

Hatan hung his shirt over one shoulder and followed behind. His knife was the only weapon he had with him. Two men from the city guard leaned against the wall of the building across the street. An exhausted crowd sat or stood around with them. They'd all worked to quell the fire. Hatan was grateful the fire hadn't spread.

Penym came hurrying up to him. "I came as soon as I heard," she said to him, her eyes assessing the damage.

Hatan sighed. "Well, there's not much you could have done. It was already out of control by the time I got here. We only just suppressed the flames." He stepped closer to her and lowered his voice. "This can't bode well for our finances."

Penym pursed her lips then whispered, "This will be somewhat ruinous. The funds from this would have helped finance the purchase of those shops we'd talked about. How did it happen?"

"This was no accident. It had to have been targeted. The assistant manager is missing. Telsala is about to check on her with me."

Penym nodded, her expression grave. "Bring them to justice. Whoever they are."

"Don't worry. They'll pay."

She glanced down at his bare chest. "I'm sure they will."

Hatan sighed within himself before turning to Telsala. "Lead on, Telsala. Men." Hatan pointed to the two city guards who'd helped. They jumped to attention. "You're with me. This might not have been an accident. Let's go."

Telsala moved with hastened steps through the cobbled streets. They were on the north end of Jehubal, near the farmlands. Most warehouses were in this part of town. It was an easy place to stash any harvested goods and transfer to various workshops throughout the city. Telsala led them straight sunward.

"Were you two nearby when the fire started?" Hatan asked the soldiers.

"Yes sir," one of them answered. "Captain Akailen keeps us in pairs of two. We patrol the warehouses. We heard the shouting once people noticed the fire. We helped organize the water and sand retrieval. We apologize that it took so long to get things coordinated, sir. Neither of us have dealt with a fire for a few years."

"That's alright. Did either of you notice anything suspicious?"

"Nothing in particular, sir," the same soldier answered.

Hatan nodded. He didn't know these men. For all he knew, they could have been involved, but he'd always want to give soldiers the benefit of the doubt.

"We're almost there, regent," Telsala said, turning up a narrow road.

Hatan rubbed a fist against his stubbly beard. This situation was out of hand. An assassination attempt directly in the palace seemed less ostentatious than burning down a Rikaydian warehouse. Whoever was moving against them, they possibly knew about the dire financial situation the throne had. That, or they were doing whatever they could to ruin it. He was too far behind. He hoped Kyel was whittling down the list of suspects. It was also possible that the coalition involved several houses. The amount of nobility that had been unenthusiastic during Migo's coronation was far greater than he cared to consider.

"Here," Telsala said, pausing outside a low stone home. The door was open.

Hatan drew his knife out. He ordered one soldier to remain outside with Telsala and had the other come with him as he entered the building. He only had to take one step inside before he knew something was wrong. The contents of the home had been scattered everywhere, as thoroughly as if a Maedari had just torn through. Among the mess was a boot beside a spattering of blood.

He saw a leg sticking out from beneath a torn pillow. "Check that room," Hatan said, pointing to a different room, not only to lead the other soldier away, but to ensure that nobody else was still inside.

"Yes sir," the soldier said in a whisper, holding his glaive out in front of him like a shield.

Hatan approached the body carefully. The home was small, with nowhere to really hide except for the room. "Telsala," he called.

Telsala shuffled into the room.

"I think she's dead. I just need you to identify the body."

"Certainly, yes."

Hatan stepped over the dead body, holding a hand over the slit throat to at least shield Telsala's eyes from the brunt of the scene.

Telsala looked down at the face then quickly turned away. "That's her."

"Thank you. No doubt her key is missing. You may go. I suggest staying with somebody whenever you go out for the next few cycles."

"Yes, regent," Telsala said. She disappeared through the door in a flash.

"All clear," the soldier said, emerging from the back room.

"We're all done here," Hatan said. "Report back to Captain Akailen. Cleanup will be needed. Murder."

Killing innocents. The people of Jehubal should have known better than to hurt their own. Hatan clenched his fists. Whoever was responsible, he would make them burn for this.

Chapter 18

K atsi hurled wind at the monstrosity that emerged from behind the stones, but it had no effect. She tried softening the ground as she had when burying R's body, but nothing happened. She could feel the magic extending out, but as soon as it reached the monster, it disappeared as if the magic never existed.

The monster charged right through Migo, the prince barely dodging out of the way, and headed straight for her.

What could she do without her magic?

She was helpless. All she could do was watch as death approached. Daggerlike claws tore at the ground and uneven fangs bristled behind its snarling lips. Her death was about to be brutally painful. What struck her most were the eyes. They didn't seem like the eyes of an animal, but rather, they were the eyes of a human, with hidden intelligence trapped inside.

"Katsi," Migo roared her name, shaking her from the stupor.

The monster lunged for her.

She summoned all her magic, the ground trembled, wind rising at her fingertips. Instinct kicked in. The ground below her burst upwards and she grasped the wind itself, launching herself over four times her own height into the air. The monster crashed into the debris left in her wake, snarling as its claws struck only the ground on which she'd stood.

Katsi hung suspended. The cool air whipped around her, but Katsi was one with it, connected in the same way as she'd done with rocks and sand.

Migo came rushing in. Emil and Rivar sprinted across to provide support but were still seconds away.

The monster had no thought for self preservation as it dove straight at Migo. He batted one of its clawed hands away, the metal hammer scraping against sharpened bone. As the other claw slashed at him, he jabbed at it with the spearpoint but it seemed to do almost nothing.

It was impervious to magic and resilient against Migo's weapon. As much a myth as enchanted silver, but it was a living creature.

The beast headbutted Migo. He roared as the spikes along the crown of its head jabbed at him, but he managed a one-armed swing with his weapon, scoring a scratch down its shoulder with the ax head.

Katsi's elevation was slowly dropping. She had to be able to do something besides watch the monster kill the young king. Then she had an idea. She hoped she wasn't too far away, but she reached out with her magic, grasping at a pile of gravel and rocks. As soon as she made the connection, she hurled them at the beast. This time, they crashed into the side of its body with dull thuds.

This only earned her a scathing snarl, but it was enough for Migo to take a step back and slash down with his ax, hacking one of the clawed nails in two.

Emil and Rivar arrived for support. Rivar jabbed at the beast's back with his two-handed longsword, but that did little more than scratch it. It spun and lunged, slapping Emil's face with the back of its claws.

Migo jumped, bringing his poleaxe down in a massive swing, severing its left arm just above the elbow. "Silver," Migo said. "Try silver."

The beast completely ignored Emil and Rivar, focusing fully on Migo. It knew the real threat. Cautious now, it dodged another swing from Migo, then gnashed out, biting the spearpoint, effectively preventing him from getting another swing in. Emil and Rivar jabbed it from either side, but those wounds were apparently paltry to such a beast as this.

Migo held onto his weapon with one arm, struggling to keep his grip as he pulled a sheathed dagger from his belt. It was the silver dagger he'd taken from R's body. Instead of trying to use it, it tossed it up in the air. "Katsi," he said.

Directly above the monster, she immediately knew what to do. She dropped her connection with the air and fell. With both hands, she snatched the dagger, throwing the sheath off as she dropped down towards the beast. She thrust the weapon into the beast's skull just before she crashed into the ground, twisting her ankle as she did so. The pain meant nothing. She scrambled away on hands and knees before looking back.

The beast had collapsed. Blackish red blood leaked from the wound in its head.

All four of them panted as they looked down at it.

"Is it dead?" Katsi asked.

"One way to be sure," Migo said. "You might not want to watch." He stood to the beast's side, and despite his warning, Katsi couldn't avert her eyes. He hacked down between two spikes on its neck. It took three swings, but he severed the head. Only then did he retrieve the dagger.

"Sleet and sand," Rivar said. Then he glanced at Migo and added, "Pardon, sir."

"What is that thing?" Emil asked, holding a hand to the side of his head where his skin beamed red from the blow he'd taken.

"Sands if I know," Migo said, setting down his weapon and dropping to one knee beside the head. "Rivar, keep an eye out. Are you alright, Emil?"

"I'll be fine. Just stings a bit." Emil frowned. "I'm usually more nimble than that. This thing moved fast."

"You were bold to help against a strange opponent," Migo said. "Whatever this is, it's resistant to normal steel. Only my silver-studded ax was able to do much damage." He regarded Katsi.

Katsi's eyes were still locked on the beast. Its very existence was a puzzle. No, an abomination. It shouldn't exist. Something was wrong. Very wrong. She couldn't shake the nervousness that rippled across her skin.

"Katsi," Migo said.

And its eyes. Why had they looked like that? They were closed now, but she couldn't deny what she'd seen there. She felt like she should have known about this kind of monster and been prepared in some way. Who'd ever heard of a creature that was resistant to magic?

"Katsi," Migo said. He was beside her, prodding at her ankle with his hands. They were so warm. It drew her attention away as she blinked up at him. "Your ankle. Is it alright?"

Katsi nodded but meant to shake her head. "I landed awkwardly when I fell. It hurts a bit, but I think I'll be okay."

"That sometimes happens in the heat of the moment," Migo said. "I once hurt my ankle during drills but kept going for another full mark. It swelled up after that and I had a hard time walking for a couple cycles. We'll want to elevate and keep an eye on it."

"Oh," Katsi said. She tried to rotate her ankle and there was definitely some lingering pain. She let out a long sigh. "Alright, I'll trust your experience."

"Do you mind if I carry you to that treeline?" He pointed at a copse of small trees with his eyes. "We can probably defend ourselves there better than we could on the open ground."

"Asking permission now I see," she teased, and then immediately wished she hadn't. It hurt him when she did that. She could see it in his eyes, though she didn't fully understand why. He looked away from her, the muscles of his jaw twitching. "Sorry," she mouthed. "Yes. That would be fine."

Migo nodded wordlessly and scooped her up as if she weighed no more than a sheet of parchment.

There was blood on his upper arm. "Were you wounded?" she asked.

"They're scratches, more-or-less. I'll manage just fine."

They were more than simple scratches, but she'd certainly seen him with worse injuries before. "Migo, that thing was resistant to my magic. Everything I tried to do directly to it simply failed."

His eyes darkened. "I thought something was up. That doesn't bode well." He set her down beside one of the larger trees. "Magical monsters that are only susceptible to silver. I feel like I should have known such a thing existed. Perhaps this is what our mysterious adversary is hiding."

"Something is definitely not right. Such a thing doesn't seem possible," Katsi said. The uneasiness in her stomach wouldn't settle. It made her want to crawl out of her skin. "The note from R said that magic and silver were needed, but if they were simply planning on killing that beast, magic would not have been needed, clearly. There must be something else my magic would be necessary for."

"True. We're certainly not done yet, but don't think I didn't notice you flying."

"Sands, I forgot." Katsi brushed a hand through her hair. "It just happened so naturally. I couldn't think of how to get away, I just grabbed the air and jumped." Come to think of it, her armlet also felt rather warm. She hadn't made the connection that it might have something to do with the magic she was using.

"I'm just glad you're safe," Migo said. "I mean, I still need you for the mission, of course." He cleared his throat. "Elevate your leg. It will help keep the blood flow down. You don't want it to swell up. I'll see if I can cross into the waste and find some ice or snow to hold to it."

He looked as though he might touch Katsi's knee, but he withdrew his hand, cleared his throat, and said, "Great work, by the way. With the dagger. That was an amazing stroke. I know you don't enjoy killing, but you saved us."

Katsi could only nod as Migo stood. She felt no remorse for killing the beast. It wasn't the same as when she'd killed the queen or R.

Migo ordered Emil and Rivar to take up positions around her as he strode off to the Frozen Waste.

"Don't you think you should have some company, lord?" Rivar asked.

"I'll be fine. Watch her." His voice faded as he took off.

Katsi wondered if the beast had been drawn out by her magic. It appeared right after she'd used the wind to blow back the fog. Maybe it was just a coincidence.

"Here," Rivar said, dropping his bag to the ground in front of Katsi. "Put your foot on this." He kept his eyes up, keeping a close watch on Migo.

The dull-headed king was walking straight to where they'd found the beast. Katsi could only hope there wasn't another one. He disappeared behind the rocks. How had that monster been hiding out there by itself? Surely somebody else had to know about the existence of those things.

"Do you love him?" Rivar asked, squatting down beside Katsi.

"What?" Katsi said.

"The king. Do you love him?"

"No."

"Do you want to love him?"

"No."

"So then you're trying not to love him." He ran the back of his hand across the dark stubble growing on his chin.

"Excuse me?" She couldn't tell what he was after.

"Oh, the two of you are just so informal, and he's rather enthusiastic to help you. We've never heard of him interacting with women, well, at all, really. I couldn't help but wonder why."

"Rivar," Emil said in a threatening tone.

Something about the idea of Migo not interacting with other women made her want to smile, but she was far from a true romantic interest if that's what Rivar was trying to get at.

"Sorry," Rivar said, "I just... you care for him, don't you?"

"Of course I do. I did save his life after all."

"Good," Rivar said. "Very good."

"The king is on his way back," Emil announced. The long bruise on the side of his face had swollen a bit.

Rivar rose from his position and watched as Migo approached.

The conversation made her wonder, though. Why did Migo care about her? She thought she knew the answer. She had saved his life after all. But it was more than that. She'd talked him away from a dark place. She'd offered him genuine sympathy and kindness, things he'd probably never received from anybody besides Hatan. It made sense that he might latch on to that, but his own words came back to mind. He'd bleed for her. Kill for her. Die for her. Defy the entire empire to keep her safe. This wasn't the first time she'd reiterated his words back to herself.

Sands. He only said that because he was ignorant to the idea that not everybody hated him.

"I didn't realize shamans could fly," Rivar said, now focused on scanning the perimeter.

"I didn't either," Katsi said. "And it was more like floating than flying.

Scales glided down from above and landed on the ground next to Katsi. He crawled up on her stomach, looked at her ankle, and then growled.

"Yeah, well I didn't see you anywhere during that little scuffle."

The brothers looked at each other but said nothing.

"Yes," Katsi said. "I talk to Scales. And he understands everything, doesn't he?" She rubbed under his neck with two fingers.

Scales let out a deep, suppressed squawk and settled down on her stomach. She hadn't seen much of him since waking up. Perhaps he'd been gorging himself on more of the strange, exploding fruit. He actually looked bigger than he had several marks ago, and the spikes that held up his webbing were longer. There seemed to be a joint at the base where it protruded from his scales.

"Don't change on me too much," Katsi whispered to him. "I still miss the tiny lizard I saved from a little rock."

Migo jogged up to them. He held a piece of ice with his short cloak.

Katsi gave a sharp intake of breath as he held it against her ankle. "Oof, where's my heated blanket?"

"You dropped it back there when we first heard the beast," Emil said.

Migo sent him off to go reclaim it. "I'll just hold this here for a while to make sure things don't swell up," he said, voice low. His other hand rested on her lower shin, warming her even through the sleeve of her pants. His thumb touched her skin, just above the ankle. It slowly slid across the surface. Tendrils ran up Katsi's leg, but not from the cold.

He stopped, suddenly catching himself. His eyes trailed up the length of her body until they locked onto hers.

She knew that look. The first time she'd seen it was right before he kissed her. It was dark and deep, filled with passion, devoid of fear and anger. A shockwave rippled through her, lifting her as though she were floating in hot water. Her chest rose and fell in two quick breaths.

"Here you go," Emil said, holding the blanket out to her. He'd practically appeared from nowhere.

"Thank you." She grabbed the blanket, though she no longer felt like she needed it, and hugged it to her chest. Scales snuggled beside it. "Sorry if this sets us back," she said to Migo. "I'm normally not so clumsy."

"Oh, I know," Migo said in an even tone, raising an eyebrow at her. "I've seen you in action. But there's no need to apologize. We suspected there'd be risks."

"In all fairness, lord," Rivar said, "I thought we'd be safer out here than in the city."

Migo smiled. "And yet, you're the only one who didn't get hurt."

Rivar shrugged. "Still plenty of time for that. I don't have near enough battle scars to show off."

"I might be missing something, but why would it be safer here than in the city?" Katsi interjected.

Migo moved the ice around gently as he sighed. "There are likely some lords working against me. Many of them would not be pleased to have such a young king, especially if he leaves them in the hands of his cousin while he looks for his father's murderer. And also," he paused to take a long breath, "if they know that I killed those men in the throne room. Apparently one of them wasn't as dead as I thought."

"Not to mention the mercenaries that nearly killed him and the regent," Emil said.

"What?" Katsi sat up. Scales jumped off her lap and flitted to the trees. What would that mean if Migo were killed? It could thrust the people back into war. It would unravel everything they'd tried to fix.

"I'm fine," Migo said. "Hatan is fine. I'm sure he can handle it. Once we find out who's moving against us, we can deal with it."

"I'm sure you will," Katsi said.

The ice in Migo's hand had mostly melted away. He tossed it aside and gently ran his fingers over her ankle. "It doesn't seem too bad. Rotate your foot. See how it feels."

Katsi did as instructed. In truth, it did seem fairly fine. There was only a small bit of pain when it rotated to the sides. "It feels mild."

Migo nodded and stood up. "It's alright to be cautious. Let's proceed, but don't hesitate to let me know if you need to stop." He reached down a hand. She took it, and he helped her stand, but she made an effort not to look in his eyes for fear of what she might see there.

Was it fear? No. It was some other feeling entirely, but she refused to analyze herself.

"We should get there in about two or three marks of walking," Migo said, releasing Katsi's hand. "To the end."

"To the end," Emil and Rivar said in unison.

They headed north, Katsi still hugging her heated blanket, wondering to what end she was marching.

Chapter 19

Nagesh popped his neck as he entered the dark cave before him. The veil over his eyes was bewitched with a unique enchantment that allowed him to see in the dark, though only in shades of gray and dark green. The warm orange light gradually faded behind him, but the heat still permeated the fiber of every substance.

Years ago. Many years now, this canyon had been their salvation.

In his hand he held the bloody mixture from those the king had killed. He swirled the contents, ever tempted to uncork the bottle and smell the fumes, drink the memories, and live the lives.

I desire self-control, a clear mind, and peace to my soul. The thought was automatic. Anytime he felt the desire to indulge unnecessarily, it came to him. A force of habit at this point. He'd been taming the inner beast for years now. Longer than most usually could when so deeply involved in bleeder magic, but he'd been avoiding the darkest spells for long enough that it no longer had the pull it once did.

Only after walking several minutes into the depths of the cave did the temperature finally change. He shivered at the sudden shift. Even his stormwading armor did little to mediate the difference.

He sensed her before he saw her. The blood pumping through her veins was like a distant thrum that vibrated in his consciousness. He stopped fast, hand over the pommel of the secula at his waist. It was not like those imitation weapons made by the Bayvana Tribe. It was the real deal, forged nearly 400 years ago. A sword of death.

Not that it would do him any good. Not against Alishara.

"You have it, then." Her voice echoed out from the depths.

What she did in here all the time was a mystery to him. How far back this cave went was completely unknown. He was never able to go any deeper than this. There were triggers all over the canyon that would signal his arrival well before he got close.

Not that he wanted to go any deeper.

Many people feared bleeder shamans—and for good reason. Their history was a terrible one. But seers? Well... he supposed everyone had to have their own nightmares, and Alishara was his.

Nagesh held out the vial, waiting for her to get closer before speaking.

"Liwana," Alishara said, touching the side of the cave wall. Activated by the magic, a ring of stones arcing overhead sparked into bluish light. She pulled down her veil, uncovering her face, etched with canyons of wrinkled, brown skin.

All part of the facade. He could only wonder what she really looked like.

"Relax, Nagesh," she said. "Now is not your time. Your purpose is yet to be fulfilled."

He held back a grimace. What did she know of his purpose? His purpose for whom? Certainly not himself. This is why he despised the seers. They always thought they were serving some higher purpose without regard to the individual lives they discarded along the way.

She stepped closer and snatched the vial from his hands.

"What did it tell you?" she asked, eyes flicking down at the vial.

"Migo killed them all. They weren't planning a coup; he was protecting the young Danan and wanted to prevent the war."

She smiled. A self-satisfied, smug smile.

"Don't tell me you orchestrated that somehow."

"Not entirely. I merely knew what was necessary for the prince to save her at the right time." She uncorked the vial with the mixed blood of those Migo had killed. "But the young monarch has served his purpose."

"I see." Nagesh kept his face as stoic as ever. Whenever Alishara wanted somebody dead, he always wanted to know why. Who could be threatening enough to make her want to remove them? It was a dangerous thing to ponder.

"I already know what you're thinking, Nagesh, but your services won't be needed. The city will solve the problem for us."

For you.

"Do you remember why you're still alive?" she asked. It was the same question every time he had the misfortune of needing to visit her.

She always expected the same answer. "You have some of my blood under blood oath."

"And don't forget it."

He never would. It would haunt him until the day she died.

A strange feeling spread down Nagesh's back, like a silken sheet slipping off his skin. It had been a long time since he'd experienced that sensation, and he knew it could only mean one thing.

He backed away. "I need to return to my client. Make up some other information about the blood."

"Avoid the city," she warned.

Nagesh did not respond, but turned and hurried through the cave. He needed no warning. He'd been hiding among the Marems for years, taking contracts from them. He even lived within the city walls most of the time. Fortunately seers couldn't see all things. What a terror that would be.

But there was something much more pressing than that. The feeling he'd gotten sent a very clear message.

His waheshi had just been killed.

Chapter 20

Migo kept a firm grip on his poleaxe as they proceeded north. The winds had shifted, and cold air whipped by them. The fog over the Frozen Waste had cleared, exposing a startlingly crisp sky. Miles in the distance, the peak of a mountain tipped over the horizon. He wondered how far he'd need to go out there to see the stars again. He doubted he'd even recognize them. There had only been a fraction of stars visible the few times he'd been able to see them. According to the astronomer, it would take three years watching the sky from three different points on the planet in order to see all the stars. Unless they could travel all the way through the Frozen Waste of course, which was impossible.

"What has you so captivated?" Katsi asked, walking up beside him and looking out at the Frozen Waste.

Migo cleared his throat, debating internally whether or not to share. "Memories. The stars are out there somewhere."

"What's so interesting about stars?"

He eyed her carefully. She was wrapped in one of her heated blankets, hood and veil on, only her eyes visible. In the clear, almost-twilight, those eyes glowed, reflecting a sliver of the light blue sky above them. He detected no guile.

"I won't tease you, if that's what you're worried about," Katsi said. "I promise. I want to know why you find them interesting."

"There are many reasons," Migo began carefully. "For one," he pointed over at the sun, "over there we have this massive, bright, powerful light, beyond anything else, and yet, because of the presence and the brilliance of the sun, we cannot see that there are other celestial lights glowing. But, even in the darkest, blackest of skies, there are still lights out there. Shining. Surviving. Despite all that envelops them. Even in the absence of the warmth and brilliance of the sun, there is still light." He paused and couldn't hold back as he whispered, "Still hope."

He looked back at Katsi sharply. Despite her promise not to tease him, he was certain she'd say something now. Instead, much to his surprise, she stared out at the Frozen Waste, her eyes as big as he'd ever seen them.

Her reverence urged him on. Energized him. "Another reason," he said, "is the unfathomable depth. Because of the moon and the stars, we know that there are other suns out there, other worlds. Who knows how miniscule we are in the vastness of all existence, but yet, despite that, it does not diminish the value of a single life. If one of those stars disappears from the sky, how many would weep? But at the passing of a life here on Malahem?" Something caught in his throat. The tear-filled eyes of Shali and Bindom came to mind. Those were lights he had ended. "Here we are. Alive and breathing. Thinking and feeling. It makes me wonder."

A long silence stretched out after he finished speaking. Katsi's eyes shimmered as she regarded him. He couldn't stand to look at her and had to turn away. Who knew what might overcome him if he looked back at her? The stars, the moon, the sun... all of them paled to the brightness that lit him when he looked into those eyes.

"Sands, lord," Emil said from behind them. "If I had a pen I'd write everything you just said into one of these poetry books of mine."

Migo groaned.

"No, Emil. Those words are not meant to be written down," Katsi said. "Some words are too beautiful to be on paper. Instead, they must remain on the heart and the tongue. The only way for others to experience them is to hear it with their ears and feel it with their own hearts."

Rivar coughed and said, "How close are we, lord?"

"Should be getting close," Migo said, grateful for Rivar's intervention. "Keep your eyes up and your weapons ready. We should be looking for two pillars made of stones. Based on the drawing, I couldn't tell you the size of the pillars, so keep your eyes peeled."

"Perhaps I might be able to see them," Katsi said. A gust of wind whipped up behind them, and Katsi launched into the air with a suppressed squeak. Scales appeared, gliding through the currents Katsi summoned as she flew forward, rising higher into the sky.

"How's that for a scout?" Rivar muttered.

Migo tried not to stare in awe. It was just a few cycles ago that he'd joked about her being able to fly, not knowing that it would indeed become a reality.

It wasn't long before she started floating back down toward them, clothes flapping around her. As she got closer, sand and rocks from the ground stretched up to catch her before lowering her down. She had so much control it was startling.

"I saw them," she announced. "It'll be hard to miss. They're larger than you might think."

"Did you see anything else?" Migo asked.

"Not that I could tell, but I suppose we'll find out soon enough."

"Emil, Rivar, you were trained as shaman hunters. I assume you must have some kind of silver weapon available," Migo said.

Rivar sheathed his longsword and pulled out a hand-and-a-half sword. "Not my first choice of weapon if we're facing any other long-armed beasts covered in spikes and claws. I wouldn't mind a good shield."

Migo wouldn't mind having his old glaive back. It would have been the perfect weapon. Such was his luck. "Emil, what about you?"

Emil sighed. "I'm not as well-armed there as I'd like. In terms of silver, I have two throwing knives and a hand knife."

Migo nodded, then asked, "What about you, Katsi? I see you have one of those... swords."

"It's magically enchanted," Katsi said. "I wouldn't be surprised if it was as ineffective as the rest of my magic. I could still throw things at it, but I couldn't control anything that was touching it already."

"That'll work, especially if you can do it from the safety of the air." As they rounded a few shrubs and topped a short incline, Migo saw the pillars. They were two solitary stones, both looked taller than him, distanced an arm-length apart from each other and carved into irregular form. The pale stone shone under the glare of distant sunlight.

"How easy is it to stay afloat, Katsi?" Migo asked.

"I could use some more practice."

"Perfect. How about providing some eyes so we don't get blindsided. Twins, the three of us should stick together this time now that we know what we're up against."

Katsi jumped and hovered ahead of them. Rivar and Emil walked to either side of Migo, keeping their weapons at the ready. Emil still held to his poleaxe but kept his silver throwing knives tucked into his vambraces.

Despite the cold, Migo's hands sweat with anticipation. His breath puffed out in a foggy mist. He listened for any sign of the enemy, but the only sound was that of the three men's footsteps pushing through the sand and dirt, slightly hardened by recent rain. Katsi glided soundlessly in the air. They made it all the way to the tall stones with no indication that anything lied in wait.

"Nothing out here," Katsi said, lighting atop one of the stones.

Scales landed on the other one and quickly spread himself out, basking in the sun.

Migo readjusted the grip on his weapon and waited. The stillness was unsettling. The density of life was significantly reduced. No more green bushes with red berries, no trees, no scaled rabbits or hammer voles. They waited in silence, but still nothing happened.

"Let's move to the east," Migo said, then felt a small vibration in the ground beneath him.

They all murmured to each other. Even Katsi felt it from atop the stone.

"What was it?" Rivar whispered.

"Watch out!" Katsi yelled before bursting into the air, narrowly dodging a head-sized boulder.

Migo looked over just in time to see a shower of stones flying towards them from the east. They all ducked, but something crashed roughly into his hip. The ground beneath him started to move, sand and dirt wiggling up onto him. He jumped back to his feet, shaking the dirt off his arms and legs.

A monster emerged from the east, charging towards them. But it wasn't alone. There were three of them.

Another shower of rocks came pouring towards them, angling down this time. There'd be no ducking.

Katsi dropped down in front of Migo and the twins, an audible pop bursting as she brought her hands together. The hailstorm of stones erupted and clattered down towards the charging monsters.

Migo wasn't about to wait for the beasts. Somewhere out there, a shaman was attacking them. A powerful one. He roared and charged forward. Something told him the beasts weren't accustomed to such boldness. The first monster bounded straight for him at frightening speed. His arms pumped awkwardly as he held his poleaxe in a two-handed grip, but he raised it overhead when he was a mere heartbeat away from the monster. It leapt at him, mouth wide open, beastly fangs glistening in the sunlight.

He brought his weapon down in full swing. The poleaxe went straight through the monster's face, tearing it from snout to skull. Its body collided with Migo's legs, flipping him over. He landed on his back just behind the monster. He quickly sprang back to his feet. His weapon was still lodged in the monster's head. The creature didn't rise. Only then did he realize that this beast looked different than the first one. It was covered mostly in scales.

Emil and Rivar whooped in triumph as they ran to meet Migo.

The other two beasts were close. Too close.

Migo jumped over to his weapon as another monster sprang towards him, but with a flash, one of Emil's throwing knives wedged into the monster's shoulder. It tripped, lashing at Migo as it fell. He dodged with a quick step and pulled his weapon free with a sickening crush.

Rivar was there, longsword in one hand, shortsword in the other. He stepped up to the third monster to provide distraction.

The injured monster rebounded and came at Migo faster than he was prepared to handle. It gnashed at him, and Migo barely had enough time to position the haft of his poleaxe, bracing the weapon on both ends as the monster bit down onto it. He fell backwards, tripping over the arm of the dead monster. The injured one withdrew and snapped again.

Wrong move.

He switched to a one-handed grip and swiped the poleaxe at the side of the monster's face then tore his silver dagger out and swung for its neck. He missed. The monster dodged. It learned. It tried to claw at him with its good arm, but he rolled, kicked the arm away, and spun back to his feet.

Emil sprinted in, slicing at the back of the monster's leg with his silver knife. It swung an arm at him, but he ducked beneath it.

Migo hacked across the monster's side, scoring a gash along its ribs.

It became reckless then, not caring if it died, so long as it took them with it. It sprang up, pouncing for Migo, legs and clawed arms all reaching for him. He spun to dodge, but it bashed him with its spiked elbow.

They both fell.

The monster was quick. It pushed up and rolled right over Migo. Its weight smashed him into the ground, forcing the air from his lungs. As soon as it rolled off on the other side, Migo lashed out with both weapons. His dagger stuck fast into its back, just beside its ridged spine.

Emil sliced the back of its leg again as it tried to rise. Migo barely had time to pull his dagger back out.

Instead of continuing the fight, it loped away from them in a broken stride.

"Lord," Emil gasped, eyes on Migo's chest. He dropped down and helped Migo rise. Pain surged in Migos' right clavicle. He looked at it with a groan, wishing he hadn't. A portion of his skin had split.

"That stings," Migo said, averting his eyes.

"Deep?" Emil asked.

"Deep enough. Let's help your brother."

Rivar stood and held off the other beast on his own, though it appeared he'd lost his longsword and the bottom of one of his pant legs had torn away.

Migo didn't see Katsi anywhere, but off to the east, a cloud of thick sand swirled like a mini tornado. She was battling the shaman. He worried that the injured monster was retreating to help the shaman against Katsi.

Not a good time to be injured. But it was only pain. As long as he didn't bleed too much. He didn't think any muscle or tendons had been struck. He hurried after Emil who was racing towards Rivar.

Migo shifted his dagger over to the right, his injured side, and kept the poleaxe in his left. Rivar fought defensively, buying time until they arrived. This monster was different from the others, with a longer body and a whiplike tail.

It eyed them as they approached, then turned to face Emil and Migo as if to attack them, but its tail swept through Rivar's legs, knocking him over. Clever beast. It had turned to them as a means of convincing Rivar that it wasn't paying attention to him. They were smarter than he initially thought, only less careful than they should be. Perhaps they didn't experience pain as normal creatures, or their imperviousness had made them lazy.

It sidestepped towards Rivar. It would attack him from the side just before Emil would be able to provide backup, and Migo was even further away. A bit of panic crawled in his stomach. He didn't want these men to die. He'd brought them into this.

Emil wasn't without options, however. He threw his second throwing knife. The creature saw it coming and ducked its head, but the weapon still wedged straight into its shoulder. It slammed a trunklike foot down at Rivar, but Rivar was quick enough to roll away and slash at the monster's foot with his silver-imbued shortsword, a small spray of its blackish blood flicking into the air.

Emil slid in to stab at the beast with his knife, but was immediately greeted by a slash from the monster's front leg that collided with Emil's hand. His knife wedged into the beast's foot, but it effectively disarmed Emil of his final silver weapon.

Migo arrived and wasted no time. There was only one way to deal with these monsters, and that was with boldness. Without fear. A one-armed swing would be enough, as long as the monster didn't dodge it. But he'd make sure it wouldn't be able to. He jumped, leaping as close to it as he could.

It must have sensed the actual danger. He even saw its eyes widen, revealing the whites that seemed reminiscent of a human's. It flinched back as if to avoid the attack, but just as he'd planned, it wouldn't be fast enough. His poleaxe arched downward. Anticipating its demise, it reached a taloned foot up to intercept him, but he was prepared for this as well, aiming his dagger at the reaching claw. His dagger slipped into the monster's claw only a fraction of a second before his poleaxe came down on its elongated snout, cleaving its snout clean off.

A groan escaped from deep within its throat, a hideous, remorseful sound.

Rivar followed up, stabbing the beast in the side.

Migo withdrew his dagger and finished it off, jabbing the weapon into the monster's neck.

Both of them stabbed it twice more until it finally fell with a trembling sigh. The last breath of life.

Emil withdrew his knives from the body.

"Hurry," Migo said. "Katsi may be in trouble. And from the looks of it, this might be our first time facing off against a shaman with actual strength. Remember your training, because now we'll need it."

"To the end!" Rivar shouted, shaking off his left hand. It looked like he'd punched a rock several times.

The three of them ran together, heading east. The swirling sand and dirt before them undulated sporadically, with rocks occasionally spraying out. It was like a living storm, acting of its own accord with no respect for the laws of nature. He only hoped Katsi was holding her own, but she'd already demonstrated great strength.

The pain from Migo's injuries tingled with the occasional spike. He knew they'd flare once things calmed down. As long as the team survived.

Migo was the first to breach the sand. He took a deep breath before entering. Earthen clods pelted him like thick rain. But he saw Katsi and the other shaman.

He was a young man, with long black hair braided down his back. He looked like any citizen of Jehubal, albeit his skin was paler. Probably from hiding in the Frozen Wastes.

But Katsi was on the ground. It looked like she was doing everything in her power not to be overwhelmed. Some rocks crashed into an invisible shield around her, but most of them slipped away as though redirected by her magic.

The shaman approached her with steady footsteps, a sickly curved sword in one hand. A secula. The injured beast from earlier lay beside him in a pool of blood. Perhaps its wounds had been serious enough to finish it off, but why had it run back here?

The shaman saw Migo and held up a hand, reddened with blood, a wicked grin on his face. "I've got your blood, prince," he said, his voice more terrible than any sound the monsters had made. "Burn."

Pain, more exquisite than anything Migo had ever experienced, tore through his body. It felt like worms feasted on every inch of his veins. He expected to die in that very instant, but his eyes locked on Katsi. She had fallen to her knees. Some of the rocks were getting through. One of them cracked her on the shoulder, knocking her over.

No.

They wouldn't die here.

Katsi. Would. Not. Die.

Everything fled from Migo's vision. Everything except for the shaman, but the shaman's eyes were set on Katsi.

He had no idea how he found any strength to continue, but he stepped forward. *It's only pain.* Something told him it was much more than just pain. Every muscle in his body felt as though it were being stretched on a rack and skewered by needles, but he stepped forward anyway. Then sprinted.

The shaman turned to him in utter shock. "Impossible," his gravelly voice muttered. His secula arced at Migo, but Migo blocked it with the ax-blade and thrust his dagger straight into the shaman's gut.

The fiery pain that encompassed him dissipated.

He withdrew the dagger, grabbed the shaman's weapon hand, and forced his own weapon into his throat. The shaman's body instantly turned black as ash.

Migo dropped the body and turned to find Katsi. Wind still swirled around, though it was less granular, which meant her stormcaller magic was still at work. He needed to know she was alright.

When he got to her, she was lying on the ground, face twisted with exertion. He grabbed her hands. "Let it go, Katsi. Release the magic. We got them."

Katsi gasped as she blinked up at him and the magic dropped. "Migo," she said with a heaving breath.

"We finished it," Migo said. "You did great saving us from the shaman."

"He was so powerful," Katsi said. "How did you do it?"

Migo reached down a hand, his uninjured side, and helped her stand. "I'm not so sure. You are the powerful one, but he was certainly skilled. Could you imagine what you might be able to do once you get more practice?"

"That's part of what I'm hoping to figure out," Katsi said.

"What kind of magic was that, anyway?" Migo asked as Emil and Rivar joined them.

"Earthmelding mostly." Then she narrowed her eyes at Migo. "Didn't he say something about having your blood though?"

Migo looked down at his hands, still surprised to see them uncharred. His muscles still trembled at the memory. "Yes. He caused me intense pain. It was all I could do to reach him."

"So, he was a bleeder then," Katsi said, she stared dully at the man's crumpled form.

"Bleeders," Rivar growled with a scowl. "We were taught that they're hated even among shamans."

"Depends on who you ask," Katsi said. "Migo," she gasped, seeing the blood on his shirt. Worry flashed in her eyes. Without any sense of permission, she grabbed his shoulder plate and pulled him down so she could see better. "How bad is it?"

"I can't really see it," Migo said, looking over at the other soldiers. Rivar and Emil were comparing their hand injuries. Rivar's was bloodied, and Emil's had at least three jammed fingers that were already swelling.

Katsi unbuttoned the top of his tunic and pulled down the collar, pushing the shoulder plate to the side.

Unwillingly, Migo's face flushed. She'd seen a lot more of him than that, but not in front of two of his soldiers.

She muttered a curse. "You'll need stitches." Her soft voice, so close to his ear, sent a warm shiver down his spine.

Not again. "You're sure?"

"Yes, but don't worry. Knowing you, I came prepared," Katsi said. "It will just need one layer." She pointed at the twins. "How are you two doing?"

"Better than His Majesty," Emil said. "We'll survive."

"He did all the killing. We were the pestering insects," Rivar added.

"Keep watch then while I sew up the king," Katsi said, pushing Migo over to a boulder and making him sit.

"Katsi, is this really the best time for this?"

"They're all dead, and you're bleeding. Yes." She pulled out her sewing kit.

"I think you just like sticking me with needles."

She said nothing, but a smile curled at the edge of her lips. She tugged the open collar of his shirt down over his shoulder and got to work.

Migo was acutely aware of the small, stabbing pain when she poked through his skin. It was so insignificant when compared to the intense pain that had overwhelmed him earlier that he simply couldn't be bothered by something so minuscule. But every time her fingers touched his flesh, it made all the pain worth it.

"You're not even flinching," Katsi said, her voice just above a whisper, breath warm against his shoulder.

He couldn't help but look over at her. Brows furrowed, eyes narrowed in concentration. She pulled out the smallest scissors he'd ever seen and snipped the stitch. "Done already?"

"I didn't have to do very many stitches." Katsi put away the stitching tools and pulled out a different vial. "I'm going to put a little bit of this restorative potion on it. It's the same stuff I used on you before, but I almost ran out." She got a little on her finger then dabbed it on the wound. "I don't suppose you have any bandages?"

"I brought some linen," Migo said, "but I don't think I can keep it there very easily. Is the bleeding bad?"

"No, it stopped mostly once I closed it up, but it might leak if you move your shoulder. Which I know you'll do."

"Right," Migo said, pulling his shirt and coat back up.

Katsi pointed at the body. "That's not the man who killed your father by chance, is he? Maybe your father was after them directly."

Migo heaved a deep sigh and headed over to the shaman's body. He hadn't even considered the possibility that it could be his father's killer. He doubted it. There was no way he'd even be able to identify the killer anyway. His memory was from years ago, and although it haunted him even still, he never saw the shaman's face. It had been fully hidden behind a veil. His concept of height and size had also changed since then, and he couldn't even think of a single prominent distinction that would signal any connection.

He bent down next to the body, observing the man's features. He'd seemed younger when alive, but the weapon had caused a sort of instant decay. Maybe death didn't bring peace for every soul. There was truly no way of knowing if this was the man who'd killed his father. That seemed too convenient. He looked at the man's weapon, a curved sword, dropped a finger-length away from the dead man's hand. The metal was darker than iron, as though it had been mixed with charcoal.

"He wields one of your magic weapons, does he not?" Migo asked, pointing to the weapon.

Katsi crouched beside Migo and picked up the sword. She spoke a word unfamiliar to him and the weapon changed, reverting back to a strange hybrid color of bronze and iron. "Yes," she said, lips curling back in disgust. "Though I think this is a real one."

"A real one?"

"Yes. The ones made by the Bayvana Tribe can pierce armor and flesh with ease, but true seculas would kill any who were cut by its blade. They are made using bleeder magic, but our tribe hasn't used that for generations. We cast out any shamans who refused to abandon such magic."

Migo nodded. "I see. Should we use it, then?"

"No." She shook her head at him, then used her magic, opening a hole deep in the ground. She tossed the sword in without another word, then covered it back up. "Best to forget you ever saw it."

"As you wish," Migo said, rising back to his feet. "Rivar, inspect the body for any other trinkets. We may find something interesting on his person. Emil, proceed with me to the wall of the Frozen Waste."

"What about me?" Katsi asked.

"You, take it easy," Migo said, mindful of her ankle and the welt that was surely rising on her shoulder. He felt somewhat uneasy giving her orders as if she were just another soldier. "Maybe see if you can find some fresh water or fruit. You're resourceful like that."

She rolled her eyes and tromped off towards the trees.

Migo and Emil headed for the wall. Whatever awaited them in the Frozen Waste, he hoped it wouldn't be any worse than what they'd already faced.

Chapter 21

Katsi dropped down from the sky, slowing her fall just before she landed next to Migo and the brothers. They all sat around, tired but alert, hunched in their cloaks. Katsi's heated blanket was tied around her like a cloak, and Emil was hugging the other one. He and Migo must have just gotten back from scanning the Frozen Waste.

Katsi hurried to the middle of the group, a bulky load in her arms. Scales trailed behind her practically drooling. She was more worried the thing would explode before she got back. "I brought one of those fruits," she said, laying down the boulder-sized fruit. It had taken all her strength to carry it. Its leathery surface had a few stretching cracks and a deep, rumbling sound emanated from it.

"Is that what I think it is?" Migo asked, slowly getting to his feet.

"Exploding fruit? Yeah," Katsi said. "It was the only food I could find. I also found some water and filled up my canteen."

The sound got louder as the seams continued to stretch and crack.

Migo and the brothers backed away.

"Oh yeah, I guess putting it down right there was a bad idea." She tried not to smile, but was also slightly concerned that it would blow up in her face at any moment.

Scales crawled up on the fruit and started digging at the cracks. Without further warning it burst open.

As quick as she could think, Katsi threw a shield of air around the fruit, but Scales still slipped through it, a chunk of fruit clutched in his eager claws. Aside from that, most of the fruit stayed contained in a bubble around it. Katsi laughed. She had no idea that would work so well. "You should have more faith in me, Migo. I'm not as reckless as you think."

"Yes, you are," he said, coming back over. "You're just lucky. And tenacious."

"I think you meant to say 'brilliant.'"

"You're right. I clearly misspoke."

Emil and Rivar shared one of their looks, but said nothing.

Katsi glared them down until they shrugged back at her. "Eat up, then. What did you find out at the wall?"

"I found a section that looked older than the rest of the wall," Emil said, picking up a piece of the stiff fruit, yellowish and soft on the inside.

Scales was practically drowning in his piece. That creature had a sweet tooth.

Katsi also grabbed a piece. It hadn't made her sick after she'd tried that small portion before. She had no idea if it was edible for humans or not, but it smelled okay. In fact, it was a rather strong scent that reminded her of the orchids that bloomed out of the trunks of trees sometimes. Right after they bloomed, a strong, sweet smell would fill the air.

"We'll take you over to it," Migo said. "I can't figure out what it's supposed to mean, but my father's agents must have somehow identified the need for silver and magic to enter, though to what end, I haven't a clue. The notes on the map didn't provide enough information."

"Lead on, then," Katsi said. "Let's get this over with." Katsi and the brothers took a piece of the fruit, but Migo avoided it.

"Not bad," Rivar said, chewing loudly.

Katsi tasted a small bit, biting the end. It was thicker than she thought it would be, like chewing on sweet, soft meat. "You don't want to try any, Migo?"

Migo breathed a laugh. "I'm not eating an exploding fruit, no."

"But Scales loves it. It must be good."

"Scales eats bugs, Katsi." Migo gave her a worried look.

Rivar and Emil burst into laughter.

"You may have a point," Katsi said. She took another bite then tossed it aside. "But some bugs are good for you."

"Somehow, I knew you'd say that," Emil said, barely able to get the words out through his fit of laughter.

"No, I'm serious!" Katsi said. "Certain grubs and larvae in particular. We even use them in potions sometimes."

"Katsi," Migo said with a smirk, "this may be one of those moments where saying less is better."

Katsi smiled. She wondered how Migo would ever survive without her to spare him from all the brooding. And they thought she was joking, but she really had eaten grubs. Nothing wrong with doing what was necessary to stay alive.

"Should be right over here," Migo said, pointing with the bottom of his poleaxe.

Katsi could feel it. Something in the air, like static, tickled across her skin. Magic was at work, though it must have been some kind of enchantment. The wall in the area looked different, as they'd mentioned. The color of the stones was a darker gray, unlike those around them that were a paler, tan hue. Despite their apparent age, they looked firmly in place. Directly behind the wall was a rocky mound that expanded into the Frozen Waste.

Migo said something else, but the words went right over Katsi's head. A force drew her in, like faint whispering on the wind, and she strained to hear it or locate where it came from. She realized it wasn't audible so much as it was felt. She placed her hand on the wall, tracing the lines of the mortar set between the stones.

The magic was old. It reminded her somewhat of the feeling she got inside the canyon at times, but this was even older. Ancient. Something was hiding behind it. She knew that much. Or perhaps it was sealed behind on purpose, like a prisoner. Maybe opening it wouldn't be a good idea, but she continued to run her fingers along the lines, feeling the strength of the bewitchings that held it all in place. It grew stronger as she followed it, as if it were leading her to the epicenter of power.

This was a state she'd never been in before. It was like she was in her body, but experiencing it from an outside perspective. All her senses were acutely focused on the magic. She could see its invisible threads like shimmering heat waves, its smell and taste were like burning ozone, and it felt both gritty and smooth like an irregular stone. But the sound... that faint whispering... it was like a single note, held in suspension. It crescendoed until it rang around her.

She stopped, her palm pressed between two stones.

"Here," Katsi said. She stepped away, dropping her hand. Her eyes slowly came back into focus, as though she'd been staring at the sun.

She felt Migo's hand settle on her shoulder. A calmness washed over her. "Are you alright?" he whispered, voice like a soft fabric brushing against her ear. "I lost you for a moment there."

"I'm fine," she said, touching his hand instinctively. "I just, I could feel the magic. It was so... palpable."

Migo nodded, eyes searching her for a moment before he turned back to the wall. "What's here? What did you see?" his breath plumed out in the cold air.

"That's where the magic is centered," Katsi said, still worried about what might be behind the wall.

"What do we do, lord?" Rivar asked.

Migo pulled out R's silver dagger. "Not sure. I don't think my father's agents knew what to do either. They just knew somebody else was looking for this." He tapped the dagger against his fingers.

Katsi fought down the knotted feeling growing in her stomach. Had the seer told her something about this? What was she so worried about?

Migo held out the dagger, pressing the blade against the stone in a cutting motion. The enchantment broke, revealing a cracked wall behind the flawless facade.

Migo withdrew his dagger and stumbled away.

The enchantment returned.

Migo looked at each of them in turn. "Silver penetrates the magic. Rivar, use your shortsword. We'll drag it off in opposite directions. Emil, see if there's a way through."

Rivar took up position beside Migo and they dragged their silver weapons across the stone to either side. Emil stepped over and tried to loose the stones, but they wouldn't budge.

"Katsi, this might be your role again," Migo said.

Katsi nodded and pulled her veil up over her nose. Emil moved out of the way as Katsi placed her hands on the stones. She grabbed the wall and threw down her hands. The bricks and mortar tumbled in a heap of sand, revealing a dark cave ahead.

"Emil, Katsi," Migo said, "you head in, Rivar and I will hold it open and come behind."

Katsi didn't even hesitate. She'd accepted her role in this. Her fate. She'd already sealed it the moment she offered Migo her help in coming here. Migo was right. She *was* reckless. "You don't need to hold it," she said. Whatever she'd done had disabled the enchantment as well. As she stepped through the threshold to the cave beyond, the air got warmer. More magic was at work. Emil followed her in, then Migo and Rivar. The light from outside lit their path forward.

Migo came up beside Katsi. Ahead of them was a bend in the path to the right. He nodded to her, then led the way.

Their footsteps echoed hollowly as they turned the corner. Before them was a small room that reminded her of all the other shamanfolk shelters she'd seen, even her own.

"Ah, you're the ones who killed my waheshi," a woman's voice said from the far end of the room. She was turned away from them, facing a body that hung upside down on the wall, blood dripping from the wrists.

Four more dead bodies laid side-by-side on the floor. They wore soldier's uniforms that looked vaguely familiar.

"You won't have it." The woman's voice was a sharp whisper as she turned to them, features obscured by a dark veil over her mouth. In one hand, she clutched a jewel, and in the other, she held a secula. She rushed them without further warning.

Katsi attempted to move the ground beneath the woman's feet, but the stones were firmly resistant. She needed to find out how other shamans used such tricks. If she'd learned anything recently, it was that her tribe's skill with magic was severely limited.

Migo stepped forward, deftly deflecting a series of blows from the shaman woman. Something metal flashed through the air as Emil threw one of his knives. It struck the woman's midsection. She stumbled, and Migo took the opportunity to run her through with the point of his weapon. He dodged back to avoid her secula, but she fell, holding the jewel to her chest as her own blood trickled over it.

The bodies on the floor started to twitch.

No. Katsi wouldn't be witness to the use of such dark magic. She whipped her sword out, took two bounding steps forward and cut down at the woman's elbow. She dropped the jewel and fell, rolling onto her back. Her eyes locked onto Katsi's, narrowing into a suspicious squint until she stopped breathing.

The bodies stilled.

That was it. No horrors unleashed. Maybe her anxiety about entering this place was unfounded.

But she'd hurt somebody again. It was becoming a regular occurrence now. If she was going to be called on to kill people for the better good, then so be it.

"Sands," Emil said, looking about the room. "What were they doing here?"

"It's that blood magic Katsi mentioned," Rivar said. He went around double checking the bodies to make sure they were dead.

Katsi bent down to observe the jewel to find that it was actually another armlet, similar to her own, except that it only had one jewel held in place with bronze mesh wiring. She touched it and instantly felt the power within, like a lifeforce pulsing with energy. The blood from the shaman sizzled and vanished, almost as if the jewel absorbed it. Her skin tingled across her entire body. Her very bones quivered at the sensation.

Migo was watching her.

She withdrew her hand, leaving the object on the floor.

"Lord," Rivar said. "These soldiers. They're imperial."

"What could have possibly been important enough to send the emperor's soldiers all the way out here?" Migo said. "I haven't seen them in Jehubal territory since I was a boy."

You still are a boy, Katsi wanted to say, but she held it back. If he was a boy, he was a very, very big one.

"They probably won't be able to tell us what they were doing here," Emil said, going up to observe the hanging body. "There are all kinds of herbs and things here in little cubbies." He was at the back wall, the darkest portion of the enclosure, and now that her eyes had adjusted more, Katsi could also see small recesses all over the wall. They no doubt contained various ingredients for making potions.

"This man was a lieutenant," Rivar added, tapping one of the soldier's boots. "They all died recently. I'd say within two cycles."

"If I had to guess what was happening here," Katsi said, "it would be that they were manufacturing some kind of potion that involves bleeder magic. From what I understand, bleeder shamans live as outcasts from most tribes." What she didn't understand, however, was why the shamans bothered using it if it resulted in everyone hating them. What was worth the risk? Why would a blood potion be valuable enough?

"Maybe it's how they make those monsters," Migo said.

"Right, what did she call them?" Rivar asked.

"Waheshi," Migo said, his voice a growl. "Could you imagine what might have happened if they had more of those? Most people aren't armed with silver weapons like we are. With twenty or thirty of those things, they could ravage an entire city."

The statement prickled the hairs on Katsi's neck. Could those things really have been made with bleeder magic? Her stomach crawled. The idea alone was sickening.

"So the emperor's men were onto it, then?" Emil said.

"Doesn't look like they had much success," Rivar said. He kicked a pile of weapons in the corner. "And it would seem they were even armed with silver."

"We're lucky we have King Rikaydian, or we might have joined them," Emil said.

Migo crouched next to Katsi, eyes on the armlet. "I'm curious what this woman meant. She didn't want us to have something. What could she have been referring to?" He tapped the armlet. "Could it have been this, Katsi?"

Katsi shook her head. "I don't know why. It's like one that I have, only it seems... stronger. Why would the emperor want something that enhances magical power? This doesn't seem like the kind of thing worth dying for."

"Unless he was hoping to separate them from it," Migo said. "Perhaps they were using it to make these waheshi. My father could have been working with the emperor to help find it. If my father was onto it, that would certainly explain why they would have assassinated him. A seer may have foreseen that he would locate them. That seer from the canyon... she must know that I'd be continuing the search. Did she only tell you to stay away from me, or did she ask you to kill me?"

"No, she didn't ask me to kill you," Katsi said.

Migo stood up. "Alright, but if you hadn't come with us, I would have died here, and we never would have gotten into this room. She's probably the one working against us."

"Do we hunt her down then, lord?" Emil asked.

"We should, but we need to consider our options."

"Lord, it has been several years since your father knew of this place, and they only had four of these monsters," Rivar said. "If it takes them that long to summon four waheshi, then it would have taken ages for them to build a sufficient army, wouldn't it?"

"I don't think we're seeing the whole of it," Migo said. "There's more to this that we're missing."

"What should we do, lord?" Emil asked.

Migo rubbed a hand through his hair. "The emperor needs to know what happened here." His dark eyes shifted to Katsi. "Katsi, did the seer tell you anything else? No other assignments?"

Katsi didn't know what to say. There was too much speculation and no facts. She was already worried that she was making the wrong decisions at every turn. But she'd sooner trust somebody who told her everything than someone who clearly hid details. She picked up the armlet and stood. "She wanted me to go to Mazanib. Meet with some secretive group of shamans there. They're the ones who can supposedly train me more in stormcalling."

"Of course," Migo said. "Right under the emperor's nose. I wouldn't be surprised if she was grooming you to murder the emperor himself."

The emperor. He was the one responsible for the mass slaughter of shamanfolk across the entire Ring. It wouldn't be any surprise if a group of shamans were planning to assassinate him. She gulped. This was a thin line she walked, between good and bad. "Who's to say killing the emperor is a bad thing? I mean, I killed the queen to save Jehubal from a war. What if killing the emperor saves the rest of the world?"

Migo held up a hand. Emil and Rivar stood still and silent. "I don't dare say such a thing. I, for one, have not met the emperor, though I know he and my father disagreed. How about this? We all head to Mazanib. You can get in touch with your contacts and see what they're planning, and we'll inform the emperor of what has transpired here. We'll leave you out of the picture. Hopefully, since we just helped the emperor accomplish whatever he was after here, he'll trust us enough to divulge what's really going on."

Katsi nodded slowly. "I do want to see how this plays out. Plus, you're the king of Jehubal, wouldn't that be enough to buy you an audience with the emperor?"

"I guess we'll find out," Migo said.

"Lord, are we really equipped to travel all the way to Mazanib?" Rivar asked. "That would take quite a bit of time."

"I'm not sure," Migo said. "But why don't you sort through those weapons and see if any are useful, preferably reinforced ones that are less malleable. I need to think." Migo moved to leave.

Katsi followed him out. She had an idea, but it sounded crazy in her head. She put the new armlet on and instantly felt the channel of energy. It was almost like it was made for her.

"What are you up to?" Migo asked her as they got outside.

"Testing ideas," Katsi said, summoning her magic. She grabbed the air and launched upwards, creating a field around herself at the same time. The amount of energy she felt was thrilling, willing her to use even more. Scales glided up beside her, riding the waves of the current she created. With a gust of wind, she moved north, steadily increasing the speed. She'd learned to create a field of air around herself which made it easier to breathe, and after summoning it, it no longer required direct focus, allowing her to keep her attention on the force and direction of the wind.

She was flying. And with the energy of both her armlets, she felt that she could soar on for cycles. She didn't realize how fast she was going until she looked down and saw the ground zipping by in a blur beneath her. It was both frightening and exciting, filling her stomach with a fluttering sensation. She slowed to a stop, bathing in the warm sunlight for a moment.

Scales had kept up with her, but without the ability to stop, he swirled around her in circles.

She knew she couldn't have been flying for very long, but when she looked back, Migo was far out of sight. She couldn't even see the large standing stones. How far had she traveled? Her armlets felt warm against her skin.

"Wow," she whispered to herself. "What do you think about that, Scales?" she hollered over to him, laughing with excitement.

Scales spun in the air and let out a croak in response. He was enjoying it as much as she was.

But now the real question still remained. She headed back, watching the ground to track her progress, flying low, but just above any trees. She didn't want to think what would happen if she hit one of those, but she flew slower this time.

Migo came into view on the horizon, but she also noticed dark clouds brewing over the Frozen Waste. She zipped over and dropped down beside him while he gawked up at her.

"I don't think I'll ever stop being amazed," Migo said as she skidded to a stop.

Without her protective bubble of air around her, Katsi felt the wind gushing in from the Frozen Waste. Migo kept looking over his shoulder at it. At least he wasn't reflexively grasping for his weapon like he used to. Instead, he'd looped it over his shoulder—the uninjured one.

"I have an idea," Katsi said. "I don't know if it'll work, but it could be a way of getting to Mazanib a lot faster."

Migo cocked his head at her ever-so-slightly. "Tell me you're not about to suggest what I think you are."

Katsi smirked. "Do you trust me?"

"Sometimes," Migo said. "Maybe not enough for that."

"Come on," she said, holding out her hand to him, "what could it hurt?"

"I could die."

"Oh yeah, that wouldn't be good." She grabbed his hand and pulled him closer. "I'll try not to drop you."

"How is this going to work? I might be twice your size. Do you expect to carry me?"

Katsi shrugged. "I'll improvise."

"Is that a storm coming?" Migo jerked his head towards the Frozen Waste.

"Sands, Migo, I've never heard you ask so many questions. You wanted a solution. I thought of one. We can at least try. I'll make it quick."

"Okay, then what do you recommend?"

"Maybe get on my back?"

Migo blanched.

Katsi snorted. "Okay, drop your weapon first, but I'm serious."

"There's no way that's sustainable, Katsi."

"Just do it!" She turned her back to him and held her arms out. She'd learned something from their interactions so far. He was stubborn, but not as stubborn as her. With enough pushing, she wouldn't be surprised if she could convince him to do anything she wanted.

Migo growled, but she heard his weapon drop to the ground. He lumbered over and put his arms around her shoulders, enveloping her like a heavy fur cloak. Katsi called forth her magic, summoning rocks closer. He would be in for a surprise, she knew that much.

"Alright, hop on," she said.

"You've been warned," Migo said with a breathy laugh.

Katsi braced herself. Migo's full weight came like a load of rocks as he hopped up. She fell face first into the gritty sand. Instead of locking herself to the air, she was too focused on summoning rocks and wind to lift Migo. Right after she flopped onto the ground, Migo popped into the air and then fell down beside her.

She looked over at him, fully expecting him to get angry, but instead, he took one look at her, rolled onto his back, and burst out laughing. She slugged him in the shoulder and joined in the laughter. The sheer pleasure of seeing him laugh so hard dissipated any sense of frustration or embarrassment she'd felt.

He clutched his stomach as he sat up, shoulders still bouncing now with a silent chuckle. "Maybe we should do a countdown next time."

"Maybe you should stop eating rocks," Katsi said, pushing herself up to her knees.

He shook his head with the biggest grin she'd ever seen. "Your face," he said, reaching out a hand. He brushed her face gently, rubbing the sand off her cheek.

Sleet and sand. But those eyes of his.

She cleared her throat and got back to her feet. "Alright, let's try this again. With a countdown."

"Alright," Migo said. He got behind her again and put his arms around her shoulders.

She got another idea. "And actually, hold onto these." She summoned two rocks that came up to Migo's hands. He grabbed them and kept his arms over her shoulders.

Migo started the countdown. "Three."

Katsi connected with the air, grabbing it not just with her hands, but her entire body.

"Two."

She kept her connection with the rocks in Migo's hand as well. Once connected, it would take a lot less focus.

"One."

She bent her knees and started a gradual lift with the air itself.

"Now." Migo hopped on again.

Katsi strained with her magic, rising with the air. She put significant energy into the stones Migo held. He caught on quickly, and his grip on the stones became iron-tight. It felt like he was simply leaning on her, with most of the weight on the stones. Conclusively, her magic was significantly stronger than her body, because they slowly started to lift off the ground, and Migo felt like little more than a heavy backpack

"Sands," Migo whispered, his lips touching her ear, warm breath sending a shiver down her neck. The higher they got, the more his thighs tightened around her hips. She looped her hands under his knees—not that it would help much—but maybe it would keep him from squeezing her to death.

Her armlets were warm, the telltale sign that she was drawing on their energy. "Take deep breaths, kingling."

"Kingling?"

"I thought it might distract you," she said. They'd reached an elevation of several meters. She could never tell exactly how high she was. "I'm going to try some synchronized movements with both the air and the stones you're holding. Ready?"

"Do I have a choice?"

"Not anymore." She slowly moved forward, casting a tentative glance to the east where the storm was definitely building. If it was a Maedari, they'd likely get hit by massive winds with little warning before the storm blew in.

Moving forward was actually fairly easy. She only needed to move with the air itself. The stones, wedged just below her collarbone, stayed in place even without the forward motion, as if she were dragging Migo through the air. With a little more practice, she'd want to move them independently so that it wasn't tugging on her body. That would definitely hurt in the long run.

"Katsi," Migo muttered.

It was possible. That was all she needed to know for now. She turned and started heading back.

"Katsi, the storm," Migo said.

Katsi realized that she'd subconsciously locked the air around them so that she wasn't feeling the force of the wind at all, but sand was fiercely blowing from the Scorched Waste while dark clouds quickly slipped overhead from the Frozen Waste.

"Don't worry, Migo. You're with me." Surprisingly, the tension in Migo's body loosened. He *did* trust her. More than he cared to admit.

Lightning flashed and thunder rumbled explosively. A white wall rolled towards them from the Frozen Waste with frightening speed.

Katsi lowered them back down, and they dropped less gracefully than she did on her solo flights. The twins were watching them from the entrance of the cave, beckoning them over.

Migo disembarked with a grunt and ran to retrieve his weapon.

Katsi held the wind at bay as the wall of glittering ice reached them, enveloping them in a dark, gray fog. The bleeder shaman's hideout would make a good refuge from the storm, but Katsi held zero enthusiasm for staying in a space with dead bodies.

Together, she and Migo trudged back into the cave, a showering of lightning bolts blazing across the muted sky. The hues of pink and yellow lit the fog around them as if they were floating in clouds of color. They reached the entrance of the cave and passed the enchanted threshold, and Katsi stopped there, turning to watch. She'd never been in a Maedari this close to the Frozen Waste. It was different than she expected, and much, much darker. Sand mingled with snow and everything sparkled under the glow of flashing lightning.

Migo stood beside her, and the four of them watched the storm together.

"It really is beautiful," Migo said, deep voice barely heard over the thunder. "When we're safe, anyway."

"Lord," Rivar said. "Did I see what I think I saw earlier?"

"If you're referring to me flying with Katsi, yes."

"It's our chance at traveling faster," Katsi said.

"Yes," Migo said, folding his arms. "But it does mean that only Katsi and I can get there. You two will need to return to Jehubal and stick with Hatan. He may need all the support he can get."

"But lord, will you be safe?" Emil asked.

"In Mazanib? I should be. I don't think anyone there has reason to hate me. As long as they don't see me flying into the city with the help of a shaman, that is." He smiled at Katsi.

"I'm sure I can be discreet." Katsi said.

"How quickly could you get there, lord?" Rivar asked.

"Katsi seems like she can go incredibly fast. I wouldn't be surprised if it only took a month."

"I predict it will be faster than that, Migo," Katsi said. "I haven't traveled that far before, but I think it might even be just a few cycles."

Emil and Rivar both looked over at her with the same, raised eyebrow expression. "That would be something," Rivar said.

"Have shamans always been able to do this?" Emil asked.

"None that I know of," Katsi said. "But I'm supposedly a rarity."

"You could have made quite a living in the shipping business," Rivar said. "When we're all done with this madness, maybe you could transport a few things for us. It would be the quickest profit imaginable. We wouldn't even need to rely on our father or brother."

Katsi breathed a laugh. "I'll have to think about it."

"Will you two be alright reporting back to Hatan?" Migo said, getting back to business.

"Yes, sir. Of course," Emil said. "I'll protect the regent with my life."

"I know you will, and hopefully it doesn't come to that. I made a promise to the people, and I intend to fulfill it. Just make sure there's a kingdom to come back to when I return."

The brothers gave their affirmations, but Katsi caught a glimpse of Scales gliding through the shroud just before he popped through the entrance of the cave, his scales shimmering with specks of sand and sleet. What had he been doing out in the Maedari? Crazy lizard. Some of the horns on his head seemed even longer, and there was definitely a joint in the webbed spikes on his back. If those grew any longer she wondered if he'd still be able to fold them back down.

"Should we get some rest then and head out when the storm is over?" Rivar asked.

"Yes," Migo said. He turned to Katsi. "Katsi, there are some bodies back there. If you don't mind, maybe you could take care of them the way you did with R."

Katsi nodded. Looking at those bodies was the last thing she wanted to do, but she'd certainly feel better once they were below the ground. She headed deeper inside, thoughts turning to the next few cycles. She'd be traveling alone with Migo for a while, his life completely in her hands. Did she dare think about his legs and arms wrapped around her, or the touch of his lips against her ear?

Certainly not. Those were trivial details at most. Necessary only for reaching their destination together.

And yet...?

She sighed, the memory of his warm breath sending tendrils down her back. This was going to be a long journey.

Chapter 22

Hatan inched the door open and slipped out from behind the secret passage. The palace was riddled with such pathways. He was positive there were several other ones that he didn't even know existed. There were probably some that were known only to Migo, and some that had only been known to his parents, but those would be forgotten now.

And that was how the regent of House Rikaydian, the ruling family of Jehubal, had to get around in his own home. Works of secrecy were the ways to survive in politics. He certainly preferred to meet his enemies in open combat. It was a simpler, straightforward approach with a singular objective to slay the opponent. But he couldn't deny the obvious use for handling things in a subtler way.

The room he'd entered was small, with no ventilation and only a tiny window above eye level that provided the only fragment of light available, which at the moment was created by flashes of purple lightning in a steady stream of constant illumination.

A figure was there, in the corner, a hooded mass camouflaged in clothes that were only a shade darker than the color of the stone wall. Hatan was sure he'd only seen the person because he knew what to look for, and he expected to find it.

"Kyel," Hatan said. "I hope you have some good information for me."

Kyel had crawled into the room from a trick opening just beside the window. Outside that was the ground level of the north garden in which they'd met last time.

"I've at least got something to go on," Kyel said.

"That works for me. What did you find out?"

Kyel laced his fingers and leaned back against the wall. "I think we can safely narrow it down to a few families in particular. Some lesser lords are involved. I think they'd see a different king as a chance for a better opportunity. My guess is that they've got somebody in mind for a potential replacement already. One of the greater lords."

"Have you narrowed that list down then?"

"I have. There are a few that sparked particular interest, like Sinteya Jenali. She more recently became the head of her house. They have some refinery ownership, but no involvement in shipping. A pair of mercenaries at a sleephouse slipped casually that they were under her bill. She has no other reason to employ them. There are a couple other ones that are similarly suspicious. We're also keeping our eyes on a few houses that have ordered weaponry of some kind within the last few cycles, which, given recent events, isn't particularly telling so far.

"Wajek Manor is on the watch list, as are any other merchant lords that were profiting from raiding shaman settlements."

"Raiding settlements?"

"Oh, yes," Kyel nodded, his dark eyes glinting in the dim light. "There were three houses involved in coordinating raids south of Cataban. Apparently there were a few shaman settlements around the swamps and lakes there. Trading was only part of their investment. I'm still not exactly sure what product they were looting from the shaman tribes other than the typical precious metals, but it was profitable enough for them to maintain a collective mercenary group together."

Hatan distinctly remembered Nedro Wajek's trophy room where he kept a stash of various trinkets, looted from the corpses of murdered shamanfolk. Even Katsi had made a point of targeting and burglarizing Nedro's home. Had there been more to it that he didn't understand?

Kyel continued. "They still traded with Asmalam at the same time, but we know there was some additional profit happening."

"Who are the other families involved?"

Kyel rolled a copper ring on his finger. "The Mayari and Kesten families."

"Kesten?" Hatan said, pulse increasing.

"Yes. You seem concerned."

Hatan rubbed at the stubble on his chin. "Rivar and Emil Kesten are with His Majesty even as we speak. I'm hoping we can trust that they act independently of their father's ambitions."

"That's how we understand it so far, unless they've been aware of our scrutiny and have been planning some kind of mutiny all along." Kyel's voice darkened. A dagger was in his hand. Hatan hadn't noticed when Kyel pulled it out. He casually picked his fingernails with it. "It's possible. Should I find them?"

"It would be too late to help Migo at this point. But I'm fairly confident that those two brothers can be trusted."

"Alright. What about here on the inside? Any idea who it is that might be compromising palace security?"

Hatan let out a long breath. He'd been too distracted to give a thorough examination of everyone yet. The acquisition of the shops was supposed to be a means of drastically reducing the onsite staff. He'd already split the palace into sections, cutting off use of certain doors to control who had access to where. Creating an environment to be able to identify any spies was hard enough work without scrambling to put out warehouse fires.

"I'm still working on it," Hatan said. "Hopefully in another cycle or two, I can make that task a lot simpler. Interrogation isn't my greatest strength. It's certainly something we could use the king's expertise on."

"Should we be watching anybody?"

"Not yet. I'll get you a list of key personnel once I finish downsizing the palace staff. I need you to keep your focus on identifying the primary orchestrator. Somebody sees themself as the new king or queen of Jehubal. That person needs to die. Publicly."

Kyel nodded. "We'll get 'em."

Hatan knew they would, if they had enough time. He felt like they were already behind. Even if he did discover who all was orchestrating it, would he have the ability to move against them? He had a network of spies and informants, not a network of assassins. He'd have to put together a coordinated arrest for the main parties and execute any traitors immediately.

What he really needed was a few more cycles to work it all out.

Chapter 23

Migo awoke to utter stillness. Air flowing in and out of his lungs was the only sound. His first instinct was to grab his weapon, but he didn't feel it around him. Had he placed it down? He didn't remember. In fact, he didn't even remember falling asleep. He'd never slept through a Maedari before.

It was dark. Darker than he was used to. Two silhouettes stood further down the entrance of the cave. They turned to look at him as he moved about.

Rivar and Emil. He couldn't see the features of their faces, but he knew it was them.

Where was Katsi and her lizard?

"Have you seen my poleaxe?" Migo asked the brothers as they came towards him.

Neither of them spoke. *Wait.* Migo's instincts rippled across his skin. His dagger. It was still looped at his belt. He whipped it out in a swift motion and took on a defensive position.

"Lord." It was Emil's voice, spoken in a sharp whisper. He held up his hands. "It's us."

Rivar also stopped short, holding his arms out as well.

"Sands," Migo said, "why is it so dark?" The hair on his arms and the back of his neck rose.

"The fog," Rivar said. "Come look."

"Why are you whispering?" Migo asked.

"You'll see, lord," Emil said.

They snuck to the entrance of the cave. The fog was, in fact, considerably dense. Some light filtered through and frozen air glistened.

Still no sign of Katsi.

There was motion in the fog. Deep, large shadows that shifted ever-so-slowly. His weapon was there at the entrance. Perhaps they were more waheshi. He snatched up his weapon. "Waheshi?" he whispered to them.

Rivar shook his head. "Wild varman."

Migo had never seen wild varman before, but why the caution? The brothers had worked with domesticated oxes to pull stormcarts. He knew them only as beasts of burden with heavy muscles and extremely thick hides. Their skins made the best leathers. But their horns were always trimmed. He'd only ever seen them with large stumps remaining.

"Where's Katsi?" He whispered.

Emil shook his head and pointed out into the fog. "She's crazy."

Maybe he was too. He shook his head and stepped out into the fog.

"Lord, wait," Emil said.

The fog enveloped him in a cold wave. It was refreshing, sharpening his senses. The dark shadows seemed ominously large. He'd seen varman before, and these shadows were larger than what his memory served. Perhaps they grew much larger in the wild or the light and fog distorted their size.

What could Katsi possibly be doing?

The ground had molded into cold clay from the aftermath of the storm. Migo's boot ground against the stone, and two nearby shadows shifted, as if great heads were turning to observe him. A deep groaning sound filled the air. It was quickly joined by others. A mild wind blew through his hair.

It was gradual at first, but he noticed it getting faster. The fog swirled about him.

He continued forward, avoiding the shadowy shapes as they lumbered about. Katsi was probably playing with the calves or riding one's back no doubt. The speed of the wind grew faster, and it became noticeably warmer. The sparkling quality of the fog ended as the air warmed. He recognized the implications a second too late.

The fog was dissipating.

He turned back toward the cave, remembering the brothers' hesitancy, but he couldn't even see the entrance. Not until enough of the fog cleared away, and he was left standing in the middle of several massive varman. Their horns were, in fact, extremely large. Not only that, they were jagged things with several tips pointing forward. He froze in place.

The varman were eating the leaves off every bit of greenery. Their thick skins were covered in a sheen coat of thin black hairs that shimmered brown in the sunlight. They were distracted enough that they hadn't even looked up to see him. He looked in every direction. There were at least a couple dozen of them, and he was dead center. Something else caught his eye. A motion, silhouetted from a tree directly in front of the sun.

Katsi. She sat on a tree limb and waved at him, pointing back to the cave.

He'd been worried about her for no reason. He doubted any animal would ever be a real threat to her.

Emil and Rivar stared at him with open mouths.

Migo moved slowly back towards them, taking careful steps, but the nearest varman looked up at him with its deep black eyes. At the sight of him, it lifted one of its cloven hooves and leaned back. Its head was completely level with his own. They were certainly larger than he remembered. He worried it would charge him, but it just stared, chewing on a leaf. He kept moving and made it most of the way back to the cave when all the varman groaned and started walking off to the north. They completely ignored him.

Katsi soared through the air over to the mouth of the cave and dropped down beside them. Scales came with her, holding on the back of her robe with his forelegs. He settled on her shoulder, but was far too big to fit there, so he hung down her back. His scales on his neck had shifted to reds and yellows.

Nobody spoke until all the varman had walked away.

"Sands, lord," Rivar said. "We've always been cautioned to steer clear of wild ones. We had a cousin get gouged and trampled before."

"Glad I didn't join him. We should hurry off," Migo said, then took a long swig from his canteen.

Emil and Rivar rushed to collect the small stash of weapons from the cave. Silver was a rare enough commodity that any weapons they could gather would be well worth it. He didn't even care if the brothers kept it to themselves so long as they put it to good use.

"Get back as soon as you can," Migo said. "Report directly to Regent Padarro."

"Keep my blankets somewhere safe for me," Katsi said. "Those are not easy to come by."

Emil smiled and nodded to her. "We'll do our best."

They clasped Migo's arm in turn.

"To the end," they said in unison, then headed south.

Migo turned to Katsi and let out a deep breath. "Alright. Are you ready for this?"

Katsi smirked. "Even if I'm not, we're going to do it anyway." She turned away from him and Scales bounced into the air, flapping his wings.

Wait, wings? When had Scales developed an extra joint?

"Please don't kill me," Migo said, stepping up to Katsi. Two fist-sized rocks zipped through the air, stopping to hover just over her shoulders. He snatched them from the air and put his arms over Katsi's shoulders, trying to act as natural as possible. It wasn't like he was hugging her, but his cheeks started to burn. He was grateful she couldn't see his face.

Katsi started the countdown this time, and Migo jumped onto her back. The rocks did a lot of the lifting as Migo rose into the air with her, and they started to glide ahead. They went slowly at first, but once they gained enough altitude, Katsi increased the speed dramatically.

Somehow, he felt no wind as they soared. His grip on the rocks tightened as he looked down, watching the ground pass by at a tremendous speed. Small pockets of water dotted the ground intermittently, and he could see deep into the Frozen Waste, a gray, lifeless plain covered in a layer of ice. Large mountains rose far out in the distance.

Seeing the Ring from this height was the greatest spectacle. A long strip of life stretching all the way to the horizon. Moving across it with such speed seemed like a privilege so beautiful that no human was meant to see it. Yet there they were.

Despite the insanity of what they were doing, Migo felt no sense of fear. Awe. Excitement, perhaps.

Katsi was right. They'd definitely reach Mazanib much faster than he'd anticipated.

"You're not tense at all," Katsi said, her voice surprisingly clear.

"It's not so bad now that we're up here."

"Yeah, try being the one who has to hold you."

"How does that work with magic? I'm heavy to lift with your body, how does the magic make lifting me possible?"

"Sands, I have no idea. I guess it feels like any other muscle, but it doesn't get sore, it only gets tired. Using magic in different ways also feels like I'm doing different stretches if that makes any sense."

"Generally, yes."

Katsi breathed a laugh. "Good enough. I don't know much about magic unfortunately, but I do know how to use it. At least a little bit."

"That's the important part for now." They flew on in silence for another mark or two. Migo tried looking around to find the moon, but didn't see it anywhere. They passed a long stretch of farmland with rows of crops, interlaced with a complex irrigation system. From this high up, it was fascinating to see how elaborate human engineering could be.

What would those people think if they looked up and saw somebody flying through the sky? How would that impact their sentiments towards shamanfolk? Maybe they'd hate them even more for possessing power that none of them ever would. That was how he might have felt had he not come to know Katsi.

He wished he knew more about how the shamanfolk thrived so well. Even after years of persecution, he got the impression that there were still so many of them. Magic played a significant role in them surviving, and yet Katsi was always seeking a way to learn more, as if her tribe lacked the information to train her properly. "Why is it that your tribe seems to have forgotten so much?"

Katsi hummed in thought. "I think their information about magic just became limited or concentrated on a few specific functions. Survival came before everything else. Growing food, bewitching clothing, safe shelter. We also banished some of the shamans from our tribe for using bleeder magic, so that reduced the number of magic users we had, which apparently can also impact the number of people born with magical affinities. Also, I'm not sure how much the tribe has forgotten. Part of me thinks that the elder shamans just don't share as much as they know, but I'm not sure why. Maybe that's just because I've been more of an outcast."

"Hm. Sounds like me and politics."

"How is that at all similar?"

"Well, I grew up as a prince, but I was never really involved in politics. My mother intentionally kept me out of it. But now here I am as the king. Politics should be second nature by now, but I don't know much about the rules."

"That must be why you left your cousin in charge."

Migo laughed. "He probably knows just about as much as I do. We're soldiers. But to me, maybe I just need to think of politics as another weapon."

"Hopefully you still have a chance to use that weapon when you get back to Jehubal. I do hope to learn a thing or two about stormcalling, but I don't intend on being anybody's puppet again."

Migo felt a parallel with her again. Both of them had been used as tools. He'd been used by his mother to enact vengeance. Katsi had been manipulated into assassinations, but to what end? He still had no clear indication as to what the other party was after. More hatred and vengeance. That was the thing about hatred. One side's success would only fuel the fire for more hatred and backlash. There was no winning. And at least to him, the losses had been heavy enough. "People must think we're too young, easy to be manipulated. But we'll be the ones dictating the future."

"Ending old people's grudges one at a time."

"Something like that."

He shifted against her. His body felt stiff and his grip on the stones made his fingers ache. Being this close to her wasn't easy. His thoughts drifted far too often to the fact that one of his knuckles was touching the skin of her collarbone. He had plenty of opportunity to move his hand somewhere else, but he never did. He told himself that it meant nothing to him, keeping it there as a means of proving it to himself, but deep down he knew it was something else.

His words to her just before she killed his mother still rang in his memory. *I would kill for you. I would bleed for you. I would die for you. I would defy the whole empire to keep you safe.* The words had been etched into his soul as though he'd been bound by an oath. He doubted there was anything he could do to purge the words from his memory. He only hoped it wouldn't be necessary.

Reflecting on it now, it seemed such a wild thing to say, as young as he was. Why had he felt such conviction? Because she was the first girl who had ever been kind to him? Was he really so fickle?

But he knew it was more than that. She'd taught him about defining himself in his own way. Finding his own path. Believing in his ability to change and become something better. It didn't matter if he was forgiven by others. What mattered was that he'd forgiven himself. What mattered was what he did now and what he was going to do in the future. The past was unchangeable, but the present possibilities were still all laid out before him. Nothing was inevitable. He'd freed his people from oppression. From rage. And there was still work to be done.

Hope.

That was the word. That was what Katsi had given him.

His knuckle touched the skin of her collarbone.

He gulped hard and tried to take a deep breath to calm his senses, but even in that deep breath, with some of her dark hair tickling his cheek, all he could smell was her. It wasn't much different from the smell of dry sand, but it also reminded him of the sweet flavor of abodas, with a sense of tang.

Sands, he was in trouble.

Katsi moved beneath him, rolling her shoulders, stretching her arms. Her hands still held him under the knees, but she was no doubt getting tired even though he was putting in his best effort to hold them up himself. They'd been flying for a while now.

A lake came into view with a few rounded buildings near its edge.

"Drop down," Migo said. "We should take a break before crossing over this lake. Get some food and water. There's a settlement down there."

Katsi slowed before lowering them down. She always seemed to need a moment to reorient their direction. Her magic had so many different parts going at once, he wondered how she was able to coordinate that. But then again, it could very well be the same as walking while talking and holding something in either hand.

They hit the ground smoothly this time. Two flights and Katsi was already doing remarkably well. She was a quick learner.

"I can't believe how far we've gotten already," Migo said, stretching out his arms and legs.

"I can go faster," she said, pulling off her cloak and checking her armlets. She poked tentatively at her skin.

Migo narrowed his eyes as a thought occurred to him. "Do they do something to you? The armlets."

Katsi shrugged. "I'm not entirely sure. I don't know how they work. I've never heard of how they are created or where the energy comes from. Any magic enhancing artifacts I've heard of are all ancient, but it's actually common for shamanfolk tribes to all have one in some form or another. Usually rings."

"But they don't hurt you, right?"

"No, definitely not," Katsi said, walking ahead on foot. "Although, it does tingle when you touch one for the first time. That's actually the first indication we have among shamanfolk that somebody has some kind of magical proficiency."

"So, by touching a magical object, you learn whether or not you have magic abilities?"

"Yes. And for me, in using these armlets, they actually get warm when I use them—it doesn't hurt—it's just warm, and it gets hotter the longer I use it."

"Is there a limit to the energy?"

"I don't know. I've never heard of one running out, but I don't think my tribe actually uses any of their artifacts other than testing for magical ability." Katsi looked around them.

They'd moved a little closer to the center of the Ring so that they weren't right next to the Frozen Waste. The landscape here was much the same as it was immediately north of Jehubal, with small ponds or lakes dotting the landscape. It was mostly flat land with the occasional bump or hill. The air was considerably humid, as it often was after a Maedari. There were fewer trees, but the scrub was dense with thick-leaved bushes that Katsi probably knew the name of.

"Is this still Jehubal?" Katsi asked.

"Technically, yes," Migo said. "The large lake beyond the settlement here is the dividing feature between Jehubal and Lazeem. Similar to the Cataban border to the south. But this lake only expands halfway into the Ring."

"So is Lazeem City close?"

"No, no. Jehubal is technically a small nation compared to most of the others, and Lazeem covers a very large territory with several cities. Its layout is nothing like Jehubal, though the city of Lazeem is smaller than the city of Jehubal, but that's because the vast majority of our population lives in the city."

"Right. Well, I have no sense of geography. If there's one thing I've learned recently, it's that I hardly know anything."

Migo smiled. "These details are trivial. You know things that people could spend a lifetime looking for."

She frowned at him. "Like what?"

"Resilience," Migo said, then added, "laughter, and hope." The hairs stood up along his arms as he spoke the last word. "Those are more valuable than geography."

Katsi held back a smile, but it split into a wide grin, and she shook her head.

Sands.

That smile.

He'd kill for that smile—to keep her laughter and hope alive.

But first he needed to find out who was trying to use her. Who was trying to pit them against each other? Could it really just be a vague, bitter old woman in the desert? His instincts told him no. It was deeper than that. Bigger. He'd get to the bottom of it and wipe whoever it was from the face of the planet.

Chapter 24

The metallic taste of copper soothed Nagesh's undulating anxiety as he rolled the ring around on his tongue. He knew he shouldn't do it. It was a bad habit. But the taste reminded him of blood. The resemblance alone calmed him down enough to assess the situation.

His body was exhausted. He'd all but sprinted for over a full cycle to get here, even through the Maedari. He was out of water and hunger clawed at him, but would any of that matter now? A rare absence of wind accompanied him as he stumbled wearily toward the ancient hideout. Everything was still.

The Maedari must have washed away anything that happened prior. He saw no signs of battle. No dead bodies. Perhaps everything was alright. Maybe the sick, twisted feeling he'd gotten was merely coincidence.

But he knew that wasn't true. The connection with his waheshi was truly severed, and he'd never be able to make one again so long as Alishara had his blood. Still, after all these years, he'd been able to keep this place hidden from her, and from everyone else. All who had approached had died. Nobody was prepared to face a waheshi. At least, nobody *had* been prepared.

He approached the hideout, noting how all the nearby shrubs were practically leafless, likely feasted on by the wild varman herd that roamed the area.

It shouldn't have been a surprise, but the sight of the hideout being wide open and exposed struck him with a terrible fear. He popped the ring out of his mouth and fitted it back over his finger. Comfort was not what he needed right now. If their hideout was exposed like that, then surely his aunt and cousin were dead. There was no other alternative.

The last of his once great family.

His feet dragged to the entrance, hand heavy upon the pommel of his secula. The air wasn't cold enough. It should have felt like ice. It should have numbed him. Instead, his heart pulsed like fire. His blood was hot, and he felt every inch of it. His footsteps echoed hollowly in the empty cave.

Whoever had entered here was no simple warrior; it was a shaman. The ancient, enchanted stones had been reduced to sand. Their strength, having stood for so many years, crumbled, and most of it had blown away with the storm. Bricks could make walls, buildings, empires. But the sand left in the wake of this destruction would build nothing. Useless.

He came to the bend in the cave and cast his weary eyes into his old home. The place he had hidden for years, living in fear. Living like a savage. Those were dark times. Before he'd allowed hope to capture him away, to venture out and make his own path.

But now he looked at what that hope had brought him.

He should have waited, as his aunt had implored. Then they might have all survived. Then he would have never been manipulated by that cursed Alishara. This was probably her doing, somehow. She must have learned it from him, even without him divulging it. He'd always sworn to her that he didn't even know his family, that he was a lone shaman, acting of his own accord to make a living among Marems.

She must have known. Seers.

His secrecy had come to naught.

And now, here he was. Back in the same cave, but it was empty. The only thing that remained were the various ingredients for making potions—including one particular potion. The most important of all.

There was still blood in the room. On the walls and floor.

Nagesh's proficiency with blood magic was supposedly spectacular, much stronger than his aunt's, but what good did that do him? Even his cousin, a powerful earthmelder, had been bested by whoever came through. All four waheshi had been slain.

All the bodies were gone. They'd been wise.

He reached the back of the room and at least had the sense to check for any food. It was all gone, of course. So they got rid of the bodies and took the food, but left the potion ingredients? Many of these ingredients were quite rare. Whoever had been through here must not have been a very knowledgeable shaman.

It struck him.

Perhaps Alishara *did* send somebody here.

The stormcaller.

The assassin.

But there was no way she was skilled enough to get past the waheshi. The waheshi guards had effectively stopped dozens of other shamans over the years.

However it happened, there was nothing he could do now. He dropped his head and fell to his knees, but one of his knees cracked hard against a sharp object. He grunted in pain and located the small object that had jabbed him. His eyes widened as he picked it up and lifted it to his face.

Could it be?

It was a small tooth. Sharp and narrow like a double-edged spike.

"Impossible," he muttered to himself.

As a bleeder and mixer, he'd grown very familiar with the anatomy of many animals. Different ingredients, especially organic ones, had properties that affected potions in countless ways. And the ingredient he held in his hand hadn't been seen for years. The animals had been thought to be extinct for a few hundred years at least, but there was no denying what he held in his very hand.

A drakotah tooth. And not just any drakotah tooth, but the drakotah was young. Possibly still an infant. That was when they were most potent.

It was a rare find. No, an impossible find. And somehow it had been delivered into his hands. He clenched it in his fist, tears coming to his eyes. Was this a sign? He didn't know what his destiny held, but the drakotah tooth meant at least one thing: he was not done. His family's death would not be in vain. This would be his chance to make one final potion. The one that created Ashjagar. Deliverance. There were other shamans out there. Others like him. He was not alone.

Perhaps he would be the means of saving them all.

Chapter 25

Katsi flew low, gliding between thick jungle trees. Migo hung on behind her. It was crazy how easily they'd grown used to each other. It was still a month ago that Migo would have killed her on sight. Probably only after torturing and questioning her, too. Yet here they were.

Friends.

If that was even the right word for it. They'd certainly moved well beyond tolerating each other. She was comfortable around him. Honest even, and true to herself. She'd told him everything. No secrets remained. He knew her motivations. Not for love, or peace, or freedom, but for power. Yes, the other things mattered too, but she understood the real reason for her actions. And he knew it too. He was too smart to be deceived.

And somehow, her desire to find her own way had inspired him to do the same. But he was nobler than her. Despite all the wicked things he'd done, he truly was out to find justice and peace, and not only for himself, but for others.

Did that mean Katsi was selfish? Was everything she was doing just for herself?

No. Not entirely. She saved Scales because he needed help. She'd agreed to help Migo with the map. She'd been the only reason they were able to enter the cave and find another hint at where to go. Not because she needed to, but because she wanted to.

"This is far enough," Migo said, jolting her from her thoughts. "Drop down."

He patted her shoulder.

Katsi brought them down, and Migo let go before she touched the ground. He'd gotten a lot better at the dismount, though she hated thinking about it with that word. She wasn't some kind of pack animal.

When she hit the ground, her feet felt at home against the soft soil. They'd crossed the lake and traveled for another couple marks before Migo suggested a place to lodge. Apparently he was quite familiar with this area.

Migo bounced ahead, clearly eager to be on his own two feet. "The town should be just through the trees. I know a good place where we can rest."

Katsi ducked under some low-hanging vines. "You've spent some time around here?" she asked.

A swarm of large, annoyingly loud, buzzing insects fled for their lives as Scales flew through them with his mouth open.

"You can say that," Migo said as they emerged into a clearing. The town ahead hugged the south-facing side of a squat, stony hill that looked like a massive boulder. The top of the hill was capped by a large castle that looked like several round spires smashed together. The buildings of the town were built close together, perhaps so their combined strength would help them hold back against the storms. They were surprisingly made with more wood than she would have expected.

Katsi felt as though she knew most everything about Migo's history, and from what she recalled, he hadn't done a whole lot of traveling. That left her with one reasonable conclusion. "Migo. Is this the place you came to learn about shaman hunting?"

"Well, that didn't take you long to figure out."

"Migo, why would you take me here? Of all places? Might that be a little dangerous?"

Migo chuckled. "No. Trust me, Rhian is the last place they'd expect to see a shaman."

"Why do you all think that? Shamanfolk are either excellent at hiding, or they're dead. They could be anywhere."

"Yes... I suppose I've thought of that before too." He glanced over at her. "So they might be suspicious, but your advantage is that you're with me. I'm well known here. They'd likely take my word on practically anything."

"And why would they do that?"

"Because I was the best student."

"And yet, when I met you, you seemed to hardly know a thing about shamans."

"Unfortunately, yes," Migo said with a sigh. "But I'm still the best shaman hunter to have attended the academy."

"So if we got into a fight, who would win?"

Migo gave her a serious look. "You would. Within the blink of an eye. I'm not sure anything could stop you besides another shaman."

"You truly think so?"

"I know so. You can control everything around me. I can fight against an actual person, but I can't slay the ground, or the air itself. At the academy, they taught us how to fight against those who were faster and stronger than us. They taught us how to predict an opponent's move, and how to counter when the opponent predicted your own move. There's a science to all of it that I took a great passion for, but I still don't think that would help me if the ground suddenly opened up and swallowed me."

Katsi shrugged with a hum. "That's true." Nevertheless, it had been Migo who defeated the earthmelder shaman, whereas Katsi didn't even know what to do. She'd tried to use the ground against him, but it didn't work. The other shaman had clearly been more skilled. She'd been significantly disadvantaged even though her power was probably greater. She needed to know how to fight against other shamans; otherwise she'd be helpless against them without Migo.

What if she ran into trouble with the other shamans when they got to Mazanib?

"Could you show me how to fight better?" she said.

Migo looked her up and down, amusement glinting in his eyes. "I was hoping you'd ask."

Katsi laughed. "Really? Just waiting for the opportunity, huh?"

Migo nodded, expression bright. He definitely wasn't joking. "I may not be the best instructor, but I could show you a few things. I'm not sure what kind of training you've had, but I'm one of the best warriors around."

"You don't have to tell me, Migo. I witnessed that firsthand. I doubt those six men you beat in the throne room were amateurs."

He looked ahead.

She still wasn't sure how he felt about that whole situation. Killing some of his own people. But it clearly affected him somehow. "How do you deal with it?"

"With what? Being a warrior?

"With killing."

Migo's jaw clenched. "Sometimes I don't. Sometimes I never think twice. But other times... I don't completely get over it. I see faces. I remember them. But even those instances fade with time. At least for me. Not all soldiers feel the same." His eyes softened as he looked back at her. "Don't worry. The remorse you feel will get better over time."

She nodded with understanding. At first, killing the queen had tortured her, even though she knew it was the right thing. But now, not a drop of regret or sadness entered her heart as she remembered the scene. It had only taken her a couple cycles to move on. It was a justified action. But with R? She didn't feel as bad as before, but some regret lingered.

Scales hung back by the treeline. She wondered how he kept track of her all the time even after losing sight of her. Scent perhaps? Whatever the case, she'd grown to expect him to simply show up whenever they got separated.

Migo stopped walking. "First lesson."

"Here?"

"Yes."

"Might somebody from town see us?"

"Yes. Again, I'm known here. Showing somebody how to defend herself shouldn't be absurd."

"Alright." Katsi placed her hands on her hips. "What would you have me learn?"

"Commitment." His eyes were hard, and he turned his body to the side, spreading his legs as though preparing to fight her. "When you fight somebody, regardless of the weapon, you must be committed. You need to be all in, focused on your objective."

His fist exploded to the left of her face, but she reacted by flinching to the side, slapping at his arm, but in the same instant, his left leg burst up, pausing before it would have struck just above her right knee. She shoved it away and kicked at his groin, but he blocked it with the bottom of his knee.

He smirked at her. "Really?"

She ignored him and punched at his gut with her left, then followed up with a right hook toward his face. He blocked both blows with his forearms, and the smirk never left his face.

"You've had some training before?" he asked, dropping his arms.

"A little," Katsi said. "While I lived with the tribe. Every shamanfolk is trained to fight."

He nodded. "There's not much I can teach without a lot more time. Your commitment is good when you aren't afraid. You could use some pacing control, but you're probably already at the point where you'd need training on specific techniques." He pointed at her sword. "I'm not about to spar with you wielding that thing, but if we ever catch a breather, I can show you some forms."

"Deal," Katsi said.

"But the last thing I'll say for now," he said, placing a hand on Katsi's shoulder. The seriousness in his eyes struck her. "Don't close or cover your eyes."

In her battle with the shaman, that's exactly what Katsi had done. She'd lost her focus, becoming more concerned about surviving than about defeating the opponent. "Got it," she said, gulping against her dry throat.

They turned and walked together toward the town. "We'll be staying over there," Migo said, pointing to a manor at the base of the hill.

"Who lives there?"

"An old friend of mine."

"You have friends?" she teased.

He smiled at her. "One or two. He and I actually go back several years. He knew me even before my father died."

Katsi whistled as they reached the streets. She half expected the few people there to acknowledge Migo in some way, but other than the quick glance, they were practically ignored. No stalls for trading. No hawkers. It was a rather quiet town, save for the clanging of metal somewhere off to the side. Children played in the streets and women milled about doing menial tasks, but she didn't see any men.

"What do people do here?" she asked, keeping her voice quiet.

Migo grunted. "Laborers mostly. There are two essential fields of employment here: working for the academy, or working for the mines."

"Mines?"

"Mmhm. Used to be a large mining operation they'd run near the Frozen Waste. Mostly silver, but they'll dig up any metal they can find. Sometimes the mines even stretch into the wastes."

"They go into the wastes?" Katsi asked incredulously, taking a second glance at all the people around her. "I feel like I should have known that there were..." she lowered her voice, "Marems that went into the wastes for work."

"Only miners and soldiers from what I know. Well," he scratched his head, "and astronomers."

"Oh yeah." She smiled faintly. "I'll have to see the stars sometime. You've talked them up so much."

Migo grabbed her arm with a gentle grip and turned to look into her eyes. "Katsi," he said, voice catching as he struggled to find words. "You are more—"

"Migo?" a voice interrupted them.

Migo released Katsi's arm but stood his ground beside her.

A young woman approached them, casting Katsi a dismissive glance. "Erm, excuse me, Lord Rikaydian." She gave him a curtsy, teeth beaming so white. Katsi had never seen such perfect teeth before. She had flawless brown skin, bare shoulders, and strong arms. Her curly black hair was held back with a tight scarf.

"Chaeyna," Migo said, his face turned to stone, but his eyes looked her up and down. Katsi could *feel* his walls go up as his body stiffened. "We were actually coming to visit you. Er, your family, that is."

Chaeyna giggled as if Migo was funny. He wasn't. He was just awkward. And big. And stupid-faced. And he was about to say something that she'd actually wanted to hear. Was Migo really taking them to this girl's home? Was this some old courting prospect of his? That seemed like a weird thing to do. Katsi wouldn't have even suspected Migo of being attracted to women at all if he hadn't kissed her.

"Come along, then," Chaeyna said. "You look as though you've been traveling for ages!" Chaeyna was practically shaking with energy, and she rocked her shoulders up and down as she spoke to him in a way that seemed extremely flirtatious. She snatched Migo's hand and urged them up the gradual slope, her vibrant yellow, orange, and white dress bouncing with her steps.

"You look taller than I remember," Chaeyna said. "And stronger."

Katsi didn't like her.

Chaeyna looked back at him with a grin. "And grumpier. Why so stoic? Did you forget how to smile after you left?"

Maybe she wasn't so bad.

Katsi was still wary but couldn't help throwing in her own jab. "I didn't know he had any other expression."

Chaeyna gave Katsi a second glance but directed her conversation back at Migo. "You knew other expressions before you left. You didn't introduce me to your companion here."

"Yes," Migo said, withdrawing his hand from Chaeyna. "This is Katsi. She's an expert on shamans. Katsi, this is Chaeyna Roqaya. She's the younger sister of my friend Yavasu."

Katsi flashed a split-second smile. The name Yavasu sounded familiar. She could have sworn she'd heard Migo mention that before. At least that was a more believable explanation than him visiting this girl.

"A shaman expert?" Chaeyna said, giving Katsi a third glance. Appraisingly longer this time. "What do you need one of those for?"

"She's been helping me with a task," Migo said.

Chaeyna giggled again. "Trying to be discreet. Well, sir, your secret is safe with me." Then she spoke to Katsi directly for the first time. "A shaman expert? Sounds dangerously fun. I'm curious to know how one becomes an expert."

They reached the home, and a single servant greeted them at the door, a woman wearing a plain tunic and skirt.

"We'll want to wake up my brother," Chaeyna said to the servant. "Tell him that Lord Rikaydian of Jehubal has come to pay a visit." The servant scurried off, and Chaeyna ushered them into the manor.

Inside was nothing like Rikaydian Palace with its impossibly massive rooms. Nor was it like Wajek Manor, riddled with gaudy decor. Instead, it was more like a large home, with wider halls and more rooms.

"You two look famished and exhausted," Chaeyna said. "I'll see if we have some food available, and I can help prepare a warm bath. You probably need it. Will you be staying long?"

"Those all sound good, thank you," Migo said. "If we can rest here before continuing on, that would be very gracious of your family."

Her perfect teeth flashed again, and she led them to an open room, a stone dining table inside, decorated with a single red cloth that rested across the length. "Have a seat in here. I'll be back in a moment."

Katsi followed Migo into the dining room as Chaeyna disappeared. A wide window on the second floor provided plenty of light. Katsi sat across from Migo, resting her pack in her lap. "I think she fancies you," Katsi said almost immediately.

Migo's brow creased in a frown. "Unlikely. She's an enthusiastic individual, that's all. However, I did get the impression that she's intimidated by you."

"She should be," Katsi said with a smile. "Even with those strong arms of hers."

Migo folded his arms and shook his head.

Katsi rolled her eyes. "You told me about Yavasu before, didn't you?"

"Yes, I played with him when we were kids. He was the friend who was playing with me outside when the Maedari came, and my father came out to try and save me."

"Oh, I see," Katsi said. Nothing like bringing up traumatic memories.

Pounding footsteps announced his approach just before Yavasu burst through the opening. "Migo!" He laughed with excitement. "What a surprise."

Migo rose from his seat.

Yavasu's smile was as white as his sister's. His hair was matted up on one side and his clothes were rumpled, but he didn't seem to care. Instead of giving Migo the usual warrior's clasp, he ran up and gave the much taller man a hug.

Chaeyna came scurrying in behind him with a basket of flat bread.

Katsi was quick to snatch one off and start munching away.

"What brings you here?" Yavasu said. "You're not going to try and rope me into sparring, are you?"

Migo smiled. "No, nothing like that. We're on our way north and wanted to come see you. We need a safe place to sleep."

Yavasu nodded. "We've got that." He gestured at himself. "Sorry for my appearance, we just got back from a dig a couple marks ago. Most of the men are sleeping."

"I figured as much when I didn't see many men outside," Migo said.

"Many?"

Migo's voice was matter-of-fact as he said, "Yes, the guard near the jungle where we came out, then another one at the edge of town and a couple more peeking down from the parapets of the castle."

Yavasu laughed. "Father prides himself on having troops well hidden—I guess that doesn't apply to well-trained princes."

"I'm actually the king now," Migo said, leaning back against the table as he folded his arms.

"Sands," Chaeyna whispered, gaping up at Migo.

Yavasu frowned in thought, touching his eyebrow with a finger, clearly contemplating the implications. "This is a good thing, is it not?"

"Better than the alternative," Katsi said through a mouthful of bread. She liked this stuff. Hadn't had much of it in Jehubal. All the bread was sweet there. Not bad, but she liked the richness of the bread here. Perhaps because it was so different.

"True," Yavasu said with a knowing look. Katsi got the feeling he was rather smart. She gave him another look-over. Grimy clothes, unkempt hair. No, it wasn't grime. It was graphite. His clothes were loose, giving him a gangly look. He wasn't built thick like Migo, but he held a strong posture, though his head propped forward just slightly enough that she could assume he spent a lot of time looking down, perhaps writing or reading.

"Your family runs the mines?" Katsi said.

Yavasu smiled. "We do. I'm sure His Majesty told you all about it on the way here."

"You think Migo talks?" Katsi said. "I have to come to all my own conclusions with him."

"I didn't tell her much," Migo conceded, "but please, Yavasu, you're my oldest friend. You can just call me Migo."

Yavasu shrugged. "Fine, but not where my parents might hear me."

Katsi glanced at Chaeyna. The girl had gone particularly quiet since Migo announced his kingship. She ogled up at him from the side of the room as though she were in the presence of deity. If only she knew that Katsi was the one to put him on the throne. If only they knew she was a shaman. She wondered how things would go if she announced that to them, just to see the reaction. Maybe she was too easily bored.

"Would it be alright if Katsi and I stay here to rest for a few marks?" Migo asked.

"For the King of Jehubal?" Yavasu smiled. "I'm not sure my parents would be able to refuse. Chae—could you help get baths ready for our guests?"

Chaeyna nodded and smiled at Migo before leaving the room.

Yavasu turned his attention to Katsi. "You aren't betrothed to the good king here, are you?"

Katsi smiled nervously and said, "No," but she couldn't help but notice Migo's hands curl into tight fists.

"Good, because he needs to marry my sister so I can officially become his brother." Yavasu laughed. "She talks about you more than I do, you know."

Migo rolled his eyes. "Yavasu."

"Right, if my family is not too beneath you, that is."

"Yavasu, nobody is *beneath* me," Migo said. "I'm no better than anybody. My father always taught that rulers and their people serve each other. We all have roles to play and values to contribute."

"Ah," Yavasu said. "I always knew you were more than a soldier."

"No thanks to the late queen's efforts," Katsi interjected.

Yavasu's response to her statement was to tap his eyebrow again. Perhaps a nervous habit when he started to think deeply.

Katsi worried he was smarter than anybody his age should be.

"I'm surprised you got here before word of your ascension reached us," Yavasu said to Migo.

"We're making good time," Migo said. "I'm heading to Mazanib to meet the emperor. I've never been there before, and neither had my mother. We also have other immediate news regarding some of the emperor's soldiers that we need to report."

"Right," Yavasu said. "Which I'm sure has something to do with why you've brought the shaman..." he gave Katsi a lingering scrutiny before adding, "expert."

"You could say that," Migo said, rising up to his full height, hard eyes staring unblinkingly down at his friend.

Yavasu grinned. "Fine. Keep your secrets, my friend."

"I'm not keeping secrets."

"Migo, I know my family just runs the mining operations here, but you know we all receive some training at the academy for both truthseeing and moderate combat techniques, right? I'm no master at either, like you are, but I can tell when you're being suspicious. You left Jehubal right after your coronation which would have been immediately after your mother's death, and you're traveling with nobody else besides a young woman armed with a sword and dressed in stormwading armor. Did you get banished?" The smile didn't leave his face.

Katsi adjusted her robe. Sure, part of the leather beneath was showing, but he'd identified it as stormwading armor far too easily. How much time had he spent in the wastes?

"Nothing like that," Migo said, "but the queen didn't die by accident. Katsi here saved my life. I swore to the people that I would discover who my father's true murderers were. That has led me up here. None of that is a secret."

"That sounds more like it," Yavasu said. "Always following the excitement." He smiled at Katsi. "And don't worry, Katsi. If Migo trusts you, you're probably doing something right. I had my opportunity to save a life years ago, but I missed it."

"Baths are ready," Chaeyna said, coming back into the room.

What did Yavasu mean about having a chance to save a life? The only thing she knew about him was that he'd been there the cycle Migo's father died... Perhaps he meant that he could have helped Migo inside before the storm came. Then Migo's father wouldn't have been assassinated to begin with.

"Migo," Yavasu said, pointing to the bowl of bread. "You didn't even try one yet. Hop to it. We can talk more after you have some rest."

Katsi was still unsure about these people. She grabbed some more flatbread just as Migo did, the back of their hands touching. There was a distinct comfort she got from him, knowing that no matter what, he was always on her side. He'd trusted the twins, and they turned out alright. This was his childhood friend. Surely he was trustworthy as well.

Chapter 26

Hatan folded his hands behind his back and nodded to the servant at the door. It was exactly the tenth mark. He'd spent what little remained of the Rikaydian's money to purchase the shops and rudimentary supplies to start up the businesses. They needed to get an income going as soon as possible. The rest of the money was being spent on this. A ball.

Expensive, yes, but he needed a good reason to get the Jehubalin nobility in one place.

The servant opened the door, and guests started filtering into the large ballroom. It hadn't been used in over ten years. Hatan had spent nearly two marks helping the staff get it cleaned up and ready. It was one of the few grandiose rooms in the palace, with elaborate, railed walkways on two sides, supported by ionic, ridged columns. Large red and gray drapes hung from the walls and a massive chandelier dangled over the middle of the room, one of the few chandeliers in the whole kingdom.

Beside him stood Captain Falshon and his wife, Briondi. Falshon looked sharp in his crisp officer's uniform. Instead of his glaive, he only had a long knife in an elaborate sheath. Hatan didn't doubt there were other weapons concealed on his person somewhere.

Briondi was an equally fitting gem. She knew how to play the part of calm serenity, her lips loose with polite smiles, but her eyes fierce and attentive. Her dress was practical, not restrictive or revealing, and it was a shade of magenta to match her husband's uniform.

"There are rangolas, and there are varman," Falshon said, raising an eyebrow at Hatan, "and I'm not sure which one I am right now."

Hatan smiled. "Varman, of course. Dangerous. Strong. And we work together."

"But isn't the symbol of house Rikaydian a rangola?" Briondi said, looping her arm through her husband's.

"Yes," Hatan said, "but I'm not a Rikaydian. Our king is out hunting, and I'm here defending."

Hatan plastered on a smile as the guests approached. Music started, light at first, as tradition held. A band of eight musicians were cluttered into an alcove at the side of the room, only two of them playing their instruments. Hatan knew nothing about music. He'd heard very little of it in his entire life, but the tune was light and cheery. Enough so that he could feel it invigorating him to socialize, even though he had no proclivity towards it. Responsibility outweighed comfort.

Hatan stood near the entrance, greeting those who came in, making sure to watch all of them. Nedro Wajek was excitement itself as he came through the door, arms flailing as he scampered up to Hatan. He wore the finest black suit with a vibrant blue robe, embroidered with gold. His sharply trimmed beard did little to hide his bouncing jowls.

"Regent Padarro," Nedro said, shaking with laughter. "I've been looking forward to this ever since I got that invitation. I can't tell you how much I've missed this old ballroom, but I can assure you, my dancing skills are as sharp as ever." He clasped Hatan's hand and shook it vigorously.

"I wouldn't doubt it, Nedro," Hatan said with a genuine smile. "I'll be watching you out there." Closely.

"But where's your companion?" Nedro said, glancing about as if baffled. "You're not here alone like some wild bachelor, are you? I know I sure am." He barked with laughter.

"I'm sure Regent Padarro will be well attended to," a woman said from behind Nedro, gracefully dodging around him to proffer her satin silver-sleeved hand to Hatan, jeweled bangles tinkling about her wrist. Light brown eyes looked up at him, framed by her dark lashes, painted red lips parting in a confident smile.

Nedro's eyes widened as he stepped aside, stifling a squeal.

Hatan took the woman's hand. Her hair, though not richly decorated, was finely styled in several braids that wound together on top of her head, revealing the smooth, light brown skin of her slender neck. She was both young and mature, with an athletic form well accentuated by her white dress, accented with black lace over the shoulders and along the bottom hems. He could only place her age at somewhere in the late twenties. "Welcome. I can't say I've met you before."

"My name is Sinteya." Her pupils widened noticeably as her eyes ran across the features of his face. "Of house Jenali. I don't blame you for not knowing—I only recently assumed the head of house. I'm sure you've been too busy putting out fires." She gasped, her cheeks brightening as she placed a hand over mouth. "My apologies, I didn't mean that literally."

Hatan smiled. So this was Sinteya Jenali, one of the names Kyel had given him. A potential insurrectionist. He knew far too well the dangers of a beautiful woman. "I'm sure everyone has heard of that. Don't worry. I take no offense, Lady Jenali." He had no doubt the reference to putting out fires was intentional. Beautiful *and* clever. Dangerous indeed. But Hatan was cautious enough to know that he could still be susceptible to deception.

"If you can forgive me for the slight, I'd be happy to share a dance with you sometime," she said. "That is, if you can tear yourself away from your duties for a moment, and the gang of women that I'm sure will be fawning over you."

"I'm sure that won't be a problem," Hatan said as the smooth touch of her gloved hand slipped away.

"I'll hold you to it," she said as she meandered off.

Nedro had enough sense to take his leave as well as more guests filtered through to offer their greetings.

Hatan was staggered at how many of them there were. Agwe had told him that there were likely to be over a hundred attendees, but he wouldn't be surprised if there were twice that. Though he hardly knew any of them by face, he'd likely recognize their family names, or even where their homes were located within the city.

Falshon leaned close to Hatan's ear and whispered, "The Mayari family just entered, sir. Green capes."

Hatan easily caught sight of the distinctive clothing. There were five of them in total. He'd studied their names beforehand, but he struggled to remember them. Lady Khadij Mayari was the first name to come to mind, then her husband, Nadim. They were entering senior years, but were still strong and well. Their oldest daughter, Rashail, was accompanied by her husband, Tasnim. They had a single son attending with them as well, Kelin. He was attending looking for a spouse no doubt.

Each of them wore a vibrant green cape that trailed just past the back of their knees. They gave Hatan little more than a cursory nod as they entered the ballroom floor. Several more patrons entered, but Hatan had his attention ready for one final group.

He worried they wouldn't show, but he didn't have to worry long.

Vitori Kesten entered with head held high, baldness shining like a beacon. His eyebrows were furry gray bushes. He wore a simple gray vest over a white shirt. All ten of his fingers were decorated with large rings, and he walked with the aid of a fine, brasswood cane, a bright sapphire caged inside the top of it. The item seemed like the sort of artifact that would have been looted off the corpse of a shaman. Knowing what Hatan knew now, that was probably exactly what it was.

Beside Vitori was his son, Avidazj. The son was taller than his father by a full head, and he carried himself with wide shoulders and a puffed out chest. His piercing eyes found their way to Hatan and stared for a few full seconds before turning his head away. He wore a wide-collared suitcoat, a golden necklace glittering on his neck where the last button had been left undone.

Hatan recognized Vitori as one of the lords who'd sworn to Migo on that first day of the coronation. Would such an oath matter if his true loyalty was called into question? How deep did the honor of Jehubal's nobility run?

As they passed by Hatan, he spoke out to them, "Lords Kesten, I hope all is well. I don't see your wives with you."

Vitori growled a response. "Ill, regent. They couldn't make it. A shame. I know they both enjoy some good dancing. Hasn't been enough of it in recent years." His face was void of expression. Avidazj was the same, though his lips were sealed.

"I'm sorry to hear that," Hatan said. "Perhaps for the next one."

"Perhaps," Vitori said, dismissing himself.

A few other guests entered behind them, and then the door was closed. Everyone was there. He'd make this simple. He raised both hands and the music stopped. "Thank you everyone for coming. We've had stressful times in the last few years. I wanted to create an opportunity for us all to turn to better times. And, yes, the rumors are true. Some of the treats available here were, in fact, made by me." He paused at a bit of laughter and light applause. "I see many young faces here. I hope to see several wedding invitations soon enough." Even more laughter and applause. He raised his hands again until silence returned. "With no further ado, musicians, grace us."

The music started immediately in the bounciest tune he'd ever heard. Though it had been years since he'd danced, he even felt the yearning to join. Only a few couples took to the dance floor at first, but the energy quickly grew and several others joined in.

Falshon and Briondi remained near Hatan but did not join the dancing.

Hatan kept his eyes on the four primary suspected families, watching where Vitori and Avidazj Kesten would settle, but Vitori crossed to the far side of the room and began conversing with Lord Obet Ilanitan, the former commerce director for the Rikaydian family. Hatan had released him from the position just a few cycles ago so that he and Penym could oversee the Rikaydian funds directly.

Perhaps he was the one who'd leaked information. It made sense. But he was no longer on the inside of the palace, so he wouldn't have access to any current data.

Kyel approached Obet and Vitori, offering drinks, dressed in the tan and maroon livery of Rikaydian servants. Most of Hatan's agents were present, disguised in one way or another. He wished more of the nobility had been part of his inner circle, but he'd been a soldier too long, disengaged from the sociality of the upper class, save for those who'd taken military roles.

He scanned the room for the Mayaris. They should have been hard to miss with their bright green capes, but among all the gaudiness of those present, it took him longer than he may have expected. They were spread about, but they were all dancing, seemingly there for the pleasure alone.

Nedro Wajek was, of course, hovering around a table laden with pastries. Hatan's eyes lingered, observing those who sampled his own pastries, taking pride in anybody who went for seconds. But he needed to focus.

Where had Avidazj disappeared to?

"Regent Padarro," Lord Melema said as he approached. He was a lesser lord from what Hatan knew, with some buildings owned along the city's central road. Not a bad trade, and he was younger in age. "It's a pity His

Majesty is not here to enjoy the festivities along with us." Beside him stood his young daughter, a pretty girl with a sheer veil over her eyes, embroidered with glittering thread.

Hatan laughed, barely sparing a glance at the two of them as he tried to keep his eyes on his suspects. There were people in this room who had tried to kill him. Who had tried to kill Migo, their king. "I'm sure King Rikaydian will be pleased to attend the next one. We're simply warming things up for him."

Lord Melema's lips twitched in a nervous smile. "Perhaps you would entertain my daughter, Roan, with a dance then."

Hatan pursed his lips. Despite the energy in the air, dancing was far from Hatan's desired activity. He wanted to refuse, but Falshon tapped Hatan on the arm.

"Sir," Falshon said in a whisper that only Hatan would be able to hear over the music. "We all have our roles to play." He shifted his eyes back to Lord Melema.

Right. The other objective. Hatan set his jaw. The other concern he had yet to procure a solution for was that if the majority of nobility were against them, they would not have the military presence to counter any sort of insurrection. He needed allies. A smile twitched across Hatan's lips. "Of course," he said. "I'd be delighted to dance with the young Lady Melema."

Roan's face split into the largest grin before she managed to suppress it, reducing her lips back into a thin line with the coyest of smiles. Hatan almost laughed. She had clearly received some training in how to flirt gracefully, but was still new to it.

He took her hand and led her to the dance floor. "Thank you, Regent Padarro," she said, her voice high, cutting off with excitement.

Hatan should have realized that by throwing a ball, most of the nobility may have suspected it would be a means of identifying possible suitors rather than just a means of entertainment, but without Migo even here, they were probably all baffled. Then again, Hatan was yet unmarried, and if Migo died, he would be the next in line, and his children would succeed him from there. It would still be an advantageous union.

He could use that to *his* advantage. Anyone plotting the downfall of the Rikaydian rule would probably not be trying to marry their daughters off to him or Migo. Or at least, they would be less likely suspects. It was equally possible that the clever spy would feign interest merely to suppress possible suspicion.

Roan and Hatan slipped into the dance with low energy to catch up. She moved mechanically, as though she'd only just had her first lessons a few marks ago in preparation. She smiled up at him nervously.

"First time?" he asked.

She laughed nervously. "That obvious?"

"It's alright. We all have a first."

She smiled again, but clearly became more comfortable as her body loosened up, allowing him to lead her through the motions of the dance. This dance involved only light touches of the hands as they crossed back and forth. Hatan kept it simple on purpose, not only for her, but for himself. He suspected this would only be the first of many dances he would have to participate in.

She seemed a sweet thing. Certainly too young for himself to consider as a possible marriage prospect, but he savored the idea of filtering through prospects for Migo. The very thought of seeing Migo married off brought a tender warmth to his heart. What a moment that would be!

That is, if Migo would overcome his infatuation with Katsi Danan. The girl had her strengths, certainly, but didn't seem the type that was fit to be a queen of one of Malahem's city-states.

The dance ended, and Roan was all smiles and giggles as she curtsied and scurried back to her father. It was only then that Hatan noticed a group of women coming together as though a line was forming to dance with him.

"Oh, sands," he muttered to himself. It would be a long party indeed.

Another lord was about to approach him, probably with a request to have him dance with his daughter, when Sinteya slipped ahead, cutting the man off.

"I see that line starting, regent," she said to him in a quiet voice, placing her sleeved hand on his forearm. "But before you start entertaining suitors for the young king, perhaps you'd entertain a different sort of prospect."

Hatan was speechless. He hadn't expected her to be so forward. All he could think to do was start dancing. "Do you mean a sort of business prospect?" Hatan asked.

Sinteya laughed. "Feigning ignorance doesn't suit you. I take it you're much more intellectual than that."

"You're bold, I'll give you that," Hatan said, leveling his gaze at her.

The dance brought them close together. "Boldness is necessary," she said breathily. "Perhaps this is why you are still unmarried. No woman has been forward enough, and you are clearly too absorbed by your work."

Hatan grunted. "And what if I just don't like women?"

Sinteya's laugh was almost sinister. "Come now, regent, I saw the way you looked at me when I introduced myself. I can tell when I'm being admired."

They came close again, Hatan's hand settling on her back where the black lace of her dress extended. He could feel the heat of her skin beneath the fabric. Her own hand touched the side of his neck, sending tendrils up his spine.

She was right. As much as he hated to admit it.

But she was a suspect. This was probably all part of their ploy against him. "And yet, you are unmarried as well? Are you sure you aren't just plotting for your own gain?" They twirled about each other at the fanfare of music, but it suddenly slowed, bringing all the dancing pairs close together.

Her eyes glinted. The smile that curled her lips might have stolen any man's heart. "That's the best part," she said, chest heaving, her voice half a whisper. "Of course I am. What woman of my stature wouldn't love to gain the affection of the most honorable, handsome nobleman of all Jehubal."

"Flattery."

"Frankness."

Hatan's heart was pounding, and not just from the dancing. His hands lingered at her waist while one of her arms settled at his shoulder. Who even was this woman? He needed Kyel to keep a close eye on her.

Applause filled the room. Apparently the song had stopped and most of the couples had paused to watch Hatan and Sinteya finish their dance. All eyes were on him.

He removed his hands from her hips and smiled to the crowd, but Sinteya caught one of his hands in hers, pressing something against his palm. "Think on it, Hatan," she said, dropping the title from his name. "I have more to offer than beauty." She withdrew her hand, leaving an object there. "I expect you to return that on another cycle." She faded into the crowd as Hatan turned back to find Falshon.

He looked down at his palm. It was a thin, silver ring with an intricate flower designed on it. Clever. More than beauty indeed. The crowd of women waiting for their turn hadn't gotten any smaller. This would be a long party. He only hoped his agents were gaining new information.

The next song started up and dancing resumed.

Something caught his eye as he approached the crowd of waiting women, planning on taking the next one onto the floor. Two men were seemingly cornering a woman against one of the supportive pillars. It was Penym. One of the men grabbed her arm. She flailed against his grip but didn't free herself. Hatan stomped over, but the men noticed him approaching and scampered away. Who were they?

They'd split up. He noticed one of his agents move to follow, but they'd need two people to track them both down. He would eagerly question them himself, but first he checked in with Penym.

"Are you well?" he said as soon as he got to her.

"I'm fine," she said, her eyes wide, breath staggered. Clearly not fine.

"Did they hurt you?"

She didn't respond.

He touched her arm gingerly where the man had grabbed her. The skin looked red. A spark of anger ignited in his chest. He turned to chase after them but she held his arm. "Please. Don't leave me," she said.

Hatan exhaled slowly. They all had roles to play. He couldn't be hunting around at his own party. He'd have to trust that his agents would track them down. Somebody in here would surely recognize who they were. That is, if they'd checked in through the door along with everyone else.

"What did they want?"

"I'm not sure. They said they wanted a key," she said. "I don't know what key they wanted. I don't even have access to the treasury if they were thinking of robbing you."

So Penym was their target. "Right here under my nose. Unbelievable. Do you know who either of them were?"

"I've never seen them before." She held his hand.

He squeezed back and put a hand on her shoulder. "Don't worry. We'll keep you safe."

She nodded, but a scream rang out over the ballroom. The music came to a screeching halt.

Captain Falshon and Briondi were beside Hatan in a flash, both of them armed with long daggers. "It was over there," Falshon said, pointing to the other side of the room where the crowd was backing away, most of them moving off in panic and a flurry of more screaming or gasps.

"Stay with Penym," Hatan ordered Falshon.

He drew his own knife and stormed across the room. The crowd parted ahead of him and some people even ran for the doors. When he reached the source of exasperation, he beheld Lord Melema on his back, gasping his last breath as blood pooled out beneath him, shimmering and dark against the pale brown tiles of the ballroom floor.

Roan Melema knelt beside her father, her shoulders rocking in silent sobs, watching helplessly as her father died. She held her trembling hands in front of her, wet with his blood.

He'd been stabbed from behind with a blade long enough to pierce his organs. He would die. There was no stopping it.

Hatan turned his eyes to the crowd. Watching them. Searching.

Avidazj stood at the edge of the jostling crowd, lips a thin line as he observed the scene.

"Avidazj," Hatan said, his voice darker than he'd intended. "Did you see what happened?

"You can't keep your guests safe, regent," Avidazj said. He shook his head and straightened the cuffs of his sleeves.

"Grit of sand," Vitori said, coming up beside his son, a frown etched across his brow. "And poor Lord Melema at that. We should go, Avidazj. We don't want to be somewhere that is unsafe." He and his son joined the thinning crowd as people hurried to the exit.

"Vitori!" Hatan called after him. They were behind this. Somehow. That cold look in Avidazj's eyes was all he needed to see.

Lord Melema stopped moving.

He'd been a target, probably for offering his daughter to dance. So much for making allies. He'd simply expanded their enemy's hit list.

"Roan," Hatan said, kneeling beside her. Tears streamed down her cheeks. "Roan, what happened? Did you see who did this?"

Roan shook her head. The blood on the floor had spread all the way to her knees and started soaking into her dress. "No. We were—we were walking, and then he stopped." She looked down at her hands and saw the blood, her eyes somehow going even wider than before.

He needed to get her away from the scene. One of his agents stood nearby, Kyel's sister, Shanon. He beckoned her over. "Get her somewhere safe."

Shanon nodded wordlessly and helped Roan stand.

Hatan rose, knuckles white around his dagger. He was done. Justice would be meted.

Two figures forced their way inside the room, pushing past all the fleeing guests. Their appearance alone led most people to dodge around them.

Emil and Rivar.

They were laden with their gear as though they'd just returned to the city. Perhaps they had.

Most importantly, Migo was not with them.

If something happened to Migo, Hatan knew he'd lose himself. Migo was the only thing left in his life that mattered. He was done with politics. He was a warrior. It was time to do what he was best at.

It was time for blood.

Chapter 27

igo awoke with a start. His body tingled with unfettered energy. He swung off the bed to his feet, reaching for his weapon, but it wasn't there. He was not alone. Several soldiers stood around the bed. Migo was prepared to fight them—he'd kill them all with his bare hands if he had to. But they weren't threatening him. Their attention was on the door of the small room.

Yavasu was there, a finger over his lips.

And these weren't just any soldiers. He saw the silver circle pinned to their vambraces. They were academy graduates. Trained in shaman hunting.

"Yavasu, what's going on?" Migo demanded.

"Sorry, friend," Yavasu said, "but I knew that girl was a shaman the moment I set eyes on her."

"What have you done?"

Migo's tone must have startled Yavasu. His friend's eyes widened with panic.

"If you hurt her," Migo growled, lunging to get to the door so he could find Katsi. Two of the soldiers moved to hold him back, but Migo twisted one's arm and threw him to the ground and kicked the other man in the shin.

Two others jumped in and it was too much for Migo to fight them off. They grappled him to the cold, stone floor.

"Migo, I had to do it this way," Yavasu said. "I could tell she has you under her spell."

"Spell?" Migo said. "What do you mean?"

"She must have had you drink a potion or something. Think, Migo. How would you ever be in the company of a shaman? Something is not right."

Migo gulped, mind spinning. Sure, he'd taken potions from her, but certainly nothing that had altered his reasoning, right? He knew shamans were capable of making extravagant potions, but nothing like that. To win his affection? His trust?

"You're making a mistake, Yavasu," Migo said, struggling against the men who restrained him. "I'm your friend. All of you know my reputation. Trust me."

"I'm sorry, Migo," Yavasu said, and his eyes truly glimmered with sorrow. "But you should see more clearly once she's dead."

There was a crash somewhere in the building and a terrible scream. The sounds of a great struggle continued.

No.

Migo roared and threw off one of the shaman hunters, but two others dragged him back to the ground.

A stillness overtook the building, with no other sounds than Migo's own panting as he tried to free himself.

Yavasu observed Migo quizzically. "They should have gotten her by now. I was hoping the effects would have diminished."

"Some enchantments take time to fade," one of the shaman hunter's said. They would have all been taught the same things. Some true. Some not.

But Katsi couldn't be dead. She couldn't.

Rage shook Migo's body. He felt it stretching at his skin, threatening to burst free.

The door swung inward.

It was Katsi.

Blood trickled down her lip.

Yavasu and every shaman hunter in the room suddenly let out a synchronized cry as the stone floor came alive, grabbing them by the feet.

One man jumped out of his boots and thrust a sword at Katsi's chest, but a brick tore from the wall and pummeled him in the elbow. They started sinking into the ground.

Migo dug his way out the grip of the men around him, kicking them away, snapping a finger, until he stood atop the bed.

"Migo," Yavasu cried. "Brother!"

Yavasu's head was the only thing left above ground. The other soldiers were half swallowed by the stone floor.

"Katsi, stop!" Migo said, stretching out his hand to her.

Katsi blinked at Migo as the soldiers stopped sinking further. She dabbed at her bloody lip with a finger then said, "I don't want to kill them."

"You don't have to. Yavasu was just doing what he thought was right. He thinks you have me under your spell or something."

"Well." Katsi shrugged. "I am rather enchanting, but not with my magic."

Scales scratched his way into the room, snarling with lizardly anger. He ran straight over and bit the nearest shaman hunter and bit his exposed finger. The man yelped. He then ran over to bite another one.

"Scales, stop," Katsi said. His jaws froze over another man's ear. "I got them, it's okay now."

Scales withdrew, and the man let out a relieved whimper. Scales growled at each of the men in turn, body poised to pounce on them at any moment.

"I'm sorry, Yavasu," Migo said, finding his things at the back of the room.

"Migo, please," Yavasu said, desperation in his voice.

"Katsi," Migo said, "head outside. We should get out of here soon. I just need to talk to Yavasu for a moment."

A few of the shaman hunters shouted curses at Katsi.

"Witch."

"Demon!"

Migo turned and punched the nearest one in the face. "If any of you speak like that about her again, you'll never see the outside of this room." He waved Katsi away. "Please, Katsi. I'll join you soon. These are still my comrades."

Katsi narrowed her eyes at him, but then shook her head and clicked her tongue. "Come on, Scales." Katsi strode away. Scales gave one last growl before scampering after her.

Migo crouched beside Yavasu's head as he adjusted the clasps of his pauldrons. "Yavasu. I'm disappointed that you would question my judgment. Know this: everything Katsi has done to win my trust has been by her merits. She saved my life, more than once. Jehubal was on the verge of destruction. She was the only thing that kept it from happening. We're taught so much that magic is evil, but she used it to heal me, not corrupt."

A couple shaman hunters growled their disapproval.

Migo shook his head. "Now look. I'm going to help you get out enough that you can help our friends out as well. Not all shamans are evil, but perhaps some are. The need for skilled shaman hunters is still there, and I want you all alive and well if that need arises. Somebody assassinated my father, and I will find out who." He was fully dressed by the end of his speech, and he started using his poleaxe to shovel sand and bricks out of the way.

"I hope you're right," Yavasu said.

Migo breathed a laugh. "You're more an intellectual than I am, Yavasu. Just think. Shamanfolk are humans. Like you and me. There are humans who make terrible choices, and some who make good ones. Shamanfolk are no different. They're not a plague to be eradicated. There's no justice in that."

Migo managed to free Yavasu down to the shoulders then helped tug his arms out.

"You still don't believe me," Migo said, seeing the frown on Yavasu's face.

"It remains to be seen," Yavasu said, "but I know you're no fool."

"Everyone in this room no doubt is aware of my history," Migo said. "You most especially, Yavasu. I've had reason to hate shamans, and I have, for years. It consumed my every waking moment. But I was wrong. If I can realize that, you can too."

Migo got back to his feet. "I'm sorry to leave you like this."

"Migo, wait."

"I'll let people know to come help you out before we leave." Migo swung the poleaxe over his shoulder. "Thank you for the hospitality. Apologize to Chaeyna for me."

Yavasu and the shaman hunters shouted after him as he left, but he wouldn't be able to trust them enough to not attack as soon as they were free. Despite the considerable mess that Migo left in the room, the rest of the manor looked fairly immaculate, save for a pair of legs that dangled from the ceiling, kicking around. They must have evacuated everyone before trying to ambush Katsi. He was only glad they hadn't managed to slit her throat in her sleep or anything. He walked straight out the open door to the outside where Katsi sat slumped on a stone bench in the yard, arms folded.

She glanced up at him, lips pouted grumpily. Scales flew around above her as if scoping out the area.

"Have a good chat there with your old *friend*?" Katsi said.

"He'll come around."

"He'd better. Shamanfolk will never really be free until we can change people's minds."

"He will."

She looked at the ground. "Did you help him out? I feel bad."

Migo laughed. She'd *dominated* them. Like nothing he'd ever seen.

"Why is that funny? I didn't want to hurt them."

"It's funny because you took out an entire squad of soldiers that have been trained specifically for hunting and killing shamans. You used the building to swallow them up in less than a few heartbeats." He shook his head. "Trained soldiers stood no chance against a seventeen-year-old young woman who still has very little experience using her power. I can't even imagine what else you might be able to do."

Katsi shrugged. "Well, let's hope you don't have to find out, but did you help your friend out or not? You never said."

"Kind of. I freed his arms."

Scales dropped down on the seat beside Katsi and croaked, looking to the manor gate, legs bouncing anxiously.

"Someone might be coming," Katsi said.

"I'll go look," Migo said. He kept his weapon on his shoulder. He had enough confidence that nobody here wanted him dead. They just wanted Katsi. He reached the opening of the low, open gate. Chaeyna and Lady Roqaya were walking up the hill together, but paused at the sight of him.

"Migo," Chaeyna exclaimed, smiling broadly.

Migo held up his hand. "Your brother and the soldiers have been detained. They are stuck in the ground. You'll need to get some help to free them. Nobody has been killed."

Lady Roqaya placed a hand over her mouth in a silent gasp.

"But... But Migo," Chaeyna said, features twisted in confused pain.

"Everything is okay. We're not enemies. I appreciate your hospitality. You've been gracious. We will take our leave now."

Katsi came and stood behind Migo. At the sight of her, the two women turned and shouted for help.

"Well, so much for hiding in plain sight," Katsi said.

Migo sighed. "Just make sure that leather armor of yours isn't showing. An armed woman isn't too uncommon, but the stormwading armor is very distinctive."

"Got it." She looked to the sky. "So how do you propose we get out of here?"

"There's nothing to hide now. Let's just fly from here."

She nodded, but walked over to the manor and placed her hand on the wall. She tilted her head and closed an eye.

"What are you doing?" Migo asked.

"Releasing your friend," Katsi said, withdrawing her hand from the wall. "I pushed some of them back out so they can help the others, but we should get going.

"Thank you," Migo said, then found a couple fist-sized rocks and assumed position on Katsi's back. It was crazy how routine this had become.

Scales seemed to know what was coming as he jumped into the air ahead of them.

Katsi did whatever it was she did, and Migo tightened his grip just before they launched into the sky. Taking off was the worst part. Once they gained enough elevation, level now with the top of the stony hill and the castle, Katsi started moving them north, tilting slightly to the west now that they'd gained more distance. He could still hardly fathom how far they'd come in so short a time.

"I have a feeling the academy is going to change its training regimen soon," Katsi said.

"Maybe, but even as a supposed shaman hunting expert myself, I have no idea what anybody could do to stop you."

"Let's just hope there's no such thing as a flying waheshi."

Migo couldn't think of anything that would be more terrifying.

"How did you get out by the way?" Migo asked. "If they'd wanted to kill me back there, they could have slit my throat as I slept."

"Easy. I didn't sleep."

"Are you not exhausted?"

"I am, yes. So if you have any other bright ideas about where to rest, I'd love to know."

"Sands, I've never been beyond Rhian. You'd know better than I would at this point. Probably best to hide under some rockberry bushes in the jungle."

Katsi turned her head to look over her shoulder at him. "You think you're a bad shaman hunter, and yet you guess the exact place I'd hide to sleep. Not bad."

"Let's get a little more distance, just in case, but I'm sure we could stop anywhere near the center of the Ring and find a good place. I think I only got a mark or two of sleep as well."

"Alright, but I want to go a little further. Maybe see how fast I can go. Ready?"

Migo adjusted his grip and tightened his legs around her waist. "As long as you don't fall asleep while we're flying."

Katsi apparently needed no further permission. Migo looked down as the ground started to pass at an ever-increasing speed. When he looked behind, trees shook and bowed as they passed.

"I think we're too low to the ground to be going this fast," Migo said.

Katsi said nothing, but their elevation went up. Her body was rigid, and her breathing became more rapid. Their speed continued to increase, along with Migo's anxiety.

He looked behind again.

Sands.

Clouds were forming in their wake, seemingly appearing from nowhere. They streamed out in every direction.

Stormcaller.

Katsi was a stormcaller.

Sands.

He was both awed and terrified.

"I think that's good," he said.

Katsi tapped his knees with her thumbs and started to descend. Her speed dropped rapidly. Migo's stomach lurched, and his thighs squeezing her waist seemed like the only thing keeping them together. Watching them get closer and closer to the ground filled him with as much excitement as charging into battle. She veered to the side, bringing them closer to the Scorched Waste.

They came right to the top of the trees and descended through a gap in the leaves. The pocket of air Katsi kept around them must have dropped because it suddenly felt warm and humid. The jungle beneath was dense. Several furred creatures with bald, boney heads scurried away through the branches. A mild buzz filled the air as though the very trees were humming at them.

"This is not the kind of jungle I'm used to," Migo said. "It seems like it should be the same, yet somehow it's not."

"I know what you mean. I'll keep us in the air until I see a good clearing."

"Works for me," Migo said, trying to pop his neck. "How are you doing?"

"Tired. You're feeling very heavy, and the armlets are rather hot."

"We can drop over there," Migo said, pointing to a small clearing. "I would have expected the jungle to be a bit thinner this close to Scorched Waste."

Katsi steered to the clearing, dodging through the branches. "Perhaps it's because there aren't any people around."

The ground where they dropped was covered in thick moss. Migo was about to let go when Katsi grabbed his hands, keeping them on the stones he held. "Wait," she said.

"What is it?"

"There's water beneath that. I can feel it." She wove through the trees, close to the sun.

It got quite warm before the density finally broke. Migo wasn't familiar with very many of the plants, but it was comforting to see a few rockberry bushes. He was most relieved to see rocks and dirt. Katsi settled down there as lizards abandoned the rocks and disappeared.

Migo dropped off and immediately laid down in the shade behind a few rocks, pulling out his canteen and taking a long swig. Unexpectedly, Katsi came and laid next to him, sharing in the bit of shade offered by the rocks.

"I wish I had any idea how close we are," Katsi said with a huff. She was shivering. And sweaty.

"Katsi," Migo said, sitting up and handing her canteen to her. "Have a drink." He pulled out the last two cookies that Hatan had made and handed them both to her. "And eat these. You don't seem well."

"I made clouds," Katsi said, pointing up over her head. "Did you see them?"

"Yes. Eat first. Sleep. We'll talk about your clouds once you wake up."

She nodded, took one bite of a cookie, a swig of her water, then all but passed out.

Migo shook his head and put the rest of the food away. No sense in attracting unwanted wildlife. He climbed up a jutting rockface and looked around. The first thing he noticed was that the moon was almost directly overhead. It usually didn't seem so close. They'd traveled far enough that they were nearing its orbital path. The city of Lazeem was famous for lying directly in the path. Every cycle, the moon eclipsed the sun, throwing the city into an abnormal shadow, even impacting the weather. It was an event Migo had long wanted to witness. It wouldn't be long before they got there.

But he too needed better sleep. He settled back down in the shade next to Katsi and slowly drifted off, the sound of her breathing lulling him into a deep calm.

Chapter 28

Katsi nuzzled into her pillow, not entirely ready to be awake yet. The jungle hummed in the distance, and she felt comforted, safe, and warm.

Then she realized her pillow was moving with a slow rising and falling motion. Her head popped up. She'd been resting on Migo's chest. He blinked at her with bleary eyes, then looked down at his chest as if he just realized. He covered his mouth with a yawn and scooted up. "So, your clouds," he said, thankfully drawing attention away from the fact that she'd been cuddling up to him.

Katsi sat up and rubbed her eyes before looking up. The sky was heavy with clouds, but they did nothing to cover the sun which forever burned over the Scorched Waste. "Yes, I didn't know that was possible, but at the same time, I could feel it."

"What did it feel like?" Migo asked, pulling his knees up and resting his elbows on them.

"Strange. I sensed a wetness, like dipping my toes in water." She shrugged. "But it was kind of everywhere, since I was connected with the air and wind. I could also feel the water in it, and it all kind of bunched up as we passed. To make us move faster, I found a way to create a sort of funnel."

"Your power was like nothing I've seen. I may be a king, but even the trees beneath bowed at your passing."

Katsi laughed. "As they should. It *was* rather fantastic. But you made the right call for me to go higher. I wouldn't want to cause too much disturbance in the Ring. I can only imagine the fright I might have caused to any animals."

"Speaking of which, I haven't seen your lizard."

Katsi got to her feet. "Scales!" she called. She looked around the trees for a while but nothing came. Her heart dropped.

"I'm sure he'll turn up," Migo said. "He rides the same air. He'd be going the same speed, right?"

"Right," Katsi said. "You really are more optimistic than you used to be."

He turned away. "I want *you* to be optimistic."

Katsi tilted her head at him. "So you say positive things not because you believe them but because you want me to believe them?"

Migo shrugged. "We should eat. You still didn't have very much before falling asleep." He handed her back the cookie from yesterday.

He was evading the question, but Katsi took the cookie and ate it. It still tasted fine, though it was a bit dry. Katsi moved slowly as they got ready to leave. Migo was grabbing some rocks when Scales finally turned back up, swirling around above Katsi's head.

"Told you," Migo said, placing his arms over her shoulders. He held her there against his chest. "I don't think you could lose him even if you tried."

She looked at Scales, marveling at the blue and purple scales of his underbelly, glittering in the sunlight, her head resting back against Migo's shoulder.

"We should fly high," Migo said. "Look for Lazeem. It would be a good place to restock on food. I brought some coin for that. We should also ask for some direction. I wouldn't know what Mazanib even looks like if we got there."

"Right," Katsi said, bending her knees and holding her arms out. She connected the stones then linked them with the air. She acted as the centerpiece that held everything together. Her shoulders and hips ached from carrying him, but she wasn't about to admit that. She didn't know how else to get them where they were going in a reasonable amount of time, and she knew Migo would feel terrible for hurting her.

They were used to the routine by now, and once they were ready, they took off. She floated all the way up to the edge of the clouds, just as a light rain began to fall, doing what it could to minimize the heat of flying in direct light from the sun.

Katsi summoned the wind. Willed it forward. Channeled it into a single, moving mass. She pushed it with all her strength, the armlets warming subtly at first. It was amazing how much of this had become second nature. She held nothing back. The nervousness Migo felt was apparent as she went faster, the tenseness of his muscles going rigid before finally relaxing once Katsi hit what she considered her maximum preferable speed.

She kept her eyes down, watching the ground so she could adjust their course. It was much easier to move in a straight line than it was to change directions. Turning required more conscious effort than she liked. She had to make course corrections while maintaining the connection with the air, the stones in Migo's hands, and also the pocket of air that kept them from getting pounded in the faces from the wind.

The armlets burned hotter than she cared to admit as well. They didn't seem to deplete of energy, but they got hotter the more she drew on their power. That alone was incentive enough to not overdo it. She flew on, determined to get them there as fast as possible. There was something so pleasing about traveling faster than the news. Where they were, nobody knew that Queen Rikaydian had been assassinated. Nobody knew that a powerful young shaman girl was the one to do it.

They traveled for three solid marks, passing over a few settlements on the way, but Migo wanted Lazeem specifically.

"How will we know when we even see it?" Katsi asked as they passed over a large town.

"I've seen it on maps before. It's dead center of the Ring, so we won't miss it, and it supposedly has some buildings that look blue or purple under the sunlight."

Katsi kept her eyes out while keeping them near the center of the Ring. The clouds around them had gotten thicker, so she was forced to fly a bit lower just to maintain visibility. She could feel the rain showering around them. All the better. She doubted anybody would look up and realize that two people were flying through the clouds, but the rain added an extra measure of cover.

"Slow down," Migo said. "That could be it in the distance."

Katsi squinted ahead and saw it. A city in the middle of the Ring with buildings of varying shades of blue.

"I'll get us closer, then see if I can move the clouds with us for cover." She hadn't controlled the clouds before, but figured it was worth a shot, and Migo didn't seem to question the possibility at all. She smiled. He probably thought she could move the whole planet if she wanted.

As they got closer, it was even more apparent that they'd reached the right place. Katsi slowed and hovered over a nearby patch of thick jungle then called up the wind, pushing it down in a funnel that looked like a tiny tornado descending on the trees. Anybody seeing it from the ground would be running for cover.

She lowered them down carefully. The cloudy cover not only kept them from being seen, but it made it difficult to see the trees below until they were right above them. It took some careful maneuvering between leaves and branches, but Katsi found the ground and severed her connection with everything once their feet touched down.

They were immediately wet. She'd forgotten it was raining, and the deep crash of thunder echoed from far away.

"Not your doing," Migo said matter-of-factly. "I think it's due for New Season. That, and the moon usually eclipses here every cycle. It's probably coming around as we speak. We should hurry to the city. Nobody would blame us for running."

Katsi had completely forgotten about New Season. She threw her hood on, and they jogged out of the jungle together. Bad weather was always a good reason for cities to keep their gates open, at least around Jehubal. She hoped it was the same here.

When they got out of the cover of the jungle, there were a few people on the road, including a stormcart pulled by charging varman. As expected, they were all hurrying into the city. Katsi tightened her cloak around her and followed after them, trying to keep up with Migo's loping strides.

The rain was fresh, so the ground was still firm. If this was the dawn of New Season though, those streets would become muddied, even with the gravel that had been mixed with the clay. It would only do so much.

A couple guards stood under the gatehouse of the city's wall. They watched people going through but did nothing else.

As Migo had said, Lazeem was much smaller than Jehubal. She hadn't seen another city that stretched to both wastes since they'd left. Maybe Jehubal and Cataban were the only cities that did that for all she knew. What she wouldn't give to look at a map.

The rain was still light, but everybody knew that could change in a heartbeat, especially with the dark clouds rolling in. They slowed to a walk as they reached the gate and Kasti moved right beside Migo. "Let's spend as little time here as possible," she said.

Migo looked out towards the sun. "Right. Let's find the markets and get out of here."

They didn't have to look long. The city had a v-shaped point that extended across the road with a gate on either side. They'd just entered through the southeast gate, while the other gate was on the northwest. Between the two gates within the city were several shops, some stacked on top of each other. The rest of the city stretched back towards the Frozen Waste.

Migo led them straight to a building with a stone sign out front labeling the shop by the name "Travelers." They went up two steps to the door and heaved it open to get inside.

Katsi was surprised when the floor creaked beneath her steps. The floor was made of polished wood. It was certainly not as rare a commodity in these parts.

"You look like my kind of customer," said a short woman behind a wooden counter. "Food stalls are in the back."

It was an odd building. The place was packed with people, probably trying to stay out of the rain. There were stalls divided along all the walls with various products on display. There were no hawkers shouting out their wares, but a person sat on a stool in each of the stalls. It was formal in a way that made Katsi feel out of place.

They walked past the first couple stalls. Migo stocked up on enough food for a few more cycles, and Katsi stored some in her own bag. It was practically all either of their bags held at this point other than some minor trinkets.

When they got back outside, the rain was much heavier. These wooden buildings had a small overhang that shielded them from most of it.

"We need to get out of the city," Katsi said. "If it's New Season, this rain won't stop, and our food will get soggy."

Migo nodded and whispered, "Keep your veil up and your head down. Let's run for the north gate. Ready?"

Katsi responded by jumping down the steps and taking off. The sooner they got out of this place, the better. Her legs relished the exertion. Flying by herself probably wasn't so bad, but flying with Migo was hard work that made her whole body stiff and tired. Migo clomped behind her on the cobbled street.

As they neared the north gate, one of the guards under the gatehouse shouted at them, "It's almost sixth mark! Where are you going?" But they made no move to stop them. It was simply a warning.

Katsi held her bag under her chest and stooped over it as she ran to keep it dry. The air was chilly with cold wind rushing in from the Frozen Waste. The rain was definitely heavier now and a white fog rolled towards them.

"There!" Migo shouted, pointing to the edge of the jungle, though if the fog closed in and got thick enough, they could take off at any moment.

The thrill of running died down after the initial burst, and now she wanted to be back in the air where her legs could hang free. They reached the treeline before the fog did, but it still came on them shortly after. They slowed to a walk.

Scales came from the mist and landed on Katsi's shoulder with a thunk. "Oh, Scales," Katsi said, tapping him under the chin in greeting. "I think you're getting too big to be doing that."

Thunder rumbled as she called up her magic again, creating a field around their group that the rain dodged around. Scales looked down at the bag in Katsi's hands and let out a low croak.

"Couldn't find any of your own food, huh?" Katsi said, digging out one of the fresh fruits. He chomped down and ate it whole.

Scales hummed appreciatively and bumped her jaw with his head before jumping off. His wings had excellent curvature to them now, allowing him to fly better with every passing cycle.

Migo was struggling to find rocks, so Katsi used her power to locate a few and brought them over to her shoulders. Migo gave his thanks and grabbed the rocks.

"Mazanib, here we come," Katsi said, and off they went.

Chapter 29

Hatan clenched his fists around the haft of the glaive that rested across his knees. Rain pounded from overhead, drenching him. Not that he minded. It helped provide some of the cover he needed.

Answers were what he was after. That's what he'd get.

He crouched atop the wall around Nedro Wajek's manor. Kyel and Shanon were there with him. Rivar and Emil were under disguise in the guardhouse, holding weapons to Nedro's guards.

Captain Falshon waited in the streets outside with eleven more soldiers.

They were all in place.

Hatan made a signal before he, Kyel, and Shanon dropped down from the wall and started towards the front door. According to Kyel's report, Nedro employed nearly nineteen people at the manor, five of whom were full time soldiers. Six of them carried out operations throughout the city and the other eight stayed at the manor doing household labor.

None of the soldiers under Nedro's pay would be as well trained as Falshon's men, and Hatan himself had provided training to Kyel and Shanon. Under the shadow of Migo's recent fame, many of Jehubal's nobles may have forgotten that Hatan was once considered the greatest warrior of Jehubal.

They would soon remember.

He marched straight to the door and tried the handle. It was unlocked. Too easy. He opened it and walked inside. The sound of rain and thunder helped provide additional cover as they fanned out. Hatan knew the layout of Wajek Manor all too well. It helped that a maid on Nedro's staff was too happy to take a bribe from Kyel and share what Nedro's routine was during the week.

The three of them went left, avoiding the stairs as they made their way through an empty waiting room. An adjacent door brought them into the library where Nedro sat behind a desk, slumped in his chair with an open book splayed out before him. The room smelled of sugared paper. In fact, everything in the manor held the slight scent of something sweet. A vase filled with half-dead purple flowers on the window sill added to the aesthetic of a room filled with more books than they even had back at Rikaydian Palace.

Nedro let out a suppressed yelp, jolting upright. "I wondered when you'd come. Is it time, then?"

Hatan grabbed a chair and placed it in front of the desk. Kyel and Shanon stood beside the two doors to the room in case anybody else showed up. Hatan dropped into the chair, the water on his clothes soaking into the plush cushions. He placed his glaive across his knees and leaned back before uncovering his face.

"Regent!" Nedro said, slapping his hands onto the desk. "Sands, lord, I thought you were somebody else. No doubt you're onto what's happening."

Hatan remained in his position, running his thumb over the groove of his weapon. "And what is happening, Nedro?"

"Conspiracy," Nedro said, eyes wide. "Other nobles claim that King Rikaydian is too young to assume the throne, that he's the one who killed his mother somehow. But we both know who it really was! That same blasted woman who stole from me!"

"His Majesty *is* responsible for the death of Queen Tilayna Rikaydian," Hatan said, waiting to see Nedro's reaction.

Nedro choked on his words. "But it was the shaman?" he sputtered.

"Yes, the king set her free so that she would kill the queen. It was the only way to establish peace with the Bayvana Tribe, since the queen refused to call off the war. The tribe was on the verge of invading the city. They would have killed everyone. It saved thousands of lives."

Nedro gulped. "I see. Terrible. Rational. He's always had better judgment, but killing a queen is, well…"

"Who were you expecting?" Hatan pressed.

"The king has enemies," Nedro said, wringing his hands.

"Are you one of them?"

"I could never, regent. You know as well as any that I've been the least prejudiced of all these prats."

"Who, then?"

Nedro blinked furiously, but his voice took on a dark tone. "The better question, regent, might be who is *not* an enemy, as that list is shorter."

Hatan's grip tightened. That was worse than he'd feared. "Do you see yourself as a king, Nedro?"

"No, regent," Nedro said, actually laughing. "I am quite pleased with my current responsibilities. I couldn't aspire to worry about any other lives."

"Then tell me, who's leading them?"

"They'll kill me, regent."

"And I won't?"

"No. You're a true gentleman. You'd put me in prison, perhaps. But I've made no act of treason."

Hatan threw the desk to the side of the room and kicked Nedro's chair. It tilted back, crashing against the bookshelf behind him, stopping it from falling to the floor. Hatan grabbed Nedro's hand and twisted, wrenching away the dagger Nedro pulled from his robe and then held it to Nedro's throat.

"Do not question the lengths I would go to in order to protect my king," Hatan said before withdrawing a step. "I know of your association with the Kestens and the Mayaris. Tell me who is leading, and I will ensure that they are no longer a threat."

Nedro cleared his throat, tried to put his seat back to no avail, and said, "They know more than I do, no doubt. They know I have no greater ambition."

"Then who were you expecting?"

"A man named Onik. He's a brute. Leads one of the mercenary groups. They've been threatening me to sign some oath against the king in support of a new leader. To claim the king is not worthy. I'll have no part in that."

So that's what they were doing. "Kyel, you mentioned various mercenary groups in your reports. Is Onik one of them you've had an eye on?"

"Yes, sir," Kyel said. "Their group has been visiting a number of manors. All of whom we've been considering as suspects."

"Who's paying Onik, Nedro?" Hatan asked.

"The Ilanitans? Kestens? I don't know."

Hatan stomped the leg of Nedro's chair, putting it back in the upright position. He tapped the blade of his glaive against Nedro's knee. "Stay safe, Nedro. I might need to question you again."

"I take it you won't be killing me, then?"

"Not this cycle," Hatan said, withdrawing his glaive. "But someone is about to die. Very soon." He nodded to Shanon and Kyel who moved to get them out the door from which they'd entered.

"As long as it's not you, regent," Nedro said, dabbing the sweat from his forehead. "I still intend to steal your recipe for those treats you made. All this lawlessness is no good for business."

"And I need you around for those tari tarts," Hatan said, throwing his hood back on. "Don't let them intimidate you. Go into hiding if you must for the next few cycles." He didn't wait for a response. The three of them dashed out of the building while one of Nedro's servants gasped as they passed her.

"Kyel, you know where Onik stays?" Hatan asked once they got outside. "I want to head there immediately."

"I'll take us there."

"Shanon," Hatan said, "fetch the twins. Let's gather up with Captain Falshon."

They moved at a run. It was best to get out of Wajek Manor grounds. For all Hatan knew, his enemies could also be watching the manor and suspect Nedro of being compromised, and they could tip off everyone else. That unfortunate event would happen eventually, but Hatan wanted as much information as possible before it happened. And he wanted to weaken them—to strike a blow where it mattered.

Shanon sprinted ahead while Hatan and Kyel climbed over to the other side of the wall. One of Nedro's other guards finally saw them and shouted across the yard, but it was too late to matter. In mere seconds, their whole team was gathered at an empty street a couple blocks from the manor.

Hatan signaled the team wordlessly in case there were any listening ears nearby. They all understood the message. Follow Kyel. Be ready for danger.

Kyel led the way, taking them through the back streets of Jehubal. The rain was heavy, and clouds were thick enough that they obscured the sun. At the sight of seventeen people rushing by, many with unconcealable weapons, anybody on the streets dashed back inside.

Hatan just hoped that they were still ahead of the game.

They wound through several streets until they came to a halt near one of the main roads. Their target was across the street, a sleephouse where Onik and his mercenaries resided. A single man lingered outside the sleephouse, casually getting drenched by the rain as if he hadn't a care. Shanon easily scaled the rounded, stone building beside them to scan the area. They must have waited nearly a full minute before she nodded and signaled them forward.

Time for blood.

Hatan led the charge.

The man outside saw them coming once they were halfway across the street. He didn't know what to do at first, then turned and ran for the door of the sleephouse. Hatan got there first and struck the man across the head with the blunt end of his glaive, knocking him down. He grabbed the ax looped in the man's belt and threw it into the street, then turned the man over on his back.

"Are you one of Onik's men?" Hatan growled.

The man groaned. "Y-yeah."

Hatan held up four fingers and gestured outside to let them know to keep four men posted outside. The rest would go in. He opened the door and stepped in, pausing just inside the entryway.

The sleephouse was uncommonly packed. The owner of the establishment was polishing a glass at the serving desk. Sensing trouble, he placed down the glass and disappeared behind another door. Several armed men rose from the tables and a whistle rang through the building. More men appeared from the bunks in the back. There were perhaps thirty of them.

"Where's Onik?" Hatan demanded.

A burly man stepped forward with an ax in either hand. "I'm Onik. What do you want?"

"Lay down your weapons and come with me," Hatan said.

"You can have my weapons when I'm dead."

Hatan shrugged. "So be it." He rushed forward. The mercenaries moved in to attack, but with a few quick slashes, Hatan's glaive drew blood on several of them. Every attack they made against him was deflected and immediately followed up with a counter stroke. A hook on the middle of his glaive made it easy to catch their weapons and swing around them. After scoring a hit on the twelfth opponent, and with Hatan's soldiers pressing in on the sides, the mercenaries grew more ferocious. Their numbers were no match for superior skill and weaponry.

Two throwing knives were hurled at Hatan simultaneously. He deflected one with his blade and the other one grazed his shoulder, but the chain shirt he wore beneath his cloak protected him from getting cut.

The mercenaries became even more furious after that. They roared and ran at Hatan's men, but that only allowed the soldiers to hack into them with greater speed.

These were the type of men Queen Rikaydian had hired. Idiots. Brutes. No more than common thugs who lacked any experience fighting true warriors. Even still, the press of bodies and their lack of experience meant they would take unnecessary risks, hoping to score a hit even if it meant getting stabbed. One man lunged at Hatan with his shortspear. Hatan caught it between his elbow and his torso then swung down with his glaive, severing the man's hand. He screamed and whipped out a dagger, diving with utter disregard for his own life. This allowed him to scratch Hatan's arm, but he took a glaive just below his neck in the process.

Hatan's soldiers didn't even need to press forward. They held their position as the mercenaries charged into their weapons.

But Onik. Hatan needed the man alive. The mercenaries had lost half their men in less than a minute.

"Onik," Hatan shouted. "Call it off!"

But the mercenaries didn't stop coming. They may have been inexperienced, but he had to commend their loyalty. It wasn't until a third of them remained that some of them finally started to surrender.

One man threw down his weapons, held out his hands and stepped back to the wall. Most followed right after.

"No!" Onik yelled at them, but Hatan jumped toward him, deflected swings from both his axes, and kicked the big man in the chest. He followed through with a quick jab that Onik managed to dodge, but Hatan pulled his weapon back so that the hook on the back of his glaive caught Onik's thigh.

Onik screamed and Hatan kicked him again, this time driving him to his back. He unhooked his glaive and smacked one of Onik's hands with it, slicing him along the thumb and knocking the weapon from his hand. He stomped down on the other wrist.

The other mercenaries had all been subdued.

"Kill me, then," Onik groaned. His body was riddled with scars. For a man who'd spent a lot of time fighting, he sure lacked the talent.

"I don't need to kill you, or your men," Hatan said, pressing against Onik's wrist with his foot. "I just need to know who hired you."

Onik laughed. "Isn't it obvious?"

"Enlighten me."

"You really can't tell? Who has the most to gain if the king winds up dead?"

"I'm asking the questions. Now answer." He rested the tip of his glaive against Onik's stomach.

"The regent hired us," Onik said.

"Very funny," Hatan said, pulling the cloth down from his face. "I'm the regent. I didn't hire you. Try again." He pressed the glaive down with a bit more pressure, but Onik's expression was shocked, eyes wide, mouth agape.

"No, I—I don't understand," Onik said.

"Explain, then. Why would you think I'm the one who hired you? Who is your contact?"

"The same person who paid us before we were expelled from the palace grounds. The woman."

Hatan felt like he'd been punched in the gut. He knew exactly who that was, and she was the last person he'd suspected.

Or Onik was lying to him.

"He's lying," Hatan said to his soldiers. "Take his men outside. Execute them for treason."

"No, sir, please," Onik said, struggling to pull his arm free. He kicked at Hatan, but Hatan only pressed his glaive down harder. Hard enough that it was probably drawing blood.

Hatan's soldiers didn't falter in following through with Hatan's orders, but the mercenaries weren't going to go down without a fight. Some of them picked their weapons back up, preparing to fight to the death. "Wait," Hatan said. Their men stared each other down.

"What were you hired to do?" Hatan asked.

"Pressure the nobles into forming a coalition. Have them sign papers affirming that King Rikaydian is a traitor, unfit to rule," Onik said.

"And who is supposed to take his place? Don't you dare say it's me. I have closely approved every transaction since assuming my role, and none of our funds have gone towards mercenaries since you were dismissed."

Onik was both sweating and shivering.

"Think carefully before you answer. Is your life worth whatever money they offered to pay you?" Hatan pressed a little harder, just to make sure his blade was breaking skin.

Onik grunted. "Avidazj," he finally sputtered. "Avidazj Kesten. His father wants to set him up as the new king."

Hatan drew back his weapon and stepped off Onik's wrist. "Very good. And you still have these papers?"

"No. We deliver them to the palace under cover of paper orders. We hand them straight to the woman."

Right under his own nose. Hatan let out a seething breath before addressing the mercenaries as a whole. "If you value your lives, throw down your weapons. We're confiscating them. You are banished from Jehubal and must leave immediately. If I ever see any of you again," he paused to look at each of them, "I will strike you down right there and then. Understood?"

The mercenaries threw down their weapons for the second time and Hatan's soldiers started gathering them up. Most of the mercenaries had already been slaughtered. The rest of them were ushered out into the rain.

He should have killed Onik. The bandit couldn't be trusted not to return. He had a feeling he'd have to kill the man eventually, but Onik would know that he'd earned his death in battle.

"Sir, they could turn right around and warn the Kestens," said Falshon.

"I know," Hatan said. "I want them to know I'm coming for them. We'll draw out their true allies." He then addressed Kyel, "Follow Onik. I want to see where he really turns to." Kyel nodded and stalked after the group of mercenaries as they skulked away through the rain.

"What now?" asked Falshon.

Hatan sighed. "We confront another traitor. I want to see those papers, and Penym will have to answer for what she's done."

Chapter 30

Lightning cracking around them as they flew among the clouds was enough to keep Migo on edge. Despite reassurance from Katsi, he still considered the high likelihood of them getting struck.

"I can feel it, though, Migo," Katsi argued. "Its energy reminds me of magic. I'm sure I could keep it away from us the same way I do the rain."

Doubtful. His arms grew tired from gripping the rocks so tightly. He decided instead to redirect his thoughts. He closed his eyes and tilted his head down, but then his nose touched the back of her neck and his thoughts assaulted him in another way instead. He took deep breaths to calm himself, but that only filled his lungs with the earthy scent of Katsi's skin. The worst part about it was that it did calm him. It transported him. The tumult of any storm was worth wading just to fill his lungs with that smell.

Sands.

He took another deep breath, resisting the urge to touch her shoulder with his thumb.

Storms.

How much longer would he be able to endure this?

"Migo," Katsi said, her voice tinged with excitement. "Migo, I think we're there."

"Impossible," Migo muttered, but Katsi was already slowing. They'd been flying for probably five straight marks without any break. Whether they'd reached Mazanib or not, they needed to stop, even if it meant just getting Migo's nose away from Katsi.

But as they drew closer to the city below, Migo became more convinced that they had truly arrived at their destination.

Mazanib.

It was like nothing Migo had seen before. It was a densely populated metropolis. Many of the buildings glittered with a shimmer of white stone, metal, and glass. It was shaped like an oval, stretching from one side of the Ring to the other, but possibly twice the size of Jehubal. Mazanib marked the northernmost tip of the Ring.

He knew that the city had once been called Silver City, but that was before the emperor took over and started a new union across the entire globe. He'd marched an army all the way around the Ring, uniting everyone under a single banner. The only battles had to be fought with minor rebellions, particularly among those shamanfolk who weren't exterminated.

It also meant wealth. Massive wealth. And the city showed for it. He doubted the Maedaris caused any problems here.

A plateau overlooking the city from the west boasted a gorgeous castle with perfectly symmetrical, rounded towers. From above, it looked like a giant flower with double-tiered towers as petals.

"Alright, not impossible," Migo corrected.

"I'll bring us down the same way as in Lazeem," Katsi said.

Migo had rarely felt grateful for the constant rain and cloud cover of New Season, but this was an exception.

After finding a suitable place to land that was a decent distance away from the city, Katsi summoned up the cloud funnel. Migo prepared himself for the dip as Katsi dropped down through the funnel and his guts hugged his throat.

They knew the drill. Once they hit the ground, they made a run for it. Despite the rain, there were more people outside than Migo expected. Work had to get done, after all. But they still fled at the site of the cloud pillar Katsi had summoned. Nobody wanted to get caught near a tornado.

What impressed Migo the most was the presence of a large storm shelter just outside the city gates. A few people stood near the entrance, watching the cloud pillar to see if it became a real threat.

Migo and Katsi jogged right by and headed to the city. For some reason, Migo had the haunted feeling that Katsi was going to be discovered at any moment. Somebody would see her armor and know, just like Yavasu had known. Maybe they should have stashed her armor somewhere outside, but he wasn't sure she'd be willing to part with it. He'd always seen her wearing it.

The guards at the gatehouse were calm, attentive, and well equipped with plated shoulders, chain shirts, and swords.

Wealth.

"Where do we go?" Migo asked once they got through the gate.

"We have to find Elen-Fidtan. It's a sleephouse."

Migo nodded and stopped the nearest person on the street, asking if he knew where they could find Elen-Fidtan.

"There are lots of sleephouses here, friend. I don't know where that one is." The man shuffled away.

Great. Of course it wouldn't be that easy to find. It took them half a mark of wandering deeper into the city and asking everyone if they knew where to find it before they came across someone who'd heard of the place. It was apparently located on the north end of the city.

They stopped to take a break before continuing on, but they were both eager to reach their destinations.

"I want to help you get squared away with your contacts first," Migo said. "Once I know you're safe, then I'll see if I can meet with the emperor."

"Right," Katsi said, shaking out her hands before stuffing them back under her armpits. "What about after that? We should plan a time to meet back up, as long as you're not late this time." She tried to shove him with her shoulder but ended up stumbling a step when met with Migo's unyielding body.

He steadied her by reaching out and grabbing her elbow, smiling shamelessly. But it didn't alleviate his anxiety. The idea of leaving Katsi behind for even a moment caused him the greatest worry. What if something happened to her? What if she missed their meeting time? Would he ever be able to find her again in such a large city?

But he had to remember that she would be a formidable opponent for anyone. What happened back at Rhial proved that.

As they got further north, they asked for better directions. More people were familiar with the sleephouse and pointed them to the right place. They paused just across the street from it, standing in the drizzling rain, their breath curling out in steamy puffs.

"Should I go in with you?" Migo asked.

"No, I think I should do this alone. So they don't get scared off or anything."

Migo nodded. It was sensible, but he didn't like it. "Alright. I'll remain close by." He went to the corner of another building, hiding under its overhang as Katsi approached the sleephouse. *This better not be some elaborate trap*, he thought as he folded his arms.

Chapter 31

Katsi pushed open the door, immediately regretting her decision to have Migo wait outside. She should have had him come along. What harm would it do? But she was too stubborn to go back out and grab him.

This was probably the finest sleephouse she'd ever seen. The front room was neat and clean. A bar lined the wall to her right, and a row of tables and chairs lined the right. A long hallway stretched ahead of her with doors on either side, indicating that it boasted private rooms for its patrons. There were seven patrons already, four at the tables, and three at the bar. One man stood behind the bar, and another serving woman approached Katsi.

"How can I be of service?" the woman asked.

Katsi gulped, trying to remember her instructions. Alishara had told her to be very exact. "Um, are you one of the cooks?"

The woman smiled. "I dabble back there, but I'm certainly not one of the true masterminds. Is there something you're looking for?"

"Well, I was rather hoping to speak with Venach," Katsi said, hopefully lowering her voice enough that the boisterous patrons wouldn't hear.

"Ah," the woman said with a careful nod. She glanced over at the man behind the bar. "Come wait back here, please. I'll see if I can pull him away from his duties." She retreated quickly, skirts rustling as she all but ran. She gestured just inside a hallway between the bar and the kitchen. It was stocked full of different ingredients.

Katsi picked at her nails. She didn't have to wait long. A burly man came out of the door just behind the serving woman. He had pale skin, a sharp nose, and light brown hair that reminded her of Damani. The serving woman went off to other customers, but Venach stopped before her.

Katsi wiped her palms on her pants, but they were equally wet.

"Did you have a question about the food?" Venach asked.

Katsi shook her head. "No."

He leaned closer. "Perhaps the ingredients? You know, we do get a root that grows near the Frozen Waste that tastes a little bitter, but when mixed in properly, it adds such an excellent accent to the rest of the flavor of our soup. Any idea what that root is?"

Katsi gulped. "Shavarani," she said.

His eyes glinted. She was supposed to show him her armlet but his eyes made her nervous. Despite that, she loosened her cloak over that shoulder and pulled up her sleeve to show the armlets.

He motioned to have her cover them up and looked over his shoulder. He held a finger over his mouth and gestured for her to follow him through the kitchen. She ignored the tightness in her stomach and followed as he led her through the kitchen then moved a shelf out of the way, revealing a door behind it. He opened it and went inside.

The room beyond was dark. The only light coming through was from a ventilation shaft, but even that was dim.

Venach lit a couple candles before speaking. "It was bold of you to come here, to Mazanib. No new shamans have been sent for a while."

"Are you a friend of shamans?" Katsi asked, feeling at the wooden floor with her feet. Even the walls were made of wood. She could feel the earthen ground further away, but it was somewhat fuzzy.

"Indeed. We've been helping run an organization here for many years, but I'm not the best person to talk to. I'm only the middleman. I'll need to get somebody else here that will help you further, but it's not safe for you to wander, especially now that other patrons saw you." He gestured at the room. "You'll need to wait here for a moment. It might take a mark to get one of the representatives here for you. I'm sorry it's not the most comfortable space to wait, but I can at least bring you something from the kitchen."

Katsi looked around the dim room. It was a dump of a room, mostly crates of various supplies and foods. There was a single chair near the wall. "I've hidden in plenty worse places," she said.

Venach laughed. "I'm sure you have. Just hold on and I'll bring you some soup, then I'll hurry off to our contact."

Katsi nodded and sat down on the hard chair, also made of wood.

Venach came back a second later with a steaming bowl in his hands. "Here we are," he said, setting it down on a crate near the center of the room. "You can scoot your chair closer. Use this as a table."

Katsi stood, and he helped push her chair up from behind. That's when she heard the jingle of metal.

She was too late.

He clamped something over both her hands from behind her back. Silver.

It was a trap.

Chapter 32

Migo was growing impatient. He considered scoping out the building. They should have devised a better plan. Migo could have gone and checked in as a customer before Katsi came. That way, he could have kept a closer eye on her. But what was to stop him from going in now?

The door opened, and several patrons left the building. Katsi wasn't one of them. He couldn't decide if that was a good sign or not. A maidservant waved goodbye to the customers from the door, glanced down the streets, seemed to notice Migo in the shadows, then retreated and closed the door behind her.

A flash blazed directly overhead and thunder rumbled a moment later. Even through the din, Migo thought he heard the sound of a stormlock being dropped into place.

He set his jaw and swung the poleaxe from his shoulder, removing the leather strap around the ax and stuffing that back into his bag. He could always go check. At least see if it was open, but if he went in now, would that compromise everything? It would potentially prevent her from making a connection with the shaman's underground network.

Migo *needed* the information from them. They were potentially more likely to know about the assassinations, and maybe even about the shamans using the blood magic.

But worry still knotted in his stomach. He didn't like leaving Katsi alone in there.

Another flash of lightning silhouetted a figure dropping rapidly from the sky, coming towards him. A shock of adrenaline struck his body but as the shape came closer, it was clearly not human.

Scales.

The lizard dropped down in front of Migo, disregarding the attention from two other people who were hurrying through the street.

Scales growled, his wings twitching rapidly.

"Scales," Migo said. "I don't speak lizard, but look, I don't like it either. We're trying to get to the bottom of this, and they can probably help us figure everything out." Had he just talked to the lizard? Katsi was rubbing off on him.

Scales gnashed his teeth in the direction of the sleephouse and let out a deep croak, clawing at the ground.

It certainly didn't ease Migo's anxiety. Scales only acted like this when he was trying to defend Katsi. Perhaps she was in trouble. Perhaps it really was a trap.

"Sleet," Migo muttered, rolling his shoulders. "I'll just interrogate the contact myself." He took one step into the street when a bolt of lightning struck the building right next to him. Everything went white. There was no sound.

Chapter 33

Katsi bellowed in frustration and tried to stand from the chair, but she was chained to it. She went to summon her magic, but it felt weak, suppressed. All she managed to do was blow out the candles.

"Don't worry, demon," Venach said, "this room is secure. And the silver locks on your hand will prevent you from using your magic."

"I don't understand," Katsi said. "Why would you do this? Why would I be sent here?"

Venach laughed again. "It's actually quite a good story. You see, whoever sent you doesn't realize that the real Venach is dead, and that we know all about their shaman smuggling efforts. So whenever a new shaman comes through, we kill them ourselves."

The door to the hidden room opened and two more silhouetted figures appeared. "What kind of shaman did we catch?" said one of the men from behind.

"We'll have to cut her open and find out," said the other.

Katsi's heart pounded like the thunder that rumbled around them. She struggled to pull her hands free. She tried to stand, to kick, to call her magic—anything.

Migo. Migo was her only chance. She screamed his name.

"Nobody's going to hear you in here, witch."

Something cracked with a vicious boom, like the building itself had been struck by lightning.

There were a few muffled screams from outside the room.

The false Venach frowned at Katsi. "She didn't come alone," he said, holding up a massive cleaver. "I'll finish her."

Katsi scooted back in the chair until she hit against the wall.

Migo would find her in time. He had to.

The other two men charged off but their shouts were ended with meaty thunks.

A new, tall figure appeared in the doorway. "Leave the girl."

It was not Migo.

The voice was deeper—more dangerous—and carried a mild accent. It struck terror into Katsi's heart. It was even more threatening than the cleaver in Venach's hand.

Venach took one step towards the figure, cleaver swiping.

The man moved with violent precision, blade glinting like a sliver of light, cutting Venach clean in half.

Katsi flinched at the scene and let out a shuddering breath.

The man sheathed his sword and walked slowly toward Katsi. "Worry not," he said. "I'm no danger to you." As he got closer, she could see him better. His face was wrapped in a black coif, but he pulled it off as he knelt beside her.

He was young, with a dark, well-trimmed shadow of a beard, highlighting a sharp jawline, angled nose, and piercing eyes under a soft, thick brow. His black hair rippled down one side of his face, his skin a darker shade of brown than her own.

He reached behind her, leaning in close to access the locks around her hands. With a sharp click, the locks clattered to the floor.

"You're safe now. Come with me," he said, rising back to his full height, towering over her.

"Who are you?" Katsi asked.

"Most call me Alyssad, but for you," he held out his hand to help her up from the chair, "I am salvation."

Katsi let out a long breath. She'd been seconds away from dying before he came. Where was Migo? She would have thought he'd notice something going on.

But no matter. If Katsi was at least able to get out of this building, then she'd have access to her power. Even if this man was a skilled warrior, he'd be no match for Katsi on solid ground. She took his hand.

"I'll take you to a safe place. A sanctuary for other shamans like your-self," Alyssad said. They went out of the hidden pantry and through the kitchen.

Katsi tried to keep her eyes away from the gruesome scene, but she kept glancing at it as they passed, worried that one of the bodies might be Migo. Alyssad had butchered them. Six men and the serving woman. Seven in all.

Alyssad led her away from the main door. "There's another way back here. Safer." He regarded her calmly, dark eyes penetrating her soul. "You have a rare gift. I intend to show you just how special you are."

A chill ran down her spine. This was him, then. What she'd been looking for. The man who would help her learn her powers.

***

Rain pattered down on Migo's face. He blinked up at it as his memory of what happened returned in a sudden flash. Katsi. He jerked upright. His poleaxe was a few paces away. He crawled over to it. There was some blood mingled with the rainwater where he'd fallen, and his head ached. He touched the back of his head and looked at his fingers. Red. He must have hit his head as he'd fallen.

But there was no time to consider the damage. He grabbed his poleaxe and headed for the sleephouse, but the door already hung ajar, smashed in by something powerful. The stormlock lay snapped in half on the floor. The scene beyond was gorey.

No.

"Katsi!" he roared, stomping into the room. Bodies littered the floor. They'd been killed with precision, like an executioner had come through, aiming a few perfect strokes. A trail of blood led straight through the kitchens to a back room that made him think of a dungeon. He rushed inside, but Katsi wasn't there. He found silver chains with a unique design... they were broken.

Katsi must have gotten away. Was this the work of her secula? He'd never seen her actually use it, but he doubted she had the skill with a weapon to do all that. Somebody else must have been here. She had help.

He followed another trail back out of the kitchen. Bloody boot prints led to another door at the back which also hung open. He examined the boot prints closely. There were two footprints that he knew were Katsi's, but there was another—a partial print. It was significantly larger than Katsi's, maybe even the size of Migo's own.

But the footprints disappeared as soon as they got outside, of course.

"Sands, Katsi," he muttered to himself. He had to hope that she'd gotten connected with the right people. That's all he *could* do. There'd be no other way to track her. All that was left for him was to play his part.

He needed to see the emperor.

Chapter 34

Katsi followed the stranger through back streets for what seemed like several marks. The route he took was a puzzle, especially for a city that was completely foreign to her. Eventually, they ended up at a door in the basement of a warehouse.

He pulled out a key and unlocked it. The air here tingled. There was magic at work, of that she was certain. So there *were* shamans in Mazanib. This was her first sign that Alyssad had an actual connection with the shamanfolk at all. But what kind of shamans were they? Like her tribe, or more like the bleeders and their waheshi? She shivered to think that Alishara would try to put her in connection with anybody who would make such monsters. And if they were more skilled than her in combat and tried to attack her, her best bet would be to take to the air and fly away.

Alyssad swung open a door, exposing a dark tunnel. He removed the cover from his face. Apparently he felt safer here, but when he saw her expression as she regarded the tunnel, his hard eyes softened. "Do not fear the dark. I will let nothing harm you. I swear it."

If she wanted to find the shamans, this was her only option. She nodded.

He entered the tunnel and Katsi came after him. This distinctly reminded her of when she followed Alishara through the dark cave in the canyons of Banadil-Atar. For being as powerful as she supposedly was, she'd needed her life saved far too many times. It was exhausting, and she was tired of it.

She would learn to use her power. She only wished Migo had been able to teach her about using a weapon as well, though there was still time to learn that. As long as she found her way back to Migo.

The dark tunnel beyond was cold. Alyssad closed the door behind them then led the way ahead, his footsteps echoing behind him. "This tunnel is straight and flat for quite a while, then it's a full ascent. You may step confidently."

Katsi didn't want to believe him. She'd stumbled around enough in her life, but when she threw out her magic to feel the earth around her, she could confirm the directness of the path. The walls were surprisingly smooth, exactly like her tribe's home in the Scorched Waste. It was no doubt carved by earthmelding. Another reassurance that she was in the right place.

They proceeded in silence for several minutes until Alyssad stopped and directed her to ascend a metal ladder. He came behind her this time. It was easily the longest ladder Katsi had ever climbed. She succumbed to the temptation of simply connecting with the stone wall and ascending with her magic. It took considerably less precision than finding each rung of the ladder.

"Clever," Alyssad said, and he started climbing even faster to keep up with her.

They reached the top, and Katsi found herself in a small room while Alyssad went to unlock yet another door at the end and pushed it open. Bright light spilled in, and Katsi shielded her eyes from it.

"We're safe here," Alyssad said, stepping into the light beyond.

Katsi followed slowly, her eyes adjusting. She found herself in a massive library with more shelves and books than she'd ever seen. The shelves were so tall that a second story balcony gave access to even more. Too many books. Nobody would ever have time to read them all. But there was knowledge contained there. Something her tribe had lacked. Only so much could be passed down orally, and the elder shaman council wasn't very forthcoming with knowledge. It was only after she'd killed Queen Rikaydian that the elders had even told her about bleeders. The books alone provided enough reassurance that she'd be able to learn everything she needed here.

Giant windows laced with iron formed an entire wall to the side. She could detect the hint of powerful enchantments like the tendrils of a spider web reinforcing it against the storms. Katsi went straight to the window and looked outside. The window faced westward. They were in a large building atop a plateau.

They were in the castle.

She whipped her head around to find Alyssad standing just behind her, leaning against the bookshelf with his arms folded.

"Who sent you?" he asked, voice rumbling. "Alishara?"

Katsi hesitated a moment before responding. "Yes." Even more confirmation.

He nodded slowly, stroking the edge of his dark beard with his thumb.

Katsi turned to face him, prepared to pull out her weapon. "Who are you exactly? Are you a shaman?"

Alyssad smirked. "I'm an ally. But I don't know your name."

"Katsi Danan."

"Katsi Danan," he repeated slowly as though his tongue were savoring the very utterance of her name. A shiver went down her spine.

A door across the large room opened, and a woman wearing a vibrant red dress entered the room. She had light brown hair, elegantly styled, gray-blue eyes, and skin the color of pale sand, freckled across her nose and cheeks. She appeared to be in her mid-thirties if Katsi had to guess, but she was decorated like a queen.

"Ah, Adrina," Alyssad said, "this is Katsi Danan. She will be your new student."

Adrina regarded Katsi with a curved smile. "Pleasure to meet you, Katsi."

"Please see to her accommodations. Give her the room on the third floor. She has not had a warm welcome here in Mazanib," Alyssad said.

"I will see to it, Your Highness," Adrina said, bowing her head to him.

Katsi mouthed the word, "Highness."

"Adrina will see to your needs, Katsi," Alyssad said, pushing off from the bookshelf, dark eyes locked onto Katsi's. "I will check in on you later to ensure everything meets your expectations, but for now I must take my leave." He placed a hand over his heart and left with a flourish, his black cloak trailing behind him.

"You're a stormcaller, then, Katsi?" Adrina asked.

"I am. And you?"

Adrina smiled. "I'm proficient at earthmelding, but I have some talent in stormcalling as well. My experience should be well suited to providing you further instruction. Come." She fanned Katsi to follow after her.

Katsi took another sweeping glance at the library before following Adrina through a separate door, absorbing it all in. This was the grandest building she'd ever been in. She never imagined ceilings could be so high. Even the hallway had an arched ceiling with ionic symbols carved into the brilliant white stone.

"Was this castle made with earthmelding?" Katsi ventured to ask.

"Much of it, yes," Adrina said. "Though everything is fitted together in the traditional sense of construction, we just used earthmelding to create individual blocks so that it looks like it was made without magic."

They made their way up a flight of spiral stairs that extended two more stories, went down another hall, then entered a room with a door that was twice her height. Beyond was an elaborate waiting room, complete with couches, a table, chairs, a desk, a vanity, a massive wardrobe, and a bed.

A bed? Sands, this was a bedroom.

"This is where you'll stay," Adrina said.

"Stay?"

"Yes, you intended to learn more about your powers here, correct?"

"Yes, but... I didn't think I'd be staying here."

"Katsi, if you want true mastery, it takes time. It doesn't matter how powerful you are if you lack the delicacy required to make precision strikes. We will unlock doors for you that you never even knew existed."

Katsi bit her cheek. It was as though Adrina knew exactly what it was she truly wanted. She didn't care how long it took, only that she had a clear path forward.

"I understand," Katsi said. "I'm ready."

"Of course you are. Otherwise you would not have been sent here. Now," she held up her hand and a chair slid across the floor, stopping in front of the vanity, "let's get you taken care of. A warm bath, some fresh food, a good rest, some new attire. Then we can begin. I'll need to see what you're already capable of."

Katsi nodded. "How did you move the chair?"

"Stones are installed on it for easy maneuvering. Many of the things here in the castle are made to accommodate our powers."

Katsi smiled and stepped further into the room. She'd like this place. "How many shamans are here?"

"Not enough. Less than a dozen. We're still trying to restore things."

Restore what? And even deeper than that question was another, one that had been burning at her since she got here. "Who is Alyssad?"

"He introduced himself as Alyssad, did he?" Adrina smiled. "Why, he's Emperor Malrabia."

"The emperor of Malahem?"

"The same."

Chapter 35

Hatan threw his wet cloak on a rack and marched down the hall of the palace. Falshon, Rivar, and Emil followed him. The rest of the soldiers went about the palace to secure the area. With his recent lockdown, the number of people in the palace was limited. More control that way. And since the altercation at the ball, Penym had been sequestered in a room of the palace. Perhaps all of that had been intentional. Penym being in the palace at all hours could have been part of their whole plan.

They approached the door of the room they'd given Penym when Hatan placed his glaive on the floor outside. "Wait out here," Hatan ordered the others. He took a deep breath, clenched his jaw, and opened the door without knocking. Penym's room had been furnished with a desk in addition to the small bed.

Penym sat behind the desk, reviewing a logbook under the light of a high window. She jumped as Hatan entered, then heaved a breath and said, "Oh, regent." She rose from her seat. "What can I do to help you?"

Hatan strode up to the desk and placed his fists down against the surface of the desk. "I want to let you know I learned everything about Onik and your association with him." Penym's lips parted and her chest heaved with a few quick breaths. "Why, Penym?" He kept it ambiguous. Perhaps then Penym might reveal more.

"Regent, I," Penym's breathing increased in rapidity, and she dropped to the seat behind her, hands flat against the desk. "They forced me into it."

"You betrayed us. You could have come to me. We could have helped you. Instead, you chose to side with them and betray your king."

"I know, regent, I'm sorry, but if I hadn't sworn to them, I would already be dead. They gave me no option."

"Loyalty to your king should supersede any other oath made under coercion. You should have come to me immediately." He understood the pull to self-preservation, but she should have had more faith in him.

"I know. I failed." She slid off the chair to her knees. "Please. I don't know what else to do."

"I need to stop whatever's happening, Penym," Hatan said. "What is their plan?"

"They will kill anyone who doesn't side with them. They've already killed a few. Once they've overturned the majority of the nobility, they will take the palace and execute the king when he returns and elect the new ruler."

"The Kestens are leading it, aren't they?"

"Yes," Penym said, her lower lip trembling, "but there's more. You must move against them, immediately. They know you are an honorable man, and they will try to use that against you. Ignore anything else that comes up. It's only meant to delay your response."

"Don't worry about that. I will execute any involved in this treason."

"Sir!"

A rushing of steps echoed up the hall. Hatan knew that voice. The soldiers at the door made way for Kyel to rush inside.

"Sir," Kyel said. "It was as you suspected. Onik returned with all his men. They went directly to the home of Sinteya Jenali. They broke in. I believe she's in danger."

"We must go there at once," Hatan said.

"Regent, no," Penym said. "They do this on purpose. They know that you are watching them. It's part of the plan, don't you see? They sent Onik to Jenali Manor because they know you are sympathetic to her. Go for the Kestens. Please, regent."

"Let's go," Hatan said, ignoring her. "Falshon, keep somebody posted at her door."

Falshon saluted in response and slammed Penym's door shut.

"Where to, regent?" Rivar asked.

"Jenali Manor. It's my fault she's in that predicament. I expected Onik to report back to his employer, not continue the job."

Rivar and Emil shared a look. They disagreed with him.

But he wouldn't stand back while an innocent person died because of him. Hatan turned to them. "What would you do?"

"Regent, we should do as Penym suggested," Emil said. "Moving against the primary instigator would mean the dissolution of their uprising. Our father and brother deserve no opportunity to rule over Jehubal. They are overcome with pride and greed."

Rivar nodded. "If we take them down, even if somebody else fills the void among the instigators, they'll still be crippled enough that we can take them all down, one by one if necessary. As long as we can keep them from uniting. It might be hard to hear, regent, but heading for them provides us the most tactical advantage, even if it means leaving Sinteya Jenali vulnerable."

They were right. Sands, they were right. Hatan rubbed his beard as Falshon rejoined them after posting somebody outside Penym's door. "Alright, here's the plan," Hatan said. "Falshon, you lead an assault on Kesten manor. Take all your remaining soldiers. We'll keep the palace locked down and manned by general staff, excepting two soldiers, one to guard Penym's door, and another to provide combat expertise should they need it. Kyel, we'll move in on Jenali Manor with your sister for a precision strike. Does that work? Everyone agree?"

"Aye, sir," Falshon and Kyel said. The twins responded more hesitantly, but they also complied.

"Right. To the end," Hatan said.

"To the end," the rest of them said. And perhaps this was the end. But Hatan would meet the end as he was supposed to. As a warrior.

Chapter 36

Migo paced impatiently. He was in the waiting room of the Silver Castle, waiting to see Emperor Malrabia. He wondered if the emperor's servants even believed he was the king of Jehubal. He didn't strike a very noble visage at present, with his muddied clothes and wild, unkempt hair, body battered from battle.

The guards at the front had him remove his weapons, his bag, and his dripping cloak. The rest of his clothes were still soaked, but he'd at least stopped dripping all over the tiled floor. He could certainly do without the squeaking, uncomfortable feeling it gave his boots however.

So far, he was massively impressed with the castle. Even if they pooled together the combined wealth of every noble in Jehubal, he doubted they'd be able to fund such a project as this.

He refused to let it limit the value of his people. Each citizen of Jehubal still mattered, and he, as their leader, had a valuable enough status to demand council with the emperor. Surely he wouldn't dismiss him, especially since Migo was so far from home. It made Migo wonder how often the emperor ever saw any of his vassals.

He'd likely been waiting for two full marks before the large doors opened up again and a servant wearing a blue and black uniform approached Migo. He held out Migo's ring to hand it back to him—well, his father's ring. It was his evidence of being part of the Rikaydian family.

"His Excellency will see you now," the servant said. He had a slight accent, something Migo hadn't anticipated.

Migo returned the ring to his finger and followed the servant as he led him through the open doors. There were more guards in the room beyond, four of them, wearing blackened steel armor, clearly studded with silver. They were no doubt trained as shaman hunters. The emperor would certainly have gone through extensive measures to keep shamans from infiltrating his own castle.

The ceiling was two stories tall throughout the whole building, but he kept his eyes down, automatically noting each door and each person, though they didn't have to walk far. As was customary, the emperor had a throne room near the waiting room for meeting with any visitors. The elaborately carved, white doors were already open as the servant ushered Migo inside.

Migo kept his head down, but noted the ten other occupants of the room, each of them armed with long poleaxes and swords. Bright light filtered down from an enormous glass dome in the roof, but he didn't get the chance to look up at it. To do so would be blatant disrespect in the presence of the emperor. Silver and gold glittered off the walls between bright red tapestries. Anything he'd ever thought of as wealth was infinitesimal when compared with the emperor's castle.

The servant walked beside Migo up until they were a couple paces from the first step of the raised dais upon which the emperor sat. The servant paused and knelt, and Migo did the same. It was the servant's job to speak first, as they would have already been invited by the emperor's request at this point.

"Your Excellency, I present to you the man claiming to be Lord Migo Rikaydian of Jehubal."

Claiming. Perfect.

"Lord Rikaydian, is it?" the emperor spoke. His voice was low, and quiet, yet it permeated the very air. If power had a sound, that was it.

For the first time, Migo looked up into the eyes of his lord, and his lips parted in utter shock. The emperor was supposed to be a much older man, yet the one seated on the throne couldn't have been older than his early twenties. The emperor raised an eyebrow as they locked eyes. After recovering from the initial shock, he nodded another bow and said, "Yes, Your Excellency. I have come a long way to see you."

"Rise," Emperor Malrabia said.

Migo stood, squared his shoulders and regarded the emperor at attention.

The emperor thumbed his beard as he scrutinized Migo. "My servant said you announced yourself as the king. Are you not still seventeen years of age? What happened to the queen?"

"I am, Your Excellency. My mother was assassinated by a shaman."

"Your family seems to have an unfortunate history with shaman assassins."

"Yes, Your Excellency."

Emperor Malrabia smiled. "I detect a hint of suspicion regarding my own appearance. I too only recently took my role as emperor. In place of my father, I am Emperor *Alyssad* Malrabia. You and I have something in common. These shamans are... persistent."

Migo folded his hands behind his back. He wanted to share everything, but needed to wait until prompted by the emperor.

Perhaps sensing the trepidation, the emperor leaned back in his extravagant throne, gripping the armrests and crossing his legs casually. "Why come here, King Rikaydian? It is no small matter to come to Mazanib and address your emperor."

"First, thank you for seeing me, Your Excellency," Migo said. "I know I did not come here by invitation, but after assuming the throne of Jehubal,

I swore to find those who assassinated my father." Migo reached into the tunic beneath his armor and withdrew the map. "My search led me to a location held by a unique class of shamans as well as some... monsters under their command."

The emperor's casual appearance grew fierce. His eyes darkened and the grip on his armrests went tight.

"After slaying the waheshi and the shamans, I found a contingency of imperial soldiers inside, all dead. They'd been... mutilated to some degree. The—"

Emperor Malrabia rose to his feet and Migo stopped speaking. The emperor descended the steps of the throne until he stood directly in front of him.

Migo was distinctly aware of the thin longsword sheathed at the emperor's waist. He had no doubt the man knew how to use it well. Alyssad was possibly the tallest person Migo had ever met, half a hand higher than Migo himself.

"Where?" Alyssad's voice was wrath itself.

Migo presented the map, bowing his head. The map's details had likely been smudged by rainwater, so he jumped to explain as the emperor unfolded it. "In the northeastern border of Jehubal, Your Excellency. On the edge of the Frozen Waste."

"You killed the shamans there, and the waheshi, and my men were already dead?" Alyssad looked down at Migo, eyes hard, filled with contempt hidden subtly behind the practiced expression of a politician. But Migo was a trained inquisitor.

"Yes, Your Excellency," Migo said, meeting Alyssad's eyes with an unwavering confidence.

A smirk slipped across Alyssad's face. "King Rikaydian came here armed, did he not? Bring it here," he said, addressing his servant who still stood beside Migo.

"Yes, Your Excellency," the servant said with a deep bow. "Two weapons. I will bring them both."

"Where did you learn the word 'waheshi,' King Rikaydian?" Alyssad asked.

"It's the term the shaman woman used to refer to the beasts that attacked us, Your Excellency," Migo said. "Before I killed her."

"How many shamans were there?"

"Only two, Your Excellency. The first was quite powerful, and the second seemed surprised that we'd made it inside their hideout. We fought them separately."

"And how many waheshi?"

"Four, Your Excellency."

The emperor looked Migo up and down. "Drop the 'Your Excellency.' It gets repetitive and I hear it enough from all these," he fanned a hand at all the other people in the room.

"As you wish," Migo said. It took all his effort not to add the appellation.

The servant returned with Migo's weapons in tow.

"Hand the king his primary weapon," Alyssad said.

Migo took the weapon tentatively and watched Alyssad with narrowed eyes. What was he playing at?

"How many men accompanied you to that raid?" Alyssad asked.

"I had two of my soldiers with me."

"No offense, but you are young, King Rikaydian. What training do you and your men have?"

"I was trained at the Lazeem Academy in Rhian. I was the top performing soldier trained in shaman hunting. The two soldiers with me were likewise trained at Rhian's academy."

"So young, but skilled?"

"Yes," Migo said, setting his jaw.

Alyssad rolled back his shoulders. Sensing the danger, Migo adjusted his grip.

"Defend yourself," Alyssad said, giving Migo permission just before drawing his blade and slashing at Migo in the same motion.

Migo stepped back with one foot, switching into stance as he deflected the blow. Alyssad followed through in rapid succession. Migo deflected and dodged, feet shuffling back as the emperor drove him. He was fast, and skilled. Migo's practice overcame the shock of being attacked by his own lord.

Reason argued that this was a strange way to perform an execution. That's not what the emperor was after. This was a test. But the emperor didn't hold back. Two blows to Migo's reinforced haft still resulted in some chipping. Meaningless damage. Migo's rage began to build and he threw in a few counterattacks, finally holding his ground.

Alyssad only smirked just before leaping in with a quick parry, slapping the back of Migo's hand with his sword before grabbing Migo's poleaxe just below the blade and pulling the weapon from Migo's grip. His sword hovered over Migo's throat.

Migo leveled his gaze at the emperor. This was the first time Migo had been bested in a duel in years. His hands balled into fists.

Alyssad laughed, a deep chuckle that echoed off the walls like soft thunder. "I believe you, King Rikaydian. It has been a long time since anyone has given me a good fight. I sent ten of my best soldiers to that shaman hideout that you cleared with just you and two of your men. I didn't believe your success at first because it seemed unlikely that you would be met with success where they would have failed." He tossed Migo's weapon back to the servant.

"Come with me," Alyssad said, walking to a door to the side of the throne.

Migo followed. Perhaps this was it. Perhaps he'd earned the emperor's trust and would learn what Alyssad knew regarding the shaman assassins.

"Migo," Alyssad said, "if I had been as skilled as you at age seventeen, I would have taken over the world. Well, if my ancestors hadn't already done so, anyway." The room beyond was a small parlor with a large stained glass window that let in a yellow, pink, and white light.

Migo felt his chest swell. Alyssad was not only his emperor, but he was the greatest warrior he'd ever met. He never thought he'd respect the emperor so much. "I am honored by your praise."

"Certainly," Alyssad said, closing the door behind them before striding to the center of the room, dodging around the plush seating. "There is one detail you failed to share with me, however."

Migo tilted his head. "Your Excellency?"

Alyssad smirked, brilliant teeth shining. "How does Katsi Danan fit into your narrative?"

Migo's pulse quickened as heat rose in his ears. In addition to the door behind him, there was one to his left. If he ran out the one behind him, he'd have to make it past all the soldiers in the throne room, then the ones outside. If he had to fight Alyssad, it was a likely death. The door to his left was a mystery.

"Speak freely."

Migo clenched his fists. If this was how he was to die, then so be it. He'd chosen his fate. He would die with honor. But why spare Migo, only to kill him later? "She's the shaman who killed my mother, at my request, to preserve Jehubal from destruction. She also assisted me in investigating the shaman hideout where we discovered your dead soldiers. Furthermore, she's the reason that I was able to reach Mazanib so quickly."

"Was she instrumental in your success in raiding the shaman hideout?"

"She played her part. How do you... how do you know about her, Your Excellency?"

Alyssad smirked and the door to Migo's left opened up.

Migo braced himself, prepared to accept whatever fate awaited him.

Katsi came through the door. At least, it looked like her, only her hair looked like it had been well brushed and tied back. She wore a white and black dress, accented with dark blue. It had a slit that rose all the way up past her knee and it left one of her shoulders exposed. Where was her armor?

"Katsi?" Migo asked, still wary. Perhaps she'd been an agent of the emperor all along. His eyes widened. This entire thing was a ruse.

"Migo?" She said, clearly as surprised as he was. She looked to the emperor. "I see you've met 'salvation' here." Her hands were held in a familiar position, as though she were about to call up her magic. "Please tell me this isn't some elaborate trap."

"On the contrary," Alyssad said. "I could have killed either of you a hundred times over by now if I wanted to, but that's not my objective."

"Then what is?" Migo said, his voice taking a dark tone.

Alyssad smirked, his eyes sliding off Katsi to regard Migo. "I intend to save my people."

"From the Maedari?" Katsi asked.

"From the bleeders," Alyssad said, folding his arms.

"The bleeder shamans created the Maedaris?" Katsi pushed.

A growl rumbled from Alyssad's chest. "They are the reason the Maedaris exist."

"So your executive order to exterminate every shamanfolk should have really just been to target the bleeder shamans," Katsi said, lips curling back. The fingers of her hands flexed, ready to swallow him up in the ground, no doubt.

"I am not as my fathers," Alyssad said. He seemed too calm and unthreatened by Katsi's apparent frustration. "Which is why I'm trying to create a safe place for shamans, like yourself. There is much damage to be remediated."

"Easy, then. Call off all these extermination wars," Katsi said.

"It's not so simple. We are still very much at war with a very real enemy. If they were to let their guard down, I fear that many cities would immediately be overrun."

Migo remembered the waheshi. He'd thought the same thing. With just a few of those, they'd be able to ravage the population. But he had other questions, and the emperor was being rather giving with information. "Your Highness, how did you know of my connection with Katsi?"

Alyssad's smirk returned. "I saw you laying in the street outside the sleephouse when I got there in time to save her from execution. I was prepared to kill you if you'd had any connection with the people who'd captured her."

"I see," Migo said, heat rising in his cheeks. He'd been unable to reach Katsi himself, due to some random bolt of lightning. The emperor had been the one to save Katsi. That bloody handiwork had been his doing.

"Though I'm sure with your skill, King Rikaydian, you could have extracted her as well," Alyssad said, leveling his eyes at him.

Migo was positive he could have, though he doubted he would have had the need to kill the two women in there as well.

"Regardless," Alyssad continued. "I'm glad you both found your way here. I have great need for both of you if we are to end the greatest threat to Malahem."

"I'm just here to learn more about my power," Katsi said.

"And I'm here to see if you know who killed my father," Migo said. "I suspected it had something to do with the bleeder shamans. My father had gone through great lengths to investigate it."

Alyssad lifted his hands up. "Our goals are one and the same, my friends. I'll elaborate on the fortuitousness of your arrival. Katsi, your power is exactly the kind of thing I've been looking for. Others have come and gone, but none with your strength. Adrina has already expressed that she senses greater strength in you than she has ever seen. Together, we'll have the power to bring peace to all of Malahem. We can solve the Maedari problem.

"And King Rikaydian, you have shown expertise that has been lacking among all my soldiers. My own general died no more than a month ago trying to locate the bleeder shamans' headquarters. We found it, but he did not survive. My need for a skilled shaman hunter and capable leader has never been greater. I want you to lead an assault against them. Strike them where it counts. This will solve all the greatest problems we've had to deal with. Imagine all the suffering, all the pain that can be eliminated by the two of you."

Alyssad unfolded his hands and took two steps towards Migo. "I knew of your father, Migo. Those bleeders are the ones who assassinated your father. They're behind all of it. Your father sought to uncover their hideout because he knew they were creating monsters and wanted to prevent it. They killed him not only to keep themselves safe, but to cause further strife between the Bayvana Tribe and Jehubal—to keep your people distracted while they raised an army—one that nobody would be able to stop."

It made perfect sense now. His mother had focused all her energy on the wrong thing. She'd succumbed to blind rage rather than looking at things logically. Even Migo had suspected that somebody wanted his city-state to be at war with the Bayvana Tribe. Now he finally understood why. His fists clenched tighter. He would destroy them. They would pay for this.

"Can I really stop the Maedaris?" Katsi asked.

"Katsi," Alyssad uttered her name with a deep sigh. "There is much left for you to learn. I have read many books regarding stormcallers of old. Once you learn for yourself... the possibilities are endless."

Migo could see the spark in Katsi's eyes. That hunger. What was it that possessed her so much to learn about her powers? It triggered both fear and fascination in him. He *wanted* to see what she could do. He *wanted* to see her completely unleashed.

"I'm ready," Katsi said, shaking out her hands. Her instinct to fight had faded.

And Migo's? It was just beginning to grow. To fester. He felt that old rage building up inside of him. That hatred. All those years he'd suffered, and he finally knew who was responsible. "What do you need me to do?"

Alyssad's smirk returned. "I have men preparing to depart as we speak." He pulled a golden cord from his black tailcoat. "You will lead them as my commanding officer. They know the location, but you must depart with them immediately. The longer we wait, the more likely they are to slink back into their holes, so we must strike soon."

"I will do it, Your Excellency," Migo said. This was what he was born to do. He'd trained his whole life to lead this charge. "I am yours to command."

Alyssad took the cord and looped it around Migo's shoulder. "Then go. Avenge your father. Bring justice and victory."

Migo filled his chest with air, but the concerned look on Kasti's face gave him pause. He almost thought she would tell him not to do it, but she said nothing. At least she'd be safe here. Migo could sense the sincerity of Alyssad's message. He truly wanted peace for his people, and this was a way to make it happen.

Chapter 37

Katsi stood on a covered balcony overlooking Mazanib, light rain showering down. Somewhere below, among a mass of some four-hundred soldiers, Migo marched through the city, heading west. His journey would take him several cycles to complete. There was a voice at the back of her head that said Migo was marching off to his death. She'd never see him again. The bleeders would kill him, harvest his blood, and burn all the cities of Malahem.

It was wild, of course. Highly unlikely. Migo was too skilled for that. She'd never seen him lose a fight, despite any odds stacked against him.

But these shamans were strong. Even the emperor's general had fallen in battle against them, and how many soldiers had died then? What made Migo's odds any better?

She should be going with him. Her magic would help them win. But even the emperor, a stranger, had more confidence in Migo than she did. Enough confidence to have him lead his army. It seemed absurd.

The smooth, stone railing rippled subtly and Katsi stepped away, watching as the words, "Feel me?" appeared on the surface.

Sands, Adrina was good. Katsi reached out with her power, feeling through the stone, searching for the source of the disturbance, but she felt blind. It was like reaching out in the dark and trying to find the wall. Maybe if she reached farther. She stretched, feeling with her magic, but made no connection.

A voice from directly behind startled her. "Interestingly enough, I'm just right here, but I could sense you reaching out."

Katsi turned and saw Adrina standing in the entryway. "Well, now I feel like a fool."

Adrina did not smile. "Focus near you first. That's where you will be most sensitive to feeling disturbance from others. Have you ever observed a spider in its web?"

Katsi nodded. Plenty of times.

"It is the same. Spiders can remain anywhere on their web, but the moment something disturbs the web, they feel it. They follow the vibration to the captured prey and attack." Her slim eyebrow arched at Katsi. "You are the spider. The ground is your web. With enough training, even the air should be your web. You will feel each disturbance. This will enable you to make precision moves you can now only dream of."

Katsi nodded again. She was willing to do it. She hated feeling inferior like she had when fighting the shaman outside the cave. She would have died were it not for Migo. Worse still, she didn't want to have another moment where she was a helpless little girl, watching as her parents were executed right before her eyes.

Never again would she be such a weakling.

"Very good," Adrina said. "Then read this book." A book popped up from the ground on a stone pillar, directly in front of Adrina. She plucked the book off and handed it to Katsi. "I want you to read it this cycle. We'll discuss after that and begin some training."

Katsi took the book hesitantly. She knew how to read, of course, but not well. How different could a book be from ingredient lists and recipes?

"Katsi," the familiar deep voice of Alyssad rumbled from around the corner. He stepped into view. "Ah, I hope I'm not interrupting a lesson."

"No, Your Excellency," Adrina said. "It was a short lesson. I have given Katsi an assignment. Her first real lesson begins in a few marks."

"Good. No time to waste," Alyssad said, leaning against the doorframe. He did that a lot. Leaning. It was like he was comfortable everywhere with not a concern in the world. It was fun to compare him to Migo, who would have been suspiciously watching every corner, prepared to stab anything that moved. "Come with me, Katsi. I have something to show you."

Adrina bowed and went her own way as Alyssad led Katsi through the castle. "Years ago, before my grandfather built this castle, there was a different castle that resided here, but it had been sitting in ruins for generations. Forgotten, even though it predated the year of Malahem's tidal locking. There had also been caves here, carved by earthmelders. They used to make the greatest structures known to man."

"What happened?"

Alyssad's eyes darkened as he took on a distant look and opened the door to a small room. "War." The room inside was filled with maps, lining the walls in sequential order from one side of the Ring to the other. "There are only a few records from the time, but Malahem was drowning in war before the tidal locking. Thousands were dying every cycle as nations warred against each other, each led by powerful shamans. Bleeder magic was at the heart of it all. Nowhere was safe. Nowhere except for Fidtan, the Silver City, the place where Mazanib now stands."

Alyssad pointed to a small map sealed behind a glass case. The drawing was somewhat faded. "Fidtan was a smaller city then, but they had lots of silver. This kept them safe from the bleeder armies, so many Marems fled and sought refuge here, despite it being a cold city on the fringes of the world. All that changed when the tidal locking occurred. Millions died." His expression became hollow. "Histories stop referencing the bleeder armies after that. A cry went out among Marems. They wanted justice, and my family gave it to them."

"The Massacres."

Alyssad nodded. "Five-hundred years later, and that event still haunts me. I want to set right the wrongs of the past, but I also want to prevent a new bleeder army from arising. I fear we are not prepared to face them if they do."

Katsi's chest tightened. Here was a man with the burden of the whole world on his shoulders. She placed a hand on his forearm. "The mistakes of your ancestors are not your own. We'll find a solution. Migo will be successful. I've never seen him fail."

Alyssad placed his hand over hers, his skin warm and soft. "I'm sure that neither of you will fail to amaze me. You most of all, Katsi. You provide more hope than you think."

Katsi withdrew her hand. Her cheeks warmed.

"I won't disrupt you any longer," Alyssad said. "You should return to reading that book. I've skimmed through it myself. It has some diagrams and examples of using stormcalling specifically." He went and held the door open for her.

"Thank you," Katsi muttered as she hurried out of the room. She'd never been so eager to read in a book in all her life. She skipped past the stairway that led up to the next floor where her room was. It was too plush and gaudy, more fit for a lady than for her. Even though she was wearing a fancy dress. She had to admit that it made her feel pretty, it fit well, and it wasn't restrictive in the least.

It was the first time she'd gone around without wearing her armor in... sands, weeks? And the crazy thing about it was that she actually felt safe. Thick walls and respite from constant danger affected her more than she thought it would.

She headed straight to the library. She'd made a point to memorize routes to different locations in the castle. Despite the castle's enormity, navigating the halls was rather simple, as everything was very distinct so as not to confuse it with anywhere else. She'd noticed a few reading nooks in the library and was eager to try them out. On the second floor was a plush sofa calling her name.

Instead of using the ladder, she simply flew up to it—after checking that the library was empty. The second story of the library was protected by an elaborate wooden railing. She slid her hand across its smooth surface before her feet settled back down. She collapsed onto the sofa, her body sinking luxuriously into its smooth embrace. She hummed with pleasure and cracked open the tomb of a book, flipping through its pages just to glance at some of the pictures.

Wait.

She flipped back a few pages.

Her jaw dropped, eyes widening as she absorbed the image and the words on the page. The illustration was that of a stormcaller commanding a streak of lightning. The page said that summoning lightning had been a common usage of stormcaller power, and that it was the most potent weapon known to man. That would be her soon enough. Flying through the sky throwing lightning.

She caught herself smiling as she turned to the first page.

Chapter 38

Lightning flashed as Hatan was buffeted by a wave of sleet and cold air. Sinteya Jenali's home was only a few blocks away, but during New Season, the center of Jehubal was subject to cold weather.

Hatan was armed to the teeth, prepared to murder every last one of Onik's men. He'd made a terrible mistake, but was far from accepting defeat. Kyel and Shanon had come with him. They would provide support from outside. Both of them were armed with small, heavy crossbows, a regionally uncommon weapon where good wood was too valuable.

"Please don't get killed," Kyel said, his voice tight.

"I'm not going to die, Kyel."

"You're going against twenty men by yourself."

"Yes, but they might as well be scaled rabbits."

"Regardless, I've already lost one father. I don't intend to lose another." Kyel didn't wait for a response, but jogged off to take up his position.

Hatan let out a long breath. Sleet. He'd always thought of himself as more of a commanding officer than a father figure, and Kyel had never seemed like the sensitive type.

But he wouldn't let it get in the way of the objective at hand. Get in, find Sinteya, extract her, kill anybody who blocked his path. The manor was not complex. The wall was barely six feet tall. Kyel and Shanon had posted up on the roofs of nearby buildings. This would give them enough of a vantage to strike at the thugs. They signaled to him. They were ready.

No time to waste. He popped his neck then signaled back to Kyel and Shanon. Time to move. He held his weapon to the side as he rushed toward the wall and jumped up to catch the top of it, pulling himself over. One of Onik's thugs was on the ground, already dead in a pool of his own blood. Kyel or Shanon must have gotten him.

Hatan didn't know much about Sinteya's home, except that there was a servant's door on the side from which he'd approached. There was one man posted outside of it, huddled under the eaves to avoid the rain. He saw Hatan too late, and when he went for his weapon, Hatan's glaive was already in full swing, taking the man in the chest. Hatan closed the distance, covered the man's mouth, and kneed his arm that went to unsheath his shortsword. He held him there until he bled out, then threw his body to the side.

Where had Onik's men managed to rearm themselves?

The door was locked, so Hatan swung at the latch with his glaive and cleaved it in two. So much for a silent entry. He pushed the door open and overheard two men arguing about who should check on the noise. It was a perfect chance to use one of his favorite attacks. He switched to a one-handed grip on his glaive and withdrew a throwing knife with his other hand, then turned the bend in the hall where the two thugs stood in the servant's dining room. They were both armed with crude axes and charged the instant they saw him. Hatan raised his glaive in a high arc, their eyes following it. He threw the knife into one man's neck, then shifted his glaive from a high swing to a low jab and hit the other thug in the thigh. The man fell with a gasp, and Hatan quickly finished him off.

He recognized all three of the men so far as Onik's thugs. They really thought this would work and that Hatan wouldn't deliver on his promise? They would all die, but only after he extracted Sinteya, of course. He retrieved his knife and wiped it off on the man's body. Jenali Manor had lower ceilings and more narrow hallways, so Hatan set his glaive on the floor and took out his sword instead, a straight, double-edged weapon that he'd brought specifically for indoor combat.

There was a shout from somewhere in the manor, but he was too far away. A few short steps led to the main floor, so he eased himself up but paused as he heard careless footsteps. They were heading away from him, so he peeked around the corner. A thug was walking down the hall, back turned. Hatan rushed in with a tiptoed jog until he came up and stabbed the man in the back, covering his mouth at the same time.

He dragged the body into the nearest room.

This hallway intersected the main entryway to the manor, and he could hear a few voices coming from there. He hoped he'd be able to bypass it, but that didn't seem a likely option. A large, potted plant at the corner gave him enough cover to peek around. Five men. And sure enough, the main staircase was there as well. He suspected Sinteya was on the second floor. Another shout came from up above as though to confirm his suspicion.

Could he take out five men by himself? *Surely if Migo can kill six trained soldiers by himself, I can take five street thugs armed with axes.* Now all he needed to do was take them by surprise.

"Hey, who are you?" said someone from behind.

Sleet.

Hatan whirled and flung the throwing knife, catching the thug behind him on the lower torso. The man screamed as he fell against the wall, pulling the knife out, eyes wide as blood seeped against his clothes. "Oh, sands," the man said. "I think... I think I'm going to die." His voice was pure panic, and there was no way the rest of the thugs hadn't heard. Further shouting from the main entry confirmed.

He spun on the group as they trotted his direction cautiously. Hatan didn't give them a chance to strategize. He rushed the closest man, dodging a delayed hack and plunged his sword through the man's gut. Another goon swung at him, but he used the other man's body as a shield as he stabbed another one, then threw the man's dying body at them.

One of them threw his ax at Hatan. It missed horribly, striking the stone floor in front of him, but it ricocheted off and slapped Hatan in the upper shin, just above his boot.

Hatan looked down at the cut on his leg. "Really?" Hatan said, looking back up at the thug who'd thrown it. He pulled out another throwing knife and, with a quick flick, buried the knife in the man's shoulder while driving back another opponent with a deft parry that sliced at fingers.

The third remaining thug shouted for help before swinging at Hatan with his shortsword. Hatan easily deflected it and blocked a kick with a stomp to the man's knee, then slashed across his face. He finished off the wounded as more footsteps came pounding down the stairs. Only four more were on the way. He met them at the bottom of the stairs, flowing through them.

This was the kind of dancing Hatan was comfortable with.

Parry, slash across the chest, push to the left. One down. Duck right, stab the knee, kick him in the face as he trips, quick stab to make sure he dies. Step back to avoid ax, parry, parry, hook the arm on one side, elbow the throat, stab the heart, shove body to the right. Startle the last man by yelling at him, he misses a step and lands awkwardly. Hack him across the thigh, follow through with a jab to the neck as he falls.

All dead.

Blood had littered his clothes and arms like hot rain. This is what they'd wanted. Unrest. But Hatan would ensure that anybody willing to fight against their king would be ended. Executed on sight. Just as he'd promised.

Now where was Onik?

He stomped up the stairs. All premise of stealth was tossed to the wind. At the last step, somebody was waiting for him. They threw an ax at his face, but Hatan had just enough time to duck. He followed up by charging at the man with a strong offensive. The thug managed to block two of Hatan's strokes before taking a sword to the neck and crumpling in a heap.

Something crashed in a room down the upper hallway. For all he knew, Sinteya was already dead, but there was only one way to find out. He marched down the hall and a door hung open. Hatan pushed through it only to find Onik holding a knife to Sinteya's throat. Two other men stood in the room with him, weapons ready.

"Let her go," Hatan said. "You've already lost. Killing her won't save you." The sweat over his brow made his skin itch. There wasn't a safe way out of this. He couldn't fight his way towards her. She would die no matter what. He could see the pleading in her eyes. This was the price she paid for flirting with him.

"Kill them, Hatan," Sinteya said through gritted teeth.

Onik laughed. "He's a man of honor, Lady Jenali. He won't attack us because he knows you'll die. So go ahead, regent. Drop your weapons."

Hatan clenched his jaw. "You're a coward, Onik."

"No, I'm a mercenary. I'm getting paid to do a job, and I mean to earn my coin. The method is not important. Now drop your weapons. I'm not sure how much more pressure her skin can take before it breaks." He pressed the blade of his knife against her skin hard enough that she flinched and it broke through, a bead of blood escaping down the metal surface.

Hatan grunted and threw his sword down, dropped his knife, pulled out six other ones and a dagger, setting them all down in front of him.

Onik laughed again. "And this is why you lose." He withdrew his knife from Sinteya's neck and shoved her away. "Don't worry, she's not in danger. She was in on it too." He pointed at Hatan's weapons. "Clear those out," he said. He kept talking, but Hatan drowned him out. Sinteya had locked eyes with him. It was a setup. All of this was a setup. Apparently his first instinct about her had been correct. She was merely a diversion.

One man aimed his sword at Hatan's face while the other one started kicking his weapons away. "On your knees," he said.

Hatan's hands curled into tight fists as he dropped to his knees. He'd been played. He glared at Sinteya, his anger boiling, but the pleading look in her eyes never faded. She'd been forced into this. But coercion or not, she'd betrayed the king.

He'd fallen for it. Just like Penym said he would. The enemy knew him too well.

But he was equally surprised as the rest of them when Sinteya stabbed Onik in the back. He grunted and spun, backhanding her, but the damage was done. The knife remained in his back, likely having pierced straight to his lung.

So she wasn't bad after all.

Hatan acted without a second thought. He palmed the sword held close to his head with both hands on either side, then slipped his leg out, kicking the man right on the upper thigh. The thug tried to jab the sword at Hatan's head, but Hatan held it firm with both hands and rolled onto his back, hooking the man behind the leg he'd kicked. The thug fell toward him. Hatan caught him with his other leg, pushing him overhead.

Hatan rolled back up, grabbing his last knife still hidden in his boot. He flung it at the thug who'd been carrying his weapons off, hitting him in the hip.

Sinteya threw a small ceramic jar at the same thug as well, hitting him square in the jaw.

Hatan grappled with the man on the floor, trying to wrest his sword away. He had it between his arm and his chest, holding it tight while elbowing him in the face. The sword twisted, scoring a cut on both his arm and his side. Hatan pounded one more time with his elbow, straight into the man's nose with a sickening crunch. He stopped moving.

Hatan got up, sword in hand. Onik lay face down, coughing up his own blood. He approached the last thug who clutched his hip where Hatan's knife must have chipped his bone. He didn't even defend himself as Hatan thrust his blade into his neck.

Sinteya's body shivered as she looked at him. "You m-must leave."

"Not without you," Hatan said. "Now come on."

"No, they're all here," Sinteya said. "They were waiting for you."

"What?" Hatan said, eyes narrowing.

Footsteps pounded toward them from the main entry, echoing off the stone floors.

"Oh no, it's too late," Sinteya covered her face, expression torn with grief.

"Look, we have to get out." He stepped toward the door. Funny. His leg felt a bit weak. He looked down and noticed more blood above his right boot than he remembered. Maybe that ax had done more damage than he'd thought.

"There's no way down besides the stairs," Sinteya said. "They knew this." She grabbed one of the axes and, without warning, threw it at the floor-to-ceiling window, breaking a small hole in it as the ax flew outside.

"What are you doing?" Hatan said, limping towards her.

"Giving you a path out." She pried open the window, clearly trying to make a display of it.

Hatan knew it wouldn't work. Even if he jumped out there, they'd catch up to him. But maybe she could at least get free. "You first," he said.

"No, we're not running." She opened a tall wardrobe, grabbed his arm, and pushed him toward it. "Get inside. I'll cover you."

"Sinteya, no."

She shoved him harder. "Now. We don't have time. Let me do this for you."

Hatan stopped resisting and huddled into the wardrobe while she closed the door and remained outside. She better not try sacrificing herself.

There was a crash from outside.

"Where is he?" a voice demanded. He recognized it immediately. Avidazj.

"He came through this room. He must have gotten out the window," Sinteya said, "but he's wounded! I tried to stab him, but it got him on the side. He's limping. You can still catch him!" Her voice was rushed, frantic.

"Get down there!" Avidazj ordered. Several footsteps trampled off, but one pair walked right past the door to the wardrobe, boots crunching on glass.

"What are you doing? You need to catch him. Isn't that the goal?" Sinteya said, her voice firmer than before.

"Of course," Avidazj said. "But I don't believe the regent made it out the window." The door to the wardrobe swung open and Hatan had a glaive pointed straight at his chest. One glance into the room was all Hatan needed. Ten men were out there. Well armed.

He was finished.

"It's over, regent," Avidazj said. "Come on out."

He'd lost. Sands. He'd lost. His heart dropped. He'd been a fool, walking right into their trap. They'd use him as bait to capture Migo, then kill them both.

He dropped the sword.

He was limping out of the wardrobe when a bolt struck one of Avidazj's men through the ear. Shanon and Kyel were trying to clear a route for him. Hatan rolled toward the window while Avidazj was distracted. Maybe with enough cover from Shanon and Kyel, he could make it out. Worst case scenario, he died. He rolled all the way out the window and fell to the ground below, crashing against the stone.

"That could have gone better," he groaned as he heaved himself back to his feet. Four soldiers had already surrounded him, weapons aimed.

"We've got him down here," one of them shouted.

Two bolts flew in, striking one of them in the shoulder and another one in the head. It wouldn't be enough. Six or seven more soldiers were coming around the manor.

Hatan watched as Kyel and Shanon jumped over the wall.

"No!" Hatan shouted to them. "Leave me."

Brother and sister engaged with the soldiers, killing two of them, but they were driven back.

"Run! Find the others!" Hatan shouted. "That's an order!" He barely caught a glimpse of Shanon turning to run before an ax pommel bashed him in the face, and he fell back to the stone, vision spinning.

He looked back up. Kyel was still fighting. His sister was gone. The fool. Why didn't he run? He tried to yell at Kyel to leave, but somebody kicked him in the gut, knocking the wind from his lungs. Another blow sent him rolling.

"We got him," somebody said.

"I'm sorry." It was Kyel's voice.

Hatan cracked his eyes open. Two men dragged Kyel over.

"What do we do with him, lord?" said one soldier to Avidazj.

"We only need Regent Padarro," Avidazj said, thrusting his blade into Kyel's stomach. The soldiers dropped him beside Hatan.

Kyel looked at Hatan, tears in his eyes. "I'm s-sorry," Kyel said, body shivering as he bled out.

The cold sleet pounded Hatan's face, but he couldn't look away. He reached a hand out to touch Kyel's arm, but he was grabbed roughly and hoisted away. Hatan roared and tried to fight back, but there must have been four people carrying him off, and somebody punched him in the face, cutting him off.

A silent sob escaped him. He'd played right into their game.

Chapter 39

Katsi sat outside on an open balcony of the castle, focused intently on the narrow neck of a bottle. She concentrated on funneling the rain into the small opening, filling it up within mere seconds. She'd been practicing for half a mark, but finally got it down.

Adrina sat beside Katsi on a chair made of remolded stones. She rolled several stone marbles between her fingers. It was like she made a point to use her magic for all kinds of random, clever things just to show off. "Very good," Adrina said, the marbles floating over her head as she stood and set down two more bottles beside the first. "Now do three at the same time."

Katsi groaned. This was all she'd been doing since Migo left four cycles ago. Small, menial concepts meant to refine her focus and "magic memory" as the book called it. If a task was repeated enough, it would be easily remembered later when it was needed.

Adrina returned to her seat and proceeded rolling the marbles in her hands.

Katsi knew the drill. She pulled the water back out of the full bottle, then tried to focus on funneling the water into all three. This felt significantly more complex. Connecting the water into one stream had been easy because she could just grab at the droplets collectively, but now she had to split it. It took her another half a mark just to get the funnels to split in two, but as she tried to separate it into three, the whole connection would break. She growled in frustration.

"Struggling?" Adrina asked.

Katsi threw up her hands. "It's easy with sand or rocks because everything is already touching, but rain is separated into individual droplets. It feels impossible to catch them all, funnel them into one stream, then split it into three."

Adrina nodded. "Focus on the end result, nothing else."

Katsi huffed. It wasn't worth arguing. Adrina was significantly more talented than her, but with enough practice, Katsi was determined to be the most skilled shaman alive. She did as instructed and focused more on the end result of water filling all three bottles. The connection came easy after that, and water started filtering into the bottles almost immediately.

Katsi's jaw dropped and she looked over at Adrina who smiled back at her. "Why did that work?" Katsi asked.

"Your magic is a part of you. It's much simpler than you make it sometimes. Compare it to running. You've been using magic like you're staring at your toes, carefully considering how to lift your leg and lean on the other leg, then swing it forward. You'll barely make any progress that way." She raised a finger at Katsi. "Keep your eyes up. Focus on the path ahead. That's the only way you'll get anywhere."

"Got it," Katsi said. It made sense. She'd been thinking about it too mechanically. It needed to be more natural than that. "Can I call lightning now, then?"

Adrina folded her arms. "It's very dangerous. That might be the last lesson you ever want to learn."

"But I think I have an idea already."

"It requires connecting two different things with immaterial energy. We'll have to try that much later."

"Let her try," Alyssad's deep voice resonated from behind.

Katsi was all smiles to see him come to encourage her while Adrina's face became expressionless. "Very well, Your Excellency." She strode out into the rain at the edge of the balcony. "Katsi, you'll want some elevation. The more clouds, the better. You'll also need to force quite a bit of air up, ideally from the Frozen Waste to help cool—"

"It's okay, Adrina," Katsi said. "I read all of that in the books." Katsi had read everything she could find about summoning lightning. It was more complex than anything else she'd done so far, and the books mentioned setting up optimal conditions for lightning, but the entire Ring was already set up for optimal conditions. The immediacy of both hot and cold air seemed to be the primary factor, which was why lightning was already common enough. Now she just needed to learn how to direct it herself.

She connected with a gust of wind and burst out into the air, happy to be free. She'd remembered to create an air pocket a little late and ended up getting pelted by a few drops of rain. She laughed at herself and rose to the edge of the clouds. Thunder rumbled around her. Could conditions be any better? Even the emperor was watching.

Fortunately, the angle of the castle blocked her off from the city so that there wouldn't be any unwanted spectators. She closed her eyes, focusing on the energy around her. The armlets on her shoulder warmed. She'd switched the armlets to her left arm so they could hide under her sleeve, since her right arm was exposed. The existence of the armlets was to be her own little secret. Well, and Migo's.

She tried to do as the books she read instructed, mainly finding the initial connection with the energy. It had a similar feeling to magic itself. It was also hard to distinguish. Practically everything around her, the air included, felt as though it had some semblance of magical energy. Perhaps, as Adrina instructed, it was simpler than she thought it to be. All she had to do was think of the end result, and channel the energy accordingly.

Her eyes snapped open. Wind rushed in and the clouds churned above her. Once the energy was gathered, she would need a target to direct it. She looked to the ground, selecting a tree that stood alone among the rocks.

"Come on," she whispered under her breath. Her hair started to rise. It was building. She could feel it. A tickle ran across her arms. She stretched a hand out towards the tree. The sensation reminded her of saliva building up just before vomiting.

A blinding flash filled her vision. It was so sudden, she hadn't even had time to close her eyes before it was gone, leaving a blackened afterimage scorched into her vision. The air around her thundered and the armlets burned hot against her skin. Her heart fluttered uncomfortably. Had it worked? She blinked a hundred times until her vision slowly cleared, then looked down at the tree.

It was cracked and smoldering.

Katsi flew back to the balcony where Adrina was giving her a polite clap while Alyssad wore his customary smirk.

"I'm impressed," Adrina said. "But next time, don't make your body the conduit. Keep it in the air."

Katsi nodded, too pleased to think of a witty response.

That was it. Katsi was a *real* stormcaller.

Chapter 40

M igo couldn't think of a worse time to be on a long march. He'd been soaking wet for twelve straight cycles, heading east of Mazanib. He missed Genda. In fact, he missed having anybody familiar around him. All the unknown faces were a peculiarity to him. They were strangers. They weren't his soldiers. Would they trust him? Could he trust them? They had no reason to believe he could bring them victory. Had the emperor really just put him in charge of his army within one mark of meeting him?

Perhaps that testing fight was all it really took.

Of course, it was only temporary. Migo would help eradicate the threat of a shaman army laced with waheshi monsters, fulfilling justice for his father at the same time, then he'd return home to his people. They'd finally be able to enjoy a semblance of peace. He'd probably even get married. He could just imagine Hatan giddily lining up potential suitors.

But the idea didn't excite him.

He didn't dare acknowledge why.

The emperor's captain, Shakairi, approached him from the front line. "Lord king," he said. "We are close to the last known location of the dark shamans." The man had the palest of skin, his hair almost white, and he was dressed in heavy metal armor, studded with silver. The value of such armor was beyond anything Migo could afford.

"Have scouts been able to confirm?" Migo said.

Shakairi rubbed his neck. "The scouts have not returned."

Dead. That's what he insinuated. "Gather the soldiers. I will speak to them."

"As you wish, lord," Shakairi said, nodding his head in a short bow. They still questioned his authority. He didn't blame them, but he expected them to at least have more faith in the emperor's decision.

Shakairi went to fulfill Migo's orders, calling the troop to a halt. 419 soldiers in total. That was all the emperor saw fit to send, even though his entire army was said to be nearly ten thousand strong. Aside from the one hundred that had recently been slaughtered by these very same shamans. But why not send more? What were his other soldiers occupied with that he wouldn't send them on this "vital" mission?

Migo climbed the tallest point near, a rocky shelf no taller than his head. He crouched and fiddled with his poleaxe, waiting patiently while the soldiers gathered around. They didn't know what to expect of him, this young king who'd been entrusted with their lives. For all he knew, he was leading them to their deaths. If there were more waheshi out there... plenty of them *would* die. But not only that, his life would also be in their hands. He needed their allegiance.

Migo finally spoke as the stormcarts came to a squeaking halt. "You do not know me," he said, voice fierce, clashing against the patter of rain. "I was once a scorned prince. I have risen through great animosity. I have fought against the enemy. I am young, but I have killed many shamans. I have also killed several of the monsters that they've created. What we will face soon may be unlike anything you have seen. Everything you have trained for has led you to this mission. To defend the empire. In Jehubal, we have a saying." He rose to his full height. "'To the end.' The end doesn't come to us, we go to it. Despite fear. Despite pain. Despite enemies. Despite all obstacles.

We are the champions of our own destiny. To the end—whether that's this very moment—or in ten years. You go boldly."

"Now comrades," Migo said, coming down from the height, unlatching the leather wrap on his poleaxe. "Prepare yourselves. The end will not come easy."

"To the end!" a soldier shouted. Others joined in, voices hollow in the suppressive rain, but a cold wind changed it into a soft flurry of snow.

A fog of breath escaped Migo's nose as he turned back to the east. He would lead the charge. Let the soldiers see him take down a waheshi. Let them know the waheshi could be killed like any other beast.

Two soldiers led the way for Migo, taking him to the site of the previous battle. They cleared the edge of the trees as they approached the Frozen Waste. A grassy plain stretched out before them, scattered with boulders and stubborn rockberry bushes.

One of their soldiers came running across the field towards them. Migo recognized him as one of the scouts they'd sent out two cycles ago. He was unarmed, and his armor had been discarded. All he wore was a simple tunic, his pants, and his boots.

He could have escaped from the enemy, but Migo doubted that. More likely, he'd been compromised. Migo held his hand up in a fist, and the soldiers behind him stopped marching as they watched the lone soldier run towards them across the plains.

Migo kept his eyes up and about. The shaman army might burst from the ground for all he knew. They knew far too little of what the shamans were capable of.

"Help," the soldier screamed just before he slipped on the slick grass and fell.

One of the two soldiers ahead of Migo moved as though to go help, but Migo grabbed his arm. "Wait."

"Lord, he's one of ours," Captain Shakairi said.

But Migo wasn't so sure. The fallen scout struggled to get up. He screamed, a sound escaping his mouth that sent shivers running down Migo's spine. It was part human, part... something else.

Migo led the way, taking careful steps towards the tortured scout.

"Poison," the scout said, still struggling on hands and knees, crawling towards them. "They poisoned me." He looked up at Migo, his eyes a milky black. His skin looked like it was stretching, expanding, and losing its color, shifting to a dark gray.

"Sleet and sand. It can't be," Migo said. "Eyes up, weapons ready!" He shouted.

The scout screamed one last time before his body began to change dramatically, arms and legs stretching, shoulders expanding, horns cracking out of his skull as his face elongated, clothes falling in tatters.

Waheshi. They were mutated humans.

A small, rocky hill across the stretch of plain about half a mile away became alive with activity as dark creatures emerged. An eerie stillness settled over the plain as the newly formed waheshi flexed its claws and regarded him with a snarl.

Migo charged it, sidestepping its haphazard swipe, and cleaved straight into its head. He let out a gasping breath and turned back to the army. "To the end!" he bellowed, and together they marched out onto the plains.

"Keep them in ranks," Migo said to Captain Shakairi. "We'll be able to fight the monsters better if we keep men together, but they move fast. Long weapons with silver are the most effective. Put them on the flanks so we don't get surrounded."

"Aye, lord," Shakairi said, turning to the lieutenants and divvying out orders.

The soldiers formed up into squads but remained together as one unit. They shuffled hastily, shouting orders up and down the lines before proceeding forward. The shaman army lingered around the hill, an intermingling of waheshi and shamanfolk. If they were bold enough to stand against the armies of the emperor, then the empire faced greater threat than he'd ever imagined. It made him even more grateful that he'd been able to resolve the tension with the Bayvana Tribe. This rebel operation of bleeder shamans—how far did it spread?

He wondered if his father's killer was there among them. He'd never know, of course. The only way to ever achieve justice was to kill them all.

As they slowly walked closer, he tried to tally how many waheshi there were. Ten? Twenty? They wouldn't stand still long enough for him to count. He'd been able to kill four with only four people, though one was Katsi. Surely they would overwhelm the shamans here, though there was still the question of what magic abilities they would use. There were perhaps only a dozen people in their ranks, but even one earthmelder would be enough of a challenge.

Migo and his little army had crossed more than half the space, and the shaman army still hadn't moved. Perhaps they wanted everyone close enough so that none of his troops could run away.

Soundlessly, the waheshi all seemed to follow a synchronous order. They stopped their shifting and began walking towards them.

"Forward," Migo shouted as some of the soldiers faltered.

The waheshi sprinted at them in unison, creating a thunderous sound as their claws and hoofs tore at the ground. Another sound, deeper, more resonant, thrummed like a drum from underground, growing closer.

They had prepared for this possibility. "Halt," Migo shouted. The order echoed down the line. He dropped to one knee. The front wave of soldiers did the same. They waited until the waheshi were close enough. It didn't take long. "Release!"

The second row of soldiers hurled a volley of nearly sixty javelins. The waheshi ignored them and charged on. Most javelins merely missed or bounced off the waheshi's skin, but a few of them managed to stick, causing more than a glancing blow. Only two waheshi faltered. Migo rose back up. "Charge!" he said, sprinting ahead of the troops, not bothering to look back and make sure they followed his order. They had to, or they'd die. Victory was the only option.

Two waheshi were aiming for him. He'd need support. He held his poleaxe low as he ran. The attack he planned was bold, but he needed to keep himself from getting attacked by two waheshi at once. He headed for one of them, only three steps away when he brought his poleaxe up in a powerful swing. His hammer met the waheshi's jaw. He dived to his knees, sliding for its legs. The other waheshi tried to claw at him, but its attack was blocked by the body of the other one that Migo was now beneath.

Migo slid on the slick ground, reversing his swing. The ax cut down across its torso, stopping just between its back legs. That had to hurt, but the beast made no sound. Migo wrenched his poleaxe free, twisting out from beneath it, dodging a hind leg that tried to stomp at him. He rose up from behind, driving his poleaxe down into the back of its neck as it tried to turn and face him.

The other waheshi leapt over. Migo dropped down, but its clawed hand still bashed across the shoulder, the blow deflected by his shoulder plate. He jabbed it with the spear of his poleaxe, but that did little more than scratch its skin. He spared a glance at the army. The line of waheshi had reached the troops, and bodies were literally soaring as waheshi tore the ranks apart.

"Come on," Migo yelled. He batted off a claw and skipped away from the other, but it dove in at him with jaw agape, jagged teeth snapping. Migo whipped his silver dagger out, slicing the waheshi across the snout before stabbing back down, wedging the dagger into the top of its mouth. He was unable to dodge as one of its hands grabbed him by the side, claws digging through his leather armor.

Migo withdrew the dagger and jabbed down two more times, one stab piercing through its skull.

The beast's grip loosened as it dropped.

He looked back at the other soldiers. They appeared to have had some success. Three or so other waheshi lay motionless, but there were at least a dozen left and it looked like fifty soldiers had already fallen.

The ground erupted beneath a batch of soldiers that were flanking a waheshi, jabbing it in the back. A shower of stones fell from the sky, battering the army. But the soldiers fought on, despite their injuries. They knew the cost of defeat.

Migo ran to help the nearest soldiers as the ground beneath him trembled. The shamans were a problem, but he didn't know what was worse, stone hail or almost invincible monsters.

Sliding in from behind, Migo hacked the leg of a waheshi clean off. It didn't help that it had six legs, but at least one less might give them an advantage. The two nearest soldiers jumped in to help, gouging the creature in the side. Migo went to the other side, bashing his poleaxe into its ribs. It let out a rare shriek, a terrifying sound that made Migo's body shiver. He rolled away to dodge a backhanded attack from it. The other soldiers jabbed at it again, one of them scoring a hit along the back of its head.

Another waheshi charged in, tackling both soldiers to the ground as Migo hacked the injured one in the head.

The two soldiers had been speared through the heads by the new waheshi's tail before Migo could even help. He climbed the body of the dead one and jumped down at the other one from above. It twitched away from him, stabbing its long tail. He changed the arc of his swing to cut at its tail instead, barely grazing it out of the way as he landed on the ground. He hoped the rest of the soldiers were faring alright. Even if they killed all the waheshi, they'd still have to deal with the shamans.

This waheshi was fast. And smart. It used its tail as a feint, then cut at him with both its front legs. His only option was to dive backwards, jumping away as quickly as he could. One of its talons slid across his thigh, tearing through the thin padding. He landed and rolled away, ignoring the pain lacing up at him as he rose and put weight on his injured leg.

The waheshi was about to dive at him when Captain Shakairi barreled into its side, thrusting his longsword through its chest. It shrieked and bashed at him with a full swing. Shakairi stumbled away in a crash of metal, but he swung at the waheshi again, severing an arm.

Migo moved in to assist, and they both aimed for its head in a joint assault that it couldn't avoid. Both weapons broke through with a thick crunch. Migo's desire for full plate mail studded with silver resurfaced. Shakairi had just taken a full blow, and though his armor looked slightly battered, the man seemed unharmed. "There are more than we thought. Heavy losses," he huffed to Migo.

"No time to worry about that," Migo said, pointing toward another group of twenty soldiers fighting defensively against two waheshi. Their line had broken into scattered groups. They'd get slaughtered.

"Regroup!" Migo shouted. "To me!"

Shakairi repeated Migo's order, their voices barely carrying over the din of battle. The troops were slowly coming together as Migo rushed to help. He glanced over his shoulder to make sure they were still clear, but the shamans were closer, coming down from the hill. A wall of rocks came showering towards them.

"Look out!" Migo yelled. There were too many to dodge them all. He ducked under the largest and threw his arm up over his head as a few rocks pelted him, one crashing painfully against his elbow.

Shakairi took a massive stone in the back and tumbled to the ground. The earth around him rose up like a wave and came crashing down. Even silver armor wouldn't save him from that.

Migo growled and spun on the shamans. He had to get close enough. Maybe if he killed them, their dark magic on the waheshi would fade away. He didn't know if that's how magic worked, but he had to try something.

They saw him coming and the ground around him started to shift. It felt like he was running through deep sand, his steps barely carrying him forward. A shaman got close enough to attack, but Migo could barely stand. The dirt itself was splashing against his shins. The shaman warrior swung for him but Migo deflected it. Their blades clashed over and over as Migo slowly sank into the ground.

"NO!" he shouted, struggling against the earth itself. He caught the shaman's blade between his ax and the haft, then twisted his grip, snapping the sword in two. Then with a one-handed swipe, he hacked across the shaman's hip.

The shaman fell with a scream before Migo stabbed him in the leg. The other shamans came forward. There were eleven of them left.

Where were Migo's other soldiers?

Migo glanced back. The troops had never fully regrouped, and Captain Shakairi was completely out of sight. He would have no help. He pulled out his silver dagger. Several of the shamans were watching him as he still fought against the ground.

"He's a fighter," one of them said.

He'd show them how much of a fighter he was. He tried to guess which one was earthmelding against him. It was a woman, eyes concentrated, hands flexed. He flung the dagger once they'd gotten a few steps closer, aiming for her chest. A rock soared through the air to knock the dagger away, but it was too late. The shaman turned to dodge, but the dagger struck her just below the clavicle.

The ground instantly stopped fighting against him. He heaved his feet free, but a throwing disk embedded itself in his right shoulder. He hadn't even seen them throw it. Something sharp struck him between the shoulder blades, and he stumbled forward, throwing a haphazard jab at the nearest shaman. The shaman skipped away, and a rock thunked into the side of Migo's head. He fell down and the ground started closing in around him.

Someone kicked his arm, and his poleaxe was thrown from his grip.

It was over. All his effort was in vain. No vengeance. No justice. He fought against the dirt, but it kept piling on until he was held down, nothing but his head and neck were above ground. The battle still raged on behind him, but it had dwindled to the sound of men screaming, emptying their lungs of breath for the last time.

A sword's blade pressed up against Migo's chin as a woman squatted in front of him.

"Wait," one of the shamans said, a man wearing a tight brown robe. He placed his hand on the woman's shoulder and squeezed. "Do you sense it?" He took a deep breath as he squatted next to her. He removed the veil from his face, revealing a scar across his forehead, and stared at Migo intensely.

"There is strength in this one," somebody said from behind, prodding Migo's head with a foot.

"King of Jehubal," the scarred one said, tilting his head at Migo.

They recognized him. Migo didn't have time to consider the implications. "Spare the men. You've won," Migo said.

"We can't do that," answered one of the other shamans.

The scarred one held up a hand. "Tell me, King Rikaydian, what brought you so far from home?"

"I seek justice," Migo said firmly. It was difficult to breathe with the muddy earth pressing against him.

"Justice?" one of them said. "By murdering victims of genocide? Now there's a claim."

"I care nothing for the extermination order," Migo said, "but one of you killed my father, and I came to seek justice."

"None of us killed your father, king," one said.

"Lies. There is no alternative."

The scarred one looked at the other shamans before addressing Migo again. "We can show you the truth. We can tell you exactly who killed your father. Your blood connection with him and your witnessing of his death can reveal enough for that."

"How did you know that?" Migo said, narrowing his eyes at the scarred shaman. Men were still dying behind him. He needed to end this.

"Everyone around Jehubal at the time remembers the story of your father's death, dying to save his son. A noble deed." His eyes softened. "We can show you the truth. No more questions. We have a skilled seer who can share the sight. Our magic can tap into the scene, remember it, and connect even more than that."

"You offer too much," argued one of the other shamans.

"He seeks justice. We will help him find it," the scarred shaman said, holding an object in his palm that Migo could not see, but the rest of the shamans regarded it with wide-eyed expressions.

"Spare the men," Migo said.

The shamans shared a look with each other, a couple of them nodding. The scarred one leaned closer to Migo's head. "We propose a bargain. We will spare the remaining soldiers, have a seer connect with your memory to reveal the truth of your father's murderer, but in return, we require some of your blood."

"You would corrupt me."

"We cannot. This kind of magic can only be done if the subject is willing."

It was insane. There was no way Migo could trust them, but also there was a reason they were asking for permission. Willingness must have had something to do with it or they wouldn't be bargaining with him at all—they could just cut him open and take all the blood they wanted. "Swear it. Swear that I will not become a waheshi, that I won't become your slave."

"We swear it. Honor still exists among the Shavarani Tribe, Migo. As surely as you still possess it."

They would turn him. He'd become a monster. Maybe this was how waheshi were made. They would do something to poison him. Either way, he was a dead man, but the soldiers behind him could still survive. Their screams tore at his thoughts. At least in his death he could spare them and a few soldiers would get back to the emperor to warn him of the danger here. Whether they'd stick to their word or not, he didn't see an alternative. "I accept."

The sounds of battle behind him stopped an instant later as the waheshi pulled back. He tried to look back and could tell that the troops were withdrawing. The waheshi must have followed some silent command. "And you won't pursue them?" Migo clarified.

"We will not," said the scarred shaman. "Though they may end up attacking us again someday. We hold no guarantee if that happens."

That was understandable, but Migo made no response.

One of the shamans gestured, and Migo's body slowly began to resurface.

"Now, for the rest of our bargain," the shaman said, rising up to his feet. He took the silver dagger from the other shaman's chest, holding a hand over the part where she'd been stabbed before turning back to face Migo.

He was surrounded, and he was pretty sure they wielded real seculas. The dark iron blades simply had an unnatural, greenish hue. His poleaxe was on the ground behind one of them, so if they decided to attack, he wouldn't stand a chance. He'd have to take it in stride.

The scarred shaman held a dagger out to Migo. It was completely clean of any blood. In his other hand, he held a vial. "It's best if you do it yourself. Slice along your arm. I'll collect it here, then I can seal the wound. After that, we'll proceed with the vision. Understood?"

Migo took the dagger, cold washing over his skin. So this is what he'd come to—bleeding himself for shamans so that he could discover who his father's murderers were. He set his jaw and pressed the blade against his arm.

Chapter 41

Katsi quickly discovered that if she flew through the halls, then Adrina couldn't sense her through a connection with the ground. She was on her way from the library to a third floor balcony on the west side of the castle. She kept her feet just above the surface of the floor so that she could drop back down if she saw anybody else. Opportunities to practice summoning lightning were few and far between. Adrina was too cautious, although Alyssad didn't mind at all. In fact, he seemed to relish every chance to see her growing abilities.

As she floated around the corner, she spotted the tail of a black cloak disappearing into a doorway. Was that the emperor? She couldn't help but go closer. Two hushed voices echoed out from the room. Katsi lingered near the door. They'd attempted to close it, but it still hung open just a crack.

"What are you doing back here?" Alyssad's unmistakable voice rumbled.

The other voice belonged to a woman, matured, almost raspy. "This is my home as well, in case you forgot. Tell me about the visitors."

"The girl is powerful. More than she recognizes. She may be the last piece we need."

A warm trickle of pride dripped down Katsi's spine.

"The boy is no shaman, but he is strong. He was born to lead. I could feel all that just by being in the same room as him, but he is, however, a shroud."

"You sense nothing?"

"Nothing at all. No outcomes."

Were they talking about Migo? What did it mean that he was a shroud?

"You killed him, then?" the woman asked. "He is a danger. We have no room for anomalies."

Katsi's heart skipped, pleading to know that Alyssad hadn't sent Migo to his death.

"He is a Marem," Alyssad's voice was a growl, threatening. Who was this woman to be addressing the emperor in such a way? "He may be the perfect general, but we will soon find out. I have sent him to wipe out the remainder of the Shavarani Tribe. If he succeeds, then he proves himself a worthy general, just in time for the girl to help finish the job with the Maedari."

"And if he fails?" Katsi said, pushing open the door and floating into the doorway.

Alyssad stood with his arms down by his side. His eyes carried a hint of surprise before he broke into his signature smirk. Every space of the wall was covered by paintings. Paintings of the sun at the edge of a sea, snowy fields, flowery hills, mountains, and even people, most of them looking like Alyssad and his family. The woman he had been speaking to regarded Katsi with folded arms and narrowed eyes. She was somewhere in her mid-forties, and her black hair had the occasional gray, but her brown skin was smooth. She was dressed like a commoner, a simple black robe and brown leather pants. Not the type of person she expected to see talking to the emperor like that.

"Katsi," Alyssad said, voice dark. "I'm not surprised to find you eavesdropping."

"Ears are for hearing," Katsi said. "Now what about Migo?"

Alyssad cleared his throat and smoothed down his shirt. "If you'll excuse me, mother, I need to show Katsi something."

His mother? Katsi regarded her with renewed interest, but the woman's expression didn't change.

Alyssad walked right past Katsi and into the hall. "Come," he said without looking back.

Katsi wanted to stand her ground just to express her defiance, but Alyssad wasn't paying attention to whether or not she followed, and she didn't want to look like a fool in front of his mother. She groaned silently and stomped after him. She'd sworn that she would not become a tool to somebody else's design. Nobody would use her again, and yet here she was, receiving training and hospitality from the emperor—and in exchange for what?

"Where are we going?" Katsi asked as Alyssad led her through a hall with three guards standing sentinel at different intervals.

"You want answers. I will give them."

"That was a mysterious way of not answering my question."

He gave her a hard look. Perhaps hearing his mother speak to him had emboldened her, but she didn't think she was being disrespectful. She was merely stating the truth.

"How much do you know of seers?" Alyssad said as they reached the end of the hall where a flight of stairs led up to a single door.

"Probably not enough," Katsi said. "My tribe doesn't have one, and I only skimmed over a few things in the books I've been reading."

They went through the door and Katsi found herself in a lavish bedroom, dark tapestries hanging from the high, arched ceiling. It was smaller than Katsi's own room, with less furnishings, but the bed looked like something people would drown in. A massive window let in plenty of light, but Alyssad closed the shades, throwing the room into shadow. He then approached another wall and pulled the curtains aside, revealing a bookshelf, though there were only a few books on the shelves. Instead, it contained ten orbs of polished stone resting atop hooked bases to keep them in place.

Each of the orbs glowed with a subtle light varying in shades of violet, blue, or red. A label was placed in front of the base, designating different names. Katsi recognized only one: Alishara.

On a shelf beneath the orbs was a row of jewelry—necklaces, cuffs, armlets, rings, a myriad assortment—all decorated similarly to the armlets Katsi wore, hidden beneath her sleeve.

"I have been establishing connections with several seers across Mala-hem," Alyssad explained. "These orbs have allowed me to receive messages from them. I've been hoping for the opportunity to connect with a storm-caller for some time now."

"Why?"

He leaned against the shelf, eyes scanning across her features as his face glowed from the rainbow of colors beside him. "You might very well be the most powerful stormcaller for centuries. You could be the very key to controlling the Maedari."

"Control them? Don't we want to eliminate them?"

Alyssad smirked. "Katsi, the Maedari can be a powerful weapon. Light-ning is one of the few things that waheshi are susceptible to."

"Yes, so are humans." This was not a good idea. The dark look in Alyssad's eyes was frightening.

"Many people have died because of me." He reached out a hand as if to touch her, but he dropped it away. "And they will continue to die unless we end this war. Once the war is over, we can find a way to perhaps end the Maedari."

"I will not be your tool," Katsi said firmly.

Alyssad shook his head slightly, touching one of the armlets on the shelf. "You are so much more than a tool, Katsi. You are hope."

"My decisions are my own."

"I expect nothing less."

"And what about Migo? If you've been in touch with Alishara, did she not mention him? Was it you that told her to keep me and Migo apart?"

"I have not been aware of that, though I understand why. Migo is considered a shroud, it means that seers have difficulty discerning him clearly. Seers have a tendency to rely on that too much at times. For some, it creates fear, but I believe in our case it can work to our advantage. It means our enemies won't see Migo coming or know what his next move will be."

"So he is a tool as well."

"Everyone has their uses, Katsi. It does not mean they are being manipulated. Migo is fighting against them because he wants to. Our wills there aligned."

"And what if mine and yours do not?" Katsi folded her arms and stared him in the eyes, craning her neck to look up at him.

He did not look away, but leaned forward slightly. His hand lingered over one of the armlets, rubbing its surface with his thumb. She was aware of how close their bodies were, but she stood her ground. "I'm sure they will eventually. I am a patient man when I have to be."

"Then I look forward to trying your patience," Katsi said, turning to leave without another word, smiling at her own cleverness. She almost expected him to grab her arm or call out to her in some way, but silence followed her as she left the room.

She wanted one thing to be clear: she would be controlled by nobody. But also, she had to wonder what the emperor was doing with so many enhancement artifacts. Perhaps that's what the emperor was really after when he'd sent his soldiers to find that shaman hideout. Would he care that she wore two of her own?

Chapter 42

Migo shivered, watching as his blood seeped from his wound and into the vial that the scarred shaman held to his arm, wondering how much of it their vile magic required. The sleet had shifted into full blown snow.

A wall of nine waheshi remained, standing in a line beside the shamans. Some of them were injured or even missing limbs, but they paid no mind. The emperor's soldiers hadn't done as well as Migo would have hoped. Nobody was prepared to fight these monsters. Nobody but him and two of his soldiers. And now he'd been captured.

"That should do," the scarred shaman said, withdrawing the vial and placing a hand over Migo's wound. He withdrew his hand a moment later, and the cut was sealed, though still visible. "It will heal quickly."

Migo pulled his sleeve down, unsure what to think of this form of magic. Katsi had used a healing balm, but nothing that could so immediately close a wound like that. Everything he knew about magic was coming into question with each new cycle it seemed. He flexed his forearm and even the pain seemed little more than a memory.

"Follow me," the shaman said. The other shamans formed a ring around Migo as he followed them to the hill. As they got closer, the ground itself opened up, and they walked into the hill. It was as though Migo were walking straight into a grave, like those of old. Many scents struck his senses as soon as he got beneath the ground. The top of the tunnel was lined with glowing stones that mimicked the amber glow of the sun. Instead of echoing, their footsteps were soft and muted. It was only then that Migo realized they were walking on a thin layer of moss.

The tunnel led them into a large chamber with a steaming hole in the middle. A couple other tunnels led away, but the main chamber was built for a community. There were beds and shelves lining the earthen walls. A few other shamanfolk hid within the large cavern, watching Migo warily.

The scarred shaman paused in front of the steaming chasm. It was filled with water, the scent of salt heavy from its steam.

A shaman who looked like he was no older than 21 came before Migo. "I will grant the vision," she said, and held out her hand. The scarred shaman poured some of Migo's blood on her palm.

"Place your hand on hers," the scarred shaman said.

Migo did so, his hand slapping into his own blood.

"Think of your father's murder," the seer said. "Remember it."

Migo's vision started to go blurry, spinning just a bit until everything around him disappeared in a gray cloud.

The storm. A Maedari raged around him. Migo hung from the ledge of the stone walkway. His father was fighting against the shaman assassin. His father's blood spattered across stones. The image warped differently than how Migo remembered it, his entire vision becoming red with the blood until it refocused on the assassin. It twisted and flickered for quite a while, as though trying to break through a barrier.

"I'm trying," a voice said as though coming from a great distance.

A person formed in the vision like a gray silhouette that slowly grew brighter and more distinct until the face of a woman finally formed, one that looked vaguely like Katsi, only a few years older. This was the assassin. The next face materialized quickly, that of a much older woman, dressed in the garb of the shamans that often skirted the Scorched Waste. Her hands were wrapped around a ball that was halfway submerged in water. The assassin stood across from her. Their mouths moved, but Migo could not hear the words.

The vision shook again as it tried to focus in on the ball. The motion was violent and Migo's head felt a tightening pressure. The pain of it increased, clouds swirling around him until the vision burst, granting him the quickest glance of a single face of a man around fifty years old, brown skin, long black hair.

Migo blinked. He was lying on the ground next to the steaming chasm. He sat up with a gasp. The shaman seer who'd supplied the vision sat across from him, trembling from the exertion.

"What did you see, Hadiv?" the scarred shaman asked, helping the seer back to her feet.

"We got all of it," Hadiv said, looking at Migo with a dark expression. "Strong blood, indeed. We should kill him where he lies."

"There is a purpose for him coming here," the scarred shaman said. "Tell us what you saw." The other shamans all stood around, eagerly waiting for the explanation.

Migo still didn't understand what had happened. He'd seen three faces, and all of them had seemed so vaguely familiar, but none of it made sense.

"The assassin," Hadiv said, "was Sirandui Danan. It was difficult to reveal her features because she's already dead. The king knows her as Katsi's mother. She received her orders from none other than Alishara. And the last face." Hadiv paused, sparing Migo a glance. "The last face was that of Ranaz. He is the one who ordered the death of your father."

The other shamans nodded as if that all made perfect sense.

"Ranaz?" Migo said, getting to his feet, the fire in his voice was stronger than he'd intended. He clenched his fists so tight that his nails dug into his palms. "Who is that?"

Hadiv took a drink of water before answering. "You know him by a different name. Alyssad Malrabia. He is not who you think he is."

"The emperor?" Migo's vision spun again. "No. That's not who we saw in the vision. The emperor is much younger."

Hadiv jerked her chin at the scarred shaman. "Nagesh. You explain this to the child."

Who was she calling a child?

Nagesh, the scarred shaman, folded his arms and let out a long breath before speaking. "Migo, most of the shamans in this room are centuries old. Bleeder shamans have the ability to create potions derived from the blood of the youth that allows us to extend our lives. Ranaz has been doing this since before the tidal locking."

Migo blinked. "That was 500 years ago."

"Yes."

A shiver sent a wave across his skin. He wanted to disbelieve them. He wanted to believe that they'd poisoned him and shown him whatever they wanted, but he couldn't. He knew it was true. "The emperor is a shaman?"

"The most powerful shaman in ages. He has made sure of that."

Another shiver. Katsi. Katsi was with him even now. "What do you mean he's made sure of that?"

Nagesh tossed a hand up. "The extermination order for starters. He's responsible for more death than you can possibly fathom. Not thousands, but millions. To maintain his power, whenever he hears of other shamans of reputable strength, he takes them to his castle, tests their power, then slaughters them to create his enchanted artifacts that strengthen his power even more."

"Sleet and sand," Migo muttered, his heart plunging. Katsi had gone to her death. "I have to go." He shuffled toward the exit, but they blocked his path.

"Migo," Nagesh said. "We know you seek justice, but you cannot defeat Ranaz."

"Then what do I do?" Migo turned, roaring at them. "I can't let him kill her!" Even without magic, Alyssad bested Migo in armed combat as though he were a babe.

Nagesh held up a closed fist. "We offer a solution, but again, this must be done willingly or it will not have the potency necessary."

So this was it, then. This was how they turned people. No matter. "I'll do it," he said aloud. "Whatever is necessary, I am willing."

Nagesh nodded to the other shamans. One of the shamans pulled out an iron pot while another went to the chasm and ladled out a scoop of the hot water, pouring it into the pot. The others scrambled off to some nearby shelves sorting through herbs and trinkets, bringing them over to the pot. Nagesh uncurled his fingers. It was a single tooth, sharp and straight, like that of a lizard.

"This is the tooth of a drakotah," Nagesh explained. "My ancestors hunted them to extinction, or so we thought, because their bodies provide extraordinary potency in potions. Pairing a drakotah potion with your unique strengths... well, it's not something that any of us have ever had the opportunity to see. If you take the potion, it will give you the strength you need to defeat Ranaz."

Migo nodded without thought. "Do it, then."

Nagesh added the tooth and Migo's blood to the potion, then stepped away.

"Nagesh," said Hadiv. "It needs to be you."

"You forget," Nagesh said. "Alishara has my blood under oath. If I perform this enchantment, she will know immediately. My life could be forfeit."

"And this was your idea, wasn't it, Nagesh? You are the strongest bleeder among us. It must be you."

Nagesh clenched his jaw and cast Migo a wary look before shaking his head. "Casting all my bets on a shrouded Marem," he said in a dark tone. "Very well." He crouched down to the pot and proceeded to stir, muttering words that from a language Migo couldn't understand. He added the drakotah tooth and emptied the rest of Migo's blood from the vial. Steam issued from the pot, and Migo could feel his heart pounding loud within his chest.

Nagesh stopped stirring, and the contents of the pot were emptied into a large metal cup. He handed the cup to Migo with a trembling hand. "Drink it. All of it." His voice was hoarse, as though creating the concoction had drained him.

Migo looked down into the contents of the potion, refusing to question what other strange chunks floated in there.

"There is the chance that it could kill you," Nagesh explained. "I've never heard of a Marem drinking a drakotah potion, but I have a strong suspicion that you will be unharmed. Or... I should say... not dead."

"Stop talking," Migo said, building up the nerve. This was it. This is what he'd come to. Trusting in a few shamans who he'd been fighting against only moments ago. Insanity.

"To the end," he said to himself, then tipped the contents into his mouth, swallowing past every unsavory flavor that burned across his throat. It was acid, poison. Surely this would kill him, but he swallowed anyway. Whatever it took, he would save Katsi. An image of the waheshi came to mind. They were once humans, but now they were slaves to their shaman masters. Monsters.

Nagesh had sworn he wouldn't turn him into one of those things, but who knew? Maybe that was their intent all along.

When the last drop of the potion went down Migo's throat, he dropped to the floor, metal cup clattering. It burned all the way through him. He may as well have consumed fire itself. His vision faded to black, and every muscle in his body seized with consuming pain.

He screamed, a terrible sound that vibrated the air, but in that sound, he recognized something distinct. The scream was only partly human. Something else within him roared. Something terrible. Something... monstrous.

"Nagesh," said a trembling voice that Migo didn't recognize. "What did you do to him? What is happening?"

"I don't know," Nagesh said with a gasp, his voice barely perceivable as each of Migo's bones felt like they would split at any moment.

It looked like he'd been cursed after all.

Afterword

I hope you've enjoyed the story so far. It has been an amazing journey for me to follow along with Migo and Katsi. I wanted to give some other characters more page-time, and I really enjoyed getting more of Scales and Hatan. There is plenty more of this in the final book.

If you've enjoyed reading as well, be sure to leave a review on Amazon or Goodreads, and don't hesitate to let your friends or family know about it. These kinds of things can go a long way toward helping out us indie authors.

Pronunciation Guide

Ailon: Ah-ee-lawn

Adrina: Ah-dree-nah

Agwe: Ah-gweh

Akailen: Ah-kah-ee-len

Alyssad Malrabia: Ah-lee-sahd Mahl-rah-bee-ah

Avidazj Kesten: Ah-vee-dahj Kes-ten

Banadil-Atar: Bah-nah-deel-Ah-tahr

Bayvana: Ba-ee-vah-nah

Bindom: Been-dohm

Briondi: Bree-ohn-dee

Cataban: Kah-tah-bahn

Chaeyna Roqaya: Cha-eh-nah Ro-ka-ya

Cosova Dia: Co-so-vah Dee-ah

Damani: Dah-mah-nee

Deliran: Deh-lee-rahn

Emil Kesten: Em-eel Kes-ten

Falshon: Fahl-shohn

Fidtan: Feed-tahn

Gendin: Gen-deen

Gindaba Danan: Geen-dah-bah Dah-nahn

Hatan Padarro: Ha-tahn Pa-da-row

Jehubal: Je-hoo-bahl

Kajina: Kah-jee-nah

Katsi Danan: Kaht-see Dah-nahn

Kelin Mayari: Keh-leen Mah-yah-ree

Khadij Mayari: Kha-deej Mah-yah-ree

Kidem Rikaydian: Kee-dem Ree-keh-ee-dee-en

Kinay: Kee-na-ee

Kyel: Kee-el

Lazeem: Lah-zeem

Melema: Meh-leh-mah

Maedari: Meh-dah-ree

Malahem: Mah-la-hem

Manahae: Mah-nah-ha-eh

Marem: Mah-rem

Mashe: Mah-she

Mazanib: Mah-zah-neeb

Migo Rikaydian: Mee-go Ree-keh-ee-dee-en

Nadim Mayari: Nah-deem Mah-yah-ree

Nagesh: Nah-gesh

Nedro Wajek: Ne-dro Wah-jek

Obet Ilanitan: Oh-bet Ee-lahn-ee-tahn

Seba: Seh-bah

Scaila: Ska-ee-la

Shali: Shah-lee

Shanon: Shah-nohn

Shakairi: Shah-ka-ee-ree

Shavarani: Shah-vah-rah-nee

Shinaseh: Shee-nah-seh

Sinteya Jenali: Seen-teh-yah Jen-ah-lee

Sirandui Danan: See-rahn-doo-ee Dah-nahn

Rangola: Rahn-goh-la

Ranaz Malrabia: Rah-nahz Mahl-rah-bee-ah

Rashail Mayari: Rah-sha-eel Mah-yah-ree

Rhial: Ree-ahl

Rivar Kesten: Ree-vahr Kes-ten

Roan Melema: Row-ahn Meh-leh-mah

Roda: Roh-dah

Tarahan: Ta-rah-han

Tasnim: Toss-neem

Telsala: Tel-sah-lah

Tilayna Rikaydian: Tee-le-nah Ree-keh-ee-dee-en

Vitori Kesten: Vee-toh-ree Kes-ten

Yavasu Roqaya: Yah-vah-soo Row-ka-ya

About the Author

Brady was born in a stronghold at the base of the Rocky Mountains. He currently resides there with his wife, their three daughters, and a few domesticated house lions of a rare breed. He set out with the goal to write fantasy that anybody could read with characters who face real life struggles. Everyone deserves to feel like there is hope.